Pharmakides

Alice Abyss

Pharmakides by Alice Abyss

ISBN: 979-8-9893669-0-3

Visit Asclepius.Press online for the author's blog, short stories, and publishing updates.

Email: info@asclepius.press

Illustration, cover design, interior formatting by author.

To those who died before their deaths.

Glossary

Please read glossary as follows:
Word: (Pronunciation) "Literal translation" additional information

Aegean Sea: (EE-jee-uhn Sea) region of the Mediterranean Sea
Akanthis: (Ah-KAN-this) "Thornette" genus of finches, species of grass
Algol: (AL-gol) "The demon" triple star system in the constellation Perseus
Alpheratz: (AL-fer-atz) "Mare's navel" binary star system in the constellation Pegasos
Ambrosia: (Am-BROH-zee-uh) "Immortality" wine infused with magical substances
Anthus: (AN-thuhs) son of Hippodamia
Apollo: (Uh-PAH-loh) "Destroy"
Aquarian: (Uh-KWAIR-ee-uhn) "Water bearer"
Ares: (AIR-eez) "Mars" ram constellation
Argos: (AR-gos) "All-eyes"
Athene: (Uh-THEE-nee) "Keen"
Baptisma: (BAP-tiz-muh) "State after immersion"
Black-Footed Buttercup: better known as christmas rose or helleborus niger
Bronte: (BRAWN-tee) "Thunder"
Burning Glass: based on Archimedes' mirrors
Cistern: (SIS-tern) "Box" an artificial reservoir that was dug into the earth or carved into rock for collecting and storing water
Cupid: (KYOO-pid) "Desire"
Delos: (DEE-lohs) "Reveal"
Demeter: (De-MEE-ter) "Earth mother"
Euryale: (YOO-ree-ay-lee) "Far-Roaming" gorgones
Gorgones: (GOR-guh-nes) "Terrible" women with snakes for hair and the ability to turn men to stone
Hekate: (HEK-uh-tee) "Worker from afar"
Hephaistos: (He-FAY-stos) "The best in his craft"
Hermes: (HER-meez) "Pile of stones"

To those who died before their deaths.

Glossary

Please read glossary as follows:
Word: (Pronunciation) "Literal translation" additional information

Aegean Sea: (EE-jee-uhn Sea) region of the Mediterranean Sea
Akanthis: (Ah-KAN-this) "Thornette" genus of finches, species of grass
Algol: (AL-gol) "The demon" triple star system in the constellation Perseus
Alpheratz: (AL-fer-atz) "Mare's navel" binary star system in the constellation Pegasos
Ambrosia: (Am-BROH-zee-uh) "Immortality" wine infused with magical substances
Anthus: (AN-thuhs) son of Hippodamia
Apollo: (Uh-PAH-loh) "Destroy"
Aquarian: (Uh-KWAIR-ee-uhn) "Water bearer"
Ares: (AIR-eez) "Mars" ram constellation
Argos: (AR-gos) "All-eyes"
Athene: (Uh-THEE-nee) "Keen"
Baptisma: (BAP-tiz-muh) "State after immersion"
Black-Footed Buttercup: better known as christmas rose or helleborus niger
Bronte: (BRAWN-tee) "Thunder"
Burning Glass: based on Archimedes' mirrors
Cistern: (SIS-tern) "Box" an artificial reservoir that was dug into the earth or carved into rock for collecting and storing water
Cupid: (KYOO-pid) "Desire"
Delos: (DEE-lohs) "Reveal"
Demeter: (De-MEE-ter) "Earth mother"
Euryale: (YOO-ree-ay-lee) "Far-Roaming" gorgones
Gorgones: (GOR-guh-nes) "Terrible" women with snakes for hair and the ability to turn men to stone
Hekate: (HEK-uh-tee) "Worker from afar"
Hephaistos: (He-FAY-stos) "The best in his craft"
Hermes: (HER-meez) "Pile of stones"

Hippodamia: (HIP-oh-DAY-mee-uh) "She who tames horses"
Hippokampos (sing.) / **Hippokampoi** (pl.): (HIP-oh-KAM-pos) / (HIP-oh-KAM-poy) "Crooked horse" horse with the tail of a fish
Hubris: (HOO-bris) "Pride"
Kentauroi: (KEN-taw-roy) "Bull-slayer" half-man and half-horse figures
Kerberos: (KUR-ber-os) "Escort dead to afterlife"
Kharybdis: (KUH-rib-dis) "Swallow and belch" whirlpool
Kheiron: (KY-ron) "Skilled with hands" half-man and half-horse figure distinguished from the rest of his kind and known for practicing medicine
Khimaira: (ki-MEHR-ruh) three-headed monster
Lampos: (LAM-pohs) "Torch"
Larissa: (Luh-RIS-uh) lowland fields of Thessaly
Magnesia: (MAG-NEE-zhuh) region of Thessaly, Greece
Mandragora: (MAN-druh-GOR-uh) known as mandrake
Medousa: (Meh-DOO-suh) "Guardian"
Murder: group of crows
Nemesis: (NEM-uh-sis) "To distribute" fall from power
Nephele: (NEF-uh-lee) "Cloud"
Nymph: (NIMF) "Girl"
Ovid: (AH-vid) Roman poet who was exiled for his controversial works
Pegasos: (PEG-uh-sos) "Sprung forth"
Pelion: (PEE-lee-on) peak of Magnesia
Perseus: (PER-see-us) "Destroyer"
Pharmakis (sing.) / **Pharmakides** (pl.): (FAR-muh-kis) / (FAR-muh-ki-deez) "Medicine or poison" refers to a witch or witches who use herbs to change the world around them
Philomela: (FIL-oh-MEE-luh) "Lover of music"
Phoinix: (FOY-niks) bird who reflects the sun
Poseidon: (Po-SYE-don) "Ruler of water"
Sarpedon: (SAR-pae-don) Island of gorgones
Scythe: (SY-the) "To cut" a curved blade typically used for cutting wheat
Sea Nymph: (SEE NIMF) "Wet ones" daughters of the ocean

Shade: (SHAYD) ghosts of the Greek Underworld
Siren: (SIGH-ren) "Entwiner" origin of harpy mythology, half-woman and half-bird creature, later evolved into mermaids
Skylla: (SKIL-uh) "Tear apart"
Sthenno: (STHEN-oh) "Strong" gorgones
Stymphalian: (stim-FAY-lee-an) birds made of metal
Tempests: (TEM-pests) "Storm" powerful wind

Table of Contents

"Bird-diviners knew the things that were,
were to be, and had been before."

Homer's *Iliad* (Book 1, lines 68-69)

1. Stork

A black feather fell from my outstretched wing. It twirled, loose on the wind, in a downward spiral towards the sea. It fell, and the fate of Greece darkened with its deceitfully innocent descent.

Although seemingly unconnected, at that exact moment, a witch's torch died out. I saw darkness fall in her cottage over the sea. An inhale caught on her lips. It was strange; it seemed as if my lone black feather created ripples through moments, like the wings of a butterfly lost in time.

As quickly as her fire burnt out, the flame reignited. Her cottage was aglow once more. I recognized the burning plant. It was bitter wolfsbane; I could smell her torch all the way from the sky.

My feather fell as her torch flickered. It was just a feather, after all. It floated down where the cliffs of Magnesia curled around the sea like a claw.

Losing a black feather, rather than a white one, appeared to be a coincidence too. Only the outermost tips of my wings were black. I'd been reckless, burnt by the flames of freedom. These very wings had carried me over Greek horizons. I chased the sun as each day was born. After many days had passed, I never caught a glimpse of one of those rare and elusive *coincidences.*

Usually, white feathers fell for newborns, from the fluffy down on my neck. All storks were called by the stars to work as midwives. We translated wishes from heaven into miracles.

Stork feathers gave life. Life was neither good nor bad. According to the skies, demons needed to be born and stars had to cross. Even black feathers fell.

Since my feather fell from my left wing, I was naturally sent on a westward circle. So I circled, watching life unfold below, in all its knowing and impartial ways. I circled above the scene, where constellations lorded in night and day. I could see them with my divine eyes, even as the winter sun peeked over the Aegean Sea.

The seawater was so still beneath me, clear as the song of a nightingale, that my shadow skirted over shallow pebbles. Winter seas glittered cyan blue. In Magnesia, cliffs hugged the sea. Land caged wind and waves, the tempests of saltwater and air.

My circle drew me from the uppermost sky, downwards, between the rocky palisades, towards my falling feather. I watched it swing back and forth like a rocking cradle.

As for the black feather, I suspect it was the work of fate and the will of celestial bodies. For I was their scribe. I made good of their promises, even in simple accidents like losing a feather.

A new life was on the way.

The dark ink in my falling feather, white frothing sea salt, and the pink lips of dawn's kiss, all slithered along one fateful path.

A noble strum of a horse's heartstring bounced through the air, but only one beat. I saw pale horses grazing along the shore. There should've been an orchestra of heartbeats— a herd. I silently wondered why I only heard one heart, the faint whirring of my feather falling from the sky, and the soft rustle of pebbles against the tides.

I scanned the herd. The horses shimmered so white they seemed blue. As I circled closer, I realized I could see through them. They were living shadows. Shades, with the tricks of metallurgy, who could walk upon the earth.

Of course, their hearts were silenced.

One horse raised her head to watch me. I saw right through her misty face to an iridescent skull. She was formless and sunlight passed through her, to the silver sage which clung onto a cliff behind her. Her ears were curved, like the horns of a delicate moon.

Only a pharmakis with the touch of Poseidon could've raised the dead. It was no coincidence these haunted horses lived in Magnesia. However, by the look of their strange ears, they had not come from Greece at all.

I heard clopping hooves against pebbles, and looked at the horse closest to shore. I couldn't see through her. One horse among the apparitions was real flesh and blood. Yet she was so white that she seemed the same ethereal blue as the others. She blended in almost perfectly, but her ears were straight like an ordinary Grecian horse and her auburn eyes were full of life. When the pink morning sunlight hit her, it didn't reveal a skeleton beneath misty flesh. I couldn't see through her. Her mane was thicker than the others too. Thicker, and more real, I supposed. She seemed as pure as the setting moon, or even a young swan. This horse alone was solid, in a sea of ghosts, in the shadow of bluffs.

I wondered about the destiny of this lone, living horse. I mused at why fate might've asked her to graze beneath a falling black feather. She was so close to the waves while the others stayed back.

I could tell she was young. Fools are always young. She didn't yet have enough years to chip away at her bravery. It was time's task to erode her jagged edges, the same way the sea whittled rocks into pebbles. I watched this horse edge towards the sea and remembered what it was like to be young and foolish. Freedom burnt the outermost tips of my wings a long time ago, when there were far less stars in the sky. I stopped being brave once fire licked my wings, and my feathers turned as weightless and as dark as ash.

The living mare grazed closest to the water's edge on salt-speckled grass, which sprang up between pebbles. Each smooth stone had been rounded by the ebb and flow of water. From above, I could see the carefully crafted pebbles, perfectly edged, like the stars themselves.

The dead horses braved the shore, but kept their distance from the water. I squawked at the irony, their fear of the material world which they had no stakes in. Perhaps the horses were scared of crabs nipping at their noses. Or maybe, they feared getting caught in a wave and tripping over a rock. It was ironic— as if they could've been touched at all. In truth, death, or the illusion of it, cast each ghost horse aside from harm.

They were cautious nonetheless. Experience had weathered them. They drew back from the edge of danger and kept close to herd. I wondered how exactly they arrived in Magnesia, perhaps through some sudden accident. Be it shipwreck or cavalry clash, these horses carried the fear of death into their eternal afterlives.

Except for the living white mare, she alone let the ocean lap at her hooves.

I saw the mare's ears rotate towards the sky. She heard the faint rush of wind balancing my black feather.

She turned her massive head upwards to investigate the noise. The mare was unbridled and free to choose her own fate.

She inhaled and her pink nostrils flared. She could sense, in the way all horses probed the unknown, something dangerous. Her serenity broke.

She took a roaring inhale and sprang into action– braving a defensive posture. She stood up on her hind legs. Her eyes broadcasted her hesitation, wondering if she should strike or flee. She froze there, balanced and tall, assessing the intentions of my feather.

Like all horses, she couldn't see directly in front of her. From above, I could see everything. Balmy air rose from the sea and puppeteered my feather. I doubted she would hear the wind over her own rushing heart and heavy breaths.

The star-white horse had no idea my feather landed upon her hoof.

If I hadn't seen her transformation with my own eyes, if it came to me as a tall tale, I'd never have believed it.

Her hoof was black and gleaming like stars do at night. It was the only spot of her that wasn't pure blazing white, light bronze amber, or soft champagne pink. In comparison to the soft brush of a feather, her hoof was already close to stone.

My feather vanished with a fizzle. As it disappeared, the blazing white mare turned into dull, lifeless rock.

She was a tragic sight to behold. The worst were her eyes. They had lost their sparkle, which was so bright I spotted it from the sky. The other ghost horses picked their heads up from grazing and stared at this horse who had fallen so eerily still that even her tail had paused mid-whoosh.

Above her, and above me, twinkling in the ancient Greek sky, the star Alpheratz disappeared. A luminaire in the black sea of sky—gone. It fizzled out like a spark or the torch of a witch.

I heard one heartbeat. Although, I imagined I should've heard none. It was softer, quieter than before, as if muddled by water.

I heard the frozen horse's heart grow frantic. Her soul must've become so scared that it resisted petrification. The heartbeat echoed within the stone, longing for freedom, even in death.

Suddenly, I felt a gust of wind behind me. I almost toppled forward through the air, but quickly flexed my wings to steady myself. Rushes of air tousled sage stems and stirred the cove's water, in the same way cavalry brought chaos over a village. I flapped higher, watching wayward winds blast through the cove. Calm waves became monsters.

Magnesia whirred with action. Waves sloshed against cliffs.

The ghost horses grew weary at the whistling air, bolted up the rock face, cramming after one another on a steep trail. I could see them pin back their ears and bare their teeth, urging the horses in front of them to move faster. They ran towards the enchanted wilds of Magnesia. They ran on bronze-shod hooves, their tethers onto the earth, and drummed a metallic thunder over the land.

The whole herd ran away, except for the stone mare.

Her life paused into a moment trapped in stone, precipitously balanced between two hooves. She stood there until a wave came and washed her away, summoned by rogue winds.

Angry ocean smashed the stone horse into smithereens. Her remains were scattered in the rocking water. I watched the rock crack apart. Eventually, after many moons, the rough edges of this horse would be carved into soft pebbles, and they would sit silently on the shore, baked by sun, as if they were never a horse at all.

The mare's heartbeat did not sink to the bottom of the sea. It was not heavy and material like the stones. It lingered and played in the water. I heard it roll in the salty froth— roll, but not sink. Where the heartbeat pulsed in the water, waves crashed overhead.

The mare's heartbeat resisted death. She begged for a new form.

Poseidon complied.

I watched one wave fold over another. It was Poseidon's hand. He stirred seas between his fingers and ushered horses beneath the touch of his palm. A piece of him walked out of spirit, and into flesh.

Life swirled forth.

A baby human, a girl, materialized midwater. Her first gasping inhale sealed a portal between realms.

She floated. She could've been a wooden plank from a shipwreck or a message in a bottle from a castaway. The child arrived in the waters of Magnesia as nothing more than a piece of flotsam with golden wisps of hair.

This newborn baby, of course, would be too young to ever remember the horse who was turned to stone and broken by the sea, to weave this into the tapestry of her life.

As the day was born, so her story began.

The girl, desperate for another breath, a tether to Greece, crawled up onto a rock. It was a piece of the mare she once was, a piece of life frozen by my falling feather. Her heart beat like the mare's, but quieter, and somehow rioting to live.

The young girl took a desperate breath. Her wish to incarnate was palpable on her lips as they searched for air.

Water pulled down her back and the young girl's fingers slipped from the rock. She tumbled backwards.

Her first lesson was about the nature of water. Poseidon was unforgiving. This lesson would keep coming back for the rest of her life, like tides following the moon, like a stork circling above. Life wasn't fair. Seafoam lapped, carrying the baby in its midst.

Forces engulfed her, nurturing her, taming her, and domiciling her. They stole her voice, her cry, and her breath. Yet, as the sea tried to kill her, it raised her. She drowned in Poseidon's forces, yet water created her.

My shadow was cast on the waves and lost in rumbling blues. The water was no longer still and clear. A girl was born, things changed. The cove was murky. I flew in circles, keeping my balance in raging winds.

Still, she struggled to breathe.

I dared not lift the baby from the sea. I dared not to even think about bringing her to land. To do so would've denied her of her own fate. This incarnation promised her a dance with Poseidon. As a stork, the stars commanded me to carry the spawn of legends into the world, but not to determine if they lived. She had to sink or swim, under my watchful eye.

As moons passed and stars twinkled, this girl born from the waves came to be known as Medousa.

Fortune favored other young maidens who sprang up from the waves. Take Aphrodite, for instance. She was carried ashore by the fish of Pisces, fully grown and ready for her first breath. She emerged much like a tear shed in reverence of her exquisite beauty— a pure, fluffy white feather fell from beneath my eye. When she came ashore, she didn't shadow a star, but rather birthed a planet named Venus. Aphrodite never winked, rather she moved around, swift as a cormorant, brighter than the stars.

Luck did not favor Medousa, at least not in the same way. She was born into a world that seemed determined to cast her aside, leaving her helpless and at the mercy of the ocean's wishes.

She was born in the shadow of Alpheratz.

Her lucky star was darker than Aphrodite's.

Salty froth rocked the girl back and forth. Each bubble around her was its own diamond of sunlight. I circled, guileless and guiltless. The ocean crept towards the shore, then retreated slightly. Poseidon carried Medousa like a thief to the sea and a hero towards land.

Her eyes were closed as she drowned in the womb of water.

Nobody but the stork and the primordial sky witnessed the birth and near-death of Medousa.

Her body twirled under the waves and she gasped in surprise. The water was unforgiving, rushing down her nose, through her mouth. I took enough plunges in my days to understand that surely it stung her throat.

Medousa gagged. She winced. She had not taken a full breath before tasting the deep, relentless power of water. It pushed air from her lungs like it could pull anything into the dark trenches of the Mediterranean, even her. The baby was still at the mercy of water, which pushed and pulled, created and destroyed. In order to live, she had to fight for every breath, swallowing more water as she struggled to reach the surface.

Even in the early moments of her life, Medousa was forced to confront her need to breathe. This was another lesson that was destined to come back again and again, painting shades of blue over her life.

As I circled over the cliff, I spotted Hekate the witch moving towards the sea with haste. Her torch, I already mentioned, winked that same morning. Of course it was just a flicker, and her torch was lit once more.

As Hekate took long strides in her leather hunting boots, a bronze key jangled from her neck. She had come to be known by birds as the Pharmakis of the Dark Side of the Moon. To us, she was royal. Rather than a crown, horns of the moon sprouted from her forehead. A silver crescent sprang from her hair with two pointed edges. I saw her figure run towards the sea cliff, battling the wind. Her black cloak rippled around her, as intimate as a shadow. The flame in her torch did not waver against tempests, and her olive-colored skin seemed warm in its glow.

When she reached the edge of the cliff, she stopped for a moment, and stuck her torch into the ground.

Hekate's torch came to life.

The handle thickened and the chamber sprouted. The blue base of the flame became undertones of heart-shaped leaves. A black poplar tree sprouted up from the torch, on the edge of the wild cliff. I watched its roots snake through exposed pebbles. The bark elongated and hardened, like honey dripping from a hive.

Hekate walked towards the sea, without looking back. Magic followed her; she didn't have to check.

She didn't need a torch near the water, where starlight reflected over sea. The ocean was a subtle luminary in that way. There was enough light for her gray eyes, thanks to the mirror of the ocean. The ocean served as her torch, especially since the moon was almost full.

Hekate stormed down the rock face and towards the sea. I wondered if she was drawn by the stars themselves. She had noticed the disappearance of Alpheratz, of course; Hekate paid close attention to the sky.

The sky had blank spaces. Back then, it was young. Stories still had to unfold. Black, primordial nothingness stretched for long distances between constellations. These blank spaces were filled in only as legends lived or died.

Hekate had never seen a star go backwards, from shining to nothing.

I knew she hadn't, because neither had I.

Stars shone for both scholars and paupers, pharmakides and priestesses, gods and mortals. They glowed, but they never went backwards. They never vanished. Sometimes they'd flicker, like a candle, but they'd never blow out completely.

Not until that fateful morning when Medousa bubbled up from the sea.

Hekate searched for something. Surely, Alpheratz's disappearance stirred her. I sensed her worries. I felt it like a current in the air of Magnesia. It chilled my skin, more so than the blowing winds. She ran down the cliff's rugged trail and, stepping quickly between rocks, came closer into my view. She had the sort of hair which shimmered like a bone in the moonlight, flowing behind her as she ran.

"Alpheratz!" Hekate shouted.

My stomach lurched, jostling me like the treacherous winds. I realized the horse must have been hers. It became obvious. The mare was a living talisman of Alpheratz, a star so white it shimmered blue.

"Alpheratz," the pharmakis cried and I swear I heard the air around her weep.

She feared her horse was gone without a ghost. Alas, she had already turned to stone and fallen into the sea. Where I brought birth, I also took death, it was the way storks flew.

Hekate made it to the beach. I circled lower over the whistling ocean. I saw her reach down to touch wet pebbles. She may have thought a tidal wave scared her horse. I watched her feet dance in hesitation, unsure where to search. She seemed about to leave and search another beach when she heard something– a splash in the ocean.

I knew it was Medousa, battling Poseidon for air. Hekate's ears caught every sound. She turned. Water rumbled. It was persistent, not like baitfish skittering across the surface.

When Hekate's eyes caught the splash they did not waver. Her pupils focused. There was another disturbance over the surface. The crashing wave was so white it looked blue, and I could see Hekate's eyes catch on rolling foam in the sea. So white it seemed blue— just like Alpheratz— both star and mare.

Without hesitation, she walked into the thrashing sea. She kept on her leather hunting boots. Each step she took, the water deepened and the splash loudened, drawing Hekate further in. Waves welcomed her. Seafoam rushed against her robes, pulling her back to shore. She walked on, stronger than water.

Hekate advanced with outstretched hands. It seemed like the waves put her in a trance.

In the splashing chaos, Hekate found Medousa.

I watched her lift the child from the sea. Hekate's hands, washed clean by the soft shallows, lifted Medousa by her ankle. The girl's lips were blue and her eyes were closed. In her sleep, she held her breath.

Hekate's hands had reaped souls in the Underworld, but that morning she saved a young life. Her horns of the moon flashed a burning red color, like an eclipse.

Hekate held Medousa, on the brink of life and death, upside down over the sea.

I watched Hekate take a deep breath and dig her free hand into her pocket. She drew a glass orb from the folds of her robes.

I veered in the sky, mesmerized by her magical object.

The dark sphere had no flaws or sharp edges. It fit into Hekate's palm. Inside the rounded glass orb, a sea frothed. Waves crested, around and around the glass. There was a sterling color to the trapped water.

At first glance, Hekate's glass seemed dark. But that wasn't so. A slim white crescent hugged an inverted shadow.

I glanced at the moon, which was missing a crescent of the same degree. The current moon was the perfect opposite to Hekate's object. In a way it was a reflection…

Then an old memory came to me, all at once.

I'd heard a story about this sphere, and this pharmakis, a long time ago when I was a mere hatchling in my parent's nest. They raised me in these woods and we nested in the arms of a black poplar.

"At first there was only the moon," my mother said, as she nuzzled us hatchlings off to sleep, "Until the witch made her burning glass. Two parts seawater, one part mercury, enclosed in a glass sphere. She used it to light fires in the dark night. Her torches in the sky never go out. As you sleep they will watch over you. One day you'll take them as your muse and call them stars."

I remember a chorus of chirps, all of us young birds were asking, "Who? Who was the witch?"

"Hekate," my mother explained, "A pharmakis created the stars."

All my mother's chicks slept soundly, under a sky that was only beginning. I dreamt about what those few and far-between stars had to say about the night. As I grew, I thought that was a poetic explanation of the stars. However, when I caught sight of Hekate's burning glass, I knew it was real.

Hekate brought the glass over her head. Her gaze followed it. She calibrated it to the stars, even though they faded as the sun rose. Hekate lined up the glass between her eye and the star of Algol.

The more I thought about it, in my circles in the sky, the more I realized. The burning glass was a talisman, like the mare Alpheratz. It was tethered to the moon. This glass was blown under an empty night sky, before any stars had yet been kindled.

Mercury's power was in its ability to reflect, just like the moon. She used the similarities, between metal and the moon, to burn stars into the night.

Medousa was lucky Hekate had found her with the burning glass in her pocket.

Hekate held Poseidon's child over the sea by her ankles. She drooped from Hekate's grasp like a plump pomegranate. Even from the sky, I could tell her lungs bloated with water.

Hekate gazed through her glass at the pink, winter morning sky. She started to move the glass from various fixed points. Her eyes scanned the sky, tracing lines from star to star. She always moved her gaze back to Algol, a pillar in the sky.

The witch was weaving. She summoned energy through the stars, and channeled it into a web. I saw strings of light move from Hekate's hand into the waterlogged baby girl. Threads of wispy starlight sunk into her skin, as deep as her organs. Medousa glowed from the inside out. Starlight forced water from the baby in a quick, clean tsunami.

Waves broke out of her mouth and nose, reversing each swallow.

She came back to life.

As Medousa sputtered, I watched the stars above. As soon as she regained her breath, Algol went dark. It vanished completely. Birth below, and so death above. This young girl stole light from the stars. With Medousa, *rather coincidentally*, came a shadow over Algol.

I watched with my own beady open eyes, the first eclipse of Algol.

A shadow was cast. I sensed mischief on the way.

As a storyteller of the skies, I interpreted the appearances and disappearances of the stars. Each of them meant something to me. Algol vanished, but Alpheratz disappeared moments before, like it was issuing a warning. I knew, in the deep knowledge all birds had when they sensed changes in the skies, that the disappearance of Algol wasn't random at all.

Medousa opened her eyes. Hekate pocketed her burning glass and cradled the gasping child. The girl's eyes were green as a dark forest, deeper with the pain of choking on saltwater. Medousa seemed innocent, even with Hekate's horns of the moon shadowing her face.

Hekate saw no monsters in the emerald eyes of Medousa, so she slithered into Hekate's trust in the same way all children warm to their caretakers.

Hekate's eyes were gray like a storm, like thunder. I'd been at the beach longer than Hekate. I summoned the arrival of Medousa. Therefore, I could tell, in the way that small children are predictable, what Medousa saw in the eyes of Hekate. It spawned from how she came to life, and the shadows that followed her.

I was sure that the baby saw Hekate's eyes as two familiar stones, gray and round like pebbles on the beach. Medousa would've seen Hekate's gray eyes and thought instinctively of the breaths she managed to catch when she crawled up a rock. I watched the child's face soften. I knew she felt safer in that illusion, which was so lucid yet impossible to ever remember once she grew up. Her pain subsided.

As soon as the girl from the sea started to feel safe, I noticed something peculiar. My flight wobbled. My peering eye made my whole body shift and sink in the air.

Water moved, but not like a wave. Poseidon spun his hand. I saw a whirlpool form beneath Medousa. A torrent ripped Medousa from Hekate. The pharmakis took a step back to keep from being pulled into the water

Medousa was swallowed by the sea and held underwater. I

wondered if Poseidon was mocking me, or if I had imprinted upon the ocean, for a small whirlpool swirled in the same direction of my circles above the cove.

Poseidon imbued her with everything the ocean's knowledge. She discovered everything a child learns in that silent, underwater baptisma. I saw seawater warp like heat on a horizon. Each drop was aging, and aging the girl in its midst.

I knew this was true, because I watched her grow. She went through the phases of childhood, adolescence, and became a woman. This odd girl grew in the sea's cradle.

The ocean glowed, as if it was the blue base of a fire, and I lost sight of Medousa.

The pharmakis watched the miracle unfold, and above her, in my circles over Magnesia, I watched too. Suddenly, the sea stopped spinning and the waters dimmed.

Medousa was spat out from the sea. She stood with haste.

She had become just as tall as the pharmakis. Robes materialized over her body. They were dark as the moon's shadow. Her cascade of curling hair seemed to be spun from gold.

Medousa faced the horizon with her back to Hekate.

"I was born in the ocean's womb and nursed by its salt," the girl spoke with a darkness shadowing her words, like a shark under a swimmer, "Poseidon's hands carved me from the water. As I've grown, I feel the pull of the land, the call of the earth."

She hissed at the horizon, baring her teeth at the endlessness of it. Her hiss sounded like the swish of a crashing wave. I marveled at her. She aged with both eyes closed, without breath, and woke waist-deep on a winter morning in the Aegean Sea.

She turned around, first with her hips, then waist, then shoulders. She moved like a fish-tailed sea nymph, as if she were underwater still.

I saw Hekate take another step back.

Medousa hissed again, this time at the very witch who saved her.

She hissed until her eyes caught Hekate's. Then, her hiss turned into a hum and Medousa sighed. Her rage fizzed away when she looked into Hekate's eyes. She felt safe, gazing into Hekate's rounded gray orbs, her eyes like pebbles on a beach.

Medousa, whose eyes shone like the emerald scales of snakes, was born from the petrified mare and the hand of Poseidon. Her destiny slithered before her, connecting horses, seas, stones, and snakes. I had to fly away. For, after her birth, the rest of her myth was for other birds to see.

Meanwhile, I was a drop of black and white over a sea of blue. When the land fell away, I was surrounded by the harsh, impartial sea. Where the ocean grew deep, where Poseidon could have swallowed Olympus, I watched the waves grow wilder. Seafoam rose and fell like galloping horses. Their flighty spirits were kindred to Poseidon and the hand he used to carve Medousa.

I flew over a salty wet desert that spanned between floating, emerald islands of Greece. I had come to Magnesia as a visitor from a distant land, and it was time to leave. Surely somewhere, in the direction where the sun set, another soul would come forth, begging to be born. I would find them by probing my long red beak between life and death and letting winds loosen my feathers. My job, as midwife to the stars, never ended.

2. *Finch*

A whisper rained down from the night sky and got tangled between the branches of my roost.

"Dear Akanthis, you must weave a nest. A girl is coming to your roost, ushered by the Pharmakis of the Dark Side of the Moon," it instructed with subtle significance.

The stars addressed me like I was still human. They even called me by my old name. I cheeped, to say that I was scared. Oh, I was frightened of Hekate's horses, dead or alive. And, I hesitated to meet the witch, look into her eyes. I feared that maybe her glance might burn me.

The stars heard my concerns.

"Her horses are shades. They cannot touch you," stars assured me, "Be brave, look into the eyes of the pharmakis, and offer a nest to the baby Medousa."

Medousa? I cocked my head at the sky and cheeped once more.

"Guard her. For she will guard Greece in her death."

The stars, even when there were few of them, always knew what was, and what was meant to be.

My wings fluttered open. I flew from the golden branches of my olive tree into the night sky. The stars, the voices of goddesses above, were intimate with me. Perhaps they recognized me as a human. Perhaps they took care of me, as I was transformed by their light. I flew back and forth, begging for more information by cheeping madly.

The message was over. Stars shared what I needed to know, and nothing more. The sky knew how to make my heart race. Stars trusted me with their secrets.

All I could do was weave.

Night passed while I was busy gathering flexible sticks and firm grasses. The sun rose and the plump moon fell. During the day it would hide. When the moon returned at night, on the opposite side of the sky, it would be perfectly full. Only then, magic would trade hands.

I knew exactly when Hekate would arrive.

I was busy building a stable stick base, looping twigs around each other, and twisting wood into a comfortable shelter. I drew inspiration from the star's wishes, and worked all through the night.

Work, but also fear, kept me awake.

I took the form of a bird after a tragedy. My mother, Hippodamia, raised a pasture of mares. They pleased my father, until our grass wilted.

The horses roamed our lands until every shriveled blade was plucked. Their hunger never stopped. They changed from homely steeds to beasts of the Underworld. Their teeth sharpened on soil and their stomachs rumbled for revenge.

Those horses grew a thirst for human blood, and one day they got what they wanted.

My younger brother Anthus was out in the field when the horses struck him down. They ate him alive. I saw the whole, gruesome act. Worst of all, I could never forget. He screamed for help, but I could not move. Fear petrified my body. I remembered the thuds of hoofbeats which drew his blood which watered the dead grass.

Hooves sounded like thunder, but there was no storm, no rain. The fields were still dry, save that patch of grass that had been watered by my brother's blood.

When Anthus died, grief opened my heart. My heart pounded like the hoofbeats that stole his life. It beat with fear. It was the only part of my scared body that could move.

Eventually my heart grew and widened into feathers, so I could reach the wind. I flew away from those monstrous horses, from the screams, from blood watering the bushes.

On the night Medousa summitted my mountain, the stars asked me to meet my fears, rather than fly away. I usually avoided the pharmakis and her steeds, dead or alive.

I worked all night, dodging the wishful gaze of hungry owls. I laced the star's whisper between twigs. By the end of my construction, the nest could've fit dozens of my own. I fluttered about to secure it, until I was sure it was big and stable enough for a human girl.

The stars knew I was dutiful. They had always trusted me, ever since they felt my pain and morphed me into a bird.

Once I finished the nest, the day had passed. The sun was setting once more and stars started to burn through the firmament. In the end, Medousa's nest glittered with gold. It was huge, spanning a branch of my thoughtful tree.

It seemed to be made completely of olive branches. That was my clever illusion. I had, in fact, threaded each olive branch with Akanthis grass. When I was a girl, I was named after grass. I marveled at the dry strands, the same substance which drove those horses mad. It brought an airy quality to the structure and made it fluffy with soft strings of grass rather than hard with bark.

The nest looked like it was baking in a warm fire by the light of the setting sun.

As the day ended, my mountain top grew darker. Eventually the inky night turned silver and the full moon rose.

Whenever the moon filled to its brim, Hekate arrived at my enchanted mountaintop. She traveled by horseback, which brought me into a state of terror each and every month. I heard her horse's heartbeat, breath, and hooves. Though I knew my lost brother wasn't on the summit, I heard Anthus' screams.

Hekate came here as reliably as a well-calibrated sundial. Every twenty eight days she would appear on her white mare. Usually she rode with her gaze fixed on the trail, and when the treeline broke, she focused on the peak of Mount Pelion. Usually I hid between leaves. But after a long night and day of weaving, I stood my ground. I stood on my new nest, with my tiny chest puffed out, and my beady eyes scanning the forest.

I spotted the witch. As Hekate rode through the forest, I could tell she was distracted.

Her gray eyes overturned every shadow. She paid no attention to where she was going. Her head moved as she ducked to see beneath thick trunks and leaves.

Hekate wasn't on her usual white mare.

She rode a silvery, translucent steed with a bronze bridle.

I heard neither the beast's breath nor heartbeat, for her horse was a shade. She used a metallurgy trick to tame the dead. A bronze bridle could reach into the afterlife. Threads of this particular metal were also woven into her saddle pad. I saw the reddish, metallic sheen between saddle and horse. I heard the horses' bronze shoes clatter over the terrain.

Another ghost horse followed Hekate, bearing a rider I realized must have been Medousa. Her robes were almost long enough to cover her bare feet. I saw her toes peek through stirrups.

I heard the clank of her horse's shoes too. Bronze kept the horses from slipping into the afterlife or rotting their flesh. These were Hekate's horses, raised from the dead.

I watched Medousa balancing in her saddle and she was enchanting. I couldn't look away.

I wondered if she guarded the secrets of the ocean's grace, for she moved with exquisite flow. To me, she looked like water. She moved like a wave, which builds-up, crashes, then fizzles. I watched her guide the necromanced horse. She would pull her hand against the reins then steady them. She pushed her legs inwards, then gripped them. It was a dance of instinct, a gift from Poseidon. She understood the tension and subtle ripples of the universe. It seemed like she was the line between stars, tracing horses to the ocean.

I thought to myself that it was no wonder the stars wished to help her. I silently wondered why the stars had called her a newborn, and I was glad I made a giant nest.

In the foothills of the mountain, a canopy laced around the two riders. Hekate and Medousa flitted in and out of my view as their horses weaved between pines, under their long gray shadows.

Whenever a ray of waning sunlight fell upon those half-dead horses, it illuminated their skeletons. I could see ephemeral ribs and skulls flashing in the light. Both horses had curled ears, like the moon's horns that sprouted from Hekate's head.

"Oh Hekate," Medousa shouted.

My feathers spread apart from each other, as if it was raining and my skin was trying to stay dry, as if an owl had caught sight of me. There was something feral in Medousa's voice that made my skin crawl.

Hekate ignored her. My spine shivered.

"What're you looking for?" Medousa asked. Every feather on my body wanted to fly away, but I stayed put, such was my duty to the stars.

"I'm not looking for anything," Hekate said, dismissively.

"Of course you are. You're looking from side to side and up and down each cliff."

Hekate stayed silent.

"Fine. Keep your secrets. Just hope I don't spot whatever you're looking for first."

Hekate rolled her eyes, but Medousa couldn't see.

"What're we going up the mountain for anyway?"

"I'm trading."

"With whom?"

"Every full moon I give a tool to Hera, the Pharmakis of the Light Side of the Moon. Our trade keeps balance between light and darkness."

"What kind of tool?"

"Glass which allows us to draw wishes from the night sky."

"Did it give you those horns?" Medousa asked.

Hekate stayed silent, but I swear I saw a faint pink glow come over her moonly horns.

"When are you going to get your glass back?" Medousa asked.

"When the moon disappears. You must be hungry, am I correct Medousa?"

"Yes."

"Here. It's lucky we came across this tree," Hekate motioned towards a grove. Quince fruits, in likeness to ripe pears, drooped so much that they weighed down their branches. Hekate pulled three from the tree and tossed them to Medousa.

They continued on the trail, with their horses walking slowly. Medousa devoured the quinces. I watched juices dribble down her face. She ate each down to its core.

After she had finished her quinces and thrown their seeds back to the mountain, Medousa's horse jumped over a root. Hekate heard the change in hoofbeats and shouted back, "I told you to stay behind me."

With a smirk on her face, Medousa clicked her tongue. Her horse broke into a gallop, and Medousa leaned forward, rushing into momentum, leaning into the danger.

There was something intense about Medousa. She bounced in the saddle, like it was her first time. Despite her loose form, there was a focus in her eyes. She was determined not to fall. She was like a wolf.

Hekate on the other hand rode swiftly, like she was one with her horse, even though she was distracted and peering between the trunks of every tree.

"Hey! Don't go ahead!" Hekate shouted.

It was no use. Medousa's horse bolted past Hekate and up the mountain.

Hekate chased the girl. As they ascended, they became closer to the stars and their breath thinned. I could hear their inhales growing closer and closer together. Everyone's breath changed except for the ghost horses, who mimicked the act, but couldn't really inhale or exhale. Breathing was so familiar and ingrained, it became the false nature of a ghost.

Medousa tore through the trees, urging her steed faster and faster along the trail, shouting at the animal. Her eyes stayed fixed between its curved ears while she moved with the steps of the beast.

Hekate followed. She was silent and seemed not to move at all on her horse, save her slow breath. The living trees brushed against her body, and traced her horns of the moon. Spiny leaves did not catch on her ghost horse's supernatural tail; silver strands floated through the vegetation.

Hekate's boots were fashioned with bronze spurs, so she could push her horse forward. Soon she took the lead from Medousa.

Hekate didn't slow down. She left Medousa chasing after her dust. My small heart beat as they approached.

As the racing horses climbed higher, pines became sparse. They broke out of the treeline. The peak was before them, and would've appeared to Hekate and Medousa as framed between silvery blue horse ears.

The ghost horses marched on, carrying their riders further up the mountain, until all the vegetation disappeared. Rocks were loose under the horse's bronze shoes. I heard the mountain crumble against metallic hooves. That particular metal had a distinct ring to it.

Only one tree, my single olive tree, stood at the top of the mountain. In it, I watched and waited.

Hekate reached the mountaintop first. Her horse leaned back and came to a slow stop. In the clearing, wind made a flag of Hekate's clothes and hair. I listened to her clothing flap, almost jostled by the sound. She turned her horse around, waiting for Medousa to come up the path.

When Medousa reached the peak, zephyrs brought her hair to life, as if it were made of living snakes. I watched, alongside fate, unseen. My breath was so short, shallow, and small it wouldn't have made a cricket buzz.

Medousa scanned the panorama. The mountains of Magnesia jutted from the earth like the scales of a great underground dragon. Only branches of an olive tree would've broken her expansive view. It sprouted from the mountaintop, lured by the call of gods in heaven. I was still unseen.

"Didn't I ask you not to run ahead?"

"Who are you, my mother?"

I let out a chirp, eager to break the tension.

Hekate spun around, searching for the source of the noise.

Before her burning eyes caught mine, I watched her gaze pause on Medousa. The wind ripped at Medousa's clothes and revealed her ankle.

"What's that?"

"What?"

"Dismount now. Let me see your ankle."

"Whatever you say," Medousa hopped off her horse with a mocking curtsy. I still sensed something sinister in her voice.

Hekate investigated Medousa's ankle. I saw starlight stuck beneath her skin.

A glowing, blue snake wrapped around her ankle. It was eating its own tail, sloughing its own skin, in a perpetual cycle of renewal.

I watched Hekate leap from her horse to touch it, as if to wipe it away, but the mark stayed.

"Starlight... under her skin..." Hekate murmured, tucking silver strands of hair behind her own ears.

"What did you say?" Medousa asked.

"Nothing."

"You said something, under your breath."

"Nevermind."

I chirped again and the pharmakis turned fast. Medousa sighed and brought her foot back to the ground.

She'd been here many times before. So naturally, she noticed the changes in my olive tree. Hekate walked closer to my tree, closer to the edge of the mountain. Reaching out a hand, Hekate gently stroked the rough bark of the olive tree. Grooves knotted beneath her fingers, and I wondered if the tree could whisper secrets through her skin.

Behind a tangle of glossy leaves, in its knotted and twisting branches, was my timely bird's nest. Hekate's gray eyes widened as she saw that it was large enough to fit herself.

Then she looked right at me. Her spacy, gray eyes caught mine. There must have been a fire inside Hekate, for her eyes were full of smoke.

Hekate moved her eyes over my blushing red face, down to the flash of yellow on my wings.

She knew I was not any ordinary finch. She knew I had once been a girl; she knew I lost my brother to cursed horses. I could tell she'd heard the stories of my sorrows. She was born from magic, and knew all about girls turned into birds. She knew who I was before I became trapped in the fidgety, round body of a bird.

Hekate shuddered.

Stars spoke to pharmakides through birds. Hekate listened, for even the smallest creatures carried stories. I peered at her. Her two eyes saw me, deep into my own human soul.

I looked at the misty eyes of her horses, ghosts of animals who were destined to serve Hekate in life and death. Their eyes were watery, even kind.

I knew, as I always suspected, a curse over the land was the problem, and never my mother's horses. Maybe my brother could've been spared. When grasses dried up, that season instilled a thirst for blood into peaceful creatures, ones with such kind eyes.

I wished to speak, but there were no words in my beak. I chirped, and I knew Hekate understood.

I told her I would do as the stars wished.

In such ways that I could never help my brother, or mend my family, I sought to protect Medousa. Cycles broke and reformed. I chirped again, motioning towards the nest for Hekate's adopted child. She understood. For the girl newly cast into the world, the stars and the birds made their offering, a soft bed of bristly grass.

I watched Hekate shiver in the whipping, alpine winds.

"Medousa, we have something for you."

"Who? You and a bird?"

"Come here."

I peeked at Medousa's emerald eyes. A veil of curiosity washed over them and led her towards Hekate. Hekate unpocketed her burning glass and held it up to her eye, gazing at the sky, then swiftly turned to Medousa. By the time Medousa reached Hekate, a spell had been cast.

"At night we sleep," Hekate whispered, brushing her hands over Medousa's eyes, calling the girl into rest. Hekate nestled Medousa into the branches of my olive tree, warmed by golden grass. Her curling hair melted into my nest. Medousa slept with a faint smile under the moonlight. Her breath was soft, going in and out like water on a languid shore.

While Medousa drifted into her dreams, Hekate used the glass to cast another spell. I looked at the dark orb. It was a true object of magic. Hekate looked through her crystal ball at the sky. Her eyes raced from star to star. She traced constellations through the foggy gaze of her silver ball.

Once she had traced over every star, as if using them as anchors for a spider's web, clouds circled Hekate. They rolled on the temperature gradient in the air like mercury spilling on glass. They swirled, stopping to twist and turn. Soon the mountaintop was like an island, and the clouds were its sea.

A pink aura radiated from the misty vapor and Hekate's platinum hair turned a rosy shade of gold. My feathers twinkled like the petals of Cupid's carnations. Even Medousa blushed in her sleep.

I'd never been so close to the unfolding staircase before, never rubied in its glow. It appeared every month, but I preferred to hide from the spectacle.

This change, from white clouds to mythic pink, compelled Hekate to sigh. She returned the burning glass to her pocket.

A spiral staircase materialized. The flight was made of moonlight, hence it only appeared during the fullest, plumpest moons. The moon reflected enough light to cast magic into clouds. Each step looked as if it were made of floating marble, with streaks in its porous white surface. The streaks moved like smoke, yet kept the shape of the steps.

Then Hekate busied herself by tying Medousa's horse to the base of the olive tree. I heard the soft twill of bronze-threaded ropes cutting into bark.

In sleep, Medousa looked like Akanthis grass to me. She was water when awake, and now a delicate thistle in her sleep. Her breath was so soft, like the rustle of grass. Her hair was golden as a meadow under sunlight. It was golden like rich pastures, before pale purple flowers bloom at the tips of their stalks, before the bees buzzed around, and before flowers dropped and rotted into the earth.

Though I was a bird, and I couldn't tell her what I thought, Hekate knew I'd stay there to watch over the baby Medousa. We made our silent promise. The fact that I was prepared said enough. Hekate hadn't learned her name yet, but I could not tell her. All I could offer was a few well-placed tweets. I'd understand, as years passed and this strange experience stuck with me, who this girl was. I spread one wing over the nest, though she was so much bigger than me, to further ease Medousa's exposure to the cold winds.

Before Hekate turned to face the stairs, she gave one knowing glance to me.

Hekate mounted her ghostly steed and ascended. Her horse stepped onto the pure white smoke in the sky, and the mysterious stairs held both horse and rider. Hekate rode her way up in a spiral, up into the sky. She went far above the mountaintops, where the air was so thin even I, living on a peak, dared not go. My small lungs were suited for weaving Akanthis which grew from the ground, never for soaring above clouds.

3. Eagle

Clouds rolled down from my post and twirled into spiraling steps. Light from the shining full moon hardened into a staircase. Only when the moon was at its fullest, could clouds reach down to the tallest point in Magnesia, and knock on the land which caged the Underworld. Stairs materialized for the moon, but more so, for the Pharmakis of the Dark Side of the Moon.

I knew she approached. Cycles marked the movements of pharmakides. I expected her after a lifetime of living by my feathers and the moon's swing.

Moreover, I heard her horse coming up the stairs. Hoofbeats had a metallic ring as they struck misty marble.

Of course, my eyes could see everything. Of all the birds in Greece, I flew highest above the earth. I tilted my head to see the stairs at an angle and I quickly spotted the witch. Hekate's crown pointed into two horns of the moon.

I focused on her horse. His fur was pale blue, and as I focused I saw that he was see-through. I stared. The horse's ears curved like the witch's horns. To me he looked more like a cloud than a living, breathing animal. I heard his bronze hoofbeats ring like the sound of a spoon striking a crystal chalice. But, he had no breath. I could hear the breath of the pharmakis, becoming lighter by the second. The horse was silent. I couldn't hear his beating heart, either.

I concluded this translucent horse must've been her experiment. He was a once-dead creature roused back to life. She must have used starlight, metallurgy, and maybe even wolfsbane to reanimate him.

I shuddered.

Hekate typically rode a different horse— a living horse. Hekate called her Alpheratz, the namesake of a star. I was not so surprised to see the pharmakis come without her, when I remembered what happened to her star. Alpheratz suddenly went missing from the sky.

When Alpheratz the star appeared, many moons ago, so did the horse. Hekate led her up my heavenly steps in training, as a black foal.

I watched Hekate and Alpheratz come and go with each passing full moon. The foal's obsidian fur shedded into dark gray dapples. She blanched whiter and whiter as each moon passed, until one day I nearly mistook her for a fallen star. She was so white. I'd seen neither dove nor swan feathers as white as her fur. I remembered Alpheratz for the way she blinded me, for my eyes were so wide and receptive to all.

I'd never seen one of these dead horses before. She was never so brazen as to bring an experiment from the Underworld up my steps, to the mouth of my golden gate. I thought it was a disgrace, but I had to let her in.

Hekate had business with Hera.

I watched over Hekate then, as I always watched over all of Greece. Her rituals were unseen by all the creatures of the earth, but I saw her. The horse stopped in front of my perch with a final scrape of his bronze shoes. Hekate was small under the grand archway, even on her horse. Though I knew it was an illusion, the horse's bronze bridle looked filthy in front of my golden gates. Alloys were such a far cry from purity.

I flew down to the latch. My feathers were as golden as the gate itself. I looked at the witch and screeched. Hekate remained stoic. She knew I had to let her in.

Usually I opened my gaze before she reached the top, but on that day I wanted her to see me. It was blasphemous to be in the presence of the dead.

I screeched again. It was a way to offload my wrath. The witch took it with a straight face.

Hekate gazed at me and I saw a familiar smoke in her eyes. My eagle eye dilated when I focused on her dark aura and dimly glowing horse. I flapped my wings and the castle gates creaked open; Hekate rode inside.

Her horse stood in front of a cloudy mote. I watched Hekate gaze between its ears, over the moat, at the decadent castle crafted by clouds. A bridge stood straight up, blocking them from crossing. On the other side of the moat, misty halls lead to different wings of the cloud castle.

Gardens bordered each pathway. Well, they weren't exactly gardens. They weren't real plants, only cloudy imitations. The only real plants in these clouds were the blue lotuses. They bloomed in the moat. The lotus blooms looked like reflections of the clear, blue sky. Hera picked them up when her clouds passed over the Nile.

Pearly white fish splashed through the hazy water of the moat. My beak longed to dig between the fish's massive scales, and rip out their meat. I resisted. Such was the way of my life. Day after day, glory grew from my discipline. Not any bird could act as gatekeeper of the skies. It had to be me. The fish were off-limits. They grew fat, old, and innocently happy. They would never know a predator watched them. The fish themselves brushed up against the edges of the moat and bumbled into each other, with the kind of glee that showed the effects of altitude, even through water. Watching the fish was like watching a slow-motion, graceful carriage wreck.

Then a larger splash caught Hekate's attention. A pink mermaid emerged, shifting her body to face the visitor. The muscles in her back flexed as she turned around. A crown of water droplets graced her head, each sparkle asked their own questions.

She looked up at Hekate with blossoming purple eyes, long lashes, and a rosy luster radiating from her skin. Her name was Nephele. She had fifty sisters who lived in the sea. She was the only one who took to the sky. Though she lived in the sky, she kept her fishtail. Cirrus wisps of hair floated from her head, as if she were still underwater.

"Where's Alpheratz?" Nephele asked, sparing not a moment for pleasantries. Her purple eyes flicked between Hekate and the ghost horse.

Hekate swayed, her charcoal robes rippling with her every movement. She dismounted her horse and waltzed towards the mermaid as if she were in a theater. Hekate's mind was becoming lost in the altitude. It happened every time she visited the clouds. Her ghost horse was unfazed, for it wasn't breathing any real breaths.

"Ahem!" Nephele blurted. She tried to sound stern, but her voice floated like the sweetest breeze to kiss the sky. Hekate's stony eyes hazed over, like gray clouds puffing up with water.

It was common for Nephele's guests to become disoriented. As an eagle, a master of thought, I could rise above the spaciness that came with thin air. I saw through the delirium, but Hekate became enchanted. I saw her stop, admire the puffiness of a cloud, before continuing, dancing along the edge of Nephele's moat. The altitude was getting to her, absolving her into mindless matter.

"Where is she?" Nephele splashed her rosy tail in the water impatiently.

"Who?"

"Alpheratz!"

"Alpheratz vanished this morning," Hekate said and her eyes started to water. I could tell she never spoke these words out loud on land. Gravity and denial would've trapped them in her throat. Everything here became transparent.

Clouds around the nymph and pharmakis rippled.

"What does that mean?"

"At dawn the star of Alpheratz went out. I stormed the beach to search for my mare, but to no avail. She simply disappeared."

A tear fell down the pharmakis' cheek, pearly in the iridescence of the cloud castle. As it fell I heard a whoosh of wind, washing away her grief. She spoke openly, as did every visitor to Nephele's baths.

"We have to find her. We must search."

"No. It's impossible."

"Impossible? Why, nothing's impossible."

"I saw a thistle finch," Hekate blurted and bowed her head.

"Where?" Nephele gasped. I heard her heart flutter in her chest.

"Perched on the peak of Mount Pelion–" Hekate gasped, "its highest point."

"If a thistle finch let you see her…at the summit…"

"It means Alpheratz is gone," Hekate said as another tear washed down her face, "We all know thistle finches flee at the sight of a horse. Well a living one, at least. For this bird to sit atop a tree, so open and brazen, means Alpheratz is nowhere in the panorama of Magnesia."

Hekate seemed far away from her words.

"No! Not Alpheratz! Every month she eats peppermints from my palms. That's a despicable prophecy," Nephele crossed her arms across her chest, "Take it back."

Even in the somber moment, under the shade of bad news, Nephele's ambiance lit up Hekate's elegant face, as if she were blushing. Her cheekbones melted into something softer. The rosy glow even lit up the ghostly horse standing behind her.

"Take it back!" Nephele urged.

Hekate was lost in the clouds. I saw her gray eyes focus on puffs of pillars swirling into extravagant courtyards.

"Even if that is the case, you can bring her back just like your other horse, right? Alpheratz can't be gone without a ghost."

Hekate shrugged. She held something on her tongue. I saw the gravity of her secret invert clouds.

"What is it? Something else happened and you're not telling me?" Nephele said and pouted.

"Oh dear, look at the moon. I must deliver the burning glass to Hera at once," Hekate pointed towards the pale moon, peeking through the clouds. It caught more light by the second.

"Anything for the moon," Nephele whispered as loyalty glazed over her eyes. Her violet eyes lightened to lavender at the very thought of the moon. She arched her human torso forward into a bow, seemingly towards the pharmakis. I knew Nephele was bowing further behind Hekate, at the moon.

"The bridge, please," Hekate said.

"Of course."

Nephele dove underwater and busied herself with the windlass. It was a massive underwater wheel threaded to a drawbridge with chains of gold. This metal was so light, the likeness of my own feathers, that it could float with the clouds. Nephele swam in circles, pushing the machinery, until a heavy counterweight of rainclouds thudded against the misty ground. The drawbridge locked into place, Hekate leapt from her horse, and rushed over the moat, towards the cloudy palace.

She stopped midway.

"I wanted to thank you again, Nephele, for allowing Hera and I to conduct our trade in your castle."

"You're welcome. My wish is to foster light and dark moons," Nephele said. I could tell she barely kept herself composed. Her voice wavered and cracked.

Hekate paid no mind and hurried onwards. She started to smile. Her smirk mirrored her horns. I sensed an unruly arrogance and ruffled my feathers. With a few quick steps, Hekate was gone. She had already left her hunting boots at the base of the bridge. I flew to Nephele.

Tears, lilac like her eyes, streamed down her pale face. Fish swam clumsily around her, knocking into her, oblivious to her suffering. She sobbed and rubbed the scales of her hips together. It made the hissing sound of a serpent.

I had seen Nephele bond with Alpheratz over many moons. When she was a filly, Nephele offered her enchanted milk from the clouds. As Alpheratz grew, Nephele fashioned peppermints for her. She made them by warping water crystals together with nectar that evaporated from the dew over fields of the sweetest flowers.

When the moon was full, she swam to the edge of her moat and patiently fed the horse, cooed at her, and whispered secrets into her ears. It was her nature to love horses, as all other nymphs who took to the ocean were tasked with taming hippokampoi. She was the only nymph of the clouds and longed for some connection to Poseidon, the force of horses.

"I miss Alpheratz," Nephele let out an anguished wail. The ghost horse watched her with apathy. She clicked her tongue, willing his approach, with a tear sparkling in the corner of her eye.

He refused.

"Where could Alpheratz have gone?"

Then Nephele looked at me with teary eyes, eager for some kind of response. Though her brothers and sisters tamed hippokampoi, I knew Nephele was the only nymph who actually talked to animals. I knew she was more gifted than other nymphs or even advanced pharmakides. They underestimated her as a sweet airhead.

Nobody realized that in her carefree manner, Nephele arrived at deep truths. While Hekate may have seen omens in the behaviors of birds, and Hera may have been able to offer us names for legends and foes, Nephele spoke to us from her heart.

I understood more than her words. I understood her grief too. Alpheratz was a special horse. She manifested as a star appeared. I remembered when Hera named her and every white peacock cooed with jealousy.

I let Nephele brush her fingers through my feathers. I wished to offer more comfort, but my mind whirred. I started to become suspicious and wonder about the coincidences between Alpheratz and the Pharmakis of the Dark Side of the Moon. Alpheratz was her only living horse, and seemed destined for a real life in the wilds of Magnesia. Suddenly, for no reason at all, the mare was gone?

I had to investigate.

I chirped at Nephele, trying to offer her comfort and a promise I would return. Then I lifted myself into the air.

I followed Hekate as silently as her own shadow. She moved through the open foyer to staircases over a court.

The castle was open, highlighting the artistry of the clouds. Where castles ordinarily displayed a painting, we had open windows. These openings allowed clouds to drift in-and-out of the pearly walls.

I heard muffled splashing from above. Hekate walked through the castle's airy, light-filled rooms to the upper levels. She had to ascend more staircases to find Hera, so Hekate spiraled, higher into the sky.

As she walked higher, her breath became thinner.

Hekate came upon a sparkling alabaster door at the end of a long misted marble corridor. In its center was a knocker shaped like a ram's head. The golden ram sparkled with the warm radiance of Ares at night. Hekate reached out to lift the knocker. With a gentle knock, the door swung open, revealing opulent baths.

Hekate walked through the tall doorway and I flew in right above her. My feathers masked me, neither pharmakis would notice my golden glow. I was nothing more than a shimmer in the corners of their eyes.

Steam greeted us first, masking me further. I felt like a spy in the night. Only the moon could see me. The moon peered through an open ceiling, through the mist, and looked down on the baths with one fully open eye.

In the baths, clouds lost their marble design. Here they articulated, divided, and sorted into elaborate mosaic tiles.

Rather than a clawfoot bathtub, the bath was hoofed and golden, seemingly modeled from the ram's face on the door. Four gleaming hooves held the bathtub aloft. Cloud water frothed over the tub's edges, drenching the floors. I could see a woman's figure through the steam.

At the clawed feet of the bath was a peacock sire. He marched away from the water as it spilled over the floor, but I saw it wet his emerald and indigo flowers. His feathers always looked like they were watching me, but I knew he couldn't see through them. His peahens lived in the gray shadows of the clouds, where Hera could fashion them to pull her golden chariot.

Hera's prized bird never left her feet. At least, not ever since she found the creature.

Technically, he could never fly as high as me. Neither peacock nor peahen could. They came here by enchantment, not by merit. Hera draped them with golden bridles and chains, so they could become weightless and ascend into the clouds.

This peacock was just an ornament. Maybe he was beautiful. Maybe he was exotic, but I could fly up to the castle and back to earth with my own wings. I was stronger and didn't need to sit in wait at the feet of a witch! I forged my own path. I didn't even look in the peacock's real eyes, and he was too much of a fool to notice me.

"You seem relaxed," Hekate said.

Hera's face became clear in the steam. I could see her honey-colored locks and amber eyes. She was golden, just like me.

Hera answered Hekate with a small smile on her lips, "I am. You know the water always has a way of soothing my soul."

Hekate nodded and walked closer to her fellow pharmakis. "What has been troubling you?" she asked. I sensed that there was something about Hera's presence that made Hekate feel at ease, as if her own problems were eclipsed.

"Sometimes it feels like my head is lost in the clouds. I lose track of my own thoughts," Hera mused. Her eyes drifted closed again as she allowed herself to sink deeper into steaming cloud water.

Hekate let out a deep sigh. Hekate understood. I knew she could see Hera's shadows.

"Oh Hekate, you take me as light and I long to be dark," Hera cooed, her voice echoed and rippled with purrs. Something about her exaggerated voice brought Hekate back to her senses. Her gray eyes cleared up, like clay as it hardened. I could tell, as clarity came back to her, she remembered the reason for her visit all at once.

Hekate fetched burning glass from her pocket. It was dark like the angry underbelly of an angry storm cloud. The glass was completely black, since the moon was perfectly full.

"It's your turn," Hekate said.

Hera floated from the bath, lifted by a cloud. The white puff carried her upwards, and obscured her, like she was a burgeoning butterfly in a cocoon.

Another cloud was at her beck and call. It draped her in a long tunic. It hung from her soft shoulders. When she returned to the floor, the fabric trailed her steps, and hardened from mist into silk. The faint murmur of the dress was something a lover might sew dreamily for their sweetheart.

"Does darkness truly serve me like light serves you? I haven't passed you the burning glass, yet you manifest matter," Hekate's words bared her heart.

"Dear, they're just clouds," as Hera spoke, a third cloud polished the crown of ivory feathers above her brows.

She reached for Hekate's offering. When Hera's fingers touched the burning glass, I saw a shadow fall over Hekate's face. Nobody else would've noticed that, unless they had the eyes of an eagle. Certainly the peacock did not notice a damned thing. He didn't even offer a bob of his head— the oblivious fool!

Hera slid the burning glass into a discreet pocket of her tunic.

"You noticed, I'm sure, Algol disappeared this morning," Hera louted.

"Yes."

"You wish to know what really troubles me?" Hera asked.

"Yes, of course," Hekate replied.

"I hear gossip from *all* the birds."

"So? What?"

"When that star went dark a stork dropped something in Magnesia," Hera said.

Hekate stepped back.

"She was meant to die," Hera continued, "You grabbed her. By the powers of the moon and starlight, you helped her live."

"Meant to die? Why would she be meant to die?" Hekate asked.

"It doesn't matter now. You went and rearranged the stars," Hera flicked her hand in the air. Her voice was thick with arrogance and annoyance.

Hekate's face was ash. She took a deep inhale before speaking, "The girl is a star-weaver."

"What?" Hera snapped, stepping closer to her counterpart, "You and I are the only star-weavers."

"You know that I consider Sthenno and Euryale star-weavers!" Hekate said.

"You know that I think that's delusional," Hera said, "Anyone can channel light down from the stars. Only you and I can *burn* them into the sky.'

Hekate huffed, "I suspect Medousa is a star-weaver, and that's why Algol vanished at dawn."

"Nonsense, star-weavers cannot make stars vanish," Hera debated.

"This one can."

The two pharmakides stared at each other in silence. I kept my presence silent as well. I floated loftily above the witches, silently turning on my feathers. I preferred to stay unknown, spying from the upper folds of the castle.

"She has a mark."

"A mark? What do you mean?"

"A tail-eating snake. It glows blue like Algol."

"Where is it?"

"On her ankle."

"Her ankle? Why her ankle?" Hera's eyebrow arched towards her peacock feather crown.

"I pulled her from Poseidon by her ankles."

"Where is she now?"

"A finch had fashioned a nest for her. I left her on Mount Pelion."

"You left a newborn baby with a finch?" Hera asked.

"She's no newborn," Hekate said, turning and pacing the bath halls.

"Like Aphrodite?"

"No," Hekate said, "She was a child when I saved her, then Poseidon aged her in the sea. It's like she spent years there, alone, in silence under the waves. I watched it all. She came out...bitter."

"Well it's good you left her with the finch," Hera smirked, "If she came up here, she might end up like Nephele."

My feathers stood on end. I hated it when Hera mocked Nephele. I held back a screech. It was better to eavesdrop— better for Nephele. Sure Nephele was open-minded and optimistic, but there was nothing wrong with her, at least not to me.

"This girl from the sea is different. I can tell. She'll have the power to write her own story in the sky," Hekate persisted.

"Any idea what role you'll play in her life?"

Hekate stared at Hera, waiting for her to answer her own question.

Hera closed her eyes and continued, "Since you summoned the stars to bring her back to life, now you're responsible for the girl. If you want a piece of my advice, she'll have to learn how to fight if she wants to live."

"I fear problems with raising thi—"

"Haven't you raised two daughters before? What's a third?"

"They were different," I watched anger bubble up in Hekate's eyes.

"That's true. They never made stars go dark. That's no matter. You have duties now, as your hands pulled her from the sea."

There was a straightforwardness, a sincerity in Hera's words, even though her words bit like they had teeth— she was real. Where Hekate was always scared to express herself, Hera's words hit hard. Hekate lived in shadows. I wondered what Hekate ate, and if she got her nourishment from secrets.

"What about her shade?" Hera asked.

Hekate rolled her eyes, "Here you go on about shades again. I suppose you're going to tell me once more that *I'm* the shadow of *you*. Is that right? Have you realized yet that shades are made of mist, and I am flesh and blood? Medousa is flesh and blood, too. Hence, why she nearly drowned in the sea."

"I can see the truth while you work to cover it up. Of course you're my shade," Hera spat, "Nevermind. How dare you question this? You pulled this girl from the ocean. Take power where you tread."

"She's a trickster," Hekate protested.

"Now she's your trickster, and she has a name."

"What is it?"

"Medousa," Hera's voice was smooth as the song of a lyre.

All at once, every bird in the Grecian isles knew the name of Medousa. It came as the whisper of a feather and a deep knowing to all of us. Thus, far below the cloud castle, I heard a thistle finch chirping in commemoration. Over the oceanic horizons, I heard cormorants surfing to the beat of her name *Me. Dou. Sa.*

"Are you sure of it?" Hekate asked.

"Yes. She is Medousa, the Mortal Shadow over Algol," Hera said the name once more and a chill slithered up my spine. I watched Hekate's shoulders tense with an electric pulse. My wings brushed up against billowing, cloudy pillars, and I circled once more over the pharmakides.

Dusk turned the heavenly castle from pink to magenta. A dark night was coming.

"I must go," Hekate said. Of course she knew better than to press Hera for details, or leave Medousa alone on a mountainside after dark.

"There's one more thing I hesitate to share, but I feel I must," Hera said.

"Go on."

"Clouds whispered to me about the legacy of Medousa. They say it will be carved into stone and..." Hera's voice trailed off, as if she had forgotten what she was saying or why she was saying it at all.

"What is it?" Hekate asked, her flushed cheeks becoming darker shades of rose by the minute.

"Oh I don't know if I should tell you the rest, but I may as well. Best if you hear it from me before plunging into your fate blind."

"Tell me. I can handle it," Hekate, ruler of the Underworld, pleaded in heaven. When she did— her voice cracked.

"Very well," Hera said, "You're going to make a monster out of her."

Hekate swallowed and blinked, stunned into silence.

"I want you to always remember," Hera said, "You could've let her die."

Hekate bowed. She hid her face from Hera, maintaining the illusion that she could, in fact, tolerate the prophecy. Then she made her way out of the baths and rushed towards the foyer. Hekate no longer took in the views from the castle, the aura of the pink clouds, the growing moon. She focused on leaving.

I flew up and out of the atrium. I could still hear Hekate's footsteps, slowly making their way through the castle. I heard them from outside, for the wind was soft. The night was calm, save the boiling emotions I felt coursing through me. Hekate's steps sounded heavier than before, and I heard them against the material mist, the smoky vapor, with a twinge of regret in her toes. Her breath sounded heavier too, like she carried something in it that she didn't bring with her up the starry steps.

I peered in through the windows at the witch, circling and passing her. Hekate didn't hesitate. She knew every bubbling fountain, she knew her way back to the gate. The pharmakis was almost as quick as me, but not quite.

Bronze trilled on her neck. Her key to the Underworld, surely. Hera didn't need any keys, because she kept no secrets. She was so honest, and trusted me to keep her gates secured. There was no lock, only the eye of an eagle. As a guardian of Nephele's castle, I flew above Hekate. I watched her leave and my golden feathers blended into the ornate atriums.

It was such a funny irony that clouds obscured the sky, yet provided clarity. Clarity was always a heavy burden.

With hurried flaps of my wings, I rushed back to Nephele.

"Thank goodness you're back," Nephele said without looking up. Her head was tucked in the crook of her elbow, awash with tears I presumed.

I perched over Nephele as Hekate emerged from the castle. She slipped into her boots, onto her horse, and down the spiral staircase. She left without taking a breath.

I did not close the gates behind the witch.

Nephele looked at me, her lip quivering.

My heart struggled to accept the grief in her eyes. Crystalline tears plummeted towards the clouds she called home. Tears even fell onto my feathers. Her tears were like diamonds. They were droplets, but as if a droplet had been carved by a chisel. Nephele's grief was calculated, while her happiness ran freely.

While tears rolled down her cheeks, they were a sweet innocent lavender color. When her grief met with clouds, they darkened. The clouds were her power, and when she let them feel her sadness they grew plump with rain.

A storm was brewing.

The fish-filled moat turned almost completely black. Silvery fish swam through it like lanterns in the night. The castle went from ethereal to gothic. Its edges sharpened. Its color turned from pink to pitch black. The castle became so dark it blotted out emerging stars. Even Nephele, with her pink tail, darkened. She wept harder than before. I watched her, bawling into the moat, and stirring a raging tempest to life. The only thing that stayed undisturbed was my golden gate, and the threads of gold that wove between bricks of clouds.

It wasn't often I felt so powerless. My beak was stronger than any bird. I could fly higher than the rest. I had power, but Nephele's heart breaking over a missing horse was out of my control. I had no idea where Alpheratz went. I didn't know what I could do.

My own wrath, my own fury, pushed me to dive from the castle. The strongest rage I felt was not really my own, it was wrath towards the injustice of another's pain.

I flew from Nephele's side, out of the golden gates. My wings were wide, until I pulled them close. I plummeted towards Magnesia and my dive lit up the earth.

4. *Crane*

Magnesia valleyed before me. I could see over the forest to an opposing mountaintop. On its summit, a spiral staircase reached towards the moon. A dead horse hurried down the steps.

It wasn't like the dead to move, especially with such a rush. I'd gotten used to it. These were Hekate's woods and mysterious things happened in the shadows of her poplar trees. I heard the soft clank of bronze horseshoes striking mist.

The staircase appeared periodically– only when a full moon glittered over my dark forest. I wondered if other creatures noticed. All through the night sleepy mosquitoes lulled between the mandibles of wasps, fireflies mesmerized bats, and crickets strummed their instruments.

I alone, it seemed, watched the moon.

The horse had a rider. It was Hekate, the Pharmakis of the Dark Side of the Moon. Other birds told me that she was as old as the sky itself. She rode down, suspended by moonlight and her own enchantments.

I watched Hekate and her horse march back down to the earth. Hekate could bring back the dead and manifest staircases into clouds. She knew a great many things, but she missed omens like anyone else. She didn't always see the messages in the birds. Perhaps a different pharmakis would've heard the quivering of my feathers. Even though Hekate came down from the sky herself, she had no idea that in that moment, she was outrunning rain.

I did. Rain spoke to me before it whispered to any other bird. I felt it between the plumes of my pewter feathers. My wings felt tempests roiling with water. Clouds swirled with blots of gray. The invisible sheen of Hekate's horse took on the anger of the sky. As clouds darkened, droplets rubbed together; light and darkness mingled.

By then, Hekate had reached the ground. I heard Hekate's horse sigh. Though he was already dead, I knew heights made all horses uneasy. The staircase disappeared behind them as if it was never there at all, as if the structure had been a glare reflecting off the moon that faded into the night.

Hekate rode towards another ghost horse tied to a tree.

She unfastened him and I watched a girl, funnily enough, step out from the branches of an olive tree. A small thistle finch chirped and hurried around their heads. It flew from Hekate to the girl, as if it carried secrets and spilled them with tweets.

Even from afar, I sensed something strange about the girl. I recognized her as Medousa, who bubbled up from the sea one day before. Hera had, on the same night, dropped this girl's name from the clouds and into my mind. Even her breath resonated with the rhythms of the sea, like waves that kiss a shore.

Medousa mounted the spare horse and followed Hekate down the mountaintop. Both horses stepped in coordinated, rapid succession.

I felt moisture collecting between my feathers, begging more to fall from the clouds.

I heralded a trumpet from my beak. It nestled between the mountains of Magnesia and the sky above. Once my first call settled, I made another.

Rain began. Soon came the first pitter-patters of water. The woodsy air, thick with musky sage, quickly blossomed with the fresh scent of rain. The moon's glow obscured behind a veil of clouds and falling water. As it rained, each drop wished to find its way back to sea.

Raindrops pelted down, drenching everything in Hekate and Medousa's path.

Medousa's head snapped up, her eyes widening with surprise as the cool droplets cascaded onto her face. Her fingers reached out, brushing against her wet cheeks. She blinked, as if trying to comprehend the sudden deluge that enveloped her. A shiver ran through her body, her shoulders tensed with unease. The sensation of the rain soaking through her clothes seemed to startle her, as if each droplet carried an unexpected touch.

Medousa was new to the world.

"Be careful in the rain," Hekate warned, "Even dead horses slip and fall."

Such was the way of mountains that their words, and even their heartbeats, traveled far below them, across the valley, and to my ears.

Medousa swallowed. Her wide eyes darted around, searching for stability and trying to regain composure amidst the downpour.

They both fell silent. I stepped towards Hekate and Medousa, yet they were still so far away. My head guided each step, the weight of my skull and my neck pulling me forwards, closer and closer to them. I always felt curious when the pharmakis came to my woods, but I had never stood on her path before. I hid in the shadows of their trail, knowing that if I did not move, they would cross my path on their way back to the sea.

As soon as I nestled into the shadows, I felt a strange wind over my back. I could tell it came from wings that flew much higher than mine, where the air was colder, where few birds dared to fly. Then I heard an angry shriek, like the sound of two enemy swords scraping against each other, vying for power.

After I heard him I saw him– a golden eagle falling from the sky. His torso flittered between the branches above me. He fell from the highest reaches of the sky, certainly higher than I have ever flown. His wings were folded against his body, in perfect position for hurtling towards the earth.

A blinding streak of lightning bursted from his golden feathers.

I saw the forest turn white. Black trunks blanched. The darkening evening sky transformed from inky purple to death-white. The eagle paled the whole forest. I swear the eyes of beetles and bats glowed, uncovered by shadows that hid them before.

The eagle's cry pierced through the wet air once again. It was full of vengeance. It was a burning warning. The eagle's storm was coming, and it would be a tempest of epic proportions, unable to be caged by bronze chains or deep caves.

A crack, a dry spell of lightning like the flick of a whip, went up my spine and commanded me to freeze. Each of my claws sank deeper into the wet forest floor. I braced for impact. I felt the eagle's fury percolate the bumps on my skin, and I felt it as my claws dug, slowly, into the thirsty earth. Though it was winter, the lightning was hot. Rain wet the forest. Heat and moisture produced all things, and on that night, strange things were coming indeed.

It was over in a flash. The sky went dark again, except for the full moon, who shone eerily through parted gray clouds and falling water.

I swear nobody else in Magnesia saw the eagle, for they were all blinded by the lightning. I alone had eyes fit for storms. I saw the eagle collect himself and fly back up into the clouds. He soared higher and higher into the sky, back from whence he came.

The eagle came to Magnesia to demand light, to uncover every shadow in the lands. Some wrong had to be righted, and the eagle sought illumination. He screeched again, asking for war between clouds and land. The eagle, from his high throne, spurred clouds to twist with rage.

I was stuck between breaths. It was as if I was a wooden part of the forest, gaining the power of invisibility by standing, so, perfectly still. Even my beady eyes dared not glisten in the dimming night.

Though I froze, this was not the instinctual reaction for Hekate and Medousa's horses. They spooked at the flash. I saw them running. I watched their heads shoot up while they broke into long gallops. Hoofbeats rocked the earth like thunder. Even across the foothills, I could see a white glimmer of terror in the horse's eyes. I saw fear strike the cold, gray stoic eyes of Hekate, but not Medousa. She was enlivened by chaos. The tension I noticed in her shoulders seemed to melt away. I even saw a smile creep up her cheeks. A chord of terror within me silently urged both her and Hekate to stay on their horses.

In those few moments after the flash, things were normal, albeit the girl Medousa was a bit unnerving. Thunder always followed a flash. On that night, when thunder came, normal went to the far side of the moon, far past the simple animation of the dead.

Creatures sprang from muddy puddles. They were called to life by rumbles of thunder, to storm across rolling hills and forests. I never heard of creatures rising from puddles. I wondered if they found a way to crawl through Magnesia from the Underworld. The notion troubled me, urging my heart to beat faster. These beasts followed a flash—- when vulnerabilities of the forest became clear. Lightning, gifted by the eagle, revealed all.

A flurry of hoofbeats erupted through the dark forest. They were born from thunder, diverged from the stillness of puddles and the rattle of rain. I felt the earth shake again.

It wasn't the shrill twang of Hekate's ghostly herd who stepped on bronze shoes. These were natural hooves, carving into the mud with no metal involved.

Strangely enough, I heard the heartbeats of horses and the heartbeats of men. I heard the shouts of men too, cutting through the trees to my frightened ears. My first impression of these new arrivals, before I understood them, was that I assumed men were riding horses.

Or even, I thought perhaps horses were chasing men. Both of my initial guesses were wrong. Either way, I stood still.

The creatures ran between trees and I heard tails whoosh behind them, like whips. The siege of rain raised the puddles which raised the creatures. The bugs had fallen asleep, except for the moths who flapped up towards the moon between sonar beams of bats. I took a breath, listening to new hoofbeats creep over the forest.

I was safest close to a tree, blending in unseen. My throat, which didn't dare call, was coated, closed by black feathers. I pretended my plumage was wooden as bark, and I imagined my eye as a subtle berry.

Animals charged between the trees all around me. I heard the noble heartbeats of horses and the manipulative heartbeats of men, somehow at odds with one another, somehow in unison. They faded in a stampede towards darker valleys.

I heard the breath of the witch in her own woods. When all the creatures fell back into the infinity of trees, I saw Hekate and Medousa coming around the trail's corner. The ghost horses walked at a slow pace and I was sure they caught no hint of the creatures who darted behind the trees. The horses and riders continued on their trail.

Rain battered the riders and fell straight through the horses. I watched the horses' silvery curving ears move to catch every sound. Not a soul knew I was there, not even those horses, with their funnily curved ears, could've heard my shallow breath.

I felt the slow steps of bronze horseshoes rattle the earth beneath my talons.

"How long are we going to be walking through this storm?" Medousa lifted waterlogged curls from her gaze. My bones shivered at her voice.

"We're riding back to the cottage."

"No way! On the other side of these mountains?" Medousa sneered. I saw fear flicker over Medousa's rebellious eyes. She shivered.

Her horse stopped. Though the colt was dead, I was sure he felt Medousa's apprehension. The sudden halt brought Medousa out of her wet saddle. She flew forward with a sudden lurch. Bronze could tether a dead horse to earth, but it couldn't tether the young girl to her seat.

Medousa splashed into a puddle, rolling over herself. Her ripples misted me, licked at my feet digging into the soil. I dared not flinch.

Medousa's wide eyes darted around. Still, she couldn't see me between moonlight and darkness. Medousa threw back her head and groaned in the dirty water. I imagined the pain of her hard meeting with the earth. I watched her hold her shoulder and I wondered if she had ever fallen before. I saw her green eyes and their reflection in the water. I saw her fear, how the water touched her, like she was grown from its very waves.

"Stop that! You're going to become soaked," Hekate demanded, "Get back onto your horse."

"I'm already soaked!" Medousa shouted. She stood in the wet forest and stomped her foot. Both the pharmakis and the girl were too caught up in their argument to notice, but I did. When Medousa stamped her foot into the puddle, a trail of blue sparks fizzled through the air. They just missed my hidden feathers

The flashes burnt out in puddles.

Medousa's horse was frightened by the sparks. They troubled his cautious, dead heart. Without a rider to reassure him, for she was laying in a puddle, he panicked. He bolted, barreling down the gnarled trail.

Hekate scowled and instructed her own horse to chase down the runaway. I could feel her disapproval of Medousa, until their hoofbeats ran far past the bends of my hiding place.

I was alone with Medousa and the stars. She looked up and I saw constellations twinkling in her eyes.

Medousa stood up in the puddles on bare feet. Robes clung to her and revealed her ankle. Streams of rain etched her skin, but underneath the streaks, I could see a mark which glowed like a star.

I saw a snake eating its own tail, encircling her ankle. It glowed with the bluish tinge of Algol. I wondered how starlight got stuck under her skin.

Medousa still looked to the stars. She hadn't noticed me examining her ankle. Though Algol flickered in the morning, was it possible that I saw it through the storm, shining in Medousa's eyes? I wondered, but I could not ask, what the starlight in her skin meant. I wondered if Medousa was chained to the stars.

I felt like I was alone with Medousa, but feeling alone in the woods was only ever an illusion. There were eyes in every crevice and, apparently, creatures waiting to spring from puddles.

I heard the slick slither of scales through a puddle. My feathers longed to stand on end, but I defied my instincts. I urged them to stay down, protect me from the rain, and cloak me in the invisibility of stillness.

From the corner of my eye, I saw a snake float over a puddle, towards the feet of Medousa. Her head was still in the clouds. I spotted another snake, and another snake, and suddenly a dozen snakes coiled at her feet. I watched them float with serpentine ease towards Medousa. Clouds dissipated light from the full moon, giving a silver sheen to each snake. I longed to bite into them, to peel their scales and rip out their meat.

It was better to stay still, better to be unseen by Medousa. My gut told me that, far deeper than my hungry stomach.

In the wet, dark, and chilled night, the snakes of Greece sought Medousa. I wondered if they could feel stars shining under her skin, and if they were seeking out their warmth. They came to her feet while she looked up at the stars. The serpents were like her roots, if she were a tree. They flicked their tongues like shadows in candlelight.

One snake slithered over the bare foot of the girl.

Medousa looked down at her feet at the creatures gathering beneath her. They all looked up at her to meet her eyes.

"Medousa," I heard a snake whisper with a hiss.

"Who are you?" She asked as if speaking to a snake was no different than speaking with Hekate.

"We are snakes."

"We know a stone cold heart and ambitious eyes," the snake's voice lisped, "We respect you for it."

"We have to tell you something," Each snake took turns speaking, but their message was collective.

"What is it?" Medousa asked. She was so young, I wondered if she knew that snakes didn't whisper to every lost girl in the woods.

"Under this moon and the grief from the clouds, creatures sprang up from the puddles."

"They will not be loyal to the forest of Magnesia."

"They'll steal from the witch."

Medousa wrinkled her brow. Each snake looked at her with yellow–slitted eyes.

"Why? What are they going to steal?" She asked. I heard her breath stop and her heart start to slow down. I recognized something in Medousa, that she was like me. As fear came over her, her natural instinct was to become as still as stone. She froze. I shivered at my resemblance in her emerald eyes. Even though the whole forest became drenched in silver moonlight, her eyes stayed green.

"They will steal from Hekate. Her bronze mirror will trade hands. Because of this betrayal on the grounds of Magnesia— you'll be dead…."

Medousa's eyes grew wide.

"You have a choice now, Medousa," the hiss begged her to listen.

"You can run into the woods and we promise you that these new creatures will protect you."

"The woods will make you stronger."

"What about Hekate?" Medousa asked.

"You must act now. You must be gone when Hekate comes back. Otherwise your fate is sealed. These creatures will steal the witch's mirror and you will be dead."

"Yes, dead before the next moon."

Medousa's stammered, but couldn't speak.

"Today creatures sprouted from the mud, half horse and half man."

"You could rule over them."

"All you must do is step outside."

"Creatures? What creatures?" She asked.

"Run into the woods."

"Go and don't look back."

"You'll find them."

I heard her heart pulse. The snakes urged her to be wild, but she stayed frozen. I heard the silence in her soul. I felt it in my bones. I heard her heart juggle the idea, but doubt crept in.

"I wish to stay here," Medousa said, "and wait for Hekate."

"Very well," a hiss of indifference.

"Such will be your fate."

"My fate? What is my fate?" She asked.

"Now it's your job to write it. You could've handed the pen over to the woods, and she would've mapped your fate for you. You could've walked a chosen path. Now, the burden of your story lies in your hands."

"What? Tell me more," Medousa pleaded.

The snakes fell silent. They pretended like they couldn't speak at all. They looked back down at each other and uncoiled their bodies. Each snake rushed into a different shadow of the forest until they had all disappeared in a shimmer of moonlight.

Medousa had a moment for one breath only, before the puddles started to ripple. We both heard the booming of hoofbeats and fixed our eyes on the trail.

Then, I spotted the creature.

He ran in moon-dappled rain. He had the focused, forward facing gaze of a human, but the body of a horse. Behind him, in the veil of silver rain, a herd of creatures with his likeness followed him.

They were horses, but where there should be a long neck, communicative ears, and a soft muzzle, was the torso of a man. Suddenly I understood why I heard the hearts of horses and men. It hadn't been horses and riders who sprang up from the puddles, but real, living kentauroi.

One heart possessed the fiery spirit of a horse, who ran first and asked questions later. The other heart pumped blood to hands and minds which could wield tools and reason.

Each animal was a living contradiction. Raindrops lingered on their fur and skin.

I realized the serpents were not lying when they prophesized betrayal from the creatures in these woods. I could see it already. Their ability to disarm lay in their dual nature. They had the ability to plot like men, then run from a heist like the wind.

These creatures were different, of course. They leapt out of puddles. I wondered about the eagle, the flash of lightning, and what act of Poseidon brought them here.

Medousa saw them too. She stood, frozen in the trail. I heard Medousa's heartbeat unravel, but she was too scared to move, to make the wrong decision, to put herself in further danger. She trembled in fear.

They could've hurt her. I saw the realization creep over her face. They were half human and half horse, but there was something more, an additional being that was more than horse and man combined.

Traitors.

She appeared calm, but I knew better. There was fear in Medousa's breath.

The beasts stampeded down the trail, narrowly avoiding stepping on the girl, and consistently splashing me between the trees.

Behind them, I spotted Hekate. Her ghostly horse was short and slow in comparison to the wild kentauroi. Hekate held onto bronze threaded reigns and brought her other dead horse along in tow for Medousa. A mossy glint sparkled in Hekate's stony eyes, for she saw Medousa trembling in a puddle on the trail, exactly where she had left her.

I heard rumors about the pharmakis. I believed them all, because of what I'd seen her do. Of course, I'd seen stairs spring from the mountaintop through her burning glass. I knew she trapped a herd of horses between living and dead. I'd seen her rule over these woods for a long time, but I'd never seen her look so worried. Her eyes were wide, her brows furrowed.

"What's wrong?" Medousa implored.

"Beasts of the Underworld are running in my forest," Hekate stammered.

"The horsemen?"

"Kentauroi! In Magnesia!"

"Those things?"

Medousa, so virginal, had not recognized the strangeness of those creatures. For all she knew they ran through these forests long before her.

"How did these new kentauroi arrive?" Hekate asked, "Did they spring up from the rain?"

Hekate leapt down from her horse.

"Medousa, hold them," She handed the bronze reins to Medousa, "I have to pull a shoe."

"What do you mean?"

"The only way the dead can walk over the earth is on bronze shoes. This one is about to fall off. Must've gotten caught on a root when he bolted. Better pull it off before he trips"

Hekate lifted the horse's foot. She unfastened her horn, her slender waning moon, from atop her head. Hekate dug the edge of her horn between metal and mist. With a swift motion, the loose shoe came free and Hekate tossed it into a muddy puddle. To my surprise, the shoe vanished with a red gleam.

Hekate wiped off her horns and refashioned them to her head.

"He's still got three bronze shoes left. No chance he'll get whisked away to hell," Hekate said.

Medousa still had not found her center. Her heart thudded.

"Mount," Hekate instructed, offering a leg up to Medousa, "We have a long ride back."

Medousa threw a leg over the horse. With a missing shoe, the horse got a little bit closer to death.

After her first rain, Medousa was a little bit closer to madness.

5. Dove

Medousa massaged olive oil through her hair with her head tilted back and eyes closed. Golden curls cascaded down her body all the way to her waist, saturated and gleaming with oil. Her fingers were slick, sliding across her scalp and down each winding lock. She took her time so that every strand was nourished. As she massaged, the curls came alive, each one with a mind of its own as they bounced and swayed with her movements.

When she finished we got to work, though it was not a demand.

I was drawn to the flowing rivers of her curls. It was my wish.

We all were. So golden was Medousa's hair; so fresh was her aura.

We fluttered together, soft plumes brushed against each other. For, what is a loving bird, without a heart beating beside its kin? I needed companions in flight.

We braided her hair into waterfalls and plaits. Somehow, she was like one of us. Her movements were fluid, her nature gentle. We flew over and under each other. A dove for each strand, fluttering about. Our flock was made of pairs, for it took many doves to weave so many curls. It was like building a nest, but even more dear. One of us carried a blooming belladonna flower inside. Its scent was intoxicating and lovely. We plucked it from Hekate's garden as soon as we saw the girl, and knew she must be adorned. From the talons of a dove to stuck behind her ear, the deep purple accented her golden locks.

Medousa's skin was so smooth she was like a pebble, carved over time by water. We readied her, adding elegance to her beauty. The small wardrobe was fashioned with a bronze mirror, which reflected Medousa's pale skin and our white feathers like gold. Her pistachio eyes yellowed, but still they glowed like the brightest stars at night. In the mirror, she looked like fluid metal under a blacksmith's hammer. Poets would've called her shiny hair *xanthos,* a color which fused red to green. She shone, in person, and in the mirror.

The mirror had its own story to tell, in silence, in reflection. Its outer edges laid out stories of the sky. The circular border was divided into chambers, like the hemispheres of a star map. Chains of constellations occupied one quadrant, and in the next, hounds chased comets. On the opposite hemisphere were embossed quails and sea-riddled islands. These were the stories of the pharmakis herself, and the stories of her mother, who fled Greece as a quail. She flew with an open, faithful heart towards the sea.

Medousa blinked, happy to see the dogs and the stars, the birds and the islands. I was sure she was perfectly unaware of their meaning.

I was sure Hekate had kept her secrets.

Her breath was like our collective coo. I drew my wings up with her inhale and down with her exhale. I flew and carried her hair. It was important to know the mirror, the room, and the cottage all belonged to the pharmakis. Her ancient walls were fixed with stories, carved runes of star signs and herbal symbols. Us doves let our white feathers brush up against deep strokes and carvings.

The wardrobe had hardly enough room for one person to turn around, well enough with a dozen birds flying behind her. As we busied ourselves with Medousa's braids, the door opened. Hekate leaned in to offer a suggestion.

"Lovely. Keep these braids in all day. You'll be learning how to fight," Hekate said, her gaze stern on Medousa's bronze reflection.

My tiny heart pounded at her last word. For, I am a loving bird who resents fighting and aggression. I, and my fellow doves, were happy in our act of braiding, if it may protect this enchanted girl.

"Why must I learn to fight?" I watched the stars fade from Medousa's eyes.

My flock had keen ears. We heard Hekate and Medousa arrive at the cottage yesterday. We heard their ghost horses run into the forests of Magnesia after their riders arrived. We heard everything in our roost. We knew the soft lull of Hekate's mysterious voice, and the new, curious questions of Medousa. We knew, when Hekate held silence, mysteries wove together and then unraveled.

"Rather than fighting, I wish to learn the ways of birds and herbs and teas," Medousa said, "I wish to read the stars."

"Without fighting you won't live long enough to learn a damned thing," Hekate said. She backed up, ready to slam the door, but caught Medousa's troubled eyes and continued, "Fortune favors the bold. You will have to fight to be who you really are."

Hekate disappeared. Medousa closed her eyes and wiped her oily fingers against her clothes. I heard her soft exhale. She stroked the belladonna we had tucked behind her ear. The purple flower was perfectly placed, as if the petals were frozen, caught licking her temples. Vivid violet was the opposite to her golden hair. We wondered if there could've been an opposite to Medousa– if this girl, golden as the light, would've ever cast a shadow. I watched her shoulders drop and her body relax. She was just a girl after all, and all girls had dreams, even girls with their heads in the stars.

We reached the end of her long coiled hair. My flock paused in wait. I flew upward towards a cupboard, near the ceiling of the wardrobe. I realized mist crawled over the door. It smelled of poppies and seawater. I cooed at my fellow doves and they understood solemnly.

From the open cupboard, I plucked a short ribbon of black silk. Maybe black could ensure luck in a fight, I wished.

I flew back down to Medousa's crown. By the time I was there, mist shrouded each pair of doves. Dewy drops clung to our ivory feathers. Medousa was oblivious to the subtle mist. Because of that, I liked her. She gave me delusional hope. She didn't bat an eye as mist fell over the door like a waterfall.

Us doves knew its origin. It bubbled up from the sea cavern beneath Hekate's cottage. The very air we breathed was a bridge, between life and death. Medousa's focus was on her fight, on keeping her flowing golden curls out of her eyes.

There was a warrior in the mirror, tainted by bronze, backdropped by doves and mist.

My partner grabbed the black ribbon. Together we tied a bow to secure the ends of her shining braids. Her hair was so golden, its glares were red and its shadows were green in the bronze mirror. Her ribbon's reflection stayed black, untainted by metals or sorcery.

6. *Vulture*

My neck curved in a graceful arc, but nobody ever mistook me for a lovely swan. All eyes that searched the skies for omens recognized me as the harbinger of death. Though I loved darkness, I always flew while the sun was high. That way, I cast a dark shadow.

I met Medousa on a dry winter afternoon while I floated over Hekate's lands in long, lonely circles.

The pharmakis' garden had no order; it flourished according to wild whims. She knew what all vultures knew— there was wisdom in the roots. Plants worked in their own mysterious ways. Hekate had no pots for seedlings. She didn't put specific plants together in rows. When it came time to plant in the spring, the pharmakis scattered her seeds randomly. If they were meant to grow, then they would, all on their own.

Although the pharmakis' methods were unruly, her plants grew. They flourished, in fact. Beneath a luscious canopy, plants whispered the secrets of the universe. Hekate grew trees that tickled the Underworld and flowers with bliss between their petals.

I inhaled the heady scent of bright red poppy blossoms. I could almost taste their bitter flavors from the sky. If I was a younger griffon vulture, with a golden coat, I may have dizzied at the scent. If I was younger and more naive, I may have even begun to imagine things.

Voices came closer and closer. I spotted two figures approaching through the tangled underbrush.

"First, you must learn the proper foot positions. A warrior is built from the ground up. Balance is key in a fight," Hekate instructed.

"What if, in a fight, I caught my opponent by surprise? What if I kicked their head and they never saw it coming?" Medousa asked. She leapt in front of the pharmakis and shot one leg into the air, falling over from the force of it.

She caught herself quickly and fell right back into step with Hekate.

I wondered how she learned to walk, for it was so strange. She seemed to me like a wave, or the tides, moving in tandem with the moon.

"You're reckless without a clue!" Hekate said, doing her best to ignore the kick.

"I'd probably win," Medousa crossed her arms.

"You don't know anything about danger!"

"Yes. I do!"

"You came from the sea without a scratch on your skin," Hekate dismissed her.

Then I saw a flash of blue in Medousa's psyche. It was an angry phosphorescence. The flash said there was some memory which clung to her ego. It needed to be reconciled. She stayed silent. She suppressed her feelings, her memories, and followed Hekate, looking down at her budding warrior feet. I saw a sweet, psychedelic belladonna flower tucked behind Medousa's ear.

They reached my commanding grove.

"We've arrived. You need to figure out which tree is meant to be your sparring partner."

A circle of black poplar trees stood still around the pharmakis and the girl. Dark trees reached for the sky, but that was only above ground. They also reached for death, for the Underworld. Black poplar roots reached deeper down than any other tree in Greece.

My grove sprang up from the confluence, the thinning layer, between living and dead.

"How will I know which tree to choose?" Medousa looked around. The trees eyed her back, though she had no idea. I circled above, a bad omen if she were to look up, but she never did.

"Your tree of choice will offer you a weapon."

I could tell Medousa's mind was open. I could sense it in her breath, which was deep and rhythmic. She didn't resist the mysteries of magic. I doubted if she even understood the boundary between magical phenomena and regular occurrences. She wouldn't ask how trees moved or sensed her presence. Medousa played along, as all the best young pharmakides did.

She looked around at the different trees. Some were old, with withered bark and tall trunks. Others were young, just sprouting and reaching towards the sun where they could find it. Some of the black poplars leaned and bore twisted branches. Others shot straight up in a steadfast defiance of gravity.

Medousa approached a slanted trunk and stroked its rough bark. From the sky I felt Poseidon on her fingertips, between her swirling grooves. I felt everything that particular tree felt, no matter where I was.

She didn't know it, but that was *my* tree. Every night I roosted between those gnarled branches. I'd hidden lucky bones between the cracks of its bark. I was its shepherd and it was mine. I commanded a battalion of roots, which crept deeper into the Underworld than I dared to venture. In its wood, I heard whispers from the dead. I circled above Medousa and the trees, feigning indifference.

I brought the black poplar to life with the help of Medousa's touch.

Above her, branches bristled. The black poplar had a mind of its own. Or so it seemed to Medousa, who never looked up to see me circling above her.

Hekate did. Her gray eyes glanced up at me. She knew.

One limb stretched down, right in front of the young girl, and broke off before her eyes. It landed at her feet and Medousa jumped in surprise.

My tree's limb transformed into a staff, fit for any warrior.

I brought my circle to an end and landed on the peak of the tree. I felt the pulse of poplar through my talons. It was the pulse of a warrior.

High above the heat of the day, in the cold abyss of sky, stars changed. A star which once shone bright started to flicker. The warrior before me, holding the very staff which I animated, was herself the Mortal Shadow over Algol. A new era of war was coming. Energies would change hands. Planets would pass each other. When shadows danced over the Algol, violence was called to earth.

As Medousa reached to pick up the staff, I saw her robes rustle. A tail-eating snake peeked from her ankle. It glowed in a shade of blue I'd seen before. Medousa was branded, blue and white-hot, like the star of Algol.

She was fit to wield stars, to cast her imagination into heavens.

Medousa held the staff, and it glowed with a blue sheen. Her pale face shimmered in the strange light.

Then the staff went dark and solidified, harder than any metal.

She needed an opponent. I could've animated the black poplar itself.

I imagined it swinging its branches in combat with her.

However, the best war strategists don't go to battle themselves. Officers sent pawns. From the woods, I could call a soldier to rise from dirt.

The ground in front of Medousa started to shake. Her eyes grew wide and she held the staff, ready to fight. She glanced at Hekate for a moment, but the elder pharmakis said nothing. She offered no reassurance. She merely watched with a hard, stony gaze. A warrior had to face her battle, whether she was ready for it or not, simply because it came time to fight.

Medousa's knuckles whitened as she held the staff. She lowered her stance. Roots loosened the earth around her.

A mandragora's long green leaves started to rise from the trembling ground. They rose higher and higher to reveal a short creature, whose body was fashioned from twisted roots. It was an earthly, humanoid figure. The mandragora stood to face Medousa, with black eyes, worms crawling over its skin, and rooty bulges where a human might've had muscles. He even sported a crown of red poppy blossoms around his green leaves.

The mandragora was armed with a long, slender root, coiled like a whip.

Medousa approached her opponent with her staff at the ready. She had all the fury of the ocean in her sea-green eyes and the weighty depth of its power.

Before she launched her attack, Medousa howled. She barked like a monster unleashed.

Her opponent was unphased. The mandragora didn't flinch. Instead, he bared his teeth, which were closer to rough, dirty, wooden stumps than fangs.

Medousa struck, aiming for the neck of the animated wooden body. The mandragora was faster. He unleashed his whip, which circled around Medousa's staff.

As the whip coiled, it created a shower of sparks that fell upon both the girl and mandragora. Medousa winced. She gritted her teeth and tugged on her weapon. The sparks gave her strength, for she was able to pull back and free her staff.

The mandragora's eyes, black as coal, locked with Medousa's and it bared its teeth again. Its wooden stumps formed a mocking smile.

Medousa struck again, this time aiming for the mandragora's ankles. Sweat beaded down her body as she swung her staff with all her might, her muscles straining with exertion. The mandragora was inexhaustible. The wooden creature leapt, high into the air, and sent its whip whistling towards Medousa. She hardly had time to dodge its lash.

Medousa's eyes darted around, looking for the mandragora's weakness.

Her opponent did not give her time to ponder. It struck its whip with increasing speed and ferocity. Medousa dodged each blow, nimbly leaping out of the way.

"Some way you have of teaching me," Medousa shouted at Hekate, who watched from the sidelines in the shady grove.

"I thought you were sure you could catch an opponent by surprise," Hekate said, her cool voice barely carrying over the sound of Medousa's labored breaths. I dug my talons into the poplar's bark and urged the battle to give way for a remarkable opportunity.

Medousa let out a battle cry and lunged towards the mandragora.

He couldn't whip her if they were too close. She pushed her staff against his chest and heaved.

The mandragora fell backwards towards the ground.

Medousa lifted her staff and punctured the mandragoras forearm with it. Splinters rained out in place of blood. Medousa pushed her staff into the earth, pinning the mandragora in place. It rolled around, trying to strike her with its other limbs.

Medousa gained control. She dodged those blows with ease. Watching Medousa fight was like watching the sea. She went back and forth between storming and relenting in the same manner that waves battered shores. She was like the ebb and flow of water. When the power was all hers, she was as merciless as the deep blue swallowing shipwrecked sailors.

There was a ruthless depth in her eyes. In the future, when she became a legend, some would say it came from Algol. In truth, it came from me. I taught Medousa to fight, and the tighter she gripped my staff, the more she picked up on the ills of war.

The mandragora cried in pain, wincing and screaming at the girl.

"You pharmakis!"

"Coming from a wilted weed!" she shouted back and kicked the mandragora in its torso. Its body crunched and splintered.

Then she pried the whip from the mandragora's hand. She lifted her new weapon, ready to strike. The whip sounded like a snake as it followed her movements in the grass.

"That's enough," Hekate said.

Medousa was tempted to ignore her, but before she could act, the wailing mandragora sank back into the earth. Quickly, the whip wriggled free from Medousa's grasp and followed the mandragora back underground. Her staff followed. I summoned my soldiers, and their weapons back into the Underworld. From my hand in her fight, a piece of the Underworld became lodged in Medousa.

She was left empty handed, panting in the center of the grove. I watched her bend over, hands on her knees, chest heaving.

"I have notes," Hekate said.

"I'm supposed to show mercy?" Medousa rolled her eyes.

"No."

"What, then?"

"Never approach your enemy with your feet facing them, always angle yourself to the side, so you are more difficult to strike," Hekate instructed and demonstrated, approaching Medousa with her body angled away.

Medousa nodded, taking a moment to practice the stance herself.

"I'll hurry to the cottage and fetch you some tea, a special blend to soothe any muscles you may have strained," Hekate said, "Stay here to catch your breath."

Medousa sighed and let her shoulders droop. Even after the battle, she still had the hardy belladonna tucked behind her ear.

As soon as Hekate turned her back, a tall figure emerged from the shadows of the trees. I had no idea how long he was there. Since he moved so quietly in the woods, I guessed him to be a hunter.

Since I was neither hawk nor falcon– I couldn't screech over the land. I grunted. I hissed. But those faint rumbles were nearly silent. Vultures are almost as quiet as the dead. Not a soul could hear me. I wanted to warn Medousa about the hunter, but it wasn't that easy. I could've animated trees, and trapped him.

I considered it.

But I'd molded this girl into a warrior. I'd given her a taste of bloodshed. I set the Underworld loose under her skin. Perhaps it was better for me to watch everything play out from above.

If Medousa defeated my mandragora, she must be ready to face the figure in the shadows.

As Hekate moved further and further away, the tall figure creeped closer towards Medousa. When he came out from the shadows I saw his thick, curling beard and piercing blue eyes. He walked silently.

There was not even a rustle of leaves under his feet.

"Young maiden with golden hair," the figure shouted towards Medousa, "You're a formidable warrior."

Medousa froze at the sound of his voice. I heard her breath catch on an inhale. A long pause drifted through the grove before she spoke, keeping her back to him.

"You watched me fight?"

"Yes, I heard the commotion and came running. I wondered if I may be of help to any fair maidens, but you handled the creature on your own."

Medousa still had her back to him, but he crept closer.

"My name is Orion and I am the bravest hunter in all of Greece. I wanted to say that in all of my travels, I have never seen anything as beautiful as the locks of your hair."

"Beauty can be deceiving."

"I am sure tha-"

"Why are you here?" Medousa cut him off.

"I came to Magnesia to hunt kentauroi. Rumors say they have arrived in these lands and I plan to draw them away," Orion puffed out his chest as he spoke, but Medousa wasn't watching. She froze in a calculated stance. Her knees bent and her breath slowed.

Medousa didn't reply.

"Are you alone?" Orion continued.

"If you saw me fight, then you know I am not alone," Medousa had a sinister edge to her voice. Orion winced at her sharp words.

"I meant to ask if you had a husband."

A blush came over Medousa's face and her heart beat against her ribs like a caged lovebird.

"So, no husband?" The hunter took another step closer.

"No."

"Young maiden, won't you look up at me?"

Medousa turned to face the tall hunter.

Her wild green eyes looked him up and down. He had four hilts on a leather belt, each holding a different dagger. Over his shoulder was a bow and arrow. His robes were navy blue like night falling over a clear day.

When Medousa worked her gaze up to Orion's face, when she looked into his shallow blue eyes, Orion yelped.

"Y-Young maiden!," Orion gasped in horror, "You're a monster!"

Of course he recognized her.

Hunters developed keen eyes to sense movement, spot tracks, and act quickly. Orion was the best hunter of all, so his eye was fixed to see past, present, and future. He saw what she was meant to become.

Orion lunged towards Medousa and sent her hurtling to the ground. He pressed her into the earth, his massive body keeping her from fighting back. Orion was huge— it was like watching a cat tackle a mouse. Medousa's body pushed against a bed of poppies, mandragoras, and sprouts of grass. She was trapped and powerless against the weight of the giant hunter.

"I am no monster! Let me go!" Medousa shouted. She had no staff in her hands and no tricks up her sleeves.

"What's this?" Orion reached for the belladonna behind her ear.

He held the flower over Medousa. She writhed under his grasp, but it was futile. He hardly noticed her struggle and focused only on the dappled lilac flower.

After a moment of consideration, he threw it into the ground. It wilted from his force.

"You're a pharmakis?" Orion asked, but it was more of an accusation.

Medousa was in real trouble. I watched from above, sure that the tables would turn. For this girl was born with Poseidon in her fingertips, and I unlocked the Underworld in her heart. She was not like Orion's other game. Medousa was not a simple monster, but one with depth. I dug tunnels into her soul, to turn her dark roots bitter.

Orion pulled on her golden braid, tilted her head back, and exposed her neck.

"Yes, you are. I can see it in your eyes, emerald like dragon scales. Green as the greediest sea. I'm the greatest hunter and I know a feral monster when I see one," Orion said, sure of himself. To the hunter, all was black and white, monsters were either alive or dead. He had no time to dance in between.

Medousa struggled underneath him, but he kept his position. Orion unfastened a dagger from his belt and quickly brought it to her throat. He was a cunning killer. One hand held the shiny bronze dagger, the other hand pulled on her serpentine locks, pushing her head back, making her neck longer for him to slit. The weight of his body pushed her into the poppies and pinned down her arms and legs.

Orion held his dagger to Medousa's throat and asked "Any last words?"

Medousa stared at him with pure venom in her eyes. Any part of me that was thinking of swooping down to help her was pushed aside. I acted from the shadows. She'd get her way. I saw it in the stars in her eyes. She was young, and a good fight would develop her into a great fighter.

"Let me go!" Medousa shouted.

She probably hoped that Hekate could hear her voice. I knew the witch was too far away. Besides, I assumed that Hekate's boiling water filled her cottage with rumbling, white noise.

Orion pressed the blade closer to her and a small trickle of Medousa's blood smeared against the sharp bronze edge.

"I will slay every beast in Greece!" Orion roared. He made this declaration so loud it boomed into Magnesia. It shook the trunk which served as my vantage point.

Ah, yes. Hubris took such a brazen form in Orion. I chuckled in my dark, arched throat. I imagined it from Orion's perspective. He had the size advantage. He had all the weapons. He already pinned her to the ground.

And, he was emboldened by his sense of righteousness.

To him, it wasn't too early to declare victory.

He knew not that a vulture watched from above.

There were plenty of bugs underground, in my roots. I could control them. I could make them grow. I was their war strategist.

Pride came before a fall. If he wished to slay every beast in Greece, then I chose to call forth a true challenge from Medousa's fingertips. I could've swooped down and defeated him myself, with my curved beak and long talons. But I preferred to move in more mysterious ways. The Underworld served its admiral.

Medousa dug her fingers into the earth, acting as if her hands were roots and she was burrowing herself, like she could've crawled into the dirt, and hidden beside her missing staff.

"Very well then, young maiden. Time to–" Orion said, but before he pressed the blade through her throat, the earth started to rumble. His lethal promise was cut short.

From above I could see the earth shake, like an earthquake was coming.

Orion hesitated, drawing his knife back, assessing the situation. The earth shook harder. Grass fell away to reveal something jet black and slick. Orion was alarmed, so much so, that he dropped Medousa and stood upwards.

Medousa took her chance to roll over and jump into a fighting stance.

She wouldn't have to fight him.

Orion watched in horror as the grass transformed into a scorpion, as big as the giant hunter himself. Its glinting black body was darker than a moonless night. Before he had a chance to draw his bow, aim his dagger, or even run, the scorpion plunged its stinger into his heart.

Orion's eyes went wide. As the scorpion rose, he set. He fell back onto the earth and squirmed with blood full of venom. Moments ago, he had been pushing Medousa against the same grove. Venom went straight into his heart, so he had one, two breaths before his eyes closed forever.

Even as he lay dying, Orion couldn't help but feel a sense of admiration for the fierce and cunning woman he had sought to conquer. A godly monster. As he gazed up at the blue sky, his final thoughts were of her, and the sting of the scorpion that pierced his prideful heart.

I could see the fallen hunter's last thoughts, and feel his final feelings. The venom of the scorpion, in some ways, the essence of my bold soul. I could move into Orion's mind in his final moments.

Medousa stood, staring at the scorpion, her heart racing. Four jet black eyes gleamed like obsidian, cold and unyielding, reflecting the creature's deadly nature. They were like pools of darkness, deep and mysterious, hiding secrets that only the scorpion knew.

Medousa stood her ground. She angled her body away from the creature, so it couldn't strike her heart like it had struck Orion moments before. She poised to push back against the scorpion's shiny black body, while protecting her most vulnerable points. I could tell strategies whirred in Medousa's eyes. She thought about where to deliver a fatal blow. Its eyes were so close to its pincers, its organs were too close to the earth, and its tail was ready to strike anything in front of it.

She didn't know her next move. The scorpion was armed to the teeth and she couldn't sneak up on it. She surely couldn't run from the beast, which cast a shadow over her. It had eight legs, where she only had two. A chase would've ended with a stinger in her back. It stepped towards her.

Instead of striking, Medousa took a different route.

"Hiss," Medousa bared her teeth.

The scorpion shuddered. It heard the whisper of a monster within Medousa. The scorpion went running for the hills, and I saw in the sky, Algol reappear.

Medousa was left with the dead body of Orion. She stared at him, frozen on the ground. I watched her. Fear caged her. She stood still until a pair of footsteps broke her spell.

"Oh dear," Hekate whispered, "Perhaps I should've brewed stronger tea."

7. Owl

I rose at evening time. My bulging eyes opened to the dimming night and the waning moon. The edge of my dreams merged into the reality of night. Day birds sang their final notes and I heard voices floating through the forest from the witch's cottage.

"It'll heal," Hekate promised, "and leave a nasty scar."

The scent of chamomile was strong. It wafted through the woods into my dreamy inhales. The sweet flower's scent mixed with the smell of misty poppies, bubbling up from the Underworld. I flew closer to the cottage to hear the conversation.

"Don't touch it," Hekate snapped.

"I just need to check that my head's still attached," Medousa protested. "Feels like I'm drifting away."

"The medicine's working. Come to your senses, Medousa. It's time to go."

"Do we have to do this at night?"

"Of course," Hekate answered. I heard her leather footsteps over the clay floor. Her cottage door creaked open and I saw Medousa creep into the garden. First I noticed Medousa's bare feet. She moved in days ago and I hadn't seen shoes on her feet yet. Then I saw the cut over her neck which shined with the soothing chamomile salve. Hekate followed Medousa into the night. Horns rose from her head, towards the moon who was missing a sliver. It was like her horns reached for their counterpart in the sky.

Hekate held two torches and passed one to Medousa. Both the pharmakis and the girl's faces flickered in the warm firelight. Hekate's gray eyes burned, while Medousa's were full of deep, green water. Flames licked the cut on Medousa's neck. The girl's hair almost blinded me for its brightness. Her braids seemed gilded by the fire's light.

They walked in silence, but there was a tangible sense of tension coming from Medousa. She spooked at the slightest sounds of bristling leaves and calls of sleepy foxes. Shadows of trees caught her attention as they opposed her torch's flare.

I flew behind the pair as they walked into the forest. During the day, all other birds flew with audible swishes of their wings. At night, they were all asleep and I alone haunted the woods anonymously. I flew in silence. I flapped, hovering above the witch and the girl. I had to swerve to avoid the erratic flights of bats. Not even their sonar could detect me. My feathers appeared like the night sky in amber torchlight, so long as I avoided ramming a bat, I remained invisible as Artemis on a hunt.

Medousa grew more comfortable as the trail snaked deeper into the dark woods. She stopped reacting to flickering shadows and the sounds of a sleeping forest. Well, she seemed less scared. I suspected she suppressed her fear and resisted the urge to push her torch towards every shadow, to run back to the cottage, or to yelp in fright. While she subdued her unease, it was still inside her, bubbling under the surface.

Hekate didn't pay attention to Medousa or the forest. She walked behind the girl on feet that knew the trail without fail. Her eyes were on the sky, darting between stars.

Soon we reached a grove of black poplars, and I perched myself on a dark branch. Other birds were sleeping between the leaves– a flock of doves nestled together. They did not stir or coo in their dreams. Not even a scraping sound manifested as my talons circled the rough bark; I was silent as the night.

But nothing is ever silent, not if you listened closely. High-pitched chirps rang through the woods. There was a soft rustle of wings. So soft, I was sure the pharmakis and Medousa could not hear. Bats flittered and flapped. They blotted out the stars in the sky. It was more than a usual gathering of bats; they came from the woods and swarmed the center of the grove.

Then, I looked into the clearing, at the center where bats swarmed. A body had fallen there. He was exceptionally tall and I had never spotted him in Magnesia before. Bunches of white lilies sprouted from his lifeless skin; clearly his death was mourned by Persephone herself. Bats fluttered over him, seeking pollen from the ivory blossoms. The bat's wings sent torrents of air rushing over the pharmakis, the girl, and the dead man at their feet.

"You will peer into his life," Hekate explained.

"Me? How will I do that?"

"First we need illumination," Hekate said, "Mirror me at his feet."

Hekate stood at the head of the fallen man. Medousa rushed, her bare feet pressing against poppy petals, to the opposite end of the corpse.

Hekate stuck her flaming stick into the ground above the body. Medousa watched and did the same with her torch at the corpse's feet. Her torch stood slanted. Both beacons were like small poplars, growing from the earth, burning at their tops.

Flames danced over his milky, lifeless skin. The flickering light made the swarm of bats look like they were on fire as well.

Hekate moved to the torso and Medousa followed. They both kneeled beside the body. Hekate ripped open the neckline of the man's wool tunic. She uprooted several lilies, until his chest was exposed. I heard roots snap as they let go of his ribcage and collarbones. Bats, previously feasting on the flowers of the dead, darted away to suckle on poppies underfoot.

The corpse's chest bore a swollen puncture wound. Then, Hekate motioned for Medousa to place her hand on the body. Hekate's dark cloak rippled around her as she moved. Medousa stayed frozen in her skin.

"Place your hands over his heart. I will ask you questions," Hekate said.

"How will I know what to say?"

"Listen to his heart."

"He's not alive."

"He was. His heart carries the story of his soul into death."

Medousa touched him.

Nobody else in the whole world watched both the sky and the witches in their grove. At that moment, the bats were much more concerned with nectar. They did not chart the stars like birds. And every other bird was asleep. None but the owl's eyes were wide enough for the moon, stars, and rituals of pharmakides. I remember what I saw.

As soon as Medousa's fingertips touched Orion's chest, Algol flickered. It winked, brief as a heartbeat in the sky.

Then the star returned, as if nothing happened at all.

Medousa flinched when she touched him, probably for the sharp coldness of his skin. Bodies were like that when their souls abandoned them for the Underworld. Medousa bent over the hunter's broad shoulders. Pollen from lilies danced in the air in front of her.

"I see–"

"Don't speak it," Hekate said.

"Why?"

"Don't you remember, I told you I'd be asking the questions?"

Medousa stayed silent. Hekate sighed.

"As pharmakides, every word we speak aloud carries meaning. If you simply told the story of his life, it would be disrespectful. You'd make too many assumptions. Since the dead cannot speak for themselves, the living must honor them with conversation."

"Two perspectives," Medousa muttered, closing her eyes, feeling for Orion's cold heart.

"Precisely."

Tiger moths buzzed through branches of black poplars. Normally I'd be chasing them and ripping into their meaty bodies with my curved beak, but a necromancy ceremony was far too interesting. My late night snacks had to wait 'till after the dead spoke.

"What's his true name?"

"Orion," Medousa's eyelids were half open, enough so that I could see her irises had totally rolled back into her head.

"What's his trade?"

Medousa flinched. She took a deep breath before continuing.

"He's a hunter."

"Who did he hunt?"

"Boars… Lions… and…" Medousa's face warped. She gasped, started to pant.

"What are you struggling to say?"

Hekate's question sparked a flood. I swear, I heard a rush above me, like wind turned to water. I heard currents swirling and whirlpools guttering. Waves crashed upon the wind itself. The black poplar trees swayed like seaweed, their hard trunks rippling like satin in the wind. I clung to the tree, but still, the doves did not wake.

Then everything was still again. Still and silent and watching, like the forest always watched at night.

"Sirens. He lured them from the sky and–," Medousa's words came like a rush of water until she stopped speaking. Her mouth clamped. A bead of sweat rolled down her forehead.

"What?"

"Slashed their throats," Medousa answered. I saw her lip quiver.

"How did he lure them?"

"Revenge," Medousa wailed, "When he openly killed one siren, another would swoop in to avenge her sister. It was a massacre."

"How did he reach Sarpedon," Hekate asked.

"He harnessed the wind," Medousa said, "It was Orion who taught every man how to sail. But, it seems to go deeper than that. The sirens beat their fury into wind, and created a kharybdis. The wind cursed sailors, turning their own powers against them. Not a sailor could fell them, until Orion came."

Every conversation with the dead went this way– I knew this ritual. Two souls knelt before the dead. One asked questions, but the other would see the story of a body and the memories they held. I'd seen pharmakides have similar conversations in this grove before— always two witches and one body.

I was sure the dead hunter showed Medousa a gruesome battle. Sirens were fierce creatures. They were strong, warrior women endowed with the wings of ospreys.

In the heart of Orion, Medousa was bound to see golden feathers splattered with blood. She must have heard cries laced with agony. I watched her face twitch. Her breath grew faster.

"Ahh!" Medousa shouted. She lifted her hand from the corpse.

"What happened?"

"More voices came through. Voices of women shouting," Medousa shuddered and wrapped her arms around herself, "They survived torture, inquisition, and even drowning, before Orion found them. They suffered, for centuries, at the hands of sailors."

"How do you feel?"

"I felt my own death," Medousa swallowed. Her throat tensed. Blood blistered across her throat like the dainty, red trail of a comet.

"Why did he hunt sirens?" Hekate brought Medousa back to the present.

Medousa sighed.

"Revenge."

"For who?"

"The sailors. He wished to cut out the sirens' throats before their winds could draw another ship off its course."

"Did any sirens survive Orion?" Hekate asked.

"No," Medousa said.

"Are you sure?" Hekate asked.

My eyes crinkled. It was a leading question and I knew exactly where Hekate was going. I was an old and wise owl. I'd been in these woods long enough to know Medousa wasn't Hekate's first daughter.

Medousa stayed silent.

"The truth lies outside of Orion," Hekate was somber, "I could tell you about the survivors if you'd like to know."

Medousa unrolled her eyes and lifted her palm off the dead man. The weight of the visions, of the gore and the blood, and the cries of the fallen sirens, was spelled out across Medousa's aching face.

"There were survivors?" she asked. She was crestfallen, horrified, and searching for hope.

"Only two," Hekate bowed her head.

"How did they evade Orion?"

"He found them as fledglings, floating atop the sea. They hadn't even learned to fly yet. They were so small, he couldn't possibly rip out their throats. Instead he tied them to stones and threw them in the deepest ocean. Both sirens sank into the Underworld. When I found them I—" Hekate's voice cracked and she stumbled on her words. I'd never seen Hekate reveal a secret that didn't take excessive prodding to reach.

"You saved them," Medousa finished.

Hope blossomed over her face. The thought of survivors soothed Medousa, who saw brutal murders of sirens, as if she had done them herself. I knew she recognized her own life as lucky, as I figured it must have been Orion who gave her that fresh scar over her neck.

"Poseidon had a cold grip over their souls. He bloated and morphed them. They drowned. I brought them back," Hekate swallowed, "They were not the same as before."

"So they aren't sirens anymore?"

"No. They became gorgones," Hekate explained, "I embalmed them with warmth from Algol. Under this strange moon, I would consider them your sisters."

"Where are they?" Medousa asked.

"They live in the same whirlpool as the sirens. Only now they're turning it to stone. They now call it Sarpedon," Hekate's voice cracked, "It's under the star of Algol, in the shadow of a trident."

"A trident?" Medousa asked. She looked as greedy as the moon longing for Poseidon's heart. Medousa would move oceans for the trident. I saw it in her eyes.

"Yes," Hekate said, "the trident is a forked, magical staff which has been with the sirens since before their wings touched the skies. Once the gorgones were dead, I used the trident to spin Algol's energy. That's how the kharybdis keeps spinning after the sirens fell."

Medousa blinked and stared at the pale, unseeing eyes of Orion.

"Let's return to ritual," Hekate ripped a few more stitches out of Orion's tunic and motioned Medousa to replace her hands over his heart. Medousa obliged and her green eyes rolled back with a flash of white.

"What did he want?" Hekate asked.

"He came to Mangesia to fell the kentauroi."

Hekate's smirk mocked her crescent horns, "Did he succeed?"

"No."

"What did he want more than this particular hunt? What was the goal of his life?" Hekate asked.

"He wanted Greece to be free of all monsters," Medousa said.

"Why?"

"Because he wanted to be remembered as a hero," Medousa said.

"Maybe we can still make that happen for him, but should we?"

Medousa's eyes fluttered back to normal, "I cannot tell if you're asking me or Orion."

"You decide."

"I have to decide…"

"Should we go and fetch that scorpion and ask what it thinks?" Hekate asked.

"No," Medousa's face went pale,

"So, what do you think?" Hekate asked.

"Orion pushed me to the ground and held a dagger to my neck. It could be my body slain like Orion."

"You want to feed his body to the wolves?"

"He wanted to be remembered," Medousa looked down at the corpse's pale blue eyes, frozen and unseeing. There was a raw honesty in her voice as she straddled between life and death.

"Are you hesitating?"

"I think about becoming older and looking back to this moment. I imagine… thinking of myself as a monster," a single tear slipped down Medousa's cheek.

"Shall you grant his wish?"

"Yes," and the girl swallowed.

"Very well. It's your compassion that allows his story to make it into the sky. Now get up. We must leave his body with the lilies. They'll preserve him. We can bury him in the stars on the new moon, after I fetch my burning glass from Hera," Hekate said, "Before we go, take the dagger from his hand. Place it back into his belt."

Medousa did as she was told, freeing the dagger's handle from Orion's strong grip in death. Her own ruby blood was crusted on its blade. The knife slid back into its bronze hilt with a satisfying swish.

Hekate stood and looked straight up at the sky. Medousa followed. Blank spaces stretched between constellations. The sky was still young, legends were still rising and falling in ancient Greece.

"The sky is so vast..." Medousa was lost in the space between the stars.

There was magic in the grooves of Medousa's skin, and destiny dripped off Orion's blade. She connected the important aspects of his form together. She spooled him into strings, and unknowingly, weaved his story into the sky. The long tongues of bats sucked nectar from the lillies, the essence of the living, and they too helped bring him into the night sky.

Medousa's ankle glowed with a bright cobalt sheen under her robes.

I looked from her bewitched ankle to the ground where I watched Orion's body disappear in a flash of light. Only lilies remained.

Once my eyes adjusted after the flash, I saw stars start to appear in the night sky. Orion became a constellation. His broad shoulders towered over the cosmos, connected by two stars. Then, four bright stars simmered next to each other, each representing a weapon from his belt. Daggers graced the sky in a perfect line. He carried his bow and arrows over his shoulder. Last, two hubristic feet stood in heaven rather than earth.

"Look," Hekate caught sight of the new constellation and pointed to the sky, "I suppose we don't need to wait until the new moon after all."

Medousa grinned. She recognized him. He towered above her and sparkled in her raging, sea-green eyes.

"The great hunter Orion— he failed to kill me and I made him immortal."

Hekate stayed silent and stoic as the stars themselves. She knew better than to interfere with Medousa, to sway her between weaving Orion into the sky or letting him rot on earth. Hekate had to let Medousa make her own choices.

I saw wisdom in them both.

Hekate faced the girl, "Your imagination creates constellations."

"Can't yours?" Medousa asked.

"No," Hekate chuckled, "I need a tool to light the night sky. When I cast constellations, I burn stars with my glass. I've made Sirius the dog, Cetus the whale, and Aquarian the water-bearer. You'll notice that not all stories have been told; the sky is still young. Do you see those unclaimed stars?"

"Yes," Medousa nodded. Algol was up there, blue, white, and glistening in her eyes.

"Imagine those stars are roots of a giant tree holding up the sky," Hekate said, "Hera burned those, to give order to the night, to hold darkness above us like the tent of a circus."

Both Hekate and Medousa stood directly beneath the constellation of Orion, but the stars weren't settled yet. The hunter's feet started to move as he nocked his arrow.

There was an audible swish as Orion ran across the sky. He leaped and bounded to the far horizon. Then the scorpion rose from the opposite horizon, curved, and poised to chase him forever.

Orion's nemesis chased his hubris forevermore, on opposite edges of the horizon.

Wrongs had to be made right.

"What's happening?" Medousa asked.

"You raised the scorpion from earth and into the sky. It's the nemesis of Orion, and wishes to chase him forever. The constellations are finding their places," Hekate said.

"How did the scorpion make it into the stars?" Medousa asked.

Hekate reached for Medousa's hand and peered at the ridges of her fingers, "The scorpion was drawn to the earth by the stars in your skin. So where else was the creature meant to go?"

"This world is a mystery to me. Everything was silent when I was raised in the sea. Here there are monsters, men, and I have powers under my skin."

"Oh Medousa, you didn't make it far enough into the sea to meet any monsters. You were born in the shallows, but there are beasts out there in the blue. No matter. Look!" Hekate pointed to Orion, "He has settled next to the star of Sirius. That constellation was once an earthly hound. Dogs are loyal to hunters. Sirius will keep the scorpion at bay," Hekate said.

Orion was positioned over the sea, where he would dance over the ocean. The scorpion rested on the opposite side of the sky, crouching behind mountains, hiding from the hunter, with its tail peeking over, ready to strike.

Once the stars had settled, I knew there was one more thing to do. Medousa peered between the realm of living and death. She spoke with a corpse. She earned passage to the shadows.

I flew over the grove and as I reached the center, two feathers fell from my tail. They were white and dappled gray.

My feathers fell in the grove, spiraling around each other.

As they fell, I saw two snakes slithering in the grass. Snakes were perceptive, they knew what was bound to happen too. They were green as Medousa's eyes but painted silver by the moon. The serpents rushed, hoping to bridge a gap between the night sky and the Underworld. They knew too, that Medousa deserved a key. I plummeted in chase of my feathers, catching the starry eyes of Medousa.

She watched me fly before her, where I hovered until my feathers fell onto the duo of snakes.

I flapped, closer and closer to the earth.

My plumes met the snakes with a shrill twang. I righted myself and landed at Medousa's feet. Moonlit scales in the grass hardened around my falling feathers. The snakes stiffened into bronze. A key materialized in the grass, its handle sporting the frozen snakes and my fallen feathers.

I wished to give her a key, a key to her own fate, if she chose to imagine it. She earned it. She peered into the darkness of death with the light of her palm. Though he challenged her, though he refuted her very existence, Medousa watched his story— even in horror.

"What's this?" Medousa asked.

"For having the courage to speak with the dead, you've been awarded a key to the Underworld."

I hooted at the pair in jest. My wide eyes saw everything between living and dead.

Medousa bent down, felt through the soft grass for a hard metal key. She looked at the snakes, and my feathers which had been transformed into bronze. She lifted the object. It shimmered with the muted, orangy-brown color of fresh bronze. As Medousa inspected it, the key swung with a twill on a fine metallic chain.

I looked up at her and at the fresh stars glowing behind her. I hooted at her feet. Medousa looked from me to the pharmakis.

"Do you have the same key?" Medousa pointed to Hekate's bronze chain.

"Not exactly," Hekate revealed the chain beneath her cloak, "Mine is marked with quails."

I looked at the ornament Hekate wore, and saw, even as it aged, it kept its bronze shimmer. It was true, Hekate had been given her key by another bird. I heard the rumors of quails serving Hekate's key, but I never quite believed it until I saw her key for myself.

Medousa strung her new key around her neck and it hung below her scar. I hooted again for good measure. Blood across her throat marked her by the hunter who couldn't quite kill her.

They stood in silence for a while, watching the moon crawl along the stars. Bats chased bugs in darkness. They watched stories integrate across the sky, including their new hero, Orion, and his belt of four weapons. Cetus, the whale constellation, tinged with rage and fury. Cetus was an homage to the sea. Though the ocean itself was impartial, its residents were on the side of the sirens. The killer of the sirens became a constellation, but his victims never made it to the sky.

"Now let's get back to the cottage before we run into anyone else in these woods," Hekate moved towards the trail, followed closely by her cloak.

"Hekate?"

"Yes?"

"Am I a monster?" Medousa asked, her voice as quiet as her steps behind the pharmakis.

Hekate's face flickered.

"No, of course you're no monster. Why would you ask?"

"Orion said I am a monster— and when I hissed at the scorpion, it ran away," Medousa said.

I saw the pharmakis' lips seal. They pressed together with a secret I would never know.

"You were doing what you had to do to survive. Look," Hekate grabbed Medousa's hand, "Here you are. You lived. You're just a girl."

Hekate's words danced around the grave. Medousa sighed. Hekate hoisted her torch into the air and Medousa grabbed the other one. She followed Hekate on the trail back to the cottage.

Nobody else in the forest saw, but when Medousa shot one final glance up at the stars, I saw the star of one of Orion's daggers vanish.

The dagger fell from the sky and into her palm. It seemed to leave no trace, save the scar it slashed across Medousa's throat. However, my eyes were wide and well-suited for the night, so no secrets crept past me. She slipped the blade beneath her robes. She moved so quickly, I was unsure if Hekate noticed.

Bronze forever danced between living and dead.

With his body in the sky, the witches left only a few new flowers and a splatter of Orion's and Medousa's blood. As the night went on, those lilies would droop into the soil, and disappear, as if they were figments of my imagination all along.

8. Rooster

Only the cosmic rooster had the right to wield the sun. I ushered in each morning.

I commanded the lightest chariot on earth. Golden wheels scraped the edge of the sky. With the sun yoked behind us, night became day.

I always imagined my fellow birds watching me from below with envy. I lived in the space between light and darkness, both before and after sunlight touched Greece. I'd seen many legends in my journeys over the sky, but I will never forget the morning when I laid eyes on Medousa.

It seemed like an ordinary dawn with a fading, waning moon. The darkness of the moon was shy. Nonetheless, moonlight waltzed through Hekate's forest far below us. The larger, lighter side of the moon wished to be chased.

So, I chased the moon, with two horses leading the way.

We crossed Magnesia at the same time each dawn.

Lampos and Bronte, pulled my chariot. Their golden shoes, lighter than air, carried them in the sky. They lived by the swing of the sun, just like me. Their pasture was the sky between inky nights and pale, blue mornings.

The sky played tricks on us. It was missing a star— Alpheratz. It disappeared a few days before, and a new constellation appeared in the sky. A celestial scorpion scuttled in the air above my chariot. On the edge of the horizon I could see new stars peeking out, but they bent over the edge of my sight and I couldn't quite determine what they formed. They clustered near the star of Sirius. Apparently, Greece saw a legendary night.

I carefully plucked the horse's reins with my beak to keep them in a steady direction. Best not to get lost or drawn off course. Then our passenger, the sun, might fall too low and scorch the earth.

The day begged to unfold.

So we approached Magnesia, dragging the sun leagues behind us.

On the morning of Medousa, we flew on time, under my careful watch. In the early morning, I spotted Hekate's abode. The pharmakis' cottage was dark as night and silver as the moon. Her abode hung out over a cliff, like it was about to nosedive into the sea. That cliff was a haunted place. Rumors from earthly birds trickled up to me and whispered stories of the dead trapped in the hollows under the stone.

Smoke brought my eyes to her cottage. Smoke I thought, until I smelt salt and dawdling vapor, rather than clawing wisps.

It was steam— hot, foggy steam from the pharmakis' eerie grotto. Bougainvillea bushes caged her home like ribs around lungs. The plant shriveled in the mist. Their thorns protected Hekate's cottage, but only from dangers on the outside. Thorns meant nothing to water. Bright pink blossoms fell. The bush's leaves grew waxy, protecting themselves from withering away in the sweltering mist.

Omens of the land sang to me, as familiar as my own hens. I knew what the mist meant– the dead were about to wage war. There was talk of mutiny down below, underwater, where only cormorants flew.

As King of Magnesia, I had a job to do. No drama unfolding in the pharmakis' could've distracted me. The sun had to come up and my horses had to run.

I cried. My long and loud call rang through dark, dewy air. It ricocheted towards the horizon.

We had to hurry up, so that the sun wouldn't run late.

My horses waited for only a moment, then I heard the noble whoosh of hoofprints brushing over the air, and our chariot lurched forwards. There was a whir of metallic wheels over trails of air. Golden manes and tails flashed like comets across the sky.

Lampos led the way. He pulled harder than Bronte. The featherlight carriage swung behind him. Luckily, we straightened out quickly as Bronte regained his speed. He could never outrun Lampos, though. None were as fast, or as bright as Lampos. Everyday was a race, and Lampos always won. Though you could probably say that I was a few steps ahead of Lampos, he remained the engine of the sun. I used my spurred toes to pull back on his rein, and keep the horses straight.

We galloped across constellations, making them vanish in our glow. The golden chariot was lighter than any other carriage. It bounced from the horse's very breath, from their hearty pulses, and the sway of heavenly winds. I held onto the rail.

Suddenly, I heard a shriek below and almost leapt from my perch.

Mornings were typically calm, waiting for me to usher action into the day. There was hardly ever any commotion during our flight.

I looked down and saw Hekate's door fling open. Mist poured out. Below me, Medousa ran into the starlit morning with mist catching on her breath. I heard her breathing and gasping.

It was moments before the day's first light would've reached her.

Medousa bolted, coughing, out of the cottage. I smelled the poppy-filled mist tumbling from the cottage, into the wild air of Magnesia. I flew over the canopy where rushing winds whisked it away.

She moved like a bird in flight. She was so nimble, springing from her bare toes, further and further from the cottage. She had all likeness to a dove, except for the worry staining her pale face.

She was graceful, even as she coughed. At first, I thought her hair was aflame, somehow kindled by mist. It was shimmering, catching all the starlight from the dark woods.

Eventually, Medousa's coughs brought her to her knees. She toppled forward onto a bed of tangled grass, between the roots of an ash tree. Heaves ripped through her as she struggled to breathe.

It was just a trick. I knew all the details of Hekate's enchantments. I knew everything that happened in Magnesia. She only coughed because she thought it was smoke. If she stopped panicking, she would've realized it was mist. Then, she could've enjoyed the sweet poppy burn. She could've laid in the grass and had dreams of nymphs.

When she fell, her robes caught on a root and her ankle caught my sharp eye. I saw a blue mark glimmer on her inner ankle. A shiver went down my spine. It was a snake, eating its own tail. I asked myself if Medousa was destined to live forever. But how could she? She seemed disarmed by the simplest spell; it'd be a miracle if she lasted the day.

Medousa collected herself and stood back up, fumbling through the forest. That's when I saw her neck. It was slashed. Dried blood sliced across her throat. I wondered where the scar came from, and whose work laid unfinished over her neck.

My attention was drawn away quickly.

I heard stallions screech in front of me. Lampos kicked out at Bronte. Sparks flew when his golden horseshoe met fiery fur. They fell to the earth as streaks of burning light, probably delighting the astronomers of Athens.

Nobody could see the horses, except for me— their master. All was invisible so close to the brightness of the sun.

"Settle down! Don't you have a chariot to pull?" I threw my head back and yelled to the stars. My voice snapped like a whip to get their attention and the feathers on my neck stood straight out. They sensed me, behind them, puffing out my dark blue chest like a lion.

To the human ear, my call reverberated and sounded like a mere cock-a-doodle-doo. Those horses understood. They straightened up and carried on.

Lampos and Bronte went back to work and the sun, in its golden chariot, peeked over the horizon. I watched the horses' muscles tense as they pulled. Slowly as our chariot advanced, night became day.

But Medousa, and the forests of Magnesia, were still in the dark.

"Hekate!" Medousa's voice was urgent.

The girl was so naive. I knew she'd never find the pharmakis on land right now. I'd been flying over Greece for a long time. If the Underworld bubbled this profusely, if the cottage seemed aflame, Hekate was surely in the thick of it.

I looked back down at the stupid, little girl.

Medousa stood up and brushed dirt from her dark robes.

"Hekate," Medousa called once more.

Though she cried for help, her voice was soft, as if she didn't really want anyone to hear. She looked back at the door. Mist floated from the cottage.

Without the beady eyes of a rooster, she could never spot horses in the sky, but they were there pulling the sun nonetheless. We pulled light rays closer and closer to her peril.

The girl stood in silence for a long time, breathing slowly. The very first rays of sunlight oranged the leaves above her, creating a halo.

"My knife..." I heard Medousa mumble. My ears were so reliable, I knew even when people on the earth whispered. I knew when they stayed up too far into the night. I knew when they acted in panic rather than pleasure.

Medousa looked back at the cottage one more time before hurrying away. She ran into the early morning woods without a torch.

I couldn't pull the sun fast enough for Medousa. I couldn't light her path. It was my duty to keep time, never rush it. Lampos struggled forward to help the girl, but I tugged at his rein with my talons.

Medousa didn't know it, but she was running straight for Hekate's cistern.

The pharmakis built her underground well a long time ago. Back then, her horses were still alive, fresh from a shipwreck, and thirsty as hell. Her cistern kept water clean and pure. Hekate aerated the water by digging wells in the woods, which opened to her pristine cavern below.

Unfortunately for Medousa, the openings for Hekate's cistern were terribly hard to see in the shadowy woods before the sun came up.

The girl with mist on her lips ran over a stone arch bridge. I wondered if she even registered changes in the terrain. Medousa moved without hesitation. She ran downhill, towards the cistern. As she got closer to the fall, each of her footsteps echoed beneath the earth.

Medousa's bare feet ran over the cistern's ancient stones.

Then I heard a scream, and a splash.

The girl didn't have my full attention. As master of the morning, I had higher callings than a patroness of Poseidon barefoot in the woods. Medousa darted below, but I couldn't see her any more. She may as well have been the crescent who ran away from the moon. At that hour, at that dawn, to me, she was gone.

As Medousa slid into the cistern, below the earth into watery darkness, Lampos balked. There was an airy screech as the chariot jolted leewards. He nearly crashed the chariot. I could see the stallion's eyes rolling behind his golden blinders. He was drawn wayward, because at that moment the star of Algol disappeared, like a burnt candle.

The winking sky frightened my horse. Stars were supposed to be steady.

Algol had been flickering for days, but the sudden disappearance stunned my lead horse. Imagine that, a sunny horse spooked by a fickle star.

My golden chariot bounced wildly and nearly came to a halt. I clutched the rail with my talons and did all I could not be flung from my craft.

"Lampos, straight ahead!" I screamed at the fiery horse. I threw my head back and shouted it to the stars, too.

Apparently, they needed to hear it as well. I told the sky, "Even if Algol flickers and Alpheratz vanishes, even if all the stars went out, you will never snuff out the sun!"

I cried to the sky and puffed out my feathers.

Lampos picked up again, and we were back on our course. Lampos and Bronte marched towards the stars in darkness, carrying the whole sun behind them.

I thought little of the girl, and the stars in her skin. She must have fallen into Hekate's cistern, where no sunlight could've touched her. In there, even in the darkness, the stars were going to teach her a lesson.

I cursed Medousa and the demon star for distracting me. *Blasted Medousa.* The sky rumbled with horse fights once again. My carriage jolted and skidded to the side.

I let out another call, and my horses carried on over Greece, under my watchful eye.

9. Kingfisher

The rooster's call woke us which, at first, was normal. He chimed with a familiar sound, as common as the days themselves. It reverberated through our cool, magnetite chamber.

The rooster promised light in shadows.

His echo brought me all the way backwards to a time when my eyes would open and we would be human. The rooster used to wake us, far above our cistern, as husband and wife. The wilds of Magnesia had always served us, until our perils with the sea.

The rooster crowed every morning. I recognized his cock-a-doodle-doo at daybreak, as well as I recognized my wife after she changed from human to bird. In that same thread, I recognized my own reflection, too. My bleeding heart turned my chest ruby red, my far-reaching optimism turned into feathered wings as blue as a cerulean sea, and my romantic eyes beaded into a deep black. Our wings were speckled with waves that already consumed our human lives.

Normally the rooster's crow would dribble over calm water, and our day would begin with crystalline stillness. We'd watch beams of light wander into the cistern and penetrate through the still water of our underground home.

As the day grew longer, we would see rays of misty sunlight bend. Water changed everything. It changed me into a bird, and it bent beams and shadows.

There was one morning where the rooster's call failed to bring in peace— when we met Medousa.

Everything was calm, until Medousa broke our spell.

Before the rooster's echo left my chamber that morning, we heard footsteps. My heart clenched when the steps reached my stony pathways without slowing down.

I let out a shrill alarm, which echoed on the walls of our cistern, as if to mock me.

We heard a shriek from above.

I curled my head beneath my wing, and took a deep breath. Then, we heard a splash.

Medousa fell through the opening.

Any other creature in the woods would've avoided this trap. Not even a fallow fawn could've fallen in. Even the kentauroi, who lauded over these lands only since this full moon, knew to steer clear of the drop. Any creature could've seen the crack in the earth and heard the calm water inside.

Not Medousa. She ran through the forest before the sun had even risen. She paid heed to no warnings while her heart pounded.

Not even the shipwrecked horses were as hasty as this girl. They were mad with thirst, but they never fell in. Hekate's horses managed to find the channel, further in the woods, where the cistern shallowed. There the water was accessible and they could drink with ease. Here, beneath the earth, water could cool. It became fresh and full of healing knowledge of magnetite.

Hekate's cistern had been largely abandoned long ago. Until one horse, Alpheratz, came to drink. But she hadn't been to the cistern since the full moon.

Medousa disturbed the peace. She fell into the deepest part of the cistern, the most unfortunate chamber.

The water was cold and deep. The magnetite was slick and wet.

Medousa's splash misted my perch. Good thing for our waterproof feathers, we were safe from chilling. I spread a wing over my mate to protect her from the sudden water. The cistern absorbed shock from the girl. Waves reverberated around corners, bouncing off walls like watery echoes.

Then the water calmed. Everything was quiet while Medousa held her breath.

Fading beams of moonlight snuck in, through the opening of the cistern. They illuminated Medousa's golden hair, which spun in the water like it could dance. The sun had barely risen and only the premiere morning birds had started to sing.

Medousa floated to the surface. She gasped for breath. I heard shock in her lungs, and nestled closer to my wife. She buried her face into my blushing chest. While Medousa struggled to breathe, I caught sight of a string of blood wrapping around her neck. I watched the scar burst open as she struggled in the water. A faint smattering of crimson trickled into my freshwater.

Her commotion felt so unexpected. No one else had come to the cistern for a few days, when Alpheratz mysteriously stopped drinking.

I looked from Medousa, up to the sky. There was only a sliver visible through the opening, but of course, I lived by it.

I saw the moon, staring down at us.

There was a curving line between the light and dark sides of the moon. It was like the harsh, dividing line between girls with legs and birds with wings. Soon, the moon would vanish. Soon, it would be day.

We could live in our hole, but other animals couldn't reach it. Humans hadn't seen the walls, the ornate pillars, since the pharmakis herself carved them with the star's light. Only a winged creature could make their way into, and out of, the cistern. There weren't even footholds for a human to ascend.

Medousa had no escape.

In fact, it was a trap. The cistern caged water in underground shade, so it never became clouds. Only Poseidon's angels, me and my lover, could brave this particular chamber. We had the gift of flight, we were nimble enough to nest between cracks, and we could dive to the bottom of our tranquil pools.

The cistern was never meant to catch Medousa. It was meant to purify rainwater, but the girl put herself in danger.

She splashed. The cistern was barely too tall for her to stand. She pointed her toes, which were only a hair's width away from brushing the stony bottom. I watched her reach, her eyes growing wider. It wasn't enough. My heart ached for the girl, for her gurgles and screams.

There was nothing that I could do. My mate shivered against me.

Medousa stayed vertical in the water, desperately reaching for the bottom. She was positioned to use all her energy– to drown.

"Kick back. Become flat," I said, but my voice echoed into chee chee. She couldn't understand the songs of birds, or perhaps her ears were too waterlogged to hear. She stayed straight up and down.

"Lay on your back. Your breath will help you float," I promised to deaf ears. My chee chee got tangled between the walls, in the still air, and floated with no understanding or relevance.

The echoes of her splashes warped around our walls. The return of every echo grew quieter. My wife and I continued to chee. Our screams, shrill against our pristine magnetite walls, couldn't save her. Nor could our ruffled feathers, or even my wife's sorrowful eyes.

Medousa moved towards a pillar with panic in her green eyes. She was too scared to notice us above her. I watched her fumble on the walls, searching for a place to grab. Everything was so perfectly smooth and wet. It was impossible to do anything but slide right off. Magnetite kept the water sweet and clean, but it was no good for girls stuck in the water. Only creatures with wings could make their way out.

I wished to help Medousa, but there was nothing I could do. I wished that my mate didn't have to bear witness to her death. She lifted her head to watch, conflicted by what she may see. I chee chee'd again, asking the cistern to show mercy, asking the magnetite itself to free Medousa.

My pleas were of no use.

Medousa's lips turned blue. Cold shock got to her. She swallowed water. I didn't want to watch her die, in such a pale, frenzied, frozen-blue panic. I had no choice. Medousa faded into the apathetic water.

Day was breaking. Surely the pharmakis would come searching for the girl? My partner chee'd and I chee'd alongside her.

Then, as quickly as she fell into the cistern, with only a flicker of warning, the fight left her eyes. She slid silently beneath the surface of the water and collapsed onto the cistern's floor.

I swear her last breath was a howl, a bellowing exhale of desperation.

She laid peacefully underwater, as if she were in a soft meadow.

From the bottom of the cistern, she stared at the gibbous moon. It was both dark and light. She watched it fade through the very same opening through which she fell, her eyes wide and unseeing.

Before the moon vanished completely, her eyes closed.

My wife and I wailed together. We hid in the cistern, away from sea monsters and storms, but girls could drown in still water. Hera turned her back on Medousa. We chee'd with the intensity of passion. The magnetite held our suffering and echoed it back to us. Nobody watched from above; nobody turned Medousa into a bird. Our chee's found corners of the cistern, they found themselves echoing through grooves, but they found no solace.

I saw her body through the clear water. I caught sight of a sparkle over her chest. It was a bronze key. The bow of the key was ornate, featuring two bronze feathers sprouting from two bronze snakes. From their union sprouted the key's teeth, meant for a lock.

I watched the key sink down the canyons of her collarbones and over the cliff of her neck.

The metal of the Underworld met my pure magnetite chamber, cleaned by Magnesia's sweetwater.

I heard the twang carry through water and into air. Medousa twitched underwater, her body asleep, but starving for breath. Then her key clattered against the floor again.

Two knocks, and a portal opened. My chamber became a vestibule between the living and the dead. A chill spread through the air.

Three dogs rushed out of the key. They were silver and transparent, as if they were made of moonlight. Each hound wore a collar threaded with bronze.

The material realm meant nothing to the dogs. Their mouths were open yet they swallowed no water. One dog carried her bronze key. It bounced on his neck while he led the way. These dogs started to climb through the air. They ran out of the cistern's opening, their twelve paws clawing into thin air, their eyes glowing red.

Then they were gone, and it was just me, my wife, and Medousa—who had no life or breath.

It struck me, all of a sudden, that I knew those dogs. My feathers stuck out with fear. I held my wife closer under my wing.

I'd heard about three moonlit dogs in myths, rumors from other birds.

This was Kerberos, three dogs who acted as one. I'd heard stories of them hunting birds to bring them down into the Underworld. They guarded the gates between life and death. I nuzzled my mate, hating to think those creatures were in our home.

In another way I felt relieved. The dogs would help Medousa. She would escape from the cistern.

She had help from those below, as my mate and I had help from those above.

Why, we weren't always birds, you see.

My lover and I lived human lives, until saltwater drove us both mad.

The ocean stole my mind and soul first. I yearned for the sea. It had a hold over my heart. Poseidon promised adventure, chivalry, and travel. The sea lured me in. I waded into the water, boarded a ship, and turned my back on my wife.

I left her behind and promised to return after some travel.

While I was gone, she was driven mad by the sea too. She became obsessed with the thought of my absence. My wife grew wild wondering if I had succumbed to the depths. In her heart, she suspected that I met my fate, like Medousa below us.

It was true.

My promise to return to her was never fulfilled. At least, not while I was alive. My boat had been ravaged by monsters and I didn't get very far at all. Leviathans tore the boards of my ship apart.

Once Poseidon had reaped my soul, I came to my wife in her dreams. I was wet, drowned, and begging for her help.

In the morning, my lover came to the sea to ask for me back. She found my body floating in the wavy water.

My poor wife who found my human body; she was driven so far into lunacy that she forgot how to swim.

The sky felt her passion while she held my bloated body.

Hera looked down on us, one lover dead and one mad with grief. Hera wished to see us reunited as lovers.

She gave us new lives as a pair of mated kingfishers.

Our flecked wings held the splash. Our red beaks carried my spilled blood. We lived in Hekate's cistern forevermore, shielded from the ocean, in eternal calm. This pool nursed shipwrecked horses and moonsick wolves. None of Poseidon's rumbles could shake our cistern's water.

The chamber sheltered me and my lover as our wings grew old together.

We looked down at Medousa and recalled our past. She reminded us of what could've been.

Medousa was frozen, still, and sunken like a stone.

My wife and I knew, through some forces darker than the ones who helped us, that Medousa would be saved. The dogs were sent to help. We wouldn't have to watch her decompose, and rear our chicks to dive between her ribs.

I felt my wife's heartbeat against mine and recalled our lives as kingfishers, and how lucky we were to live with intensity in passion.

Medousa was still, the sun crept higher, and warm light shone down on her freezing body. I saw her clearly. Her robes lifted up in the water and a faint blue light glimmered near her ankle.

I leaned over the edge of my column. My wife chee chee'd, but I had to see. My heart leapt. I flew from our perch and towards her sunken body.

I landed on the surface beside the girl, well above her. Her still body was underwater. I watched over her like I was her angel.

My eyes could see through water, but I didn't believe what I saw. I thought it was a trick of my eyes, or perhaps a glare underwater.

I dove below the surface, using my wings to propel me downwards.

It was true. My eyes hadn't deceived me.

Starlight was stuck underneath her skin. A glowing snake, blue as my own feathers, wrapped around her ankle. The snake swallowed its own tail, forever, trapped under her skin. I wondered if she was really dead, and if she would rise again.

The dogs might've saved her, but water would drive her mad forevermore. I knew what that snake meant. One baptisma would lead to another, until her final plunge.

In the end the dogs did help Medousa; they led Hekate to retrieve her.

As time passed, our cistern was changed forever by that morning. Sun turned into shade.

Over time, a wolfsbane plant sprouted where the Kerberos passed through. I'd never seen roots take hold of water, but they did. They wrapped themselves around each other to form a lattice. The plants drank our water, but its brown roots were not strong enough to carve magnetite. It bent around the structures. Their roots coiled around pillars and bulbous nodules floated on the surface.

With lobed leaves and drooping purple blossoms, our cistern was transformed. Wherever rays of sunlight pierced before Medousa's visit, bushels of wolfsbane tangled together and gave us shade.

The sunny sliver where Medousa fell through was colonized by wolfsbane. Its seeds may as well have been the clattering key, the terror of Medousa, or our own pleading chee's.

Eventually, we could no longer see the moon or the sun from our cistern. When we grew older and it was time for us to rest, the flowers crept over every exit, to the point where we couldn't fly out even if that was our dying wish.

10. Peacock

A merchant smuggled me to Greece alongside what would become Hekate's herd of ghost horses.

They were rounded up in the same faraway desert as me. We crossed the Arabian Sea, where coins glittered over the backs of whales alongside our ship. Upstream against the seven-streamed Delta of the Nile, skirting between sandy banks, we were carried closer and closer to Greece.

Traders bound my spurred toes and tucked me into a cage. I was stacked like merchandise between bushels of dried saffron. They fed me at sunrise and sunset– mere handfuls of millet. I missed scratching for worms in sandy dunes.

My striking plumage and my azure face would surely fetch the merchants a high price in a new land, or so they thought. Ultimately, beauty was my curse. Merchants saw my feathers. My feathers saw them back, but I could not fight against their ropes and cages. Iron bars trapped me and took me from the desert.

The horses were kept in the ship's hull. I could hear their fiery breath through the deck. They hissed at each other like the waves which crashed against our ship.

Things didn't go to plan. Poseidon marred the merchant's course.

Our ship was struck down before we reached our destination. Tempests pushed our vessel against hidden rocks. Our wooden hull cracked and left us at Poseidon's mercy.

It was random, certainly unplanned for us to crash into rocks. The merchant sailors had made a mistake. Chance brought us to wreck on Magnesia's shore.

Men drowned, weighed down by their wishes for riches. The horses, the harbingers of chance, saw their opportunity and bolted through the broken hull and into the rocky sea. The horses were fast– faster than water. They rushed to shore before the waves.

They came to this land with no owners. So Hekate looked after them, even after each horse died. Their souls belonged to the Pharmakis of the Dark Side of the Moon.

The horses made it to shore, the sailors fell into the sea, and I was left alone with wet saffron, spilling out of its bushels and into my cage.

My cage protected me from the crashing rocks, but not from water. It flowed between the bars and snuffed out my breaths with waves. I couldn't fight Poseidon with my talons, even if they were free.

I cried and cooed. I imagined it was my final song.

My voice was so exotic and strange, so unknown to the lands of Greece, it piqued the attention of a cloud, or rather, the pharmakis enchanting it.

I'd been spotted. In Posiedon's merciless ocean, I was protected.

Hera made a plan for me. She saw my indigo and emerald feathers, the pupils in my plumes, and decided to steal me. In a tempestuous display of power, her clouds descended upon the ship, forsaking every man and welcoming me into the embrace of Hera.

I found my refuge in heavenly order rather than devilish chaos. Come to think of it, she probably knew the ship would come and I would be there. She could see into the future. She could see clearly across horizons, further than the bird's eye. I had been sought out by the meticulous eye of the Pharmakis of the Light Side of the Moon.

While Hekate's horses were promised an animated death, Hera granted me an eternal life. She rescued me from the jaws of the sea and promised me safe haven. I became the champion of Hera's chariot, the counselman who resided at her feet, and the sire of her silver hens. I'd been drawn from the realm of earth to a position in the sky.

Whenever someone considered crossing over into the afterlife, they were either ushered to Hekate's or Hera's realm.

If they were ushered to the clouds, I was there too, bathing them, and preparing them for a new life. I watched everything from Hera's feet, where she stood next to the golden-hoofed bathtub. The sweetwater bath was a portal where the living lingered before they died.

I saw both beauty and ugliness pass through Hera's bathwaters. Souls came here in fear, as scared as I was before Hera saved me from drowning in a cage.

I was not alone in being cursed by beauty. I saw many souls come and go, and pour through the baths like water. They either passed through or returned. They never stayed for long, but I got to know souls in their most vulnerable moments.

The most impressionable of all the souls was Medousa.

Hera and I were gazing at drifting pink clouds when we heard a splash in the tub. We turned and rushed to the bath. I lead the way. She followed the scratches of my claws over misty floors.

Medousa appeared on the morning of the shrinking moon. Her soul sought counsel, wondering whether to live or die. I gasped at her beauty. I stopped breathing, frozen for a whole moment.

Her hair dripped out of the bathtub in mad coils, ungodly colorful in the pastel morning sky, in the calm, white castle.

I peered at her pale skin. She was as smooth as the sea after a storm, but I struggled to take in her neck.

Someone had tried to slice open her throat, but their blade did not cut deep enough. She must have been in a brawl or some sort of fight. I wondered if she was lucky for surviving or unlucky for nearly dying in the first place. The slash was not deep enough to bring her here, to the brink of death.

No, it wasn't a blade which brought Medousa to the golden tub. It was water. I could hear her true killer sloshing around in her ephemeral lungs. Her breath rippled. Her lips paled. She must have drowned. I could sense the silence of the deep muddying her consciousness.

Hera examined Medousa through the burning glass. The orb had a small sliver glowing on its surface. Half of the time, Hera examined the dead with her bare eyes, conditioned by judgment and bitterness. With the burning glass, between the full and new moons, Hera could see Medousa as the moon saw her.

Such were the natural rhythms and cycles of power, that it waxed and waned. If Medousa was unlucky to get the scar across her neck, she was lucky Hera had the burning glass at that moment.

The sea inside Hera's burning glass recognized Medousa.

The water in the glass didn't hang down towards the earth, as it usually did. It was attracted to Medousa, in the same invisible fashion as the draw of the magnetite stones.

The water in the crystal glass orb sloshed towards Medousa, splashing flecks of mercury in the moonlight.

Water was naturally attracted to Medousa.

Hera and I had never seen this before. Hera was bewildered. Her jaw unhinged like a hungry cobra. I heard her exhale with disbelief. She leaned around the side of the glass to confirm it was true.

Hera stared in disbelief. We both took a deep breath and waited. Medousa was asleep in our baths, but somewhere down there on earth, she was fighting for her life.

She had time to bathe between life and death.

I could tell Medousa a story.

"I was once a human," I whispered to Medousa, "with one hundred eyes."

"You're filling her head with nonsense," Hera chuckled.

"With so many eyes," I continued, "that I was considered the finest guardian in Greece."

Medousa slept in the warm bath. She would never remember this, but at the same time, she always would. She wasn't physically in the baths, but on a subliminal level, she heard my story. Some parts of her took it as real, though I fabricated it with the levity of clouds. Some part of my story even predicted her future.

In another time and in another story, I could have had one hundred eyes.

"A guardian protects that which is precious. Hera asked me to protect her ivory white heifer," I whispered, "so I grazed her in remote plains, below the forests, and on the sea."

Hera's cheeks blushed and she swallowed her laughter. Medousa breathed in both my story and the entertainment of Hera's observation. She breathed in the bath and I heard her lungs bubble.

I knew it was better to lie, to tell a story, to enchant. I spoke with a whisper so soft it sounded like the rustle of sand dunes.

"We were far from other nomads, farther from civilization. No man reached our plains. No mortal was tempted to steal the heifer. That didn't stop the gods. Hermes, a trickster with winged sandals, passed by the remote plains. He spotted Hera's secret white heifer," I cooed, "Hermes wished to steal her."

"I did not fear Hermes. I was a giant, a man with a shadow as tall as a god," I said, "I always watched him, but he tricked me all the same, right before my hundred eyes. He traveled with music and he was cunning. He played a flute that carried lullabies in the wind. The whole world resonated with Herme's song. Grasses swayed to his meter."

Medousa's eyes were closed. She was in a sweet slumber. My words were hardly above a hum.

I looked at Medousa's sweet sleeping face and continued, "He put me to sleep with his song. As soon as I drifted off, he cut off my head with a silver dagger."

Medousa flinched.

"Never trust a trickster, Medousa," I bobbed my head up and down before her hooded eyes, "Never, ever."

My story became lodged in Medousa's psyche.

"I was lucky," I continued, "Hera's clouds rolled over the plains and witnessed my massacre. She found one of my hundred eyes rolling away. With her gift, with light off the moon, she made me into a bird."

"What a nice story," Hera grinned.

Hera placed the burning glass back in her robes and pulled out blue petals.

"Hold your breath, young girl," Hera whispered. I watched the Pharmakis of the Light Side of the Moon kneel next to the hoof-footed bathtub, and dump blue lotus petals into the water. Medousa's skin tinged with goosebumps. Blue lotus grew between living and dead, water and air, rather than a normal plant that dug its roots into earth. It could bridge the gap between the skies and land. It gave the dying their final breaths.

Medousa's green eyes opened halfway. She became lucid in her dream. I knew that in the baths at that moment, under the pale morning sky, Medousa with her eyes half open, saw me as pale and misty through the steaming bath.

"Hera crafted me from the clouds themselves. I am an ivory bird with silver pupils watching from my long trail of feathers."

I liked to make up stories. It started when I was younger, when I had been trapped by the merchants. Those cowards could cage me, but they had no control over my thoughts. I spun stories in my head, where I was the champion, where I escaped their grasps.

Explorations of the desert, the feeling of freedom in endless sand, played over and over in my head. I embellished my own stories during captivity.

Once I had been saved by Hera, I learned the myths of Greece. I learned the way she saw the stars and talked to birds, so I came up with my own story. As I whispered it to Medousa, I had a strange feeling she would invent her own story one day.

I was, after all, a master of deception. In my homelands, before coming to Greece, I could chase down spitting cobras. I could run across deserts. I even fluffed up my feathers to trick leopards into believing I was a hundred-eyed giant.

Oil seeping out of the blue lotus petals glinted in the hot water. The sheen caught my gaze and something purple caught my eye. It was not blue like a lotus or the sky, but purple like royalty. The only purple in Nephele's castle was on my feathers. It was strange to see such a rich color in this white castle, if not in my reflection.

My neck was tall enough to careen over bath rails. I peered at the girl's ankle.

My heart thudded like an angered minotaur. It beat against the cage of my ribs with madness. I spotted a snake on her ankle. It glowed against her skin, and seemed so alive.

This girl, so seemingly beautiful and angelic, had a dark side. She had a tail-eating snake emblazoned on her skin. In the rosy baths it appeared deep purple, so I guessed that outside of the pigmented water it must have been blue.

How mysterious, for Medousa to be branded with the light of a blue star. Perhaps she was meant to be a trickster.

Medousa relaxed into foamy water. The slick essense on the surface faded into white and pink bubbles. Medousa blushed, even over her closed eyes, and the tip of Hera's nose was rosy. My own beak glistened like burning poplar.

It was almost time for Medousa to make a choice.

Her physical body was drowning on earth, under the shadow of clouds. In the clouds she had to choose whether to return to her body, or move on to a new form. Her body was so still in the airy water.

I knew what was coming. I'd seen this play out over the years at Hera's feet. When someone was on the brink of going up into Heaven, Hera always gave them a choice.

I heard rumors from other birds. I didn't know if I should trust the words of jays or ravens, but I heard when souls came through the Underworld, Hekate gave them no choice at all. I heard she left them to the whims of Poseidon and didn't examine them or let them choose.

Hera looked down into the tub, and I looked alongside her.

"If you wish to live, exhale, and let your human heart beat," Hera said to Medousa in a hushed voice, "Choose to die, hold your breath in, and I'll welcome you into the skies."

Medousa exhaled and vanished, in a puff of starry bubbles, back down to her body.

11. Heron

I watched light pass through water.

One of my eyes faced a stony bridge. The other looked into the riverbed. When light slipped beneath the surface, it played. The more I watched, the more I understood the dance of light and water. Everything moved in a different way once it passed into the liquid realm.

I lived in this space, between the lightness of air and the heaviness of water. I lived in beams of the sun, yet also in the shadow of the bridge.

After a lifetime of watching the water, I understood its magnification. I saw past its warp. I could reach for a fish here and catch it there.

When I stood still enough, the fish would happen upon me. Simple catfish worked their way through water. They perceived danger with whiskers, but they never felt me and my watchful eyes. They swam with sweet strokes, naively seeking protection in the shadow of their villain. All kinds of fish hid in my shadows, coming closer and closer, before their final moment when I whipped my arched neck around and snatched them up into my beak.

The fish felt safe in my shadow when I did not move. They didn't understand that even in stillness, I was a hunter.

That's who I am and who I have always been– the false protector.

It's been my fate and Hera has mocked me by turning me into a heron. Even before I became a bird, I was just a shadow of a protector, never the real thing.

If I could've protected the children, Akanthis would've never have become a finch, and her brother would never have been ravaged in a pool of blood under maddened hooves.

For, I was the nanny of Hippodamia. I was her children's guardian. I watched the horses attack Anthus, but what was I to do? Break up a bloody horsefight?

I shrieked and tried to shield the other child from watching, poor Akanthis. I don't think I even succeeded in that. Looking back, I wonder if she stood on her tiptoes and saw past my quaking palms.

I was an ordinary nanny. My heart was not cast for greatness or bravery. It wasn't my fault Anthus got mixed up with those damned horses; I told him to stay away.

That was a long time ago. I spent many moons as a bird, scouring Hekate's river for morsels.

My white feathers ruffled in the breeze which snaked towards the cistern, one curve at a time. Air raced water, and air always won. It was lighter and faster, and tickled foam onto waves before the water became cold and still in a marble chamber. My gangly legs stood still in the breeze-chasing water.

The river was always the same, but these woods around the stream were wilder than ever before. Since the full moon passed, new creatures sprang up in Magnesia.

Something wild came out of a rainy night. I heard hints of hoofbeats, not from the dead horses of Hekate. Suddenly, there was a herd of real, living horses in the woods. They shouted like men. I caught glimpses of fast fawn coats darting between trees. Somehow, between the trunks, above the rushing water of my creek, I felt more vulnerable than ever before.

Then, I saw three beasts outrunning the wind. They looked like living mist, see-through like ghosts.

They moved without a sound. I heard not one single pant, not one single paw rustle over stone.

They had wild, piercing red eyes. Bronze collars lined each dogs throat. They stormed with padded feet over my stone arch bridge. When I squinted my precise eye, I saw their paws float over the stones. My heart shuddered in my chest. I watched them yap, moving their mouths as if to speak, but nothing came out. They were already dead, misty, and silver like dark moonlight.

One dog ran before the rest. A chain and a key dangled from his chuffing neck. It flew behind him like a kite, for he was running so fast.

I'd met these dogs before.

My ivory feathers stood on their ends at the memory. I recognized the three shades as Kerberos, guardian of the Underworld.

I met him before I crossed from human into bird. They'd been growling and frothing their mouths at me when Hera took my hand and led me away from a deep, dark cave. She arranged a deal for my soul. She took me into the clouds.

Hera spared me, even though she knew I was a coward.

She traded my skin for feathers. She traded my lips for a beak.

Hera let me live as a bird, in the shadow of the human I was. She wished for me to meditate on the ripples of water, and the air which bore them.

Quickly, the dogs were back, with Hekate in tow.

I could hear the pharmakis' steps when she ran over the bridge, following the misty dogs. Robes billowed behind her.

Hekate was flushed. She dripped with bullets of poppy-soaked mist.

She ran over the stony bridge, downhill towards the cistern, and disappeared from my sight.

I watched the sunny water, wondering if I should move downstream. Chaos on the bridge could ruin my chances of catching a fish, but I was curious.

The pharmakis was vulnerable in this phase of the moon.

I stayed in wait, willing the fish to come my way.

Small silver fish swirled at my feet, in my shadow, but they were out of reach. I heard a distant rumble coming from underground. It sounded like splashing and shouting in the cistern.

A crab braved a path close to my stance. My stomach growled when I saw the crunchy, bronze-colored morsel. It had beady eyes that caught on when I stretched my neck a hair closer to him. The crab scuttled away.

I waited until I heard more footsteps in the woods, coming towards the bridge.

Hekate walked in front. Her cloak was dripping, the thick wool dragged behind her. Her wet clothes collected dirt on their hems.

The girl, Medousa, followed. Her gaze was low. She was soaked too, but it went to her bones, like she had been stripped of sunlight and warmth. Her blue lips stayed slightly open, inhaling and exhaling. Wet, blonde hair draped around her like a waterfall. On her neck was a pale red slash.

When they reached the stony bridge, Medousa spoke.

"You need to *protect* me," her voice was soft.

"I need to do what?" Hekate whirled. For a moment, her stony eyes flashed with burning amber.

"You need to protect me!" Medousa shouted. Desperation made it sound like it was her last breath.

"Didn't I just save your life?" Hekate's face stiffened into stone.

Medousa inhaled sharply then erupted into a coughing fit. She fell and her knees hit the stone bridge. Her coughs were so loud and startling over the river bank, every fish near my feet darted away to quieter bends of the river.

Medousa coughed again and water spilled from her mouth onto the stones. She choked on Poseidon.

"Why can't you save me," Medousa struggled to speak between breaths, "like you did before?"

"Oh," Hekate bowed her head, "how naive..."

Medousa started to cry. Rivers flowed from her eyes into my creek. Drops of her grief rushed down magnetite rocks, into the water, and towards the very cistern from whence she came.

"You do not understand magic," Hekate pulled her cloak over her head, and started pacing to the side. She hid her face, her emotions, her very identity, but her words were as clear as the river's water.

"I'm the Pharmakis of the Dark Side of the Moon. When the moon vanishes from the sky, when my forest is darkest, when the stars shine with all their will, I have the powers of a dark moon. On the full moon, I already told you, I always give my tool to Hera."

Medousa coughed again and more water came out of her mouth, out of her nose, and I watched in horror– her ears.

"Everything has its place. Look around. Water falls to earth while air is left in the sky. Greece was nothing, nowhere, until water became heavier than air. The tool we share has a light and a dark side. It must trade hands."

The witch walked off the bridge and into the woods. Medousa heaved the last waves of water from her lungs. They splashed into the river. I watched her struggle, but there was nothing I could do to help. I watched her, once again, a false protector.

Hekate returned. She carried round fruit with matte, red skin and pointed horns. The fruit was the likeness of her very essence. Every bird knew that Hekate had blood on her hands; her crescent horns curved like the crown of the pomegranate.

"How about protecting yourself? I bet you forgot your dagger in the cottage!"

"How do you know about my dagger?" Medousa growled. She

came to her feet. I saw a sinister flash dance over her emerald eyes.

"I can sniff out bronze better than Kerberos," Hekate said, "No matter the phase of the moon."

Hekate reached into the pocket of her robes. With a flick of her wrist she withdrew a bronze dagger. Medousa stared at the knife and shivered. Her eyes were like the winter leaves all around– chilled and longing for light.

Hekate held the pomegranate and drew the blade to its bulging skin.

"That's my knife," Medousa said.

"You stole it from the sky, so I stole it from you," Hekate pierced the fruit and drew bullets of red juice.

"How could I steal it? It left a gash across my neck."

"Ah well, it doesn't really matter if you stole it. It was the right thing to do," Hekate smirked, "It's great work, Medousa. The constellation looks so much better without that particular dagger. Orion's belt is easier to spot with three perfectly-spaced stars; four was overkill."

Hekate continued to slice the pomegranate. First she cut it in half. Then she divided both halves into wedges, into smirking slices like her horns.

"Greece was one round and whole— as stuffed as this fruit. When elements divided—" red juice squirted from another incision, "they created duality. Then, from duality came trinity. Light is opposite to dark. But while that is true, there is light in darkness and darkness in light. Nights are illuminated by stars. The sun casts shadows. Water gives us life, but the sea is ruthless."

She handed the wedges to Medousa.

"Eat. The forest made this fruit for you."

Medousa devoured the tangy, red bulbs of pomegranate. She was so hungry she even swallowed the white membranous ether, which was like the sky between red, tart stars.

Medousa ate each of the six slices, every bit of pomegranate, all except the peel. Juice stained her chin and the tips of her fingers. Even the juice was matte, as dull as liquid could've been.

Pomegranate made my own mouth taste dry whenever I found them cracked open on the riverbank.

Medousa tossed her peels into the river. I watched them pass my feet and flow down the creek, towards the cold underground pool.

Hekate dropped the bronze knife onto the stone bridge and Medousa snapped her head up at the alloyed twang. Hekate kicked the dagger towards Medousa. It clanged against the rough stone bridge and clattered to a stop at Medousa's feet. She pocketed her dagger quickly and looked down at the clear water beneath the stones, flowing beneath her bare feet.

I spotted the dog and his shades. They trotted over the stones and laid themselves at Hekate's feet. Hekate jumped back, dishonored.

"Kerber- " Her voice was like a whip. She didn't have to finish the name before the dogs remembered, they had a job to do, somewhere else to be, and ran back to the cottage.

The dog left behind a bronze key, on a glistening chain, at the foot of the pharmakis. It shimmered red. I stared at the key, at the feet of Hekate, protector of Medousa.

My mind wandered. I couldn't help it. I thought about my last breaths as a human, watching Anthus' blood spilling out into the horse pasture, the day they ate him alive.

"Missing this?" Hekate tossed the key towards Medousa. She hurried to catch it in the air. She rolled the chain between her fingers. The soft bronze links whispered with every movement.

"What does this key unlock?"

"I suppose your eyes were closed and you were asleep under the veil. During your baptisma you had no idea, but your key summoned the guardians of the Underworld."

"Who?"

"Kerberos and his shades," Hekate said, "Best wear it around your neck, Medousa. Guard it."

My focus didn't waver. I stared at the water in silence and stillness. A bright orange fish swam under my shadow. I leapt forward and snatched it up in my beak with a splash. I swallowed my fish and it coursed down my arched neck. My splashing hadn't drawn Medousa or Hekate's attention. The pharmakis and the girl stared at each other.

"I suppose I should show you the lock before you lose your key again?" Hekate asked.

The pharmakis didn't wait for an answer. Hekate turned on her heel and stormed into the woods. Medousa followed, meek as a turtle dove.

12. Stymphalian

An articulate click rang down our winding tunnel. I heard the shrill rustle of a bronze key fitting into its lock. It searched for the right alignment, clicked, then popped.

I had excellent hearing, especially for metal. The key sounded so much fresher than my feathers, which grew heavy under a layer of corrosion.

My fellow stymphalians screeched. We rattled the salty, wet air.

We didn't sing the songs of light, organic birds.

Our feathers, our beaks, our feet, our ears and even our souls were cast with metal. Bronze, the link between dead and living, gave us feathers and needle-nosed beaks. We lost the copper sheen of freshly melted bronze from living in a misty grotto. We turned green. Each member of the flock, myself included, had a patina.

Our hearts beat with the levity of gold, and with every beat, they rattled our iron ribcages. We ticked. Our hearts set the pace of time around us, and beat together with the other stymphalians. Sometimes our hearts beat in time with the crashing sea. Those were the luckiest days.

Our eyes were silver like the mist in which we lived. We'd been drafted and enchanted, not hatched like normal birds. We were not meant for blue skies, but for shadows. We lived where the ocean met an underground sea cave.

More echoes snaked down to my perch. I heard the swing of a latch and the creak of old wood.

It was the trapdoor.

I felt black poplar's roots quake beneath my iron talons. My fellow stymphalians stomped their metal feet on husky spines throughout the grotto. We were all connected. Roots snaked down from the sunny earth and stretched through the Underworld. They carved magnetite rocks. We perched on the dark roots, watching over the liminal space between dead and living.

It was always dark in the grotto. We lived in a never-ending night. The black poplar roots whispered to me about sunlight, but I had never seen it for myself. Hekate had enchanted the crack where the sky and ocean met our cave so no sunlight could have entered.

We watched the moon and the stars too, which we could see through the thin crack in the rock that connected our grotto to the outer ocean. Since the most recent full moon, the dead had been troubled. They rioted and bubbled. Something was amiss, but I could never decipher their intentions.

While we did not have light from the sun, there were always six small, laser-focused red glowing eyes and three polished bronze collars.

Kerberos swam in the grotto.

We hardly ever saw all six eyes at once. The dogs chased each other through the crests and valleys of waves. They surfed beneath the surface, creating flickers like fire.

Of course, there was the silver shimmer of shades swimming over the surface. They didn't cast much light anyways.

As the trapdoor creaked further and further open, voices scurried down our tunnels like rats in their nests.

I recognized Hekate's voice, but she spoke to someone else. I looked the stymphalian next to me in the eye. We both eavesdropped. We listened because Hekate was our master. Unlike ordinary, egg-hatched birds, we were crafted from Hekate's bloody hands.

There were hundreds of us in the mist, but we couldn't see far. We heard the scrapes and clicks of other birds, but the mist hid most of them. We clung to outcroppings of dark magnetite and roots of black poplars. We clattered and creaked, unseen, save by the closest stymphalians with their silver eyes.

The pharmakis must have touched our tree's upper roots, near the mouth of the cave. I felt her magical pulse. Metallic squeals echoed through the cavern from the throats of my kin.

Our roots moved and twisted. Far above us, a torch handle materialized in the pharmakis' palm. This happened whenever she visited, but we still squealed with shrill clicks and whistles when we felt our roots come to life in her hand. We clanked our metal feathers against our flanks. We worshipped our maker.

She spent her night in our grotto. We saw her busy herself with crushing dried poppy petals and tossing them into the churning waters. She did this to soothe the dead, to quell their rebellious spirits.

Hekate had created us. She molded us from the hummingbird, a creature she told us chased rainbows. I never understood her until I saw prisms of moonlight catching on misty waves. I wondered what our kindred spirits were like. Did their organic hearts beat to the same pace as our golden ones?

Tick. Tick. Tick.

"Let's see what you unlocked," Hekate said.

"We're going inside?" Asked a girl's voice that paused over each vowel. She sounded unsure of what her next word would be. She sounded hollow and filled with water– like a vase. Her heart trembled like a drowning bee.

"Yes. I must get back to watching over the shades."

"What are shades?"

"Shades are souls who are meant to stay underwater— in the Underworld."

Both the girl's and Hekate's voices boomed through the magnetic chamber, as if they were speaking over and over. *Underwater… In the Underworld.*

They were imperfectly alive. Their voices were simply not as sharp, not as clear, as the mechanical clicks and hisses of metal.

I heard footsteps over the slippery crystal floor and the crackle of Hekate's torch.

"They're like those horses we rode to the mountains, Medousa. They cannot touch the earth– not unless they're tethered to the ground with bronze," Hekate added, "and they truly cannot breathe."

As their voices got closer, I realized the slower one, the younger one, the one who sounded tentative and who had never once come to this fateful grotto before— that was Medousa.

The black poplar whispered to me through its roots that it had already taught Medousa the lessons of war. I recognized Medousa as a budding pharmakis. I knew she could use plants to change the world, but I didn't know if her plants had found and identified her yet. As they walked down the tunnel, her heart beat in time with the sea.

Though the cave was nearly pitch dark, sound traveled well. It carried even faster when the mist was thick. I heard the steps of girl and pharmakis, the clocklike tick of stymphalian hearts, and waves crashing around the cave. Waves were so fierce, they were almost like fire.

Then I heard Medousa's breath hitch. Mist got stuck in the crook of her throat, I supposed.

"You haven't even told me why the cottage is on fire," Medousa coughed, "Where are we going? This tunnel is full of smoke."

"Oh Medousa," I could hear the smirk in Hekate's voice, "That's not smoke."

"Not smoke?" Medousa exhaled sharply, "Then why was I ousted at dawn by smoke in my lungs?"

"It's an illusion. The mist smells of burning poppies. It's made to trick you," Hekate explained, "This tunnel leads to a cave where the shades live. When they swim to the surface of the grotto, and try to breathe, they cannot inhale the air. Instead they exhale mist, as they cannot escape the sea. When shades swim over the surface, they create mist, the vapor between water and air. There's been so much mist lately, I'm certain that there's an escape attempt on the way. That's why I spent my night in the grotto. Now that I've had to leave, and save your hide, maybe I already missed the escape."

Our grotto frothed; the scent of poppies grew heady in the mist.

"How come I can breathe the mist now without coughing and choking?" Medousa asked.

"Because you heard my suggestion that it's not smoke. Now it cannot trick you. Don't trust anything in this grotto— except for me."

I heard Medousa sigh and her heart pitter-patter behind a cage of calcified ribs. Her heart rioted. It ebbed and flowed like Poseidon himself. How unpredictable she was, especially to us birds who were brought to life by mechanics. Our hearts never missed a collective tick.

"What's that sound?" Medousa asked.

"The birds," Hekate answered.

"How can that be birds?"

"I used the burning glass to build a flock of metal birds to guard the grotto. They're synced to one heartbeat."

Tick. Tick. Tick.

Firelight lapped down our tunnel. I saw a flicker of warm flame in the cool, foggy air. The stone was dark, even under a torch's light. Magnesia housed enchanted lands. The ground itself was magnetized with dark crystals. It pulled on metals purer than bronze, on our iron bones. The dark rocks were even said to attract mischief.

I watched Hekate and Medousa taking their last steps from the tunnel to the lip of the grotto.

Medousa's hair glowed like warm gold. Though the young girl carried no torch, her hair reflected Hekate's light. Her coily serpentine hair flattened in the moisture. I could see the remnants of twists straightened out by water.

Hekate's hair was light as well, but cool like the sea. It reminded me of the oldest flakes of my patina. I saw slender horns of the moon rise from her temples.

When Medousa came closer I saw that her neck bore a strange scar, like she had nearly been beheaded. The slash was only as deep as a strand of her radiant hair.

Hekate's steps were timid and thoughtful, searching with her feet before she transferred all her weight to the other leg. She came here many times before, but it was treacherous every time.

Medousa took more chances. She stepped quickly behind the witch, constantly adjusting her feet to move through puddles and rocks.

Medousa looked around with wide eyes, but I knew she could not see very far through the thick vapor. When she reached the end of the tunnel, at the grotto's dropoff, what she could see was the living dead.

Dark, gray water frothed and bubbled like a pharmakis' chalice. Wisps of the dead slithered into view. Silver manes, pewter scales, and chalky talons roiled in the water.

Medousa looked into the grotto, where Kerberos ducked between the swelling waves.

Then she turned and saw my silver eye spying on her. She jumped back and her feet slipped on magnetite. I watched her catch herself quickly.

"Everything in the grotto functions to shield the dead from the living and the living from the dead. The mist serves to warn me when the shades get too unruly. See–" Hekate pointed through the mist to the hissing waves, "They're impassioned."

Their voices were direct, but not loud enough to bounce off the walls of the massive grotto. I heard them speak only once; Poseidon ate their echoes.

"What's that?" Medousa pointed to a pair of glowing red eyes before they dashed back underwater. I heard a gurgle, a rumble, and a snap from the wave.

"Your savior," Hekate said, "Kerberos."

Red eyes appeared again, glowing in misty vapor. Kerberos and his two shades surfed through the waves like otters with bared teeth.

Shades swam from them. I could see silver forms racing through the water.

I watched Medousa lean over the edge of the grotto, looking down at the churning water. My eyes, as well as the eyes of every nearby stymphalian, were fixed on her as she leaned, further and further, over the edge.

Medousa squinted.

In the pale mist, under Hekate's warm torchlight, the sea moved up and down. Swell brought the grotto to life. It bubbled with the beasts of past lives— horses and humans, dolphins and sharks, lions and bears. They splashed over the surface in silver forms, wishing to ascend back into life.

It would never happen. Not under my silver-eyed watch.

Water rushed in through the mouth of the grotto.

Us stymphalians lived by the rhythm of waves. Our existence in the grotto was never silent. The ocean was always humming, stirring, and entrancing us in the sounds of bubbling water. We knew how it was meant to flow, and we heard an outsider. We heard water even when the ocean was veiled by mist. Outsiders could not understand whispers of our caged waves, but we knew.

Something was off.

A rogue wave stampeded into the grotto, as if it had been dealt by the hand of Poseidon.

I couldn't see it through the mist, but I heard water warp from the outer ocean, through our grotto's crack. I heard swell become swallowed by the monstrous wave. I clicked my bronze beak in wait.

Stymphalian hearts never missed a tick. Our rusty joints squeaked in the misty air. I could hear every metal bird becoming alert, waiting for a crash.

I squealed, asking Hekate and Medousa to stand back from the tunnel's edge.

They did not listen.

I watched them lean closer towards the ocean. They strained their eyes to see what their ears could not. In mist, both the old witch and the young girl were blind. They knew not what was coming.

All the birds started to rustle. Our feathers stood up.

The ocean was issuing the growl before a roar, but Hekate and Medousa were oblivious.

In a whistling huff, I flew before the pair. My green feathers flashed in their eyes and they stepped back.

It was at the right moment they did.

Poseidon licked their previous foothold. His wave slurped up the tunnel and sloshed back towards the sea. It left a puddle over the slippery floor.

I returned to my perch, but as soon as I wrapped my talons around my root, I realized the wave carried a passenger to the lip of the tunnel. A silver body writhed in the puddle.

The creature stood, floating on the surface of the puddle. Mist foamed from its skin. He was a common weasel, or rather, the ghost of one. A stripe between his white stomach and silver body ran along his side to his slender tail. He had wide eyes and the soft ears of a mouse.

Medousa saw the ghostly form and yelped. He looked into her green eyes and I watched the creature change.

The weasel mistook Medousa as its natural enemy, the snake. I'd seen enough weasels pass through here, living and dead, to know which creature they resented.

The ghostly weasel went from confused and forlorn to preparing for a fight. Mist poured off his back in raging funnels. His nose curled back in a snarl.

The weasel couldn't hiss. Shades were silent. But the grotto behind the creature wheezed and sputtered instead. The rogue wave had fallen back and natural swell took its place.

"What should I do?" Medousa asked. I could hear fear bubbling in her voice.

"Ignore it. It can't touch you."

"Why is it so aggressive? Hekate, it's looking right at me!"

"I said it doesn't matter. It's all silver and no bronze. That weasel's thinner than mist."

I heard Medousa's heartbeat quicken. Before it was steady and in-time with the ocean, but it quickly gave into her fear.

Magnetite crystals all around the tunnel, and stretching across the grotto, absorbed her raging heartbeat and channeled it into the earth. The cave magnified her madness.

Medousa's eyes darted from the weasel to the water behind it.

"Can we get out of here? I want to go back to the cottage," Medousa said.

"Yes. We can go ba–"

Medousa's shriek cut Hekate off. The weasel was swimming in its puddle, in the same serpentine motion as the slithering snakes it hated, towards the feet of Medousa. She leapt in fear and cried in terror.

When she landed, her bare feet slipped over the dark magnetite.

She couldn't catch herself.

Medousa rocketed down the tunnel. She fell feet first, from the lip of the grotto towards the foaming ocean. The wily weasel leapt after her, flowing with the water that cascaded in Medousa's wake.

Medousa's heartbeat spiked. I heard it whisper 'panic' inside her veins. Her heart thudded against the bronze key hanging from her neck with a shrill twang. Each thump came faster than the one before it.

As I observed her, a lump formed in my throat. A metallic taste coated my mouth like a silver tear. In the erratic rush of Medousa's blood, I detected memories left by tumultuous encounters with the relentless sea. Her memories were etched deep into her being.

Water left a scar much deeper than the faint slice over her neck. I gulped, swallowing the drop in my throat.

I feared the wrath of Hekate if her guest were to drown.

I heard Medousa's splash.

It was time to act. I hissed and creaked with metallic fervor. Calls resonated from my rusty windpipe. I hoped it would soothe the panicked girl. I swooped down to keep my silver eye on her.

For a normal bird it would've been too dark to find her, but I made do with light from Hekate's torch and the splashing red eyes of Kerberos. Orange and red spread through the mist, so that I could see Medousa clearly. Her hair was still glowing, but bobbing as she struggled to breathe.

Shades bolted away from the splash, and swam in fervor around the edge of the grotto.

I saw something moving in the water below her.

A glowing silver membrane peeled off of Medousa's body. I wondered if my eye, or the illusion of splashing water, was tricking me.

Then Medousa split in two.

The silver veneer started to take form like every other shade. I watched it break away from Medousa. It was a part of her, lost, into the sea.

I watched her shade in awe. Medousa's real body stayed on the surface, splashing and gasping for air. Every breath she managed to catch must have been tainted by salty mist.

I'd never seen a living soul deposit a shade in the Underworld before.

Normally shades took the living with them into the depths. For example, when Hekate passed through the veil and into the deep Underworld, she took a new form.

I saw, beyond the pale silver of Medousa's shade, a bronze glow in the water.

There was a metallic rustle above me. I looked up and saw it was Hekate. I heard the sound of her key swinging on a chain around her neck. She jumped into the grotto.

Hekate splashed next to Medousa with her torch in hand. Magic flames were unphased by the ocean, as they always were.

Her torch illuminated the underwater world, even Medousa's lingering shade.

She had the silver, scaly tail of a sea nymph. She had glassy, white eyes, and skin that looked like silver mist. Her hands were different from other shades; they were gloved in bronze.

I shivered. I wished not to challenge this shade. I wondered if her scaly hands could dismantle my ticking heart.

I needn't have worried. She disappeared under the light of Hekate's torch.

Hekate didn't see the shade. She swam quickly towards Medousa, kicking her leather hunting boots in the water.

Hekate grabbed the girl and whistled. Her high note echoed through the grotto and brought me into action.

I crackled in relief and rushed towards the witch.

I didn't have to watch them struggle. Hekate, with a shrill, metallic whistle, gave us permission to help her.

Dozens of stymphalians appeared from the mist.

We swooped down towards the splashing bodies. I wrapped my talons around the warm flesh of Medousa's arm. Water sloshed against my iron feet. Each bird grabbed wherever they could hold, and we lifted them upwards.

Hekate held onto her torch with one hand and held onto the writhing, slippery Medousa with the other. I watched Hekate. She stayed calm even in the chaos, but I could hear a change in the beat of her heart. I tightened my talons around Medousa's arms, enough to keep her in my grasp, but not enough to break her skin.

We couldn't lift her back to the tunnel's edge. It was too high to fly with the weight of their bodies. Instead, we carried them to an island of magnetite in the center of the grotto.

With all the shades swimming around the grotto's edges, a

whirlpool started to form in the grotto. The island became the calm eye in the center of chaos.

"Catch your breath here, Medousa," Hekate said.

Hekate and Medousa both steadied themselves. They slipped over the dark rocks, which were wet from the rogue wave which washed over the island.

Medousa had returned from the waters of the dead— at least a part of her.

This island was not here by chance. Hekate rose this rock from the seafloor with her burning glass. I watched her summon starlight, which shone through the crack at the mouth of the grotto.

The island served as the station for a dock. I knew that outside of Hekate's torchlight it jutted into the grotto, cut from black poplar planks. It was a place to moor a ship tethered to the stars.

Hekate pointed her torch towards Medousa.

Medousa inhaled slowly and exhaled slower. She stood to her feet beside Hekate. Us birds who brought them to this rocky shore were gathered at their feet, clicking and hissing from our bronze beaks.

I heard an inhale and cocked my head towards the mist. It was not the inhale of the young girl or the pharmakis, for it came from outside of our torchlight. It was not the breath of a stymphalian, for we never breathed. We were powered by metal rather than air. It couldn't have been an ordinary shade either, for they were trapped in breathless eternity.

It sounded like the inhale of a man. Every stymphalian knew him by breath alone.

"What was that?" Medousa asked.

"Probably the intruder," Hekate said.

"I thought you said shades couldn't breathe," Medousa said.

"This one is more than a shade. He's fallen from the craft of medicine."

"What?"

"This one's will is pooled into his mind. I allowed him to save face. When he became a shade, I gave him the powers of speech and breath. It's something I have since regretted," Hekate rolled her eyes in her flickering torchlight.

The girl, the witch, and the mysterious breath were silent for a moment.

Then stymphalian hearts ticked.

"His name is Kheiron. He's been killed by his own medicine, and he's going to stay dead," Hekate shouted into the mist.

I heard the scrape of metal over stone, but it was muffled by water.

"Was that metal?" Medousa asked.

"Kheiron must have paid a visit to a blacksmith, but his flesh is silver mist," Hekate's lip curled.

There was another whine, another wail of metal against rock. It rushed through the air to my aluminum ear drums. It wasn't the iron clank of a stymphalian's talon.

I knew bronze when I heard it.

Hekate heard it too and pointed her torch towards the sound.

We couldn't see anything in the mist.

"Why can't he leave the Underworld?" Medousa asked.

I felt the cold silence of Hekate after this question. I saw Hekate's fist tighten around the torch's handle.

Waves whirred around the island.

Tick. Tick. Tick.

Medousa and I were still waiting for Hekate to answer.

Another wave made its way along the shore. We waited.

"I must uphold the laws of plants."

There was another sound of metal scraping against stone. This time it was closer, and sent electric shivers down my metal bones. Misty torchlight flickered over Hekate's scowling face.

I heard four rapid hoofbeats and turned.

Hekate's torchlight followed my gaze.

The disgraced kentauroi stood before us. His eyes reflected Hekate's fire.

I looked at his feet, and I saw, sure enough, bronze shoes supporting his silver feet. My mind ticked and whirled, cursing the blacksmith he colluded with in the Underworld.

He'd tried to escape many times, but Kheiron was a more formidable opponent than ever before. He had the potential, with his newly shod hooves, to strike the witch. Or, he could've made his way onto land, and ran wild in Magnesia.

Medousa stood behind Hekate. She was like her shadow in the misty air. I watched the young girl shiver down to her bones.

I screeched from my beak. I flew to the eyeline of Kheiron and saw a mad, frenzied veil over his eyes.

Neither Kheiron's equine nor human heart beat. They'd been frozen in his chest since poison struck his blood. There was a twinge of blue to his silvery, misty form. It was his suffocated, stagnant blood.

Kheiron's face was bluer than the sea, and floated over his misty human neck. He turned blue from poison, cursing him in eternal death.

Kheiron could breathe in, but never exhale. Once air moved through his mouth, it rose like mist out of his lungs. Since wolfsbane brought him the kiss of death, he never exhaled, he never purged the poison.

Kheiron swatted me away from his raging, blue face. I fluttered to Hekate's shoulder. My talons rested on her collarbones. I could feel her pulsing anger beneath my iron claws.

"I heard the news. There's a new herd of kentauroi in Magnesia," Kheiron said, "I wish to meet them. Hephaistos fashioned me these shoes so I may go."

"So that's the root of the mist?" Hekate rolled her eyes. Wet, silver hair draped over her shoulders. It felt cool and light against my heavy feathers.

Kheiron yelled. It was a man's deep, guttural yowl– not the light whinny of a horse. He was once a living contradiction, until dying forever as a mythicized paradox.

Kheiron had the bronze shoes, he knew the path out of his tomb. He struck his hoof against magnetite.

"Pull yourself together!" Hekate snapped.

Kheiron took a step towards Hekate, who brought her torch between them.

I watched his eyes dart behind Hekate and grow wide. He must have spotted Medousa.

"Who's this?" Kheiron asked and walked behind Hekate towards the girl with glowing gold hair.

He towered over both of them, standing on equine legs. With each step he took, stymphalians clattered and moved out of his way.

"My name's Medousa," she peeped.

Kheiron didn't hesitate. He lifted onto his haunches and struck her with his bronze shoes. She fell back onto the hard rocky island.

"Hey! Leave her alone!" Hekate said.

"I would. If only you let me pass into Magnesia," Kheiron threatened.

"I don't make deals with shades," Hekate spat.

"Hekate," he said, "we already made a deal. That's why I can speak."

"That's something I've since regretted."

"You wish for me to draw her blood?" Kheiron rested his bronze hoof on Medousa's cowering body. He forced her against the rocks.

"You're underestimating the powers of my grotto, Kheiron."

"Well you're overestimating me," Kheiron said, "What harm would I do among the living? Just let me go!"

"Never!" Hekate said, "Letting you live would be disrespectful to the wolfsbane who killed you!"

I knew Hekate and I knew the poplars. I knew Hekate served plants before she served any horse or any man. I listened to their debate, but of course I couldn't weigh in.

The truth was, I enjoyed Kheiron. Each of his attempts to escape became a challenge for me and my flock. Kheiron provided battles for my fellow birds to bond over. Even warriors with metal souls needed enemies. What would a guardian be without a gate-crasher?

At any moment Hekate would give us a sign to end Kheiron's escape. Our bronze beaks probed between living and dead.

I heard the faint exhale of Medousa's breath against Kheiron's bronzed hoof.

Kheiron could impale her, but he wouldn't. It was only a bluff. If he hurt Medousa, it would backfire. Kheiron wanted to make the point– that he was harmless– that Hekate could trust him on land.

Medousa's blood would have proved him wrong.

Kheiron stared at the witch, who looked right back at him. Medousa whimpered on the stones. Poseidon lapped against the island, impartial to all.

From misting water, glowing red eyes emerged. The silver dogs of Kerberos climbed up the rock. He snarled with three sets of bone-white teeth. The dog maneuvered. He wasn't playful; he was trying to herd the kentauroi back underwater.

"You have chased me long enough through the waves, silver hound! You're not so tough on land, not with my bronze shoes."

The placidity he had, the bluff he carried when pinning down Medousa, disappeared. I could see his true intentions. Endless fights in the grotto kindled a rage for Kerberos within the unbeating hearts of Kheiron.

Before the pharmakis or the girl could speak, before they could even draw their breath, the kentauroi struck Kerberos.

His bronze shoe cracked the dog's skull. A howl echoed in the mist. It rattled my bones. It was not the howl of the dog, for Kerberos was silent, but the howl of Hekate as she watched her loyal companion fall.

As soon as Kheiron lifted his hoof, Medousa rolled free. She hurried back behind the witch. Her bare feet rushed over the slippery rocks.

The dog fell beneath his metal hoof. Silver blood pooled on magnetite rocks and clung to Kheiron's bronze shoes. Kerberos' blood looked like melting mercury in the torchlight. As one dog fell, the two other misty dogs toppled.

To hurt one shade of Kerberos seemed to hurt them all.

Hekate screamed.

It was not a whistle, like the way she normally commanded us, but the wrath in her scream which called our attention.

We had to do something.

I summoned the troops.

I took flight, to the highest reaches of the grotto, and I whistled. I whined like volcanoes under the cracking, boiling pressure of the earth.

I whistled from my beak, and the other stymphalians understood.

I told them about our enemy. *Kheiron.* We had to attack him with our bronze beaks, for his skin was mist.

Metallic wings jostled all around me. We knew our target. They swirled around me in a rush. I took flight, leading the flock. I took aim and my fellow stymphalians spiraled in my wake.

My sharp, needle-like beak aimed downwards. I fell like an arrow, pointed precisely at Kheiron.

Metal whisked through the air, I heard the soft click of bronze feathers behind me. The kentauroi couldn't see us coming in the mist. He stood up, and tried to turn, but he simply couldn't move fast enough.

With a simple tweak of our wings, we adjusted for his attempt to flee, and our beaks made landing. My beak pierced his vaporized hide, and dozens more stymphalians were behind me. Silvery, blue blood pooled from mist.

We withdrew, but the damage was already done.

Kheiron toppled. He fell right over his withers, rolled forward, and rested at the pharmakis' feet.

Metallic flaps came from above.

Seven stymphalians came down from the highest enclave of our roost— the weavers. They lived at the pinnacle of the grotto, and pulled bronze ores, alloyed and fraying from magnetite rocks. They carried their finely woven bronze thread and flew down to the kentauroi at Hekate's feet. She watched the metal birds work quickly, to tie up Kheiron before he took a breath. They looped their thread around his human neck, his equine legs, his misty form which was solid against their Underworldly metal.

The stymphalians darted around each other and formed a binding knot. One stymphalian handed a thread to Hekate, who grabbed it, and winced. I heard the hiss of metal and smelled the singe of flesh. The malleable thread was red-hot.

Hekate did not let go. Rather, she fastened the thread onto the handle of her torch. I heard it hiss against her fingers and scorch the poplar handle. She'd been burned before, so she tied the knot unphased.

Kheiron was restrained before he could even take a breath. Winded from his fall, with legs hobbled together, and arms bound— he couldn't run or strike.

As soon as Kheiron fell, the dead surrendered to their depths. Mist fell from the salty air. Silver forms of shades disappeared. The whirlpool in the grotto slowed.

He'd been controlling them, subtly convincing them, through the silent language of the dead, to ascend and riot. They fell back, into the depths where their iridescence grew murky. Since the full moon, they worked hard to blur the edges between life and death. Their leader lost his power and their battle was over.

Mist fell from the air. I heard it cloak the ocean with a whoosh. It rained onto my body and onto the skin of Medousa and Hekate. Mist fell right through the fallen Kheiron, but drops bubbled over his blue face and pooled on the bronze threads which bound him.

The faint glow, iridescent as the mist itself, of the dead animating and bubbling the water, sank into the waters of the dead.

The grotto was calmer than it'd been since the moon filled.

Without mist, we had clarity.

I saw the whole dark island and the stymphalians who stood in wait. On the shore of the island, I saw the dock crafted from dark wood. I watched Medousa's eyes trace it, all the way to the skiff, chained by its bow. Hekate's flame flickered against the faraway walls of the grotto, gnarled with black poplar roots and nesting, cackling, ticking stymphalians. Silver eyes watched each other without blinking.

Waves ceased their sloshing against the grotto's walls. The cavern fell still, with only a gentle sway of tides.

Before silence settled, we squawked, and clicked, and hissed at each other.

Our mission was done, but it was easier to hunt than to heal.

Hekate's job was only beginning. She tended to her fallen dog. She frowned in a perfect opposite to the horns of the moon rising from her head. Her hands held all three misty, canine corpses by their collars. Hekate held her torch in the other hand. She turned and faced Medousa, with the dog's silver blood dripping like tails of comets down her wrists.

I heard Hekate consider. Her mind wasn't like Medousa or even Kheiron. Her thoughts sounded like ticking heartbeats to me. My silver eye could see into her emotions, her feelings, and her intuitions. I could resonate with her problems, as a fellow defender of the grotto, as a craft which came from her hands. She knew, deep down, that even though she ruled the Underworld, she was never meant to control it. I knew she struggled with this, whenever chaos inevitably bubbled up from the depths. The very foundation of reality was its uncontrollable nature. I heard her desperate attempts to wrangle with the concept, to explain to Medousa what she must do.

"Kerberos is dead," Hekate said with a storm in her gray eyes, "I can bring him back."

"How?"

"With his body, and a trip to the Underworld— that's how a pharmakis raises the dead, not to roam the stars, but to live in their own bodies again."

"To–" Medousa stuttered, "the Underworld?"

"Yes, but you cannot go."

I screeched. Oh, the irony! Hekate was blind!

Medousa was already in the Underworld. I saw a shade split from her living body! I wanted to shout at the pharmakis, but all I could do was screech and whistle.

She looked at me, and considered, but only for a moment.

"Magnesia is not safe for you either," Hekate swallowed, "not without me."

"Where am I to go?"

"You have no choice but to visit your sisters."

"You said you would protect me."

"Now your sisters will protect you, and the ocean will protect you on the way."

"The ocean has done nothing but hurt me!"

"You're mistaken," Hekate said, "You've grown bitter. The ocean nursed you on its salt and aged you in its waves."

Medousa stepped towards the warm torchlight of the witch.

Medousa's lips sealed and she exhaled out of her nose.

Hekate slipped the corpses of Kerberos into the leather belt around her waist. It gave her one free hand, while her other hand still carried the burning poplar torch.

"I need you to go quickly. If you're escaping to Sarpedon, and I'm going under, we'll be leaving the grotto unlocked. It shouldn't take me more than one night to raise Kerberos. The stymphalians should be able to hold off any intruders until then. You wouldn't want to be here if there's another rogue shade."

Medousa stood, waiting for the witches' next instructions.

"Hurry," Hekate said, "Board the boat on the edge of the dock. Every bronze nail in its hull is a talisman to Algol. It can only take you in one direction– to Sarpedon."

Medousa walked away from Hekate. She ran quickly over the dock's dark, splintered wood. Medousa jumped into the skiff. She landed with such a jolt that she had to hold onto the rail to keep from flying overboard.

I flew towards the bow. I had to see Hekate's command turn true. My talons dug into the aged, wet wood. Grooves of the fallen tree resonated with my iron talons. I could feel the nails through the wood, begging to drift towards the star. It was a dark energy, even to a bronze bird.

I pecked the chain with my metal beak. I split the metal quickly, as it had also aged in the salt and mist. The skiff's heavy chain fell into the Underworld.

The boat started to move. I perched on the bow, watching tides rush against us, but they were unable to draw us off course. The skiff cut the water like my beak pierced flesh.

Medousa ran her fingers through her hair, mindlessly pulling strands out of her loose braid. She looked around the grotto, and she asked Hekate, "How can I get out of here?"

"There is a crack between the rocks that leads to the ocean. I've enchanted it so no sunlight may enter. You cannot see it. but your boat knows its way. Let the skiff find its course."

Medousa swallowed and hung her head.

"Medousa?"

"Yes?"

"You must stop living in fear," Hekate said, "Your sisters will protect you. So will the... journey."

Without another word Hekate bent low to the ground. She sprang forward, diving through the air and into the water. Kerberos was on her belt and the lightweight shade of Kherion followed her, tethered by a bronze thread. He was still winded from our attack, and didn't even try to resist.

Once Hekate splashed beneath the surface, Medousa leaned over the skiff, watching the glowing torch disappear into murky water.

"An underwater flame?" She asked, but not loud enough for the massive grotto to echo an answer. She asked it to herself, questioning her own understanding of fire and water. I listened to the drip of mist from the sharp grotto walls, the crackle of stymphalians, and I heard the breath of the girl struck by fear of the unknown.

Hekate was gone. She left the lock at the top of the tunnel open, and Kerberos was gone too, so my flock was the only barrier between the dead and the living. We defended Hekate's grotto with our mechanical lives. We never slept and our silver eyes had no silver lids.

"Hekate?" Medousa shouted. Her breath quickened.

I saw a flash of a serpentine tail. Hekate descended into a torchlit abyss. She was gone.

I saw fear and hunger in Medousa's eyes. The boat carried us towards the dark crack in the grotto's wall.

We passed through the veil, into the sunny, endless world of the open ocean.

I had never dared to fly out of the grotto before. That wasn't the way of a stymphalian.

I wanted to see Medousa through. I wanted to pass her onto another guardian.

Medousa started to clutch herself. The skiff moved forward, impartial to fear and hesitation. I watched waves split at her bow. Waves were fiercer outside the grotto, and there was no backlash from waves bouncing against cavern walls. I saw the infinite horizon.

I felt sunlight over my bronze feathers. I'd never felt so flustered, blinded. Before darting back inside, I caught a glimpse of a strong bird overhead. She could cross the sea under his shadow.

13. Phoinix

"Medousa has a shade too, you know," I said.

Hekate didn't know.

She hid her surprise well, but I saw through her mask.

Hekate looked at me with her gray eyes. Those same eyes which were once round and human looked at me with the cold, sharp slits of a cat. Hekate still had her same face, her robed torso, and the same horns of the moon clinging to her forehead. But her legs had been replaced. The thick, bronze tail of a snake propelled us downwards into the depths.

Underwater she kept her Hekatean soul, but she navigated depths inside the serpentine bodice of skylla.

Her long, python-like tail swished. Soon we were deeper than the sun could shine. I watched her gills, like gashes on her neck, flare for breath.

"She has no shade," Hekate dismissed my claim.

"Would your own phoinix lie to you?" I insisted.

Hekate lowered her stony gaze and swam in silent resignation. Silver hair trailing behind her turned blue as we sank deeper.

"I saw her shade," I said, "She looks like you, like skyllax."

The pharmakis rolled her catty eyes. I could press her, because I knew she needed me to light the Underworld. She'd have to face the truth.

Though Hekate hadn't summoned me in a long time, I heard the whispers of birds while I was embodied as ash, floating over the lands of Greece. Every bird knew of Medousa roaming the earth on her way to legend. She was tangled up in the strings of the stars, and she had to swim, battle, and run her way through.

"A part of Medousa split," I explained, "That part of her became a shade. Medousa has taken silver form."

"Don't mock me. I saw Medousa in flesh board the boat to Sarpedon," Hekate's voice was as cold as the deep.

"When Medousa fell from the cliff, a shade split from her skin. You jumped in after Medousa, and when your torch was submerged, I spotted her shade. She was a mermaid, silver as the counterpart to your moon," I said, "She had bronze hands and white eyes. She swam away, into the deep, as soon as I spotted her."

Hekate was silent. My flaming feathers cackled.

"Nonsense, she can't be a shade and keep on living. She's on her way to Sarpedon, not down here."

"You know I'd never lie to you, Hekate," I winked, "Medousa has a shade. Medousa is not one, but two. I won't make you admit it, so you may keep your pride."

"Let's not talk about it," Hekate said. As skylla, she slashed her tail through the water. My flaming, enchanted feathers quivered against currents as we plummeted.

"So, why are we swimming into the Underworld tonight, Hekate? It seems you've been spending your time in other realms lately. What brings you to the deep?"

"Here," the pharmakis said.

Hekate untied something from her waist and brought it closer to my burning eyes.

She held three dogs together by their tails. Their fur was misty, and though my torchlight was warm, their bodies didn't warm in my light. They were as cold as a whisper on a dark night.

"Kerberos," my own voice was a stunned whisper.

A silver rivulet trailed down the face of the biggest dog. His skull had been split open and his moonlit blood poured out.

She fastened the dogs onto a bronze belt around her scaly waist.

"What happened to him?"

"Kheiron tried to escape," Hekate said.

"Yet again," I hissed from my molten beak.

"He was seeking a new herd of free kentauroi who now roam the wilds of Magnesia. He even got bronze shoes!" anger bubbled in her voice, then Hekate's eyes scanned the craggy grotto, "Shall we keep from discussing this? I fear someone might overhear."

"How noble," I cooed. I judged her intentions. Noble, yes, to preserve a life, but a gray area loomed in that Kerberos was a gatekeeper, and his life meant the imprisonment of the souls of the dead. Perfectly contradictory, so I let my flames roar.

"We must hurry," Hekate said, "I've left the grotto unlocked."

"Oh dear," I replied.

She swam deeper, and my light colored the grotto's edges. This trench.would take us to the depths, but I needed answers first. Where I shone, there was always a contradiction. I was an underwater fire, after all.

Hekate knew if her task was pure, with no shadow, I wouldn't help. I had to see both sides, wherever she took me. I saw Hekate and skylla. I saw the living and the dead. Likewise, if her mission underwater was perfectly evil with no silver lining, I would've vanished all the same.

I shined light in dark places, never for purely noble causes. That's why Hekate alone could summon me, because a nefarious shadow followed everything she did.

"I've taken Kheiron as my prisoner."

Yes, even darker. I grew stronger. Light stretched deeper into the shadowy depths.

I did what my mortal likeness, the peacock, could never dream of doing. I traveled into the depths of the dead.

"Oh?" I careened my head to see the kentauroi, restrained by bronze threads, trailing behind us in the water. His misty body wavered like my flaming feathers. He resigned, and accepted his imprisonment. I felt the threads cut into the torch, the link between me and Hekate. I watched the limp body of Kerberos, in all three of his forms, and the resigned body of Kheiron being dragged into the deep.

"Hephaistos gave him bronze shoes, but let's wait until we get deeper," Hekate said, "I don't wish to be overheard."

Just as Hekate spoke of eavesdroppers, a herd of glittering, silver horses came into my light. They'd been sentenced to the Underworld, into their home at sea, in the palm of Poseidon. They floated, trotting through liquid, as if there were steps in the water column for them. The herd swam fast, their narrow shoulders cut through the water, their soaring hearts like the wildest fish in the sea. Their eyes were wide, and they staggered. I was sure my light blinded them, for they probably spent eternity in shadows.

I watched the horses bow and shake their heads, vying for dominance among me and the pharmakis, who ignored them and took us deeper.

The herd disappeared. Their silver bodies faded into dark water around us.

We were in the deep ocean. The trench under Hekate's grotto stretched for leagues under the sea. The water was calm, and under so much pressure, it pushed us down.

"I pray we can make some conversation, Hekate. It has been a long time since you brought me underwater. I must inquire...In your human form," I asked, "are you hurt? I could taste flesh burning during your metamorphosis."

"Yes," Hekate said, "My palm was burned by Kheiron's chains."

"Pity," I said.

"The thread was hot, but I didn't let go," Hekate continued, "I'm not taking any chances this time."

"Yet another sacrifice from the caretaker of the abyss," I assured her, "Someone has to do it, Hekate."

When she went underwater, and morphed from Hekate into skylla, I felt her palm against the torch change. Burns turned into bruises. She was safe to swim underwater. Hekate left her human body behind, in the frothing water of ocean waves. She left it as a memory between her and the sea. Down here, with me, she was in the body of skylla.

I transformed, too. We were the same that way. When she took me underwater, my flames sparked into feathers, and I became a phoinix.

The truth was, skylla and Hekate were one. Hekate would have to surface and she would have to heal.

"Worry not, your human form will heal by the burning glass' light," I said, "Where is the moon now, my dear?"

"Waning gibbous," Hekate said.

"Some time will pass before the glass trades hands. Well, you must have healing salves in your cottage," I mused, "That will help at least."

"Yes," Hekate submitted, "My chamomile salve is prepared."

In truth, I loved talking to Hekate. I loved speaking human words with an avian tongue. It was better than my life above the sea, where I silently floated as ash.

Even with my light, creatures of the deep tried their best to hide.

There were much more than Poseidon's horses down there. Octopus couldn't speak or understand the words of a pharmakis, but their eyes watched from every crevice. Tentacles curled up behind those eyes. I was sure of it, though I couldn't see them. I could never bring light to the labyrinth of octopi in the grooves of the trench.

All I ever saw were their goat-like eyes flickering in my torchlight. The octopus, so strange and unlike every other creature of the ocean, reflected a myriad of colors back into my eyes, never the same one. They were truly odd.

Yes, the octopi were strange, even for myself, a bird without a mother or a father, and who never ate nuts or seeds, or flew on wings, like my fellow birds. I felt disarmed by their unearthliness. Their monstrous nature was evident when they reflected my own torchlight back to me.

The octopi had the same mysterious glimmer I saw in the eyes of Medousa's shade. I knew there were parts of her I couldn't see. I knew, from the way her shade swam, quickly, naturally, and instinctually into the abyss, that Medousa was the daughter of sea monsters.

We sank deeper and deeper. Then, a hole appeared in the cliff face, and Hekate swam inside, allowing my light to lead the way. The passage was plenty big for me, the three bodies of Kerberos, the fallen kentauroi, and the swishing tail of Hekate as skylla.

The cave slithered before us, as if it was carved by a leviathan snaking his way through stone. Hekate as skylla held me in front of her, casting light over every crevice. I saw red dots flash to green flash to blue; they were eyes. Octopi watched from every turn in the tunnel.

Tunnels branched in several directions, but Hekate knew the way. She kept to her path, with me leading the way, and Kerberos and the kentauroi in tow. Hekate knew better than to get lost down an offshoot where a creature lurked in the shadows. I didn't know exactly where we were going, only that we were going down. Then the labyrinth leveled out into a deep canal.

When we reached the bottom, a vast chamber the size of a stadium opened up. The walls were lined with doors and openings. There were a myriad of ways to go, and hallways that crawled under the Aegean Sea like mad rabbits.

Hekate moved faster in the wide open space. She flicked her tail with purpose.

We moved past doors made of iron, but those didn't interest Hekate. She swished her reddish tail and propelled us further, past more doors she wouldn't open.

We heard a click, a bang, and a hiss thunder through the water. Hekate stopped for one moment to listen, then moved faster, in the same direction, like she knew exactly where to go all along.

Eventually we came to a gilded door. It was ornate, as if someone had spent a lifetime carving it. The designs on the door told the story of a boy falling from a mountain and being swallowed by the sea. I knew whose story it was and I knew exactly why we came. A blacksmith lived here. I had illuminated Hekate's visits with him before.

Perhaps, *he* had shod Kheiron, I thought.

The bronze door reflected my torchlight back to me with the same fiery glow as skylla's scales. I heard another loud bang rumble behind the door.

Hekate didn't bother to knock.

She barged in, nearly taking the door off its rusting hinges.

With a creak, then the smack of the door rattling the underwater chamber, we entered the forge of Hephaistos. Hekate slithered inside, holding me in front, her dead dogs strapped to her waist, and the bound kentauroi drifting behind her.

We entered a hall so vast that my torchlight couldn't reach the walls. Before us stood a sunken ship half-buried in sand. Its jagged hull bowed like the ribs of a fallen whale.

Where the ship's wood rotted away, it had been replaced by beams of bronze. My light licked over the wood and glistened on the metal.

Bang.

Skylla's tail swished and led us into the wreck, into the bones of the ship. My light warped around underwater halls and rooms. In a few turns and a flight of stairs— we were upon Hephaistos.

His metallic gills flapped as we caught him by surprise. I saw a flash of silver along his neck, the metal of breath.

Hephaistos dropped his tongs and cursed as a red-hot hunk of metal fell into the sand, barely missing his foot. His wide eyes seemed like they couldn't see at all.

Perhaps my light blinded him. He worked in the dark, over hot water rather than flames.

Perhaps Hephaistos didn't hear the door smash open. He must have been too absorbed in his work. He stood next to a torrent of bubbling, hot water-- his Underworldly forge.

He was like the gilded ship, but a man, broken and mended by metal. He rubbed his eyes with an intricate metal hand. Half of his face shone with the red glow of bronze. There was not one flake of green patina on his mechanical skin. I knew Hephaistos' tricks. He was protected by wax, which he harvested from sea kelp. I'd seen him make it down here before, melting the seaweed on his forge.

The rest of him was obscured by work clothes, but I knew he was more metal than human.

Hephaistos squinted at me bringing light to his shadowy affairs. He wasn't alone; nobody was ever truly *alone* in the Underworld.

A tall figure emerged from the shadows. Auburn hair framed his cherub-like face.

"I see Aquarian still pulls all the strings in the Underworld," Hekate sneered.

"Oh, love," Aquarian, the tall fellow, said, "I beg you to take the reins from me."

"I'd rather not," Hekate said, "How pathetic a court is this? Only half a blacksmith and the shadow of an angel?"

I saw the pupils in Aquarian's blue eyes shrink as he adjusted to my light. He looked at me and scanned the long body of Hekate. I watched his eyes linger on the three dead dogs and the bound kentauroi, who tried to look back, but the threads binding him were too tight.

"My love, that's why you'll never be invited to court in the clouds," Aquarian chuckled, "Too much despair can be found in your wake. The dead have a funny way of following you around."

Aquarian was playful, but testy, like he played a game he felt entitled to win before it even started. Anger spilled over skylla's face, but Hekate kept her lips sealed.

"You know the upper court of clouds, or so you've heard of it," Aquarian continued, "Far above Nephele's castle, my heavenly counterpart is pouring drinks for Artemis, Athene and all the other pharmakides who don't wish to control each other."

I imagined them floating, in the bright sky, where all truths laid out in the open. Nobody up there would need a phoinix to see. They could chase sunlight forever, drinking sparkling ambrosia across horizons. I'd never shine up there. I belonged under pressure. I was Hekate's bird, not Hera's peacock.

"You'd never fit in up there," Aquarian went on with a cunning wink, "In the sky, we tend to bliss. Down here, in the realm of your creation, we're all sadists."

"I don't want to play court in the clouds and I'm not here to see you," Hekate spat.

I knew her statement was only half-true. Deep inside Hekate, she was enraged at being excluded from the highest reaches of the clouds. Hekate kept jealousy as her precious secret, but I could see inside her heart. She loved the darkness in herself, but she didn't love to entertain the darkness in others. She could not trust them, for dark shadows were always twisting and turning and changing alliances. She wondered if, in another life, with less secrets in her heart, if she could've gone to the highest realm.

I knew her well.

"My dear, I sense a tinge of jealousy. Worry not. Hera's not allowed at the Court in the clouds either. Not after what she did to our poor Hephaistos."

"That's who I've come to see," Hekate focused skylla's gray eyes on Hephaistos, "So he may take back what he did and chain Kheiron to the seafloor."

Hephaistos recoiled. He stood behind his bubbling forge, as if he was willing his workplace to protect him. How pitiful he looked, under Hekate's wrathful eye, my flaming light, and Aquarian's quip about his mother. He was, after all, a victim of Hera.

Even the most talented witches sometimes made all the wrong choices. Hera threw her own son from a mountaintop. Instead of nurturing the boy, she saw the face of her scorned lover in her own child, and saw him gone. She flung him from the peak of Pelion, into the sea.

Hephaistos was injured by the fall. The young boy's body was disfigured. He sank into the Underworld to rebuild himself.

Hekate pushed past Aquarian. She moved towards the Hephaistos and thrust me into his face. My torchlight revealed his beady eyes and smooth, bronze skin. He had the look of a worker, who spent lifetimes hunched over his craft. Where he still had human flesh, his face was lined by focus and grit.

"Hephaistos!" Hekate bared her fangs.

He took a step back, but Hekate surged forward, for skylla's tail was so powerful, she could chase any man through the depths of the Underworld. His forge was no obstacle for Hekate as skylla. She would slither her way around anything.

Hekate flicked her wrist, like a whip, and the bound kentauroi snapped in front of her, between her scaly tail and Hephaistos' chaps and boots. His eyes grew and he began to stammer.

"You are only to put bronze shoes on a beast with my permission," Hekate said. He stared at her, into her catty gray eyes.

"Do you understand?"

"Y-yes, Hekate."

Kheiron was broken. His soul, which longed to be free, which longed to see kentauroi in the wilds of Magnesia, had stopped stirring. His human mind stopped dreaming and his equine body stopped fleeing. He did not speak nor struggle.

"How could you betray me after all these moons?" Hekate asked.

"Not me... It was..." Hephaisos stammered.

Bronze shoes glowed in my firelight. They arched on the undersides of Kheiron's hooves, as if to mock Hekate's horns of the moon. Hephaistos glanced at the kentauroi's feet. His metallic body shuddered and I heard his skin click like the rattling of a stymphalian.

"Oh, spit it out already!" Hekate shouted. Her voice would have echoed on land, but dark water muffled it.

"It was ambrosia!" Hephaistos admitted. He swallowed and blinked.

Hekate turned and gave a sharp, knowing glance to Aquarian. He had a smug grin, and clearly, didn't fear Hekate like Hephaistos did. If the root of the problem was ambrosia, Aquarian was the sure supplier.

"You'll give him bronze chains and anchor him to the seafloor," Hekate turned to face the blacksmith once more, "This was Kheiron's last escape attempt."

Hephaistos forge bubbled, Aquarian watched with amusement, and my flames flickered over the scene. The blacksmith stammered, searching for words.

"Do you understand?" Hekate growled.

Hephaistos nodded.

"What are you waiting for?" Hekate asked.

Hephaistos swallowed. He fumbled through gilded drawers, drawing out pure bricks of copper and tin. His hands, one metal and one flesh, threw the materials into his forge. He got to work melting metals to forge the bridge between life and death, the alloy of bronze. Hekate watched him and didn't blink.

"Come now Hekate, must everyone down here be your prisoner?" Aquarian asked joyfully.

Hekate took her eyes off the blacksmith and moved towards the blue-eyed man. She was dragging Kheiron by her torch. Bronze threads dug into the kentauroi with every movement of her body. His blue blood dribbled onto the sand. I felt the pull of the beast against my black poplar handle.

Then, in the corner of the shipwreck, my flame illuminated something silver. Everything was polished bronze and waterlogged wood in the wreck, I didn't expect to catch the light of silver. It was gone in a flash before I could really look at it.

I figured it must have been a shade, but I had the strange feeling that it wasn't the first time I saw that swift, silver flash.

Before I could consider it, Hekate was upon Aquarian. With her mighty tail she could stand taller than him.

Hephaistos forge hissed as compounds collided.

"Water, water everywhere," the water bearer whispered, "I found for you, a drop to drink."

Hekate rolled her eyes. Aquarian held out a golden goblet. Red liquid swirled in its center. He was playing. Hekate knew it wasn't water and so did I. Of course, it couldn't be water. It was far more dense than seawater, sinking in his golden goblet, glittering the ruby color of healthy blood.

"I'm not here to get drunk," Hekate snapped. Aquarian and Hekate's eyes were locked. Hephaistos' hammer boomed in the background, but neither Hekate nor Aquarian paid attention.

The liquid steamed under Hekate's turned-up nose. It was ambrosia, alcohol for the dead. Brewed in the depths, I knew it to be much stronger than whatever Aquairan's counterpart served in the clouds. Pressure made everything stronger— hatred and haste included.

The bloody liquid carried a curse. One drop, and Hekate's mission in the Underworld would've fallen apart.

I'd seen it all before. Hekate once frequented these depths, with me as her light.

"Please, take one sip. Dark little pharmakis," Aquarian wiggled his eyebrows, "You seem thirsty."

"No!" Hekate shouted, "Now that Hephaistos is crafting chains, I am meant to resurrect Kerberos. There's no time for me to waste."

Hephaistos' relentless hammering stopped for a moment. He adjusted hot copper with his tongs, and got back to work.

Aquarian brought the ambrosia to his lips and hissed, "Mmm... delicious. Heal thyself— Kheiron taught me that."

Hekate screamed. I felt her fingers pulse in frustration against the torch's handle. Her rage was so fierce, so fresh. She mourned for her dog and for every minute she left the grotto unlocked.

It was the scream of someone bubbling with so much frustration that it became a blistering pain.

Hekate ripped Aquarian's goblet from his hands. She held the goblet for just a moment. Then she threw it to the ground. Metal landed in sand and crimson contents spilled over the sea floor.

Since she wasn't acting clearly, since she was fueled by rage rather than reason, she failed to think about the splash. A flood of dense liquid coated her scaly tail.

All it took was one drop to work its way through her scales, and she was gone.

Ambrosial spirit took over her. The hunger of the Underworld laid her down to rest. She sank into its intoxication, her body falling back onto the shadowy sand, a curtain of unconsciousness falling before her eyes. Still, her dogs were belted around her waist. Still, all three of them were dead.

The splash hit Aquarian too. He staggered and dropped beside Hekate into the sand.

When Aquarian and Hekate were asleep, the silver flash returned. It was Medousa, or rather, her shade. I watched the nimble nymph come to *Kheiron's* aid. She floated past the sleeping drunkards, and with bronze gloves untangled bronze threads. Her eyes were white as death itself, and I could hardly stand to look at her.

The kentauroi smirked, but kept silent.

In a moment, the bronze threads fell to the seafloor, and Kheiron was free. Medousa's shade was gone once again, disappearing into the shadow Underworld where this part of her belonged.

As Kheiron stood, I heard the soft slosh of his bronze horseshoes in the sand.

First I saw his scars, burnt where hot bronze threads touched him, bleeding blue against his misty skin. Deep gashes lined his human arms and his equine haunches.

A smirk crept over Kheiron's aquamarine face.

He was free.

He could see no better than a rat. He had the eyes of a man, and not of an illusive octopus. Nonetheless, he managed his way out.

Neither Hekate nor Aquarian stirred.

How he escaped was a secret I would never tell Hekate, she'd wake up eventually, and assume Kheiron escaped on his own accord. I didn't wish to turn her against Medousa. The girl shouldn't suffer for the treason of her shade. So in ash or flame, I never spoke of Medousa's shade freeing Kheiron. Hekate would never know. She would blame the cunning mixture of horse and man, an alloy as malleable as bronze. She'd never guess it had been Medousa's silver shade. I would tell Hekate; even though I shed light, all light had shadows.

Still, Hephaistos hammered, too focused to notice the commotion.

His work would go to little use. Chains couldn't lock down a missing prisoner.

As Hekate fell deeper into her drunken stupor, her grip on my wooden handle loosened. The torch slipped from her fingertips, my flaming body melted into ash, and everything went black.

14. Osprey

A boat emerged from a narrow crack in the cliff.

Waves battered the skiff, but it trudged forward, unrelenting, unphased by the pull of swell. The small boat stuck to its course.

I caught sight of a girl, sitting near the stern, clutching her knees to her chest, rocking like the sea. Wet, dark clothes stuck to her skin. She held a long gaze at the ocean. Her eyes scanned the patterns of waves and the course of the wind. Her eyes darted over crests and across the horizon.

She looked to the sea with no cage or shelter. She sat on the edge of her skiff, a tempest to the elements. Her locks glowed like freshly minted coins. She was so bright. Had she taken me by surprise, she could've blinded me and knocked me out of the sky, like a swordfish in the sunlight.

I heard a metal whistle. I saw some kind of green, nimble hummingbird dart back between the rocks from whence the skiff came.

I dove down from the sky, riding the wind closer to the mysterious boat and its passenger, and I spotted a thin scar over her neck and a bronze chain dangling below it.

That's when I realized who she was.

I remembered Orion the hunter who appeared, days ago, on a night filled with bats, and the scorpion that chased him. There was more to the myth than made it into the sky.

I heard the truth in bat's chirps. They squealed stories of girls and monsters. Their chirps were so high, so similar to mine, that I understood what they were saying.

It was her– the girl who raised Orion into the sky.

I recognized the girl in the skiff as Medousa.

"Algol," she looked to the sky, which was clear and sunny beyond the mist. Her brows furrowed, as if trying to remember something.

Medousa sank low onto her heels, balancing on the skiff's boards. She gazed from the skiff's bow along a straight line, back up to the sky. I watched her look up and down, several times in long, visual strokes.

She pointed dead ahead at a faraway cloud. All seabirds knew the places of stars. Far behind that cloud was Algol, fixed but hidden in the light of day. Then, seemingly content with her findings, Medousa sat back, and held her knees to her chest once more.

I noticed she had no paddle and no sail, but her small ship moved on its own accord.

Water rippled behind Medousa's skiff. I swear I saw a moonlit mermaid cast the ripples. There was a flash of silver, and the dull glow of bronze. When I looked closer, she sank into the deep, blue land of dreams.

I could hear Medousa's heart pounding. She bit her lip when a wave crashed over the skiff's rail. She shrank from the salty spray. I guessed that she was scared of water.

Medousa dared not move, save her heart and her breath. Suppressing fear made her freeze, as if she was made of stone.

Though she was frozen in place, her skiff carried onwards.

I flew behind Medousa.

Her golden hair was bright, but did not reveal her true nature.

Each osprey chick had eyes as blue as the sea. As we matured, our eyes yellowed. Medousa may have been golden, but she was not aged like an osprey. She did not seem old in the world. I felt it was my duty to protect her. By my golden-brown feathers, flecked with salt, and aged by the sea, I saw her as my fellow.

My heart opened to the task of protecting Medousa, as if she were my fledgling.

We set out towards the horizon. Waves grew calm, but swell grew thicker. We drifted towards the deepest blues in Greece, where trenches fell into other worlds.

Eventually I lost sight of shore and Medousa became a drop of gold in endless blue. Her glint was so bright, I wondered if she might be like a burning glass, which could've started a fire by reflecting light. I'd seen Hekate wield the formidable tool before. I wondered who she was, and where destiny might take her.

Apparently, fate ushered her to a star hidden behind sunshine and clouds.

Algol.

I swallowed.

The star was a legend among ospreys.

We flew towards the place, the whirlpool in the ocean, where women who shared my wings were slaughtered. My heart flummoxed with grief. At least there would be no mass grave, I assured myself. Poseidon would've swallowed the winged women the moment they stopped flying.

Little did I know, he had spit two of them back out.

After hours of travel, Medousa sighed and began to relax. The tension in her exhale left her body and carried over horizons. She even stood and gazed at the sea, which stretched forever in every direction. I couldn't spot land from the sky.

There was nothing but the sun, sea, wind, and my shadow over Medousa– until I noticed something fall from her hair.

It was a black ribbon, dislodged by scurrying winds. It landed behind the skiff and disappeared beneath a wave. Medousa's messy braid unraveled, and her hair became animated by tempests. I saw her hair like my own golden feathers, begging to take flight.

It was strange, after we lost sight of shore, I still smelled sage. The earthy aroma lingered in the sea, and reminded me of the Pharmakis of the Dark Side of the Moon.

Meanwhile, her skiff stayed on course to Algol, even after the orange and pink cloud which covered the star turned gray and purple and faded into a faraway rain shower. Clouds glided across the sky, but behind their show, the star Algol stayed fixed. The star was out there, beyond the pale veil of day.

I heard Medousa's stomach rumble. There was no fruit for Medousa to eat on the journey; she had no drinkable water. In the open ocean, I didn't spot any fish I could've caught for her either. I wished for a bushel of grapes to offer Medousa.

I could fly far with no water and no food. My wings stretched to horizons, and my strength knew no bounds.

But Medousa was just a girl.

Clouds parted and the sky sweltered.

I realized that the open sea offered no shade, save my small shadow. Though I was cooled by the wind under my feathers, Medousa grew hot in the skiff. I watched her skin blush and burn. The sun beat down on her.

I chirped, asking Medousa to please take care of herself.

I spoke to a place deep inside of the girl. It was deeper than logic, deeper than language which would seek direct meanings in chirps. This was the way of birds and humans in Greece. Us birds wove an intricate web, carrying the subtleties of nature. Humans followed our wishes, without knowing exactly why or how.

She took my advice. Medousa leaned over the railing of the boat. I supposed that she was too hot to mind her fear of the ocean.

She splashed cool, salty seawater over her face.

As she leaned over the edge, the hem of her robe revealed her ankle. I saw a faint blue glow and strained my eyes to see the details. Emblazoned on her skin was a snake eating its own tail. It wrapped around her ankle into infinity. I wondered if she was meant for infinity too. I assumed that one day, I would look into the stars, and see Medousa shining back at me.

She would never die.

Medousa doused her upper body in salty water, baking in the hot sun. The long sleeves of her robes absorbed the sea, cooling her wrists. I watched her and saw her relax more.

It wasn't the right moment to let her guard down.

Her splash attracted a beast.

A shadow materialized beneath her. It was long, slender, and dark blue in a sea of crystalline turquoise. Sunlight struck the beast and revealed it, but only to my eyes in the sky. I followed from above, watching the dark leviathan lurk behind Medousa's skiff.

We traveled over waves, deeper into the blue.

The shadow came closer to Medousa, so close that its wake shifted the skiff's course. It corrected itself, but none of the other waves had moved her ship. I swallowed. Medousa looked around. She lowered her head again and scanned over the bow with precision. I flew overhead, consciously watching the girl with my yellow eyes— sharp as an archer's.

The beast followed her, like the sun followed us across the ocean. It swished its tail slowly.

The leviathan never wavered in pursuit of Medousa. I stifled an uncomfortable chuckle, wondering if it was also bound to Algol. In that way I was bound to Algol too. I was free, a bird of the sea, bound not to the stars, but to their warped, glistening reflections.

I saw the reflection of Algol in Medousa. I wondered if the leviathan saw it too.

I watched the beast lift his head out of the water. His scales were the same kelp green as Medousa's eyes. The monster's own eyes were yellow and piercing, as bright as Medousa's hair.

The beast was watching her.

She had no idea. Her gaze fixed over the bow. Her heartbeat quickened at a large wave that frothed over the rail of the skiff. It was the leviathan's tail who put that wave into motion.

The leviathan pulled his head back under. He followed Medousa in perfect invisibility. Even if she looked right at him, she would've seen only the expansive sea. The creature knew how to hide. He kept himself between the sun and Medousa. Only I saw his shadow in the water. The leviathan was as big as a hundred skiffs. To Medousa, the whole sea behind her was dark.

The leviathan dove down, so deep its body disappeared.

I had a sneaking suspicion he wasn't gone. Not at all.

My feathers stood on end.

I chirped, wishing to warn Medousa. She looked around, but there was nothing to see.

Out of the blue, the leviathan lunged, up into the air, right in front of her skiff. His head towered so tall over Medousa, it almost came to my height in the sky. I swear I could feel his breath over my feathers and shuddered.

Medousa's frozen nature changed when real danger struck. She moved so quickly, as if to make up for all the time she spent curled up in fear. She jumped onto her feet. I heard her breath catch in her chest.

The Leviathan hissed at her. He bared rows of curved fangs and flicked a three-forked tongue.

I swooped down to intervene, but I wasn't as fast as Medousa.

I never expected that the girl would've had a knife, or that she could pull it out and wield it so quickly. I watched it glimmer in the sunlight, neither copper nor tin. I heard the scrape of bronze over scales, then a slick click when her blade slid between them, and a flush when she drew blood from monstrous flesh.

I saw Medousa tuck her bronze knife between the folds of her dark robes.

Her secret was safe with me.

Red liquid sloshed from the beast and into the skiff. The torrent was thick. His monstrous blood was heavier than impartial seawater.

Blood pooled in the bottom of the skiff, and pulled it downwards.

Medousa shrieked. But she didn't panic. She was calculated. She kicked the rail of the skiff. I heard the thud of her bare flesh against wood, and a plank shot upwards. I saw bronze nails, glittering, in the flotsam's black wood.

Good thing she thought quickly, because before she took another breath, Poseidon swallowed her boat.

I swear, when her ship sank, it sank in the direction of Algol.

Medousa took a deep breath. Her fingers clung to the plank and she pulled her body over the board. It was the last remnant of her vessel.

She was miniscule compared to the beast, and yet she had bested it. Medousa and her plank were hardly bigger than a few of the creature's scales.

The not-so-mighty leviathan wailed. There was no cliff or forest to echo his cries, but I heard his screams reverberate through my mind for moons to come. The creature thrashed his massive head and cried to the sea. Poseidon's waves curled.

Medousa beat this creature and bore no trophy, no glory from her battle.

It was a wrong I could right.

I hurried. I shot downwards. My wings folded against my body and I plummeted towards the sinking beast.

He may have been throwing its head in pain, but I was faster. I could adjust to his movements. I was the mighty osprey, who plucked the fastest fishes from the sea.

I flew towards the beast's eye. He couldn't see me approach. The monster's eyes were closed, quaking with pain.

I reached the creature and did not hesitate. I dug my talons around his scaly lid and took out his eye.

I had to flex my talons to their full width to carry the monster's eye. It glowed like yellow torchlight in my claws. I flapped, away from his wildly thrashing head.

The leviathan slinked back into the sea, bubbling with a sigh. I had no idea if he was slain or crawling into the depths to heal. Either way, he wouldn't bother Medousa anymore.

A whirlpool swirled in the leviathan's wake, but it did not draw Medousa's remaining plank off-course. She floated towards Algol.

I flew, holding the leviathan's monstrous, yellow eyeball. I clutched it with the strength of both of my feet. Medousa stared at me for a moment, registering that I carried something. It was for her, but without her skiff, I would have to carry it until we reached wherever laid ahead of us.

I felt no remorse for my theft, for blinding the beast on one side. I saw evil in the eye which I stole. The beast may have lived, with half his sight, or he may have bled out and died. I imagined his massive bones haunting the trenches of Greece forevermore.

Flying above took far more effort, for I carried the weight of a monster's eye.

My breath became rapid. My wings grew tired.

We traveled until the sun sank low and the sky turned gold. Whenever Medousa's waterlogged plank started to sink, I willed the wind to lift it from the water.

The wind heard my whispers, and bent to my will, as I flew between skies and stars. The wind heard my wish, and kept waves from breaking over her face.

Waves rocked Medousa and I heard her heart sync to the rhythm of the water. She clung to the driftwood like it was part of her. I floated above, drifting on mere air.

As soon as the sun dipped below the horizon, stars began to tell their stories. I saw the new scorpion, glittering like she was always there. I saw Algol from its lonely perch in the sky,

I saw Medousa watching Algol the same way I watched a fish I wished to catch. Her gaze was steady and hunger fumed in her green eyes.

The ocean was predictable, even when I flew to far reaches where I'd never flown before.

Waves followed the wind, and wind followed the spin of the earth.

When I followed Medousa, she led me towards a strange phenomenon.

I noticed waves curling, instead of rolling in long barrels, they curved. I looked over the blue sea and noticed a spiral, as if waves were drawn towards an eye, like a storm.

We left the watery, blue desert and approached a kharybdis.

I wondered what lay in the eye of the whirlpool and shivered. I remembered stories of women with my wings, beating fury into the sky. Legend had it that they were all gone, but their whirlpool was still spinning. I started to get nervous.

Fate brought me here, to lead Medousa to this spot in the ocean. She had, after all, gotten revenge for the sirens.

I noticed several small silver fish. They swam downstream of Algol towards Medousa on her plank. The fish were curious about her bare feet dangling over the edge and her robes billowing in the water. I watched them school around her.

The fish were a sign. Tiny bait fish didn't frequent open oceans. We were leaving the deep, though I didn't know exactly what we approached.

A mound sprouted from the horizon. I'd heard stories of Sarpedon as a whirlpool.

I hadn't ever considered that there would've been a physical island. Legends spoke of wind, water, and feathers lost from Orion's slaughter — no stones, no land.

Wind started to pull on my feathers and lift Medousa's hair. Her golden locks came to life, as if snakes sprouted from her head.

Wind blew us along, and shifted the water below. Medousa's plank drifted in a new direction. She floated away from her course towards Algol, into the whirlpool.

I chirped, marveling at the phenomena.

There could've only been one explanation. Each drop of water was a talisman. Each individual liquid bead held the intentions of Algol. A spell had been cast, when Algol was in a favorable light. Luck lingered in these waters.

As we got closer, I saw tentacles of stone stretching from the mound. Shallow water rustled as it moved over the labyrinth stretching out before us. The water and the stones spiraled around the mound in the distance. We moved around Algol, rather than towards it. Waves gurgled as depths shallowed.

The strange thing was, there were no stones in Medousa's path. On course towards Algol, from the land of Magnesia, we could not crash. Waves ushered us above underwater canyons and cliffs, as if our course was planned.

Tunnels peeked out of the sea. I noticed that each stone was crafted from dark, magnetite rocks. Those same stones formed the lands of Magnesia from whence we came. I heard crushing waves, and the whoosh of wind. Tempests sang over stones. Wind whistled in the distance, as if the island was calling us over the sea.

Medousa looked at the rocks. I watched her turn her head. She pointed her toes and tried to float, like a leaf, flat over the water.

So the plank moved in an arc, and the labyrinth sprang up around us. Rubble rose from the ocean in long ridges, all curving, all guiding waves and wind towards the center, the eye. I imagined, in these strange winds, sailors from any direction becoming entangled within the kharybdis. All the stones were dark as shadows.

These were not like brick stones which were crafted for a function. Every rock was seemingly misshapen, seemingly born from chaos, or even destruction. A few stones caught my sharp eye, for they bore such an uncanny resemblance to fish.

The stones were dead, but housed so much life. Birds scuttled and nested in nooks and crannies. Crabs, as blue as the deep, scuttled to and fro. I swear I saw the flash of a juicy octopus tentacle, coiling around a rock. I didn't stop to hunt. My stomach rumbled, but it was not the time to quench my hunger. It was time to see my mission through. I carried the heavy eye in my talons, and was slated to bring it to Medousa when she met the shore.

At first the rubble walls were short and barely rose from the ocean. Then, as we got closer, the walls grew taller. Eventually, I was sure Medousa could not see over the walls of rocks. She was encircled, ensnared, by stony cliffs.

Dolphins whistled, clicked, and exhaled plumes of air in distant tunnels. I heard their chatter and saw their misty breath. Medousa couldn't spot them over the rising rocks. Fear clouded her green eyes.

The mound on the horizon came closer. I realized that it was the eye of the kharybdis, staying still where everything around it was in constant motion. Water rushed quickly between the tunnels.

When we got closer, I recalled the myths I heard as a fledgling.

The women with wings of ospreys had a name. They'd been called sirens.

Rumor had it they were the children of Poseidon, born from the wild, free spirit of osprey feathers that fell into the sea, and the feminine nature of deep oceans. Oceans were impartial, but oceans couldn't suppress life. Poseidon fostered the strongest and the strangest. Sirens were born wild. These women were called to stir up the winds of the wildest seas. As legend had it, they wreaked havoc on sailors.

Until, of course, Orion extinguished them.

I had never known them to build land, to craft a whirlpool of stone. They were women of the wind who never rested to sleep and never stopped flying. They flew on clear blue days and in roaring gray storms.

They battered winds, shrieked, and howled, until Orion silenced them– every last one.

I inhaled quickly, my wings straining against the weight of the monster's eye. I could feel it losing firmness in the heat and melting into my talons. The rubbery membrane around the monster's scaly lid became supple. Stealing the eye was much more cunning than stealing its heart. I blinded the beast, the long snaky creature of the deep. The leviathan, the most perceptive and cunning creature, failed to perceive an osprey.

I imagined sailors, pulled along by tempests, winding into these stony tunnels. I imagined the slow ebb of their freedom, and losing their ability to turn around, the further they wove in between the channels the less likely it became that they would've ever escaped. I wondered what, exactly, laid at the eye of the storm inside the stony hive.

I watched Medousa float into the labyrinth. In a way, the fallen monster watched from the clutches of my talons too. It was forced to see Medousa's bravery, even after she drew its blood.

Stones arched over the sea. I saw Medousa's path from the bird's eye. She was bound to disappear into the caves. Her plank approached the lip of the tunnels, where stones were destined to obscure her from my sight in the sky. I had to leave the upper sky to follow her.

Medousa shimmied on the driftwood for a better look around her. Her face turned stony, like she wore a mask which was frozen with fear. She floated into darkness. I heard her heartbeat choke her throat.

I shook my wings out and took a deep breath.

My eyes saw a flash of gold at the mound's zenith. It was a forked trident, gold as the sun and the hair of Medousa. Three prongs pointed straight up towards the star of Algol. I shivered.

Medousa's driftwood carried her into the tunnel. I dove down, in the same way I dove towards the leviathan, into the mouth of the tunnel. Wind rushed, pushing me in its angled arc.

In the tunnel it became clear that the entire structure wasn't made from stones, wood was stuck between rocks in a funny fashion. Long planks stretched between rocks. In the tunnels wood became trapped, frozen, in holds of stone. I saw the light, sunbleached planks of cedar sticking through dark, magnetite rock. There were slits, where we could peek into other tunnels in the labyrinth, where it seems wood had rotted away.

I thought, for a brief moment, of the sailors whose ships were eaten by these tunnels.

This strange island was rich with soft, rotting wood, but the island was barren. There was no sign of living plants. There were no green leaves or brown roots as far as I could see.

It was dark, but I could still see Medousa's golden hair, which reflected all available light.

It was much harder to fly in the tunnel. Floating in the open, building off of the energy of the sky, was easier. There I could stretch my wings and glide, whereas in the tunnel I was flapping, rapidly panting, all while carrying the heavy monster's eye. In a small tunnel I had to work harder, and my wings grew tired. I lost my breath rapidly.

I couldn't go as slow as Medousa. I couldn't float above her like I did in the open sea. In the tunnel, I had to rush ahead.

I opened my heart and stretched my wings as far as I could with each flap. My feathers skimmed over irregular stones. When all the light disappeared, I heard the whisper of wind telling me how to turn. I knew, relatively, where to go, because I saw from the sky how the tunnel was bound to curve.

I flew into the unknown, but I did not fly in fear. I flew with my heart wide open.

Eventually, a chamber materialized before me. There were cracks between stones in the ceilings, which let starlight shine through.

I sighed and drifted downwards. I set the yellow monster's eye in the ocean, and balanced it between my legs. I imagined it like an egg, but rather than heating it with my body, I was letting it cool down in the water.

I watched wisps of blood pour from the monster's eye and saturate the water. A small, suppressible horror rolled through me. I imagined my own yellow eyes. Surely there were fish in the sea who would've taken me as a monster. If they had their way, they may have wished for my own eye to roll bloody underwater.

I watched the eye in wait, waiting for Medousa to catch up.

In my patience, in that small moment to myself and the quiet rustle of waves, I realized what made Medousa and myself different from the monster.

Where our pupils were round, and I could see circularly, the monster's eye was a slit. It looked like a cat or a snake– creatures born with cold blood and narrow eyes. Yet one of his eyes was Medousa's prize. She outsmarted the beast of the deep.

I stood in the chamber and listened for Medousa's breath. It traveled down the tunnel to my finely tuned ears.

Eventually I saw her approach and heard the crunch of her wooden plank against stones.

Medousa stumbled over wet wood and slippery rocks.

Her tired feet didn't touch pure stone, like walking on pebbles, or standing on a solid rock. She stood with a tilt, on uneven ground. Everything was chaotic at this howling island in the sea. I'd found a nook where I could balance myself and the eye.

Once she found her footing, she glanced at me and I chirped.

She looked closer and saw the yellow glow I was protecting like an egg.

I gave her a sideways eye and beckoned her to take it, and she recognized it as hers.

Medousa reached down and grabbed the monster's yellow eye. I recognized something familiar about the way she held the circular object. She held it between her hands like a pharmakis may have held a burning glass. I'd lived in Hekate's forest for many moons, and seen all her tricks.

When I saw the girl holding the eye, my ancestors whispered to me. I heard them through the blood in my veins. This was not an island of sirens– I entered the realm of monsters. *Gorgones.* I shivered and my feathers begged to shoot up, but I pushed them down.

I flew to Medousa's shoulder. I rested on her collarbone and tried not to pierce through her robes, and her skin, with my talons. We both stood in wet, cold darkness. We listened to drops of water over rocks, waiting for something to happen, until it did.

The roar of a lion sliced the air. It rumbled through our bones and under our skin. Medousa whimpered and surely held back a scream.

A freakish animal, with many faces, lunged towards us. I heard the hiss of a snake and the bleat of a goat. I heard the scrape of claws over rock and felt a warm breath over my feathers. Goosebumps erupted on mine and Medousa's flesh. The creature was upon us before I could see each of its faces or understand its monstrous form. We felt the brush of its whiskers and Medousa shuddered beneath my grip.

She moved through her fear. Her shoulder steadied and she cleared her throat. It echoed through the cave walls, spliced by the sound of waves crashing at the cave's mouth.

"Greetings sisters. It's me, Medousa. I am a girl raised by Hekate."

At the mention of Hekate, the creature fell back onto its haunches. I realized why, even in the wildest ocean, I smelled the lingering smoke of sage in the air. It came from Medousa's skin, for she had been touched by Hekate. Surely that was why we were safe, uneaten by the lion. Surely it too could smell the sage on her skin, and was loyal to the pharmakis. I thought to myself in amusement, that only the Pharmakis of the Dark Side of the Moon could've created a creature such as this.

"Khimaira, be gone now. You'll meet our guest in the morning," a voice echoed from inside the dark cavern.

The strange lion let out a long sigh and walked back towards the sea-filled tunnel. We heard plodding paws over stones and the distant, relinquished sigh of a tame beast. She jumped into the ocean, and seemingly disappeared. I looked for her, with my piercing yellow eyes, but there was neither a swish of waves nor one head coming up for breath.

Then I heard two sharp inhales and two women came into my view. Both of them had circular faces. I couldn't see them clearly in the strange light of the cavern, but I could see massive, silver wings folded behind their backs. I stared at them and wondered if they really were who I thought they were, if any sirens had indeed survived Orion.

Though their bodies were hidden, I should have seen twinkles in their eyes. No light shined from their eyes, none at all.

"Greetings Medousa," a voice said with a peculiar metallic lisp. It was a fiercely feminine voice, the soft voice of a woman who, I sensed, could roar like the lion who pierced the air.

"We welcome all friends of Hekate," said another voice, with a whistle under her tongue. Of course, they too could smell the scent of the pharmakis' herb on Medousa's skin.

Medousa bit her lip in anticipation. Though they stood in the back of the cavern, I could tell that both of the winged women were much taller than Medousa. Her crown reached their clavicles.

"Trust us," the first voice said. There was a metallic whistle to their words.

"I do trust you," Medousa said, her hand still clasping the monster's eye.

I heard the faint rustle of cloth, the whisper of snake scales rustling together, and the tide kissing the cave mouth. Cool air of the cave tingled both me and Medousa.

The women stepped closer, into a cascade of starlight, and I was able to see the details of their forms. Their skin was silver and see-through, like the ghostly horses who haunted Magnesia. They wore no clothes, but their bodies were misty, and obscured by the veil between water and air.

Their noses were flat and their jaws bulged, as if they had been deformed.

Black blindfolds covered both of their eyes.

Medousa's eyelids fluttered. She looked at the two strange women. Their lips were glowing, solid bronze unlike the rest of their silver bodies. Their hands were crafted from bronze too, as if to mimic scales rushing from their fingertips towards their elbows. Both women had slender bronze slippers on their feet, allowing shades to stand on the stones.

One woman stood with her hands on her hips. The other stood with her round head cocked to the side. It was easy to look at Medousa, but harder to look at these undead who she called her sisters.

When Medousa saw their hair, she gasped. I followed Medousa's gaze and realized it wasn't hair at all. Each woman had a living nest of snakes resting upon their heads. The snake's bronze scales had red luster. They were made of metal, too. Serpentine bodies blended into misty skulls. Though the snakes were crafted from metal, and seemingly neither alive nor dead, I grew hungry. My stomach growled, as quiet as the hum of water on the shore. Nobody heard it rumble. I wished to rip into them, strip pale meat from beneath their scales. I resisted. I came here to be a hero, not to find my own snack. To contrast their bronze scales, each snake had foggy eyes, like they hadn't shed their skin for a long time, like they'd be easy to hunt.

"Your hair…" Medousa's voice trailed off into a wilderness where no words could've captured her surprise.

"Do you like it?" one woman asked, flaunting and turning her head so Medousa could see them all, writhing and staring at Medousa. Her words carried a metallic twang.

"I-I…" Medousa stammered.

"Don't worry. They don't bite," the other woman promised with a subtle crinkle in her face that looked like a wink beneath her blindfold.

Medousa watched the snakes yawning with nature's widest mouths. Their jaws unhinged to reveal delicate, curved teeth. Sunlight sparkled on their reddish, copper teeth. I wished to fly away with one, for my hunger, on the way home. Another rumble came from my stomach, masked by the gently rocking sea.

Those snakes wouldn't make a good meal anyway. They were crafted of moonlight, mist, and metal alloys.

"You must be thirsty. You've had a long journey across the sea."

"Yes," Medousa said, in a whisper like a desperate, crashing wave.

"Here," a bronze hand stretched towards Medousa and pushed a shell into her hands, lacking all finesse as her eyes were covered.

Medousa held the spiraling shell in her hands and lifted its cusp her lips. Medousa was so salty, so hot and thirsty, she didn't question the contents of the shell. She chugged the contents and sighed. Medousa swallowed the water.

In a few gulps the shell was empty. I wondered what it would have been like to be human, to be much more vulnerable than a bird of the sea.

The bronze hand reached back and scooped the shell from her.

"Let's introduce ourselves. I'm Sthenno," one of the silver women said, stretching out her hand. Medousa looked at the disfigured face of her sister. When she grasped her hand, Medousa shuddered.

The misty, metal woman recoiled, but I couldn't hear a rustle of feathers. She was eerily silent, like the horses in Magnesia with no hearts beating in their silver bodies.

"Icy?" Sthenno asked. Medousa lowered her gaze in response, of course unseen by Sthenno.

"I'm Euryale," the other woman said. Medousa shook her frozen hand too, this time braced for her chilled touch.

Reaching forward for pleasantries caught Medousa off-balance and she slipped over the uneven ground. I flew up, off of her shoulder, trying not to drag her down. She caught herself from falling onto the stones.

Medousa steadied herself and looked at the ground, which happened to be a particularly ornate stone. It looked like two human faces. Their eyes were wide with surprise, their mouths gasping. I looked around at the cave and saw that every inch of it was completely carved. Each surface showcased some depiction of a creature. There were animals too, seagulls with frozen feathers and fish stuck between them like tiles.

Euryale grabbed Medousa's body and pulled her back to her feet.

"Are you alright?"

"Cut yourself?"

"No, I'm okay. What's the story behind these carvings?" Medousa asked.

I realized she was naive, a doe in a lioness den.

My stomach turned. I felt in the trenches of my soul that there was a dark secret behind the carvings. I suddenly wished to be back in Magnesia. I tried to screech, but my voice twisted in knots.

"This little girl is so sweet!" Sthenno cooed, pursing her bronze lips.

"Carvings? Oh dear," Euryale said with a bittersweet laugh.

"Hekate didn't tell you too much about us, did she?" Sthenno asked.

A shiny forked tongue flicked from Sthenno's lips.

I flapped my wings and flew back to Medousa's shoulder.

"Hekate only told me that you're my sisters. She brought you back after Orion drowned you," Medousa answered. Her eyes were wide, and nobody else could've seen them, not the winged women, not the faces frozen in stone, not even the khimaira who was nowhere to be seen. Only I saw the fear in her eyes, and also recognized, she had nowhere else to turn. Medousa crossed a sea to come here, and her ship sank on the way.

"Of course," Euryale said, and it looked as if she were rolling her eyes beneath the blindfold.

"These carvings could communicate better than that pharmakis," Sthenno said, drawing out the word *carvings* with a sarcastic tone.

Sthenno snorted at Euryale's remark, "Yes, Hekate lives under an aura of mystery."

"Hekate can be read easily as the faintest star on a full moon," Euryale said.

"Oh Pharmakis of the Dark Side of the Moon, let not a spec of her inner workings touch the light of day," Sthenno said and threw her head back, with her palm to the air, to mimic fainting.

"Everything's a secret to our mother," Euryale exhaled sharply.

"Hekate had to...leave. And she-" Medousa stammered.

"Leave? What do you mean?" Sthenno asked, her voice growing harsh.

"She's gone into the Underworld," Medousa said.

Both gorgones became serious, stone-cold even. I pressed my feathers against my skin, holding in my own warmth.

"When?" Sthenno demanded.

"Today. She told me-"

"Why?" Sthenno pressed.

"Kerberos is dead," Medousa said.

The gorgones sisters turned their heads towards each other, as if guided by habit. They could not see through their blindfolds, but the news drew them to search for connection. Euryale grabbed Sthenno's hand and I heard a bronze click.

"Well if they're not carvings, what are they?" Medousa asked again, pointing her foot towards faces in the stones. Her toes lingered over a realistic eye, popping from the head of a screaming man.

The cavern fell silent for a moment. Both women stopped their antics, as if they had forgotten what had gotten them started in the first place. I turned to face them with my yellow eyes.

"There's a reason we have to cover our eyes around you," Euryale explained, "Our snakes may seem menacing, but our eyes are truly deadly."

"All living things we look at turn to stone," Sthenno cut straight to the point.

My feathers prickled in fear. Medousa looked around the cave as I did. Birds, fish, and men stared back at us, unseeing and dead. I wondered what could have ushered them out here to Sarpedon to meet their fate as lifeless stones. I suspected that some of the men were explorers and sought a dangerous fate. Others, surely, had gotten lost in a storm.

"Some of these stones are humans!" Medousa said, "You've killed men!"

"Yes," Euryale said, "We make traveling treacherous for men who try to pass near our kharybdis."

"Does that make you monsters?" Medousa asked.

Both gorgones laughed and their snakes hissed.

"These sailors," Sthenno said, "were monsters in their own right."

"What about the khimaira? Why hasn't it been turned to stone?" Medousa asked.

"You'll see in the morning," Euryale explained.

"How come you haven't frozen each other?" Medousa asked.

"I'd turn her to stone if I could," Euryale said with a playful punch aimed at Sthenno's shoulder. Her bronze hand could touch Sthenno's misty form.

"Please, you'd be totally lost without me," Sthenno spat from her metal mouth and turned to Medousa, "We're both gorgones by blood, so we can't be frozen."

"Yes, not anymore than we already are," Euryale added.

"Now that you're here, and you're our sister, I suppose you're a gorgones too," Sthenno added.

"Not from the stars or Hekate's hands," Euryale said with a sly laugh, "she's a gorgones by chance."

"I sense that you brought something from the sea..." Sthenno said, "You carry something you collected from a challenge along the way."

I screeched and my voice echoed into a dark cave.

Medousa looked between me and the gorgones. The yellow eye started to melt and warp in her hand. I held my breath.

"How do you know?" Medousa asked.

"I cannot see, but the stones can. I sometimes hear thoughts of the souls trapped inside," Sthenno folded her hands in front of her, as if she were regal.

"This eye came from a monster," Medousa explained, "There was a creature, with a head like a giant lizard, and a yellow eye. We were crossing here to Sarpedon when we met it. I..." Medousa's voice trailed off.

She felt for a lump under her robes. The winged women couldn't see her, but I could.

Medousa felt for the knife which caught the beast between its scales. I could hear the bronze shiver against its sheath. I screeched again, to cover up the metallic sound. If Medousa wanted to keep a secret, I was determined to help her.

My feathers stood on end again. How modest, how innocent for her to leave this out, to let her voice trail off, like she had never slayed a beast in the deep seas of Greece.

"Then this screeching bird captured its eye for you?" Euryale asked.

"Yes," Medousa said.

I chirped again. Medousa handed the yellow monster eye to Euryale, who gasped at its touch. I watched Medousa and the blind gorgones. The eye of the beast passed between the trio.

I heard whispers. They came from the drips of water over the dark rocks, speaking a familiar language of birds, water, and starlight. My blood ran cold. Voices urged me to leave. I couldn't protect Medousa any longer.

She would have to be her own protector. I didn't understand how she would fit in on this strange island, but I sensed she would.

I knew the eye of a beast was all Medousa needed for protection. It may have changed hands among the gorgones, but it was hers. My gut swirled with this truth, and I knew I had to let her go.

I opened my wings, grabbed the air with my brown feathers, and lifted off. In the air I took one last look at Medousa, and her rippling hair.

I flew away, down the dark tunnels and back into the open ocean. I flew high into the clouds, where I could see nothing, neither dead or living.

I ushered Medousa across the sea, and she needed me no more. I left her, in this wild spec on the sea, with multi-headed beasts, and the ghosts of sirens who passed.

15. Seagull

The mainland of Greece disappeared behind me. I left in the morning, while the sun was still hiding underneath the horizon.

I flew between stars in the sky, and stars reflecting over the sea. The moon receded like the tide at dawn, going on her own path, impartial to my journey. The moon disappeared and the sun lit up the Aegean Sea.

Water sprayed my wings. I flew on, into the howling winds, ever curious of what may have been over the next wave.

The day passed, and I was still flying. The stars started to shine once more, and I was still in the middle of the sea. It was then, the moment when I should have turned back, when I wondered why the waves below me curved. Water moved against the hand of Poseidon, moving like the crevices in a nautilus shell.

Other gulls warned me to never fly there, but they could never give me a reason. I asked *why, why, why?*

No gulls knew *why*. They said, *don't go there.* I had too many questions and never got any answers, so I flew into the sea, seeking gnosis.

I felt strong enough to cross the ocean. I was young and wanted to see what my fellows feared.

I was a fool, but I didn't know that yet.

I flew close to the water. Wind pushed me as it pushed the waves. I followed the water in the same way a moth was drawn to a spiderweb, glistening and dewy in moonlight. Tidepools flashed underneath me, and pulled the waves further off course.

I peeked over a wave and glimpsed an island, seemingly rising out of the depths of a barren sea. It reached towards the sky and the stars.

Three golden fingers stretched from its highest point. Around it the tidepools formed tunnels and underwater cliffs. I was pulled along the tempest's labyrinth, closer to the eye of the kharybdis.

Wind ushered me towards the island and suddenly I looked above me. I saw an osprey battling the wind, fighting to return to the mainland. His strong wings pulled against the air. I imagined my flight home, against the tempests, and swallowed. I called out to him and he chirped back.

He did not tell me what he saw, or what I was flying towards.

"You've had a long journey, Medousa. We'll let you sleep," a woman's voice carried over the water.

"First we want to protect you," another woman spoke slowly.

"How?" a girl asked.

"We need to cast a talisman by imprinting your face onto the sea."

"Can it wait until morning?" the girl asked with sincere exhaustion.

"We must act now, in case Algol winks again. It has been strange, and flickering lately."

Their words floated over the waves and I had a bad feeling about the island. It was too early to turn back. I wanted a story to boast about to my roost. I wanted to return as the bravest among them.

Waves crashed. My wings flapped.

As I flew closer to the rocky island, I saw locks of golden hair and their owner standing with her eyes on the sea. She knelt towards the ocean, as if in prayer to Poseidon.

Two women stood behind her.

On second look, I wondered if they were really women. I squinted. Their faces were as round as the stars themselves. They were made of mist. They wore no clothes, but the details of their bodies faded into wafts. Their skin had a shimmer and I could see through them. Strangely enough, these women had wings, which folded down their backs.

Their hair... was moving. When my eyes finally focused, I noticed their hair wasn't made of hair at all. Snakes writhed on their crowns.

Blindfolds, with a strange reddish-brown shimmer, covered the misty women's eyes. But I saw the eyes of the young girl. They were sea-green with tired, purple circles resting beneath them.

A broken plank rested on the shore, beside the girl and the misty women. Splash marks stained the waterlogged wood. I saw, in the secret language between watermarks and birds, that water always warped around this island. I saw it too, beneath me, the waves still curving.

I landed near the shore. I stood over a shallow pool of uneven rocks. It was a long flight from the mainland. My heart fluttered. I finally had a chance to breathe and steady myself.

One of the misty women held a giant yellow eye. She held the eye upwards, as if it were a torch in the dark. The eye, detached from its beast, gazed at the endless sky. Both of the misty women looked up– into the night.

I blinked.

I wondered what the mysterious women could see, and what they couldn't. Blindfolds covered their eyes, but they saw beyond them.

Their occulted gazes followed a pattern. They looked at constellations and weaved them together, calling their power down to Greece, through the eye.

Their living, snaky hair paid no attention to the stars. They yawned and hissed and writhed around each other.

I watched them weave the eyeball between fixed positions of stars I knew, and continuously return to the star of Algol.

The women shifted their faces together, rapidly moving, following the hand which held the eye.

Then, both of the women were still. The girl knelt before them.

A pause hung in the salty air.

"Medousa, sit still. This may hurt."

Both of the women shoved Medousa forwards. Their bronze hands clicked from the force.

She fell, face-first, into the ocean. I stood on the discordant rocks, with a sense of unease bubbling in my stomach.

I was starting to understand why my fellow gulls avoided this place.

The girl's face dipped into the water, and when it did I heard a sizzle. I watched steam rise from the splash. Bubbles boiled up around her blonde curling hair.

She stayed like that for a moment, searing her face into the waves.

When her lips left the water she howled in pain. I heard her scream. It rattled my sea-sick bones. Her eyes were clamped shut, crinkled with shock.

I thought about turning around. I thought about flying back home to my roost and never looking back.

I froze in fear– something I'd always regret. My wings stuck to my body. For several moments my heart ceased to beat.

Wind came in from the sea, tossing me with it. I stumbled, landing on a rock in the shallow tidepool. I preened my feathers for a moment and looked back at the girl.

I let out a squawk.

It was a fleeting call into the unknown, wondering, begging how the moment was about to unravel.

That small noise was my downfall.

One of the misty figures slipped her blindfold beneath her eye to see, looking for the noisemaker.

I saw, from the shallow tidepool, the white light of death. She saw me with one frozen eye, so cold, it petrified my body and soul.

She was the last thing I'd see with my living eyes.

My body fell into the sea like a stone.

16. Mallard

As soon as the seagull appeared, I knew he was bound to fall.

I'd seen the same dance a hundred times. He splashed into the spiraling matrix of tidepools around Sarpedon as a rock among the rest of us.

He landed next to me.

I'd already been trapped there for eternities. Poseidon's hand slowly chipped away at my bill and plumes. The seagull would spend forever as a stone, right beside me. He fell where he once stood, where I once felt a pulse coursing through the webs of his feet.

My frozen fate mismatched my fiery soul. How I wished to tear the gull apart with my bill! I wished to puff out my chest and chase him away from my territory.

There was nothing I could do. Nothing belongs to those who cannot fight for it. Nothing belongs to souls trapped in stone.

In my living days, if a gull came too close to my space, I could've attacked him.

As a frozen rock, my anger simmered, but never boiled.

I wished to have my own territory, but stone never gets its wishes granted. I watched the gull through the water, forevermore, waiting for our eyes to turn to dust.

I saw the weary, anxious look in his eyes when he arrived. I could almost see the string of fate tying him to this rock. He was no different from the rest of us. For if the sea whispered to the wind to bring him here, he would be delivered.

I couldn't see the seagull by looking at him as he flew by. I couldn't turn to face anything, not dolphins in the tunnels nor birds on their way to die. My gaze was fixed, until Poseidon took my sight too. I expected that one day the perpetual, sweeping tides would erode my eyes, and I'd finally be free from witnessing the world as a stone. I saw the gull only because he flew over and landed on me. He stood right over where my heart used to beat.

I remembered the moment my fate was sealed, just like the gull's. If my heart could still beat, if it was more pliable than stone, then it would've broken at the painful reminder of my own folly. There was a reflection of myself in the gull.

I'd been petrified by Sthenno's eyes. My birdy bones morphed into brick, but that was many moons ago.

I watched life all around me, but my heart never beat again.

I watched the gorgones and all the creatures who passed by Sarpedon. I even watched that osprey, and I envied him when he flew out of the kharybdis.

When I stumbled up onto Sarpedon, before I looked a gorgones dead in the eye, I had a crown of glossy green feathers. Of course, they were stiffened and dulled. I'd been touched by the heavy hand of magic.

After the gull's splash calmed, I saw Sthenno's forked tongue flicker from her mouth, fast as lightning. Of course, I saw through the veil of water. I saw only as slowly and with as much distortion as Poseidon willed me to see.

Poseidon, the ocean, shielded these monsters from the mainland of Greece. The salty expanse isolated the gorgones, allowing them to become more and more monstrous.

Poseidon protected, but he also harmed. He lured me from my home, as a sacrifice, to spend eternity as a stone in the sea.

I heard, through the muffle of water, the never-ending lullaby of Poseidon to his fishes. There was a deafening silence in the shallows. There was always a soft crash rippling through channels, cresting atop me, originating from somewhere faraway. The ocean was so loud, so talkative, so fluid and conversational, so connected to each part that I dissolved into it. Sometimes I forgot I was a mallard at all. That was, until a brazen gull splashed before me.

I saw Medousa stagger and fall back from the rocky shoreline.

Sthenno reached underwater. I saw her metallic, scaly hand splash into the tidepool. It was the very hand of the gorgones which served me to my death.

I could not bite her, or chase her, or even quack. The underwater world held me in its spell. Sthenno reached for something below me, something which I couldn't see. She lifted a mask from the tidepool.

It was cast from bronze and the salt of Poseidon. I could see it, I could see it with my stony eyes. It looked like Medousa.

Wings sprang from the mask's temples. Her hair, in the mask, was made of vile snakes, like a gorgones. I saw white marble eyes on the mask. They were so white against the reddish bronze. I saw cold, misty vapor, in their piercing whiteness. The mask's eyes were like stars on the darkest night, like the last sight of my living days.

"No, Medousa, don't look."

"This could be dangerous."

The gorgones warned Medousa. Then both of the misty women huddled together. Snakes from each of their heads coiled around each other. Their bronze scales clicked against each other. Their voices dropped to hushed whispers, as mysterious as eyes behind blindfolds.

Their whispers mixed with the waves, until I saw another hand reach into the water. Bronze fingers grabbed a tiny silver fish and ripped him out of the sea, stealing him from Poseidon.

More whispers from the gorgones floated into the water, until they were punctuated by a soft splash. I saw the silver fish, but he was no longer silver. A moment ago he was swimming through crevasses, but he had been turned to stone. He would swim no more. The fish sank to the bottom of the channel next to me. He'd spend eternity as stone there. I was sure that he would always remember the light of the mask which stared him dead.

I stared at the two new stone arrivals, and the stars shining above us.

"You may not be a gorgones..." the woman spoke to Medousa again.

"You'll have the powers of one."

Medousa started to question them, but they quickly ushered her into the dark cave. They could see, as I could see through the water, the tiredness lurking under Medousa's eyes. I heard Medousa yawn. The gorgones left her to sleep on the cold, hard stones. She slept for days on the brink of the cave, while stars twinkled and suns passed. I observed with envy.

I wasn't asleep, but I could never wake up.

I stared at the sleeping waif and wished to escape those shallow pools.

17. Falcon

The spiraling tidepool drew me in, but I stayed high above. I never dared dive down to snatch prey, though game was plentiful. I never dreamed of calling out, soaring down to the birds wading in the shallows, or scooping up a fat mackerel in my talons. No matter how delightfully delicious fowl and fish seemed, I never tried to go for them.

I came to witness the kharybdis.

This chaotic space was a monster in the tides, and a talisman to monsters in the sky. Algol was watching, far higher than I could fly. The kharybdis and Algol were mirrors of each other, whirlpools with the virtues of Poseidon.

Waves moved in a circle. Stones stuck out from the sea, and winds curled around the eye. I saw planks of rotten wood, where shipwrecks met stones.

I imagined sailors, carried by those fallen ships, becoming petrified. I imagined their bodies sinking into blue, while their vessels floated above. Nothing grew here, but mystery and disaster. There was rotten wood, stuck in the tidepools, but no living plants and no digging roots.

Sarpedon was barren, but it was hard to make out all the details. The island was far below me. I flew so close to the clouds that I could hear the sweet coos of Hera's white peahens. For I knew, to soar down to Sarpedon would mean to risk my feathers turning to stone.

I heard legends of gorgones with snakes for hair and eyes that brought the kiss of death. I knew, even entertaining the idea of letting the wind bring me here, was a dance with danger. Visiting Sarpedon was fun, so long as I kept my distance. I flew so high nobody could see my eyes. It was like hiding behind a veil, like being an observing cloud, drifting over the sea. I longed for these dangerous solo flights, because bravery and fear were like plumes on the same vane.

I didn't look too closely at the stones. I hated to see their frozen, dead eyes staring up at me.

A movement caught my eye far below. It wasn't like the splash of a gray dolphin or the ripple of fish.

I saw the distinct reddish glow of bronze. I narrowed my sharp eyes.

A mermaid hovered over the deep. She was as silver and misty as the living dead. Her hands caught my eye, for they were cast from bronze. I thought she was so strange, and so peculiar, I tried to get a better look. But she was gone. As soon as I spotted her, she darted below the waves, away from the enlightening sun and my peering eye.

I looked ahead towards the island, where the golden trident sprouted from a rocky hive. Tentacles of tunnels branched from the mighty fork. The fork pointed directly at Algol, glittering beyond the light of day.

"Shh! Medousa is still sleeping. You're going to wake her up," a woman's voice said. I had ears so finely tuned that I could've heard a mouse stepping in a puddle.

Her name was Sthenno and she came here by the light of Algol and the hand of Hekate. The gorgones' voices carried into the sky. I heard an echo, and a sleepy girl's yawn.

I dipped down to peek into the cave. It was risky, but I felt lucky. There were plenty of cracks and holes in the stony structure that I could see through. I spotted strands of curling, reddish-gold hair.

Oh Medousa, I was enchanted by her very breath. I heard her stirring from her sleep. As a bird of the stars, I already knew she was a living legend. Hera whispered her name to me when the moon was full. Medousa's breath, the way it synced up perfectly with lulling waves, made me wonder if she could have melted into the ocean. She breathed in time with the sea. I could hardly even hear inhales and exhales, hardly even distinguish her existence from the ocean.

She opened her eyes. I could see, all the way from the shadows of the clouds, their green shimmer. I'd seen that same green before, in the leaves of the oldest oaks, aged and properly attuned to seasons changing and stars aligning. The girl was a fledgling with the spark of an old soul burning inside her pupils.

Then I saw fear cross over her face. Her eyes narrowed. Her mouth opened and she started to breathe a little faster. It was like she remembered where she was, and how the walls were made of souls. She looked at the petrified people. She startled, sitting upright, glancing at their still, unseeing eyes.

Sarpedon unsettled her. I watched her stare at the sea. She'd never felt the ominous matrix of ocean surrounding this cursed place, feeling waves coming from every direction like they were crawling under your skin. I shuddered, even in the clouds.

It was such an unusual place.

Medousa was such an unusual girl. As she sat up, I saw a gash over her throat. It was a scar.

I spread my wings and flew a few strokes higher, losing sight of the scene, higher. I was ever-curious, but eager to avoid trouble.

"Look! You woke her!" said one of the gorgones. It was Euryale, the counterpart to Sthenno.

I assumed Medousa saw the women, but I stopped watching. I knew better than to look at the gorgones. I heard the whir of metallic snake scales rub together and averted my eyes. My gaze rested on the horizon, blue in every direction. I flew a bit higher.

"Good morning," I heard both gorgones chime in unison.

I heard Medousa take a sharp inhale.

"You have slept for days, Medousa!" Sthenno said.

"Are you hungry?" Euryale asked.

"Of course she's hungry!" Sthenno quipped, "Come Medousa, let us show you how we collect our breakfast. Follow us."

I heard their footsteps through the cave, then I heard the barefoot steps of Medousa. The gorgones walked on bronze-embossed slippers, which clicked against stones with each step.

I circled, just enough to see them from above, for my heart to race with the thrill of the stalk.

Medousa appeared at the edge of the tunnel. I watched the girl. I circled above her like the kharybdis around her. I felt no fear looking at her, at her curled hair which was wild and blowing in the wind, tossed by salt.

She may as well have had snakes for hair, too.

It was safe to keep looking. If Medousa was with the gorgones, their eyes would've been covered. She was human, and the winged sisters would protect her.

"What about that thing?" Medousa asked, squinting at the rising sun, "Was it a lion?"

"Shhh... You will see," Sthenno said and I caught sight of her.

A blindfold, with a dark red shimmer, was fashioned over her face. She had no real form, mist obscured her body and feathers trailed down her back.

My heart raced. I knew that a slip of a blindfold could seal my fate. Snakes wriggled around the dark cloth, but it stayed in place. Perhaps if I was spotted, the thin veil of clouds in the sky would've protected me. I imagined with a shiver of my feathers, fortune misfavoring me. What if the gorgones decided to look up, searching for omens in the flights of birds?

Danger thrilled me. I couldn't look away.

The closest tidepool to Medousa and the gorgones, started to bubble. It seemed shallow to me, far too shallow for what happened next.

A massive beast burst forth from the water. It was the khimaira, a creature of magic.

I'd seen this creature before, and it was one reason I kept coming back to Sarpedon. Many of my fellow falcons feared the kharybdis, but I felt pleasure in seeing such a beast, yet remaining hidden. I may as well be invincible in this world if I could pass by the mighty khimaira's notice.

She was a female, fit to protect and guard a family of women, but had the long, snaky locks of a male lion. Her bushy mane tangled down towards her withers, where sunkissed locks turnt into a deep, burnt, ember brown. Out from her back popped a curious goat head, with swirling nostrils, pointed ears, and a long neck. I watched from the sky, as the goat's head unfolded from the lion's back, and her tail swished with a literal mind of her own.

She emerged from the sea without a drop of water on her fur, locks, or scales.

"How did it hide in shallow water?" Medousa asked, gaping towards the mouth of the cave. She stepped back from the animal, wrapping her arms around herself.

"Our khimaira is a magical creature, we cannot always understand how she does things, or even why," Sthenno explained, "She's always here, in every drop of water. She's a talisman, like the sea around Sarpedon. All three heads protect us from unwanted visitors."

"That's why she roared at your arrival," Euryale added.

"How come you haven't turned her to stone?"

"See for yourself."

I came here to feel alive and feel breathless and dangerous in the sky. I never before got close enough to catch the eye of the khimaira, or ask the gorgones their secrets. They'd never had a guest, questions to answer, or a reason to cover their eyes before.

I squinted and looked at the khimaira. Where there should have been the piercing yellow eyes of a lion, were deep ruby slits. I looked quickly at the other faces. The khimaira didn't have a single eye where she should have had six. My beak almost fell open in surprise, but I steadied myself in the empty wind.

Medousa dropped her hands by her waist, took a deep breath, and stepped towards the khimaira.

First she examined the lion's face. The creature's breath was so strong that her exhale sent Medousa's hair flying upwards. The khimaira cocked her head to listen closely to Medousa's breath— just like me. Medousa looked up at the goat, which did not look down at her. Then Medousa gazed at goat udders hanging between four clawed lion feet. I saw Medousa, for good measure, turn to look at the khimaira's serpentine tail, swishing rapidly back and forth.

She looked at each of the khimaira's three faces, a trinity in one animal. It crossed the boundaries between a hellish lion, a lively goat, and a cunning snake. The lion had a soul meant for the clouds, the goat remained grounded in earth, and the serpent could make her way in the Underworld.

"All her eyes are missing," Medousa said

It made sense, how this one living creature could've lived on Sarpedon without being killed by a glance from the very entities she was destined to protect. Lion eyes, goat eyes, and snake eyes were all fixed in a permanent, bloody blink.

Another mystery of the kharybdis had been revealed to me. I understood the sacrifice of the gorgones' khimaira. The three-headed beast gave up her sight to fulfill her task. I was closer to understanding the world underneath me. I sought to see it all, so I may offer a better rendition to whisper to the stars.

"Now we milk her," Sthenno explained. She knelt before the beast.

When Sthenno was so close to the khimaira, the snakes on her crown eyed the snake on the khimaira's tail. Sthenno's coven of snakes stared at the khimaira's lonely tail. I heard hissing like the frothing of waves or the ebbing of tides.

Sthenno lifted a shell from the flat waters of the tidepool and brought it beneath the khimaira. Even from the sky, I could tell it wasn't an ordinary shell. The inside was polished to a blinding alabaster white, and the outside bore bright orange spurs, sharp enough to have been a weapon in its own right.

"This is the spondylus shell. The khimaira will only produce milk into this shell, which represents her true nature. Pure, white on the inside, but seemingly ferocious on the outside," the gorgones said, smiling at Medousa. She turned the shell, so Medousa's green eyes could take in the whole thing, from the spiraling, pearly interior to the orange spines.

From the sky I could see Sthenno's eyes crinkling underneath her blindfold. Euryale stood behind them in wait, hands on her hips, overseeing the passing of knowledge. Her snakes seemed chilled. They coiled into a braid, and remained still, as if trying to absorb the each other's warmth.

"We do not milk the khimaira with our hands," Sthenno said, "We are far too cold. Our hands would chill the milk, stop it from flowing. This creature was made by Hekate, so she's been bewitched by the stars. Milk is magnetized to starlight and wishes. Look into the shell and visualize a star, a lone star in a night dark as black."

Sthenno delicately tugged at her blindfold until it fell around her neck. I held my breath, tantalized by the threat of death.

She looked down, at the glimmering shell. I was tempted to avert my gaze, but I watched for the sheer thrill of it.

I was behind her, so I was safe.

I knew Sthenno would never turn around. I knew she was trying not to threaten Medousa.

Milk streamed into the deep shell. The khimaira stood and relaxed as it streamed. Once the shell was full, Sthenno closed her eyes and lifted it towards Medousa's parted lips.

"Here, you take the first sip," she offered.

Medousa sipped milk from the shell. One timid draw turned into a hefty gulp. I watched her throw her head back and sigh with satisfaction.

A smile crept over Medousa's lips.

"That was delicious," she said.

"Oh yes," Sthenno promised, her voice trailing into a subtle hiss.

"The khimaira milk is powerful," Euryale added, "Not even Hekate herself could brew a potion this strong."

The gorgones took turns milking the beast and passing their spiny shell to Medousa. So long as I circled in the sky backdropping Medousa, the gorgones would never give me a final, fatal look. My heart shook like the wind beneath my feathers.

"What does the khimaira eat?" Medousa asked after several helpings of khimaira milk.

"No food," Euryale said.

"She only drinks ocean water," Sthenno said.

"Then the stars above sweeten salt into milk," Euryale smiled.

"Hekate made this creature special for us. Not only for protection, but also for nourishment. The milk reminds us to love the sea."

There was a thoughtful pause and I wished to try the milk for myself. That, of course, would've been far too risky.

"How can we drink water? Like when I arrived?" Medousa asked.

"From another shell..." Euryale hissed, reaching into the tidepool to fetch it, "Drink from Triton's trumpet and no salt will touch your lips."

Medousa used the ridged shell to drink water from the sea. I could see a salty crust form on the brim, but not pass through her mouth. My vision was clear, even compared to my fellow sharp-seeing birds.

"Now it's your turn to milk the khimaira," a gorgones said, nudging Medousa gently.

I heard Medousa sigh. It sounded of relief, not fatigue. I guessed she was happy to be welcomed into the fold of gorgones. How funny, for such a sweet-looking girl to long for acceptance from monsters?

Medousa knelt on the stony cave floor. Her knees touched. They fit into a groove, the elbow of a man turned to stone. Medousa looked back and forth between the face of the lion and the face of the snake. I knew she was imagining exactly how vulnerable she was, kneeling beside the beast.

I laughed for good measure, thankful the winds were in my favor to blow me here on this morning of all mornings.

Medousa took a sharp, deep inhale and looked at the shell in her palms. The khimaira's lips rolled back and revealed a mouth full of sharp teeth.

All at once I heard a growl, a bleat, and a hiss.

Medousa jumped, falling back towards the gorgones' bronze slippers.

They rubbed her shoulders gently, as gently as metal fingers could, and hummed softly in her ears. They were so quiet, a lesser bird may have thought it was the whisper of waves. When the gorgones hummed, their shrill bronze lips mystified the sounds. They soothed Medousa. She regained her breath.

The khimaira grew calm once more. Each head was cocked,

listening intently to gather what couldn't be seen.

Medousa stayed for a moment, leaning back into the gorgones' metal arms before they coaxed her back into kneeling.

"Hmm... How strange," Sthenno mused.

"Normally the khimaira loves to be milked," Euryale said.

"This time think of a different star," bronze lips instructed.

Medousa repeated the action, but before her gaze fully rested on the shell, the ocean grew angry. A crashing, thunderous wave rolled over the matrix of tidepools. I watch it swing into the gorgones' lair, so tall it could have crushed any of the waves that came before it. It soaked the khimaira's clawed feet and even cast salty water over her udders. Medousa stood and the gorgones hissed.

I heard a yowl, a baa, and a swish from the khimaira.

"What's wrong?" Medousa yelped.

"The forces of nature will not allow it," Sthenno snapped.

"Poseidon refuses!" Euryale said.

The gorgones swooped in and tried to take the shell from Medousa. Both women grabbed blindly for Medousa's hands.

"W-wait," Medousa stammered, "I have an idea."

The gorgones couldn't see through their blindfolds, but through the cracks in the stony hive. I looked at the eyes of Medousa. She had returned to kneeling before the khimaira, but there were no shining, greedy emeralds.

Her eyes were closed.

She held the shell out for the khimaira, blind as a bat.

In silence she waited.

A stream of milk flowed right into the spondylus shell. Medousa grinned and the khimaira purred. Still, she kept her eyes closed and milk continued to flow

"What did you do?" Euryale hissed.

"How did you make this work?" Sthenno begged.

"I thought of an eclipsing star. I thought of the darkest night."

I felt a chill in my bones.

I remembered, in nights that had passed, new stars had been born and others disappeared. Those were certainly legendary times I was living in.

Quickly, the spondylus shell brimmed with milk, and Medousa passed it to her sisters. They didn't hesitate to drink.

I circled and stared and another mystery became clear to me.

With Medousa kneeling, the hem of her dark robes rode up. I could see a cerulean glimmer on her ankle. It was a snake, the same shade as the star of Algol. That star had been flickering since I heard Medousa's name fall from the clouds.

Like the snake, she could work her way into the Underworld.

She could be reborn.

Medousa may shed her skin, and start a new life. I knew what Hera could never whisper. I knew Medousa was special, that she was a talisman to Algol. Her very flesh was drawn from the star.

The gorgones couldn't see the snake glowing on Medousa's skin. They knew Medousa from sound alone.

The gorgones wrinkled their foreheads, thinking deeply about the girl, but allowed her to continue. I watched their round faces contort behind the blindfolds. Medousa collected shellful after shellful, and shared the milk with her sisters.

"Milk her more, she has more to offer you," a gorgones said.

"We drink a dozen shells' worth every morning, take more," said the other one. She nodded her misty head and bronze tresses. Though her head bobbed up and down the snake's faces stayed still, their eyes fixed on Medousa, staring as if to challenge her. The snake's eyes were silver as the moon, like dewdrops against their misty scales. I'm sure centuries had passed since the snakes had time to gaze upon the living, anything other than each other and the beast with three heads.

Medousa took her final sips of milk. The khimaira sank back into the sea without a splash.

"Toss the shell after her," Euryale instructed, "It will always be in the tidepools when you need it."

So Medousa tossed the spiny shell into the sea. Its spines didn't crack on the stones underwater, because as soon as it touched the surface, it vanished, just like the khimaira.

"You're still hungry?" Sthenno asked.

Medousa looked up. I could see shallows under her cheekbones.

"Yes," she admitted.

"Do not worry, Medousa. You can eat fish," Sthenno said.

"Sea life is bountiful here," Euryale continued, "Poseidon will feed you."

"How?" Medousa asked.

The misty women looked at each other, out of habit rather than vision.

"She could use the trident," Euryale suggested.

"Yes, I suppose. Go fetch it."

Euryale unfurled her massive, misty wings, and rocketed into the air.

She flew without eyes to see, but I supposed she knew her way. I watched her wearily, balancing in the sky above her.

"We're not exactly like the living," Sthenno said, gesturing to her braids of snakes, "Clearly, but there's more than meets the eye. We never sleep, we never feel cold, and we don't have normal human tongues for chewing. Milk is the only nourishment which can pass through our metal lips."

The gorgones flicked her bronze, forked tongue. Medousa stared at its flash. I squinted at the details. Still, like a sea-green patina, I could see Medousa's eyes. I saw the flicker of a trickster cross over her pupils. I watched her rub her eyes, as if blinded by light.

The gorgones never developed a patina, the winds of the kharybdis must have peeled it away before it ever grew. Wind eroded everything — minds, hearts, and souls.

Euryale reached the pinnacle and grabbed the golden trident. I heard the clink of her bronze fingers grabbing the light metallic shaft. Then, she dropped back in a plunge.

There was a swiftness in Euryale's flight, holding the trident along her body. She reminded me of the way a spearfisher would've held his spear beside him, to be like an arrow in the water.

Euryale landed in front of Medousa, her misty form rippled when her bronze slippers touched the dark stone.

"We can let you borrow this trident. You'll have to hunt for yourself; anything we catch might turn to stone."

The gorgones stuck out her skinny, flat tongue after speaking. Both gorgones had dually forked tongues, while their trident was divided in three.

If you looked for hints about the origins of Greece, if you developed your eyes to be sharp like a falcon, you would see the entire universe in small details.

"It's amazing," Medousa exclaimed, staring at elaborate golden fixtures and pointed prongs. The trident was as tall as the gorgones themselves and much taller than Medousa.

Euryale grinned with her bronze lips, "Are you ready?" She asked, facing Medousa.

"For what?" Medousa asked.

"Catch," She said, throwing the trident.

The golden trident flew through the air, hurtling towards Medousa.

She watched the sharp points fly past her and grabbed the handle. Medousa lunged and braced herself.

Medousa lifted up so quickly that she nearly fell back. The trident wasn't heavy. It was light as a feather. She staggered and caught her balance on the uneven ground.

"Whoa," Medousa said, twirling the shaft around her fingers.

"Hekate enchanted it," a gorgones said, "She anointed this trident with seawater and cast a spell for levity."

Medousa wasn't listening. Her green eyes were focused on the tidepools.

I had no idea what Medousa stalked, but I knew that she was moving towards prey.

"She enchanted it long before we were ever born, before there were ever stones in this spot in the sea..."

Medousa completely ignored them. She stepped closer towards the tidepools which kissed the cave's mouth. The winds of the kharybdis pushed her knotted hair from her face.

Medousa was on the hunt.

She crouched, lower, towards the stony cavern floor. On an exhale she leapt forward and sent the trident hurtling through the air. Watching the trident fly towards its target was like watching an archer fire his arrow. It quivered in the air with a flash.

I saw a blemish of blue in the tidepool and Medousa darted towards her catch.

The gorgones heard the splash and the clank of the metal trident's strike.

"Medousa!"

"Did you catch something?"

The blindfolded gorgones looked back and forth as if they could see.

Medousa waited to answer. She lifted the trident from the water.

An octopus dangled from the center prong. Tentacles twitched as life passed.

Medousa drew the trident closer towards her eyes. White flashes appeared and disappeared from the octopus' skin, as if it wished to hypnotize its killer.

"Yes," Medousa said, "A slimy thing… with chalices for fingertips… with a writhing body… a bulbous head…. and the eye of a goat."

Clearly the octopus was new to her. The creature was so peculiar, she didn't know its name. The gorgones gasped with the faint ring of metal as wind rushed past their lips.

"No..."

"Medousa, that's so strange! You caught an octopus."

The misty women started to laugh. It was hollow, shrill laughter that was too dark to come from their dead hearts. They spun haughty laughter from their throats.

Medousa's catch was strange indeed. Blue blood streamed down the trident.

"Go ahead," Euryale said.

"Mortals eat the damndest things," Sthenne said.

Medousa looked at the creature before her. The octopus struggled for only her eyes and my eye in the sky. The gorgones mocked Medousa's catch, but they couldn't see the creature trying to crawl its way off the trident.

"How did you even spot the octopus, huh?" Sthenno questioned Medousa.

"Yes, I thought they were the masters of disguise!" Euryale taunted.

"Its eye gave it away," Medousa watched blood fall from her catch.

Her green eyes were locked on the blue rivulets. I could see her mind, working through her eyes, trying to understand the unusual sight.

Though she was naive, she did have a scar over her neck. I was sure she knew that blood was supposed to be red.

Eventually the octopus fell limp, and its malleable body sank down the trident, weighed down by its own lifelessness.

"So, what did you expect me to catch?" Medousa asked the gorgones. Her voice revealed she was hurt.

"Medousa, you think too much," Sthenno said and reached out to rest a metallic hand on Medousa's shoulder.

"We thought you would catch a big fish," Euryale said.

At her remark, both gorgones breathed a sly chuckle.

"Hey be fair," Sthenno mockingly pleaded, "You know she'd have to go deep for a big fish."

"I am... I am a little scared of the ocean," Medousa peeped, "I don't want to go deep."

Both of the gorgones broke into laughter. They lifted their wings and floated off into the upper reaches of their stony hive.

Medousa was alone, alone save my eye watching her from the sky. She didn't understand that the gorgones were joking. Medousa fixed her gaze onto the horizon.

"Then, I will go deep," she swore to the sea.

Then Medousa dug her teeth into the octopus. It was like a serpent writhing in her mouth.

Medousa chewed the tender pieces, and swallowed them. Her promise of the ocean was heard by the Underworld and the beast in her belly.

I wished to keep flying in circles. I wanted to watch what would happen in this fateful kharybdis, but a storm brewed over the horizon. It was dark, gray, and told me to head back to shore while I still could, while my wings were made of feathers rather than stone.

18. Swallow

I saw a gleam on the horizon.

At first, I took it for a mirage. Poseidon tricked me before, but as the sparkle grew, I wondered if a star was lost at sea.

Eventually, my ship's men saw it too, "A light! Off the bow!"

"Fire!"

"Yes, fire! There must be land, behold!"

In my avian form, I never wielded fire. But in a strange way, I knew more about fire than the men. The men who lit torches and cooked their food needed a bird to call their bluff. I warbled at their folly.

My instincts never waned. I remembered how to smell an ember over the sea, how to spot smoke on the wind, and how to avoid chaos rather than create it. The glow was warm, but certainly not fire. At least the sailors had me as their guardian and usher.

I squinted and peered at the horizon and it blurred under a veil of mist.

But the glow was everlasting. It caught my eye, and the hopes in my heart.

I had a secret wish for the light. I thought we might discover, in some lucky stroke, treasure glittering in the waves. I'd heard stories of gold floating on the backs of whales in faraway seas. I thought, maybe, those lucky whales were migrating across the Aegean Sea.

As I flew on my course over the sea, I wondered why it felt like winds pushed me towards that golden gleam. There was a curve in the wind, and I let it carry me.

My men didn't resist either. They didn't try to steer away from the supposed fire. They let their vessel drift along, following my lead. I was sure they were curious, for they probably wondered why was there a fire in the open sea. Perhaps they even felt called to put it out.

If I'd only known what the star really was; I'd have gone mad, fluttering in front of the oarsmen, pointing towards the rudder, and urging them to turn around.

I didn't know. I could never go back to save a sunken ship, or petrified men.

As the glimmer appeared, we were cloaked in mist. It was hard to tell where our ship was going, or how we got there. I imagined a cloud bathing around us, coming down from heaven to rest in the warm Aegean Sea.

I let out a brave warble and flew ahead of my men.

"There goes the swallow," they said.

Their curved ship disappeared behind me in the mist.

I wanted to be the first to spot the lucky whale. I was no braver than my men, because I could fly ahead. I wasn't scared of the light, I knew it wasn't fire, but I should've been afraid.

My feathered crown was blue as a summer sky, my cheeks blushed like an eager lover, and my forked tail never led a ship astray. I finally did cast an unlucky shadow, on that day I led my men towards the golden light. I was not following my internal navigation, but I was following the star lost in the sea and an arc in the wind.

Perhaps I could've stopped the ship. I could've given the sailors a sign to man their oars, and steer away from the light. I wonder if it would've even helped, or if Poseidon had fixed our course. I had no idea that the golden glimmer was a legend, a monster, who would make her way from the sea back into the stars.

My feathers, and the white lines of seafoam rolling over waves, all coursed towards the fallen star.

I saw the gleam bounce over the horizon. It rose, then fell, then darted, then remained still. My heart fluttered watching its dance. I started to realize it wasn't a lucky whale.

Eventually I got close enough to see the source of the glow.

It was a golden staff, with three prongs, reflecting the sun.

A bewitching girl stood ankle-deep in the water. I'd sailed many seas on trades and voyages, and still, I'd seen nothing like her. She floated in the mist, like a drop of gold in endless blue.

It was Medousa, wielding a giant fork.

I'd heard about her in stories. I was a traveler, so I talked to birds on every shore. Storks claimed she bubbled up from a falling black feather, and Poseidon aged her. Word from the kingfishers was she died, water held her, but she rose again. I've also heard an osprey claim Medousa sailed on a maiden voyage all the way to a rocky spot in the sea.

I supposed that's where we found her, ankle-deep in the blue.

I knew all the rumors were true from the stars in her eyes. There was something respectful yet careful in them when she looked at the ocean. The girl was on edge, on the edge of the world.

Medousa's hair, dripping in knotted curls, sparkled like the trident. Her strands were thick as snakes, enlivened by the wind. I could see how salt had its way with her hair.

Dark robes whooshed around her. Her gown took to her like the coarse linen sails that pulled our ship across the Aegean Sea. I could see her torso rise and fall with her breath.

Her gaze was fluid, sweeping from horizon to horizon. Her green eyes followed fish in the water. She was scanning, looking into the blue. She caught every dolphin's ripple and every school's flutter.

She did not seem like a typical huntress, who scanned for prey, hunched in ambush, quiet on the earth. She was like a sailor with an open heart. She scanned the horizon, the depths, the skies, as wide as the eye could see.

From the sky, I spotted the fish that she hunted. A sailfish was taunting her, flashing his reflective fin, smirking with his long nose, and casting waves over her feet.

The fish was fast and fearless.

I wondered how she carried such a massive staff of gold. For it was taller than her, and I noticed, though she tried, she couldn't wrap her fingers all the way around it.

Still, I thought Medousa would've been interesting for my men to meet. This girl was stranded in the sea. I thought my chivalrous men may have been able to help her. I thought they may have even been able to tame her.

I hovered over Medousa, waiting for my men to arrive.

Medousa launched her trident at the shining sailfish. Gold hurtled through the air, but the fish darted away. She missed.

Medousa leapt in, after her trident, and I swear before she grabbed it I saw something unbelievable. My eyes may have deceived me, but her trident rose out of the water, as if searching for her hand. I had been wondering how she carried her trident with grace, and how her arms didn't grow tired from wielding it. Perhaps, I thought with folly, it was truly weightless.

I circled effortlessly over the girl, like I was a spark of her missing halo. She floated back to her rock, clinging to the sunlit staff. My tail, with its own forks, helped me twist in the air. I was so curious about the girl, and more so, curious about the way the sea crawled around Medousa. When I circled above her, I saw strange patterns of water. From each direction I looked, waves flowed towards her.

I saw my men gain speed. They moved towards the craggy underwater rocks upon which Medousa stood.

Swift winds pushed the boat. Her sails were full, and she moved so quickly, there would've been no way to stop her. The currents were too strong, and the winds were too mad. One man, at the rudder, pulled back and tried to slow our approach. Then the rudder snapped, and came up, floating behind the vessel. I blinked and sent a silent prayer to the stars.

The sails were still flush. Poseidon had his way.

I witnessed my men's speedy approach with no way to stop them.

So did Medousa.

Her gaze was no longer on fish nor on the sea. She watched my men, with her hand grasping her golden trident.

The ship curved over Poseidon like an evil grin. As they got closer, my oarsmen spotted her too.

One of my men called out, "What are you doing out here?"

Another shouted, "Girl, do you need help?"

Their voices carried over the water.

Medousa pulled locks of hair from her eyes and stared at the ship. I shivered in the sky when I saw venom in her green eyes. I flew, quickly, down to the bow of my ship. I heard some of the men sigh, relieved to see their allegedly lucky bird was still on their side.

"I was hunting," Medousa shouted with malice, "Until your ship's shadow scared away the fish!"

Medousa looked at my men as if they were the fish who outswam her. I saw fear turn her mad, but my men didn't notice.

All they saw was a girl, not a monster.

Our boat rocked with laughter. Some of the oarsmen clutched their bellies. Others tilted their heads back, as if their joy was meant for the clouds. I had to dig my claws into the wooden bow to stay on board, as the ship rocked with their laughter.

"That's just silly!"

"Oh, she's been disturbed by the sea!"

"We have to help her, she's no hunter!"

"Is that so? If I'm no hunter, then how did I bring down the best hunter in Greece?" asked Medousa.

My sailors fell silent, save their roaring hearts. I heard the soft lull of waves against our bow, leading us towards the self-proclaimed killer.

After the silence, outrage erupted like seafoam in a storm.

"It was you?"

"How could it have been her?"

"Who is she against Orion?"

"You want proof?" Medousa jeered.

Men laughed, gasped, and argued among themselves. Not one among them could compose himself to answer.

Medousa lifted a lock of yellow hair that was wrapped across the front of her neck. She revealed a scar which trailed over her throat.

"Orion gave me this," Medousa said.

At that moment I, and all my fellow sailors saw a beast emerge from the water next to Medousa. It bursted from the sea, with three heads, roaring. One head of a lion, another of a goat, and a hissing snake for a tail.

The roar had me shivering beneath my feathers and shook me like I was in the Underworld. I looked at my men. Some of them paled at the sight. Others looked on with wide eyes. Each of their hearts beat to a frantic song.

The creature with a lion's roar swam straight towards Medousa.

There was a moment of silence, while the ghost of a roar hung in the air, and the hybrid cat stretched with each stroke of its massive paws.

Each man recognized danger in the beast, but not in Medousa.

Chaos broke out.

My men yelled. Some screamed in fear, running to the other side of the boat like cowards. Others were pleading, begging Medousa to run away, to swim to our boat, to find safety while she had the chance.

Medousa let the calls of my men roll over her shoulders and back out to sea.

She ignored them and approached the beast like an old friend. The dark, matted mane of the lion met her slender fingers. She cupped her hand around its feline ear. I was sure she whispered something to the creature, but shouting men, lull of water, and brooding chaos was too much.

I could not hear her, but the creature did. It obeyed.

It slinked back into the ocean. All three heads disappeared underwater. Neither splash nor ripple was left in its wake.

Medousa looked back to the ship with an evil grin. I'd seen the expression before, on sharks who swarmed injured gulls flapping in the shallows. Such a grimace never graced a swallow, and I'd never seen it before on a girl.

"We haven't even introduced ourselves. My name is Medousa."

My men stayed silent, in fear of the girl who could've tamed a beast.

She claimed to kill Orion, and that's when we all started to believe her. Water hissed against our boat, and the whole ocean breathed only there, only as our vessel rocked closer to Medousa. The ocean sputtered in wine-dark, frothing bursts.

My men only stayed silent for one, collective heartbeat, then chaos broke out again.

"Pharmakis!" men shouted at Medousa in panicked confusion.

"Oh, she's going to turn us into swine!"

There was tension, a string of fate almost, connecting the green eyes of Medousa to the frightened eyes of my men. I wondered if that same thread had reeled us in from the open ocean. Our ship, curving with the strange pattern of the sea around the rocks, shifted, so our curved bow skirted past Medousa, and the boat pulled leewards, closer to her.

Medousa kept quiet, in respect to the ocean. I could tell she feared it. She feared the men who crossed it. She feared the helplessness and the endlessness of the ocean, but she was tied to it. Chained to it. Standing in it. Imprisonment, wet in her eyes, veiled the way she saw my free men.

Her fear metamorphosed into distaste for her intruders. I saw her emotions in the depths of her sea-green eyes.

Then there was the screech of wood, and the crack of oars as they brushed rock.

"Men, collect your oars!"

The damage was already done. Their paddles floated away.

Medousa smirked. Wind howled in fear. Waves curled to her will. Her grin cut through my heart like our ship cut through the waves.

The hypnotic ocean, seemingly magnetized to Medousa, as if she were the moon itself, pushed our craft towards the dark rocks. If this girl was a star, then we were bound to her.

Silence broke, like a weak mooring line in a tumultuous sea, and we crashed.

The scrape of our hull grinding against rock felt like a savage rending of flesh.

My men shouted and abandoned their benches. They ran across the ship, to the starboard side, piling up against the edge, huddled in mass. I fluttered from the bow, slipping into a small hole in the boards. It would've been the perfect place to hide, if only my blushing face and blue feathers were muted.

Poseidon followed a relentless beat. Each wave pushed the wooden ship harder against the rocks. It creaked and rumbled.

Only one manned his oar. Though he was sitting alone, abandoned even by the paddle which floated away, he stood tall.

Then, I heard the uncanny shiver of a blade sliding out of its sheath.

His name was Ovid. He'd been a stranger until we picked him up at the previous port.

He brandished his weapon towards Medousa. She looked up at him from the sea. She smiled, wider at him.

I burrowed deeper between the wooden planks, my heart beating frantically. Medousa laughed. She reached into a fold in her robes. The trident was no burden to her, she twirled it in her arms like it was made of air.

"She's reaching for another weapon!"

"She's going to kill us all!"

"Hush now..." Medousa whispered, at the same volume as hissing waves, but her voice rang in my ears, "Let me show you my trick."

Medousa took one step towards the ship, and Ovid leapt from the deck. He plummeted into the water. Ovid landed on a shallow rock, and toppled for a moment before catching his balance.

My body shivered between the planks.

Through the frothing waves, amidst screams of my men, and past the brave stance of Ovid, I saw a plan form in Medousa's green eyes.

"I promise, you'll be awarded for your bravery," Medousa said to Ovid.

Before he could respond, she charged him. She brandished the trident. She was so flippant with the weapon that it whirred in the air. Ovid stood no chance at disarming this wild girl; anyone could've seen that. He stepped back, but slipped. He fell into the ocean, below the waves.

Medousa leapt aboard. She sprang from the sea, into our ship.

Medousa was not the same girl who stood in the waves. Or at least, she didn't appear the same.

She had put on a mask. It had been hiding in the folds of her robes.

Medousa's new face was bronze. Not in color alone, but also in texture. There was not a blemish on her face, or a pore of flesh.

Sunlight beamed across the smooth, red surface. Wings sprouted from her temples. A nest of serpents was like a wreath around her face. She didn't look straight at me, and now I can thank the stars for that.

I saw the corners of her eyes, the edges of her face. Her eyes, no longer ocean-green wells, were as white as pearls.

Ovid flapped in the water. He beat his arms against the sea, just like I beat my wings against the sky while I was flying. I mused, how his bravery landed him in the sea. Yet, he was the safest of all my sailors.

At that moment, all the other men on my ship took their final breaths. Their lungs hardened into stone. Their hearts collectively paused forevermore.

Silence hung in the air, while I waited for their hearts to beat again, but they never would. Their faces, which were once sunkissed, darkened into magnetite rock.

Screams solidified in their throats.

Ovid saw their faces turn to stone. I watched his own face contort in horror, confusion, and misery.

The boat leaned backwards.

I leapt from between the boards. My wings grabbed air. I flew up into the sky, and watched the whole ship, mast and all, disappear into water. Before it submerged, Medousa leapt from the boat, carefree as a dandelion loose on the wind.

The weight of stone corpses brought down the vessel which had been their homes, their seat for adventure, their way of livelihood, and a beacon of brotherhood for each sailor as they crossed the seas.

"I pray for my men who have fallen into Poseidon's grasp!" Ovid shouted as he struggled to stay afloat. Saltwater washed into his mouth.

Though the sun was shining and daylight was passing, the moon, white as a skull, yet also hidden as a phantom, watched Medousa kill the men. It had a hard line between its two halves. The moon watched Medousa in neither light nor darkness. The moon watched with such impartial observance, no interference, just as a witness.

I prayed to the lighter half of the moon, prayed that I might return to the mainland of Greece.

I could not be impartial. I was not like the moon, too far away to care. I had led sailors over waves. I steered the oarsmen towards fortune, towards love, and suddenly to their deaths. I shivered. I held my breath from crying out as the men died. It was I, their lucky swallow, who had ushered misguided deaths.

All of them were gone with one glance from Medousa. Except for Ovid, who floundered in the waves, swallowing water. I was spared too, unseen in the chaos. I dipped into the water and floated, resting, hiding behind cresting waves. I pleaded that my blue feathers would blend in, and my cherry red face was hidden in mist.

I watched Medousa. Though, just thinking about those glances at her makes me shiver. I should've looked away. Thankfully, she didn't look into my beady eyes. I watched Medousa remove her deadly bronze mask, and return it to the folds of her robes.

Poseidon echoed the sound of creaking wood. I heard a slow rumble. It was the sound of petrified bodies shifting underwater. Fallen statues toppled, and overturned their vessel. The upside-down wooden hull shot up and breached at the surface.

When our ship floated right-side up, both ends of the vessel curved towards the sky. When our ship was upside down, the curved hull was flat, barren, and submitted to the sea.

I watched Ovid scramble through the water towards the wood. I swam out of his way, knowing I was too small to help him, but his thrashing arms could drown me by accident. He was desperate for something to cling to, and I didn't want him to cling onto me.

Ovid struggled. He pulled himself up onto the hull, grabbing a hole that the craggy underwater cliffs carved into wood. He used it as leverage to hoist himself out of the water. I noticed then, as he climbed up the overturned hull, that his blade was gone. Ovid looked down, into the whirlpool of water that swallowed his friends, his weapon, and spat out his ship.

The man gulped. He was unarmed. I could hear his heartbeat over the waves. Medousa stood on an underwater outcrop, as if she was standing on the ocean itself.

"Your ship won't go down without you," Medousa said. Without the disguise of her deadly mask, I saw her creepy smile again.

"What happened to my crew?" Ovid cried.

"Now they're stone. Your friends sank to the bottom of the sea!"

"Why would you kill my men? They did nothing to you!"

"Your boat scared away my fish. Is it not my right to protect my hunting grounds? These are my tidepools. What were *they* doing *here*?"

"Hey! You're a pharmakis! You bewitched these waters to bring us here! How dare you ask why we came! The winds and currents are so strong; it was like we had no choice at all."

"Nevermind your conspiracy," Medousa hissed, "Your friends will rest on the ocean floor. Fish will hatch off their flesh."

Ovid pressed his body against the hull and sighed. I floated in the water, like an angel above our men in their graves below.

"Besides, why do you care what happens to them?" Medousa asked, "They hid like cowards while you fought for their lives!"

Ovid's heart raced, like a chariot around a track. Disarmed and alone, he begged to be spared, even if he begged with a frantic heartbeat alone. Ovid had no words.

"Don't worry," Medousa promised, "It won't happen to you."

"How on earth can you turn men into stone?" Ovid asked.

"It's my trick. I can't reveal it to you. Why don't you just call them metamorphosed?" Medousa grinned.

"You're speaking in riddles. If only I had a way out of your spell, pharmakis!"

It wasn't going to be that easy for dear, lion-hearted Ovid. For just as beautiful as the shallow cyan seas could be, and as innocent as a dolphin's breath, there was always an abyss. Poseidon had a dark side. There was always a crashing wave and a perpetual, sacrificial death within the tides.

I heard a hammer that shook the ground like thunder. I blinked. Medousa had struck the rocky tidepool beneath her wet feet, and stuck the trident upright like a flagpole. Then, a splash. Medousa dove into the water towards Ovid's ship. A wave followed her and I rode over it.

She surfaced in front of Ovid's dilapidated, overturned vessel. Medousa floated without kicking, as if she were part of the water rather than an autonomous girl.

"How come I'm not stone yet? I'm looking at you."

"Because I want you to tell all your friends about me. Warn them about the girl in the sea," Medousa pulled herself onto the ship. It rocked under her weight. Ovid leaned back, steadying the ship, and distancing himself from Medousa.

"You killed all my friends!" There was pain in Ovid's voice.

"Make new ones," Medousa's eyes were green like a rotting kelp bed, she crept closer towards him, "and warn them about Medousa. Tell every soul in Greece about what you saw and about her eyes that can turn men into stone."

I floated in the water. I was the silent observer to a story's origin, before the first pages of Ovid's poems were ever written.

"Tell them I was ravaged by Poseidon," Medousa lifted a lock of matted golden hair from her eyes.

Medousa was caught up in creating a story. She didn't notice the way her robes rippled in the wind. She didn't notice Ovid's eye catching on the blue mark of a snake on her ankle. She certainly didn't see Ovid's eye's creep up, along a tear in her robes, to a bronze dagger in its sheath.

Only I could see everything that was going on. Medousa was not so observant. She grew comfortable as she thought she was in total control.

"What do you mean, *ravaged by Poseidon*?" Ovid asked.

"I was born in the ocean's womb and nursed by its salt," Medousa said, "Poseidon's hands created me. As I've grown, he's tried to rob me of my life, and use water to draw my last breath from my lungs."

Ovid didn't care about her answer. He only half listened. He asked the question as a form of distraction. I could tell what he really focused on. As Medousa spoke, Ovid's fingers, stealthy as an octopus tentacle frisking a crab, unsheathed the bronze dagger from her hip.

"I am no mere girl, but a creature of the seas," Medousa continued, with no idea that she was being tricked by Ovid, "Have you got the story straight?"

"Y-yes." Though he had the upper hand, the sharp edge, Ovid's heart beat like stormy waves in a sea cave.

"Good," Medousa leapt from the ship and swam away from him, "Now I'll let you live if you tell the rest of Greece that I am a monster. Nobody should come here if they value their beating hearts."

With a crackling snap, Medousa lifted the golden trident out from the rocks, and ran back towards the misty horizon. Her feet were nimble over the tidepools, as if she were the ocean itself who rolled with ease over the sharpest stones.

When Medousa was gone, I flew out of the sea and burrowed between planks beside Ovid.

Suddenly a wave came and whisked us away. We drifted away from the island, from the evil girl, and back into blue. Winds shifted in our favor and pushed us away from the pull of the kharybdis. In the silence that followed, the stunned Ovid clung to wood, and I took to his shoulder. I knew we were sent towards land, and we would reach it in the end. When I looked back, I swear the mist that shrouded our men's final moment's appeared like a cloud on the horizon. Then it moved, and twirled up into the heavens, as if, it too, were alive.

We floated away on the ocean, bringing us all the way back to the shores of Magnesia, the mainland of Greece. I wondered if it was the fate of all sailors for the sea and the sky to drive them mad.

Well, that is, the fate of sailors who survived their travels.

As soon as his feet touched the stony beach, Ovid set out towards Athens, with a story bubbling on his tongue, and tears for our fallen men brimming on his lashes.

I followed the newfound poet to Athens, lucky for Ovid alone.

19. Bat

I heard the words of birds, though I was not feathered. I knew the phases of the moon, though I never saw the sun. I knew the habits of pharmakides, because when the moon went missing they staged their trades in my forest.

I waited in the woods for the witches. Usually, Hekate never kept me waiting for long. On the night of one particular new moon, while spring was budding, the witch was running late.

Hera was already there, tapping her fingers against her golden chariot. She flicked strands of luscious honey-colored hair out of her face. Her snow-white peahens, regal as the pharmakis herself, scratched at the dirt. I watched them as I darted in the sky above. Those birds only got to touch the ground when the moon went missing.

Hekate appeared and left her cottage door open behind her.

"You reek of ambrosia."

"If you look hard enough for anything, you'll always find it."

There was a pause. A judicious pause. A moment of silence lush with thought.

Then I heard a sniff and a sharp inhale.

"I'm right," Hera said.

Hekate sighed, "I'll only let you be right, because the ambrosia's made me too tired for tricks."

"It's cute how you think your tricks still work on me," Hera was regal, "I already looked to the stars, listened to the birds, and knew where you were."

Hekate was silent, but I could hear her heart strumming an orchestra of regret. There were ashes in her eyes.

"What brought you to the Underworld?" Hera's brow arched.

"Kerberos," Hekate admitted, "He's the reason I went down to begin with."

Hera stepped out of her chariot, her gleaming, bare white feet touching the dirt for the first time since the last new moon.

"I had no idea the Underworld lost its guardian," Hera said, "With all the birds who spill their secrets to me, you're still full of surprises."

"That's because the phoinix and stymphalians keep my secrets, Hera," Hekate said.

"What happened to Kerberos?" Hera asked.

"It was that damned kentauroi, Kheiron, drunk on the possibility of mingling with the new herd in Magnesia."

"Tell me what happened," Hera said.

The beady eyes of Hera's peahens and the silver pupils on their feathers, watched her every step. She placed a hand on Hekate's pale shoulder.

I watched from the sky, twirling on my silent wings, chasing nothing but my own curiosity, my own secret admiration for the pharmakides. Myths bounced back to me from the stars. They whispered the stories of bats long ago, cheeps lost as time passed.

"A bronze horseshoe cracked his skull. I carried him through the Underworld…" said Hekate

"And?" Hera asked.

"Kerberos has risen. He's back in position at the grotto."

Hera dropped her hand, dug into a pocket near her waist, "How did you raise him while the powers were mine?"

"No, not me alone. Poseidon reanimated Kerberos and I carried the bodies," Hekate said.

"You speak of Poseidon like I speak of the birds."

Hekate turned to her fellow pharmakis and winked, but I knew it was too dark for Hera to see. My wings grew tired and my heart grew fast.

I wanted to rest, to leave the sky. Besides I didn't want to stand in the way of Hekate and the stars and the dark orb of the moon crawling over them through the night. I could eavesdrop better when I was still. I swooped down to a cypress tree and clung on with my claws. Nobody in Greece, not even the peahens saw my black eyes. When the moon darkened, so did the border between me and the night.

"Looks like my cottage has been ransacked," Hekate said, "I suppose it was the kentauroi. The living ones. I didn't have much time to look around, but it seems that they stole almost all my metal, even my bronze mirror."

Hera cast her eyes over the cottage, "Yes, I suppose it has. The stars have been fiddling with us here on earth in such strange ways, isn't that true, Hekate?"

"Yes," Hekate yawned in the night.

"At least your trip to the Underworld was fruitful. The trinity's guardian has returned," Hera said, "and no souls escaped."

"Well…" Hekate's voice trailed off.

"What?" Hera snapped.

"The last thing I remembered… Kheiron was shackled. When I woke up from the ambrosia, he was gone. I've been searching for him in the Underworld. I rushed here now to meet you about the burning glass."

"It seems like you're having difficulties managing the dead," Hera said.

"I've no idea how he got loose, my senses were dulled," Hekate said.

"So dear," Hera asked, "why did you drink the ambrosia?"

Hekate's gray eyes boiled, "You haven't got a clue how courts run in the Underworld!"

Hera giggled and her peahens cooed, with soft sweet drumming calls.

"I suppose you are right. Nonetheless, you do seem alive as ever," Hera said with a roll of her eyes, a flash of white in the darkness, "I sense this won't serve you much. I suspect you'll spend the phases of this dark moon in a slumber."

Hera pulled the burning glass from her pocket. The orb was fully illuminated, in opposition to the missing moon. Hekate reached for it, and the burning glass changed hands.

Hekate winced upon touching the glass.

"What's wrong?" Hera asked.

"Nothing but a minor burn," Hekate mumbled.

She held the orb between her palms, and stretched it out. Hekate gazed at the stars, summoning light to heal her hands. There was a flash of light, and she sighed. Hekate quickly slipped the piece into her gown.

Hekate remarked "At least I'll have the moon in my dreams"

"I'm sure you've been too busy with the dead and their dances to hear the new rumors about your girl."

"My girl?"

"Oh come on Hekate! I know you haven't forgotten her already. Surely you remember Medousa," Hera said.

"What rumors?" Hekate whispered and a crinkle of regret fluttered over her face. I heard a murmur in Hekate's heart, a longing to protect Medousa, but a deeper drowsiness.

"It's all the buzz around Athens. Some sailor named Ovid washed up on the shore, claiming the rest of his crew was turned to stone by the beautiful, the dangerous," Hera drew out her words, "Medousa."

Hekate blinked.

Hera continued, "I even heard it from a swallow who witnessed the whole thing."

"It must be a trick," Hekate said.

"A trick?" Hera asked.

"Yes. Medousa is no monster. She's a girl not a gorgones. There's no way her glance could turn flesh to stone."

There was a pause, a lull in conversation, while I heard the clicks of my kin.

"She has a mask," Hera said.

"A mask?"

"Yes, the swallow claims that Medousa's mask is made of bronze."

Hekate rubbed her bleary eyes. I could see the world spinning in front of her as she staggered.

Hera continued, "Ovid was drunk and boasting of his escape from Medousa. He claims to have won a prize," Hera pulled a bronze knife from her robes, "One of my nymphs stole this from him. It must have been Medousa's. I thought you should have it."

Hekate held the knife and fixed her gaze on the constellation Orion.

"Let's get back to what's important. Ovid's story has spread across Greece. It reached a young boy, eager to prove himself. He wishes to bring honor to the lives Medousa ended by stealing her head. His name is Perseus. He is arranging travel to Sarpedon as we speak. Ovid told Perseus how to find his way there."

Hekate adopted a vague, contemplative look. Her eyes were cloudy rather than starry.

"Medousa has frozen, flown, and fought," Hekate whispered to the stars. I knew her words were not meant for Hera, or even for bats huddled in cypress trees.

Hera averted her gaze, looking at her peahens' talons stirring the dirt.

"I must warn Medousa," Hekate's eyes grew wide and dewy with starlight.

"Do you think so?" Hera was calm. She didn't look up from the dirt.

"Yes!" Hekate spat.

"Of course," Hera cooed, "Medousa should be warned. but that's not your duty."

Hera sighed.

The gentle release of her breath coursed through the forest. I heard it bounce through the trees and stir sympathetic ears. A sweet brown bird flew to its source, swift as the wind, and landed in Hera's palm. Its beady eyes were malleable, searching for meaning. She wished to take Hera's instructions, no doubt.

The brown bird chattered and peeped. I recognized her as a nightingale when she started to sing with the voice of a dreamer.

"Good idea…" Hera said, as if she understood the song, "It's much better if Medousa thinks it's her own idea that Perseus is coming. Guide her while she sleeps."

Hera looked at Hekate with one arched eyebrow. Hera whispered to the bird, so softly I was sure the other pharmakis couldn't hear, but bats caught every sound.

"Make sure," Hera whispered, "This girl doesn't hurt Perseus. He seems like an honest boy."

The nightingale rattled off a series of chirps.

"I suppose," Hera murmured, "Medousa could give Perseus her mask in place of her head."

There was a swish of tawny feathers. The bird fluttered into the dark forest, with a divine secret in her beak.

"Thank you," Hekate's voice was warped by a yawn. I wondered when she would head into the cottage for her sleep, where I peered into her dreams.

"There's one more thing," Hera continued.

"What is it?"

"Nothing to do with Medousa, but my dear Nephele has not stopped weeping about Alpheratz since the past full moon. Have you found the mare? May I give her good news?"

"No news of Alpheratz," Hekate looked at the stars. I wondered if she saw any guidance in their silent counsel.

Hera chuckled, "I suspect the inception of the new herd of kentauroi was the work of Nephele."

"How so?"

"She's a sea nymph, you may remember. She carries the touch of Poseidon, even if she hardly understands it."

"She's a lot like Medousa, I suppose," Hekate said.

Both pharmakides stared up into the night sky. Bats fluttered above them like butterflies of the night. I watched between sprigs of cypress. The tree grounded me. Though its branches reached towards heaven, it was rooted in the Underworld.

I heard the faint wings of moths, the chirps of their hunters, and the sound of bats rustling into flowers. Then I heard a rumble like thunder, or a crushing ocean. The sound became louder and I realized it was the prattle of hooves over earth.

I sighed and huddled closer to cypress bark. A metallic twang echoed in the steps.

I caught sight of a blue head floating between the branches of the trees. I shifted for a better look. The silver body of a horse came into my view. He had the torso of a man, and the body of a horse. I couldn't hear his heartbeat, or his exhales.

I only heard the rush of his inhales.

"Kheiron!" Hekate shouted.

"So we meet again," the misty kentauroi said. I peeked down and saw bronze shoes glittering on his silver hooves, "You must be wondering how I escaped."

Kheiron laughed and Hekate watched in silence. Her fists clenched.

"I didn't come through your grotto," Kheiron said, "No, I evaded your beasts and your tricks. I ended up on a pebbled shore, but freedom wasn't enough. I came here to find you, Hekate. I wanted to mock you for thinking you could chain me forever."

The wild horseman bucked. His back hooves shot upwards in anger. Then he stomped his shod hooves. They clanked against the forest floor.

Kheiron stepped closer towards Hekate. I could hear his inhales, steaming his ideas, and fanning the flames of his soul. His blue face sported a smug grin.

Hera took a step back, towards her chariot, and made herself subtle in the confrontation.

"Did you find those damned kentauroi you were searching for?" Hekate asked, "It seems to me like they left these woods."

She spoke only to enrage him, to get under the misty skin of the beast.

"No," Kheiron stepped in place. I heard the scrape of his hooves over the ground, "They're gone, but can you blame me for escaping?"

"You think you're free to run wild among the living because some horses started to think like men?"

"Well, I should be!" Kheiron stuck out his tongue. It was as blue as his face.

"You know I'll never let you live," Hekate said, "Wolfsbane took your life, and I will not give it back."

"I thought it was medicine," Kheiron said.

"Well you thought wrong," Hekate said and bared her teeth.

She waved her dark robes around her.

Kheiron jumped back. He moved so quickly, with such haste. Though Kheiron had the industriousness and willpower of man, he still had the instincts of a horse. He spooked at her sudden movement.

I saw a shimmer of bronze and heard a metallic whistle. Medousa's blade, which just traded hands, whooshed through the air.

Hekate threw her knife at the kentauroi.

Kheiron ran from the spinning blade. He bolted from earth, into the heavens, closely followed by the flying knife.

Kheiron ran so far and so fast from the wrath of Hekate that he became a comet in the sky. Medousa's bronze blade became the red tail which followed him forevermore. He was no longer a shade. Kheiron became a legend.

Though the kentauroi was exiled from the earth, he was free to run wild across the sky.

Hera watched from her chariot, "Charming, Hekate."

Hekate sighed and pressed down her flowing robes.

"I'll be on my way. You may sleep," a smirk brightened Hera's lips, "Before we part, I must say one thing. I was right. Medousa became a monster indeed."

Hera turned on her heel, sat onto her golden, feather-light chariot and crossed her legs. Her fingers grabbed the peahen's reins, and with a subtle flick of her wrist, they were off, running into the woods, and then, flying like another comet into the sky.

Hekate swayed beneath the stars, looking up as her counterpart and opponent both disappeared into the dark sky. She turned on her heel too, in the same manner as Hera. I flew down from her cypress, and before she closed the cottage door behind her, I floated inside on the whirl of wind the door created.

Hekate nestled into her silky bed and I scurried underneath. I was careful not to let my talons scrape against the wood, not to let the pharmakis know that I was there.

Soon she was asleep. I watched her dreams play out like a drama before me, like constellations in the night. I knew Hekate better than she ever knew herself, for I could peer into the darkest parts of her psyche.

In sleep, Hekate's world became our world. My wings flapped from revelation to reflection. I knew that she orchestrated Greece, she connected the dots, and the phases of the moon aligned for her. Myths were in the palm of her hand.

She dreamed of white swan feathers and hoofbeats like thunder. She dreamed of innocence lost and gained. She dreamed of life bubbling out of the sea. And Poseidon was there too, his hand crafting the finest horses, blowing life into the strongest wings.

20. Lark

A question weighed on me. It kept me up late into starry nights ever since Hera transformed me into a bird. I was once a woman. The Pharmakis of the Light Side of the Moon ruffled my flesh into feathers. She hardened my lips into a beak, she brittled my bones, but she never answered my one, urgent question.

If she was powerful enough to metamorphose my heart's enclosure, surely she was powerful enough to answer a simple question.

I heard Hera's whisper in the wind. I followed them, and beat my tiny wings against the air. I heard her recently tell all the birds Medousa's name. I chirped my question to Hera, over and over again, but she never answered.

If I had a moment with Hera, where she was bound to answer my single question, I would've asked…*Is every hero a fool, or is it just me?*

I asked everyone, not only Hera, but nobody could answer me. Some people didn't even believe that I was a hero. They said if I was a hero, then I would've saved Anthus, I would've had something to prove for my deed.

I stayed resolute. I wished to be called a hero for the simple act of trying to save him, while everyone stood aside.

I know there is a stitch of truth in this, for my feathers are fit for war. Hera transformed me into a hero among birds. I had a shield emblazoned upon my chest.

Some even said I was a villain. I refused to accept that. I resisted the urge to cast myself in shadow. How was I to know a curse fell over me, and spread like a plague over my family?

Maybe, if there were only more heroes in the world, if someone stepped in to help me, together we could've saved Anthus.

Is every hero a fool, or is it just me?

I asked myself this question, because I had nobody left to ask. My beady eyes couldn't shed a tear for my fallen son and my lost daughter. I was stoic, in a way. I could no longer release grief like a human. As a bird, everything changed. Instead of tears, I carried sadness in my song. Tall fields of grass bristled in the wind as if they sang my song's chorus.

Suddenly, an answer came to me.

I heard a rustle in the grass. It wasn't an answer like the one I always expected. I expected words. I expected a clear-cut yes or no.

My answer took the form of a boy. A *hero*. He reminded me of my son Anthus, if he ever had the chance to grow up. Anthus had eyes that were blue like the winter sky, like the boy approaching my fields.

It was Perseus, a boy with a clean face, and a rhythmic heartbeat like a warrior. I could tell he was on a mission to be a hero. There was a purpose to his step, a fixture to his gaze.

As Perseus looked around, marveled at the plains, examined the position of the sun, and noted his shadow, I guessed that he had a purpose, but he may have been lost.

Perseus marched his way through a sea of tall barley. He carried nothing but a small sac. Blades and flowers tugged on his light linen clothes, but he walked on. Curly hair bounced as he stepped. Perseus saw over the barley, but had to stand on the balls of his feet to scout the horizon.

The pasture was gold, so gold that it brought out the defiant blue in his eyes. I looked at his hands which pushed his way through the meadow. They were calloused. I recognized them, since I could see into humans deeper than other animals, for I was once a fair woman. Perseus had the hands of an honest boy longing to become a man.

He had the sort of hands that if you were to shake on a deal with Perseus, the bargain would be kept.

I flew to him. I flew high into the air, circled, and chirped a high-pitched note. Then, I plummeted down with my wings folded against me. At the last moment, just before I would have struck Perseus' head with my beak, I swerved upwards.

"Argh!" Perseus said.

He jumped at the sudden flash of my feathers. I turned, quickly, and circled him.

"Oh lark," Perseus mused, "What am I to do?"

I chirped again, so he knew I was listening. His face wrinkled with worry. He was in such a plight, I could tell, he had no choice but to be authentic.

"I met a man named Ovid who told me a horror story from the sea," Perseus explained, "He met a girl— nay, a monster. With one glance she turned his entire crew to stone. Yes, it's a wild story. He arrived on land on an upside down ship, for it had been overturned by the weight of his fallen men. He gives everyone who listens to him a warning, and a story that might perplex even the gods."

I chirped and nodded, flying right in front of him, twirling, looking into his blue eyes.

"How is it possible," Perseus asked, "For a girl to turn men into stone? Do you think Ovid is telling the truth?"

I chirped again. Then, I fluttered down to settle on Perseus' shoulder. He smiled. I felt his heartbeat through my feet.

"He claims that she killed Orion. Ovid even suspects she is a witch! She killed the hunter and cast him into a constellation above the horizon!"

I sang, softer, right into the ear of the budding hero.

"We spent so much time talking, me and Ovid," Perseus said, "I promised him that I would steal the head of Medousa. I made a drunken vow! We shook on it."

His pace quickened, grass thickened, and clouds blotted out the sun.

"I was drunk! I was brazen! I wished to go into the sea and come back with a story on my lips," Perseus said, "It sounds easy to kill a girl, but how can I kill a monster?"

I paused for a moment, lost in thought.

"I-if I killed a girl, would that make me a monster?" he croaked.

Was it heroic to slay a monster? What if she was a girl?

I suspected it was true, that even girls could become monsters.

I was no stranger to innocent souls turning evil. I once loved my horses. Their inky eyes pierced into my heart. Until, they became possessed.

Probably, so was this girl. I bet there was something inside of her, something that wasn't quite a girl. She'd been corrupted. Her soul shattered. For, how could she fell a hunter, if she was an ordinary girl?

I'd seen stranger things happen before, surely Medousa could walk the line between monster and girl.

I never thought a horse could become a monster. When I saw this happen before my eyes, reality shattered. It continued to shatter when I lost my body and became a bird.

I supposed that a girl could be a monster. This girl, Medousa, may have been driven mad. She may have become savage as my horses.

Sometimes a pure soul ate twisted roots.

I didn't judge Perseus. If Medousa's head was his mission, then that was his hero's journey.

I made up my mind. Perseus was a hero, this was his quest, and I was his helper.

One day he'd think of me, the brave bird who met him in the fields.

"Take her head! Go all the way!" I sang.

Surely, he only heard my suggestion as a melodious song. I hoped he heard the call to adventure in my voice. Regardless, I could tell he caught the spirit of my song. In every bird's voice, there was a deeper truth, be it an oath or a warning. Perseus' eyes lit up like a warrior before battle.

"I will take her head," Perseus said.

He took a deep inhale and his chest puffed out. His heart opened to the barley.

"Ovid told me it'd be easy to find a place in the sea, under the lonely star Algol, where the ocean would suck me in, then spit me out. I'll follow through on my promise, but for that I'll need a boat and a blade," Perseus said, "Here I am, lost in the Larissa lowlands, where I've never been before. Oh lark, I don't even know my way to the sea!"

Of course I could lead him wherever he needed to go.

I saw from the bird's eye view, I could direct Perseus across these lowlands. I knew them well.

For, before I became a bird, I cultivated these fields. They called me Hippodamia, and I was a master of horses.

I'd roamed these plains by horseback and settled the fields with my family.

That was, of course, before my horses became monsters, and my family was stripped away.

These lowlands of Larissa, they had once been my pride and joy. Here, pastures sprawled over lands.

Everything was perfect. I bore children from my husband. We had a nanny, plentiful grain and crops, and our lives were sweet.

So, so sweet.

I couldn't even think about those early days, when my family was still together, without wishing to tear the universe apart. I used to think birds could fly anywhere. But as a bird, I could never go where I really wanted.

I wished to wind back the moon and the sun, fly against the currents of time, and emerge in the past.

There was a time I was happy, a time before tragedy struck.

The horses were meant to protect us. They kept the lands healthy. They were strong in numbers and warded off unwanted visitors.

They were meant to be housekeepers, and pull bushes back from our humble hut. That way my children could dig into the earth, freshly overturned from horse hooves, and plant seeds for vegetables.

Everything was perfect, until my pastures wilted.

I'd been cursed. It must have been Demeter whom I had unknowingly wronged. She issued a season where all my grasses died.

I remembered the slow fall of all my barley. These fields became a bowl of dust.

With no grass to eat, my horses became mad with hunger. It did not take very long for everything to change.

The horses refused to pull a carriage or be ridden. I was brave enough to keep trying, but after several falls, that was all. Barren fields yielded rotten horses. There was nothing left. I could not even leave, to find a farmer with cut hay, because the horses became too dangerous to pull a carriage.

They ate everything— every dead strand of grass. It was never enough. My horses were still hungry.

Under a baking sun they dug roots up from the ground. There was something in those roots, something evil that darkened their hearts.

I was inside, tending to our home, while the nanny watched over my children. Then I heard a scream.

I ran outside. Wind and dust rushed across the desolate pastures. My gaunt horses gathered, and I heard another scream coming from the mass of horses.

I ran towards them. I ran past the nanny and my daughter Akanthis. I ran to the screams, for they sounded like my son Anthus.

I heard the beat of the hooves against the hollow earth.

Close to the horses, kicking hooves neared my face. Ears folded back. Sharp teeth were bared.

I squinted and saw blood spilling over the dust. The horses did not cower against my screams. They kicked back. My own horses, striking me, missed my face by barely a hair.

I danced behind my kicking horses, trying to muscle my way between them. It was impossible. The frenzy had fired up their spirits. They pushed me aside. They were hungry, each horse's bones hollowed out their skin.

My boy became their food.

I saw one horse lift his small body off the ground. The horse carried him away.

He wasn't screaming anymore.

I was left standing, for a moment, in a puddle of my son's blood. It already became powder, saturated in the dusty land.

I chased them. I chased them until my son was gone, and the horses had eaten his bones.

The fight was over, and the horses took Anthus.

I turned around. My husband was nowhere in sight. He left me to storm into this battle on my own. The nanny, and my daughter, had disappeared too. I'd never see them again.

I searched for my daughter, in vain. A mad finch twittered around me, but there was no sign of the girl who once was. It was as if the horses had staged a double attack.

I wished I could have done more, but at least I had tried to do something. My children were gone; all things came and went.

That's when Hera found me, and performed her metamorphoses upon me. I became the lark and I stayed in my fields. Eventually, my herd of horses died on fields with no grass. By the next season, these pastures were rich and bountiful once more, as if the blood of my son had nourished the earth.

Thus, I always thought I was cursed. I was born to lose everything—my son, my daughter, my marriage, my horses, my reputation. It was all destroyed.

Thoughts of my lost family never left me. They followed me across fields. I tried too hard to be their hero, to keep everyone alive. Gods and goddesses had their own wills. My family had been squelched out, and I was left as a lonely lark in Larissa.

Perseus was so sweet. I wondered, for a silly moment, if he was my son. If Anthus's blood had sunk into the Underworld, maybe he sprang up in the form of a budding hero. I sighed, wistfully, into the boy's ear.

If I turned into a bird, then why couldn't Anthus be reborn? Who was to say what the gods had in store? Perseus had the same crystalline blue eyes as Anthus.

Yes, I would take Perseus to the sea. I would take him as far as I could. He answered my question about heroes. He may have been a fool, but it didn't matter. The brave idea that we could do the impossible, is what made us heroes.

I was a hero for running in to save my son, even though I didn't win. Perseus was a hero too, because he sought a monster's head. He wished to keep his word. His hands, calloused by the labors of his youth, kept the promises he shook upon.

I flew in front of Perseus and darted forward with a song. I wanted to invite him to follow me. I wanted to tell him that he could trust me, that the sea beckoned on the edge of my wings.

Perseus understood.

I redirected our course, only by a few degrees, so we would've reached our destination faster. Perseus followed me in the grass, pushing apart the tall grasses in the same way a swimmer pushes aside water. He followed me for a long time, and we fell into a flow between his steps and the flaps of my wings.

I still imagined, as I led him towards the sea, that I was leading Anthus. In my mind, the Aegean beckoned him, for a baptisma, which he was never granted in his short life.

The sun fell from the pastel, purple sky. Breeze carried salt in the air. We were steps from the sea. I flew back to Perseus' shoulder with a sigh. I heard the nearby kiss of tides against the shore.

Hoofbeats stirred me. The unmistakable sound thundered from the beach. I shuddered in my feathers. I hoped that it wasn't my savage herd, returning from hell to finish me off. I curled into the crook of Perseus' neck.

"Don't worry, little lark," Perseus said, "It's only a few horses."

The boy stroked my feathers. I trusted him. I felt safe in the bosom of his neck.

We didn't know it yet, but they were far more than just horses.

Hoofs beat louder and louder. Perseus was unbothered, which helped my heart slow down. He was curious, in fact, about the horses. He reminded me of my children, before the curse fell over us and our horses went mad for blood. Children always had an affinity for horses.

Perseus, risking his life on a voyage to become a man, looked up and down the beach with a boyish gleam in his eye.

Alongside hoofbeats, I heard clanking metal and shouting men. That's when I realized these were not ordinary horses. At first, I suspected they were warhorses. It sounded like men riding in full armor. I thought, there must be some unrest, for cavalry to trot along my lowlands.

No... They were more than a troop of dragoons.

I peered over bristling, moonlit grass, and spotted them. I'd never encountered their kind before.

Horses raced on the beach before us, horses indeed. Yet, they were more than horses. From their withers burst half formed men. They ran across the beach, three gray-bodied horses, with each man wielding weapons. They had shields, and behind them, curved blades. Blades that were curved like the crescent moon were slick in battle. They could arch around the rim of a protective field, and strike.

They were like me, for I bore a feathered shield over my chest.

Only, as the kentauroi ran over the beach, they were not wearing shields over their chests, and they were not coordinating a strike.

The three kentauroi ran with hearts open to the wind. They held shields overhead, banging the handles of their blades against the metal like drums.

My head started to spin.

I heard the clanks of silver against bronze and iron against tin. It was a cacophony of frequencies, the sound of their wild drumming galloped across the beach like the horses themselves.

My heart beat in my chest, as if to mimic drumming hoofs. The horsemen ran alongside the sea, and echoed into my fears, back to the day that my son's blood spilt over the lowlands.

Their weapons glimmered. The sun was setting fast, casting its last golden rays upon them. Perseus turned to face the mysterious kentauroi. He was brave. He could have hidden in the tall grasses.

He stared at the kentauroi, and marveled at their otherworldly forms.

Perseus was a seeker. He wished to make his way across the sea, we were almost there, and I intuited that he hoped the kentauroi were there to help him. I peeked from the crook of his neck.

Three gray horses galloped between us and silver starlit waves. Both horses and the ocean moved with the same forces. I wondered if Poseidon animated these horses and if, like the sea, they were pulled by the moon.

The moon was a small crescent, a mere smirk of mischief, over the inky night. The sky was dappled as the horse's hides. As light was fading, clusters of constellations and splotches of empty night were unveiled in darkness. Each horse was gray, with splotches of white. Each had ornate patterns, like the down of my own feathers.

"Hey," Perseus shouted.

The beasts halted. They slid across the grainy sand, leaning back, and sighing.

The men held their plates over their chests and turned to face us. I hid my face beneath my wing. I hoped to blend in with Perseus' earthen tunic.

"Who goes there?" one of the kentauroi asked.

"I am Perseus," He stepped forward, "I mean you no harm. Look, I've got nothing here but a small rucksack. I must ask, if my eyes are deceiving me? Men, can you dismount your horses, I'm afraid I'm not seeing straight."

Laughter rolled off the kentauroi's tongues. I shivered and felt Perseus' skin prickle with anticipation.

"It's no trick, young man," a kentauroi said with a chuckle.

The three beastly men gathered around Perseus. They stood with their backs to the sea, and Perseus stood with his back to fields of grass. He was a boy grounded to the earth, tethered to the land, and pursuing the natural course of his life.

There was not enough sunlight to see their faces, to judge their intent. I peeked out from between my feathers, willing for them to favor Perseus.

"What brings you here, lad?" a kentauroi with kind gray eyes leaned down towards Perseus.

"I am on a quest," Perseus said and inhaled into his chest.

"A quest? Who are you— some kind of hero?"

"I suppose I am," Perseus stood tall, "I am seeking help in my journey. I seek to capture the head of Medousa."

That got their attention.

"Medousa?"

"Medousa, you say?"

"Yes, that's right," Perseus said, "I made a vow to Ovid to travel the sea and return with her head. The only trouble is I haven't got a—"

"How are you going to get her head? Why, she's a monster!"

"You're bound to get turned right into stone."

"How do you know about her?" Perseus asked.

"We came from Magnesia," a green-eyed kentauroi explained, "Every songbird in those woods sings about her, telling stories about Medousa and Hekate, the witch."

"We can hear the songs of birds, and also the words of men."

"Yes, Ovid's tall tales have reached our ears," an amber-eyed kentauroi explained, "Clearly Ovid's tales have also touched your heartstrings."

A chuckle rippled between the three man-horses. Who was more monstrous— horse or man? What could these men be hungry for? They had fields of treasured grasses, but did it satisfy their human hunger?

"I need your help," Perseus pleaded.

"Oh yeah?" a murky whisper in the dark.

"Why should we help you?" husky words from a man who wasn't fully man at all.

"I am seeking honor for the men who have fallen! For Orion, the greatest among us! For the innocent sailors who are trapped in stone beneath the sea!"

"What is it, lad, that you seek?" the green-eyed kentauroi begged to know.

"I need a boat!" Perseus piped, "And I need a blade!"

"You say you come bearing next to nothing. Well, what's that?" the green-eyed kentauroi asked.

He pointed towards me. I saw his finger looming in front of my vision. I lifted my crested head and warbled a song, right into his inquisitive face. Then I curled back up and nestled into the safety of Perseus' skin.

"Why that's a lark!" the green-eyed kentauroi exclaimed.

"What's the meaning of that?" the gray-eyed kentauroi asked.

"Can you not see that this is a crested lark?" he explained, "Did you see the feathers atop its head, and the flash of white over its chest? That flash of white is a shield! This bird is a warrior!"

"You call this bird brave, but look here! It's scared of us!" the gray-eyed kentauroi said.

They had voices like ordinary men, but wilder, huskier. There was a growl to their voices and an edge to their words. My heart beat rapidly.

"It's fate," the green-eyed kentauroi said, "It's a sign from the gods. To have a crested lark by his side, means this hero will succeed. It is a sign. We ought to help him."

The other two kentauroi shifted their weight. I heard sand loosen beneath their hooves.

Night fell fast. Moonlight gave the horsemen a silver glow.

At that moment, I realized that each kentauroi bore two hearts. One of a horse, and one of a man. I could hear their manly hearts racing, clamoring to unnerve Perseus, to comfort him, to understand him. Their equine heartbeats were smooth, and flowed in time with waves crashing towards the moon.

"This bird is not brave!" one kentauroi said to another, "Look! This is no symbol of a hero! That lark is hiding from us now."

I thought my heart may have bursted from my chest.

I unfurled my wings with a huff. I flew right before the kentauroi who accused me of cowardice, right before his storm-gray eyes. If I ran into a feeding frenzy, where my own son was ravaged in the middle, how could I shy away from anything else?

I flew before him and twittered, I promised that Perseus was true, that he could secure Medousa's head indeed.

"Well," the gray-eyed kentauroi admitted, "at least the bird believes in you."

"I say we help him," the green-eyed kentauroi suggested.

"Now, if we disagree and split up, our herd will become even smaller," the amber-eyed kentauroi said, "We're only three of us. We already broke from the rest of the kentauroi. Act with some sense, will you?"

"Destiny calls us to help this boy," the green-eyed kentauroi insisted.

He rolled his amber eyes, but it was so dark, and tensions were so high, I was sure none but me were able to see his silent act of defiance. I heard the whoosh of irritated horse tails.

"Boy, where did you say you were going?" asked the gray-eyed beast.

"Sarpedon. An island barren of life and hope. I must go into the sea, towards a whirlpool," Perseus pointed, "It lies under that star, the star of Algol."

"Let's just help him! What harm can it—"

"Enough! We can't help him!"

Their fighting ran each man in circles. Yet, they weren't running with their equine bodies. They weren't galloping, breathing, and pounding their spirits into the earth. It was much worse. They were running around in circles in their minds. They wished to catch each other, to make him see the way he was seeing.

"We're meant to help the boy!"

"Don't be a fool!"

Such a human-like squabble. They inherited the best and worst of the creatures that made them up. As they squabbled, the kentaurois glanced at Algol. For it was so dark, and they only had a few stars for light. On the beach, they aired their grievances with each other to the cosmos.

"You know not the meaning of a lark!"

"You—"

The debate was over, before any kentauroi could've gotten another word out.

The stars weighed in.

Golden streams rained down from Algol. They arched across the sky. It was like a dam had broken and a gushing flood of liquid gold rained over the heavens.

I looked from the sky to the three kentaurois. Moments ago, one kentauroi had green eyes, another gray, and another amber. Under that mystical sky, however, each beastly man had golden eyes.

"Golden rain…" the kentauroi mumbled. Where the ego of man was evident in his voice before, he sounded humbled. He sounded moved, like he could've stopped for a moment, and kissed the earth.

"Helping you will bring us good fortune."

"You will be a hero, Perseus."

All three of them, towering over Perseus, embraced him. I felt their chiseled armed brush against me, and I froze. I wished to fly away, to be gone of these men who were neither horses nor men. I was so scared, so relieved, so in awe of the heavens, that I could not move.

All was still for a somber, reflective moment.

Rain still fell in golden streaks, not wetting the earth, but burning the sky. I saw, as the shower went on, Algol disappeared. The star eclipsed, as if all its light had been poured out and dripped over Greece.

"Medousa is the daughter of Hekate," a kentauroi said, "We have stolen all alloys, ores, and minerals from the witch. There's not a stitch of metal left in her cottage. Go forth Perseus, steal the head of Medousa too!"

"Yes! Steal her head!"

"Your quest is our quest! The stars have asked us to help you!"

"Let me offer this to you," the gray-eyed kentauroi said, "If her gaze turns men to stone, then use this to outwit her."

There was a shrill twang.

I looked down. He offered Perseus a bronze mirror, which doubled as a shield. It laid at Perseus' feet.

It was more than an ordinary mirror, and I didn't need to be a pharmakis to know that.

Constellations had been thoughtfully carved into the rim. The carvings told a story. Hounds chased the stars around the edge of the mirror. Birds fluttered over seas and waves kissed their feathers. I could see the details clearly, for they were so sharp, even in the little moonlight that was available.

Perseus picked up the mirror, holding onto a makeshift handle that had been fashioned to its inside. The bronze was so reflective, so intricately connected to everything around it, that I heard Perseus' heartbeat reverberate from the spherical surface.

"If you're going to cut off her head," the green-eyed kentauroi chimed, "Then I will offer my silver blade."

He extended a scythe and Perseus reached for it.

I shivered deeper in my brittle bones. The blade mocked the small, silver crescent of moonlight hanging in the sky. It smirked up at me. It was the weapon of the moon, the collector of Demeter.

I wondered if my curse would follow me forevermore, if I would see Demeter anywhere there was an echo of her.

I swallowed. I allowed the sickle to be a part of the journey. I let go of my fear, as we all had to let go of something to come together on the beach.

"Our hero, now you have a weapon and shield."

"We will go now, to fell a tree."

"We will find the other kentaurois and commission their help. Surely they saw the golden rain. We will, at once, tell them what it means, and they will volunteer their hands and their hides for the task of making you a boat."

"Perseus wait here, where grain kisses the sea."

"We will work day and night to bring a small sailboat back to you!" a kentauroi shouted.

The trio was already running away. Their equine hearts did have agency, for when it came time to run, they gave it their all.

Hoofbeats thundered away, and for the first time in many moons, I did not wince at the sound.

Perseus sighed. He tousled a free hand through my feathers.

"Thank you," he whispered, but I couldn't tell if it was meant for me or the stars.

The boy laid down, onto the cool sand. He fell asleep with the heavens as his blanket. Stars looked down on him between vast empty spaces of sky. He had nothing, but the scythe, the mirror, the promise of a boat, and me. I watched over him as if he were my own son.

The boy dozed off, but I was sleepless, lost in similarities and synchronicities. I noticed Perseus' light, beige clothes catching on the night wind. His skin rippled with bumps. He was cold.

I got to work. I gathered grasses and quickly wove them together. Before the moon had moved a full degree in the sky, I had a blanket for Perseus. I sheltered him as if he were a fledgling in my nest or a child in my past life.

More than promises, and more than his new weapon, Perseus had a mission. He could never be stopped. He would lay his own life down before he quit, before he made ill of his word. That's why, I took him as a bird of my own feathers. I prayed that Perseus wouldn't end up like me, a failed hero.

The kentaurois did come back, and they did help the boy set off into the sea. His desire to cross over to Sarpedon never died.

I met Perseus as winter melted into spring. Before spring passed, news of his victory traveled to me, but not as a boy or a man.

Soon after he set sail, Perseus lit up the sky as a constellation.

By the time summer returned, sparks rained down from his stars.

Golden rain, like streaks of grass, or burning embers, showered across the sky. Perseus came to life on short summer nights, reminding me of his voyage through my lands.

21. Cuckoo

I lived in the walls of Sarpedon, between petrified faces of sailors. They gazed forever upon Poseidon, who betrayed them by leading them here in the first place. And they gazed at me, nesting atop their petrified faces. I watched over the tidepools every day.

I spotted a girl, Medousa, carrying Sarpedon's giant trident in her grasp. I noticed, as wind whipped her face, that she bore a scar across her neck. I wondered where it could have come from, and if she was destined to lose her head.

She darted across the labyrinth of stones and water. Curly hair bounced with her bounds. From above, I saw rocks burst from the head of Sarpedon like they were real, live constrictors stretching into the sea. Medousa, since she was in the maze herself, all she could see was her next step.

She moved with purpose.

Medousa was hunting, but I knew she was mistaken. Her purpose was channeled in all the wrong directions.

I watched Medousa ready her trident. She inhaled, honed her aim, and released her weapon.

Clank.

Three prongs struck rock. Medousa moved quickly to collect it. All the fish darted away from her, scared by her hasty mistake.

Poseidon tricked the airy eye. Every seabird, or cuckoo imposter, knew that Poseidon distorted our vision. In dealing with the ocean there was the real, and there was the reflected. It was easy to be misguided.

Medousa was learning that fish were never where they seemed. It was a mistake every young bird made when they learned to hunt in the sea. I saw her, days before, catch an octopus. It was much easier to catch an octopus, but the hard part was spotting them. They were normally as motionless as stone.

Fish were quick, and fled from her trident.

Somewhere, off in another tunnel, dolphins gossiped about Medousa trying her hand at hunting. I overheard their musings and chuckled to myself. Medousa was so much like a baby dolphin who fishes outswam, or a young bird with no experience. She balanced on the edge of flight.

I saw myself in her. You could say it was the way all cuckoos were forced to see themselves in others. It was part of our assimilation. I saw her as a cuckoo too, not raised by her own.

She'd clearly been set out into the world with a hungry mouth and nowhere to fly. Born in the wrong nest, just like me. There was something oceanic about her, there was a grace under her skin that I saw only in the waves.

I wondered why she had legs. Was she meant to be a sea nymph? I sensed she didn't have long in this realm. At any moment she would leap into a tidepool and merge with Poseidon.

As the sun fell, the ocean became wine-dark and my stony roost cooled.

I watched Medousa continue in the dimming light.

She had grit, there was no mistaking that.

Her tenacity, and desire to persist, reminded me of a tricky cuckoo too.

For it was in a cuckoo's blood to never give up. That very first cuckoo was able to trick Hera, and we all took after him. He never floundered from his trick, not until Hera was totally lovesick and fooled.

There was once a time when the Pharmakis of the Light Side of the Moon rejected all suitors. She stopped meeting with men who were looking to court her, and she hid herself away in Nephele's baths.

Hera's heart may have been closed off to men, but she couldn't turn away a cuckoo fledgling. The young bird was lost, somehow, amongst the clouds. Hera became enamored with his gray down, gold-rimmed eyes, and striped feathers. She nursed the fledgling as her own, and wished for the young bird to grow up healthy and strong.

As that original cuckoo fledgling grew, he did not turn into an adult bird. He grew into a man. By then, she couldn't turn him away. The bird had already wedged his way into her heart.

Hera was supposed to shed light on any illusion and expose the truth, but the cuckoo tricked her.

Each cuckoo followed the original. None of us were raised by our parents. We were all implants in random bird's nests. We mocked our way through life.

For, my own cuckoo mother had planted me into the nest of the mightiest seabirds, the ones whose feathers sprang sirens. Funnily enough, like those ospreys, my eyes shone gold. But the similarities stopped there.

Something innocent in the other osprey chicks was missing from my face. Though our eyes were the same color, there was an arch to my eyelid. It made me seem inquisitive.

Why don't you trust me? my expression begged. Always, cuckoos kept their secrets. As an imposter, I struggled to accept myself.

I shuddered. I huddled between dark magnetite rocks. The cracked stone face of a wayward sailor looked up at me. I wondered if his soul could still see me, a bird with no eggs, nesting on his terrified, frozen expression.

Medousa continued to pillage the tidepool, or at least, tried her very best.

I wondered where Medousa hatched. I felt a chill over my feather-light bones. Shivers nestled me closer to the rock, towards the stillness of the fallen sailors, while I watched her dancing in the waves.

The sun started to set. Failure after failure taught her the trick of water. I watched until her hair stopped glowing and she became a silhouette. Medousa howled. She bellowed over the waves.

She wanted more than food.

She wanted glory. She wanted to understand the trick of the water.

Suddenly Medousa sank low over the tidepools. She bent her knees. I felt like I was watching a lioness press her hungry heart against the earth. There was a ferocity in Medousa, which was something I could appreciate from the safety of my misfit nest.

I saw three fins crest out of the sea. Medousa struck. She made a hit, an alignment between prey, predator, and a setting red sun.

Medousa raised the trident from the water. One fish on each prong squirmed against her weapon. They wriggled until their bodies became stiff, then three souls rushed from their bodies, back to the ocean.

Their blood dripped into the Aegean sea. I witnessed her transfiguration from golden-haired maiden to sea-huntress, but I wasn't alone.

When blood spilled in the sea, it never went unmissed. Blood attracted beasts.

I saw a bronze and silver shimmer in the water. I caught sight of two bone-white eyes staring at Medousa. I wondered if it was a sea nymph, a cormorant, or maybe the ghost of one.

It disappeared before I got a better look.

Medousa walked back, oblivious to all but her catch.

The fish's blood ran down the trident like rivulets, searching for the ocean. She stepped over the stones, towards the hive, and fish blood pooled behind her. It was a slow trickle, until her trail across the tidepools was perfectly clear. I saw little streaks of red blood over the dark tidepools, blotting the water, and marking her path.

The sun fell beneath the horizon. In a slow moment, the sky shifted from roaring red to dark purple. Medousa moved through the tones. Her hair became muted. Her skin blushed with bruises from racing across stones.

"Are you blindfolded, sisters?" Medousa called towards the cave.

I heard a rustle.

With closed eyes, I listened.

"Medousa," a gorgones' voice said with a hiss, "You have killed fish."

"It was easy," Medousa laughed, and I laughed too. After all, tricksters were destined to lie.

Stars shimmered in arcs across the sky. Algol reappeared, since it vanished the night before. A smirking crescent moon materialized in the night. As the world darkened and constellations burned, I began to wonder, if myths danced like shadows over the tidepools.

The sound of rustling scales drifted through the air. I sighed and listened.

I heard, in darkness, the gorgones hiss and coo over Medousa's kill.

One of them said, "She's ready to go deep."

"I am?" Medousa asked.

I fell asleep wondering if Medousa was fit for the sea or the stars.

22. Cormorant

Silver flashed before me. Each scale luminesced like the moon, pearly and pewter.

I chased a school, trying to isolate one of its fish. I used my long neck to navigate water and change directions as rapidly as my prey. They could swim in any direction, but somehow they always swam together, like stars bound by constellations, schooling side-by-side, night-after-night.

One fish finally relented and lagged behind the rest. I was about to snatch it, but something caught my eye.

Gold floated on the surface. I stopped midwater. My webbed feet acted as rudders and my wings as brakes. Water rushed against my feathers as I slowed down.

The flaxen sparkle was so unlike all the silver fish in the sea.

First I spotted the trident. It normally rested at the peak of Sarpedon. I lived in its eternal shadow and never left. When I stared at it directly, it nearly blinded me for its golden brightness.

The trident wasn't alone. A girl held onto it. She floated on the surface. I noticed that her fingers were too short to wrap around the shaft.

It was Medousa. Her hair melted into the sea like gold on a forge. Her eyes were closed and bubbles escaped from her lips. Medousa exhaled, slowly, face-first into the water. Then she looked up and sipped air to inhale.

As she moved, I saw a bronze chain and a key hanging from her neck. Snakes and feathers decorated the key. It reached downwards, below the girl, and towards the Underworld. My gaze caught on her neck, where a thin slit wandered over her skin. I wondered what blade may have delivered the damage, and I wondered how she survived such a blow. I shivered. Medousa's dark robes floated around her like she was hiding in her own shadow.

I watched Medousa for too long. I'd been mesmerized. Suddenly, I remembered, I had to breathe. My body tensed, begging for air. I had to go up. I had no choice. My lungs forced me.

I turned to rush towards the blue sky from the dark, deep sea. Suddenly, I was about to run into Medousa.

I looked quickly. I spotted the two gorgones treading water. Well, they didn't need to tread. They hovered, floating without effort, without holding their breaths. They were immaterial. Sunlight pierced through their misty bodies and into the sea. Their skin was as silver as a mackerel's scales. The gorgones were made of ephemeral mist, not blood and flesh. Nonetheless, my heart thudded in my chest.

Not even the gorgones' snakes noticed me. I was like a shadow of the ocean below them. My body shook for breath. Both gorgones flattened their immaterial, misty wings over the ocean.

Skillfully, swiftly, I darted around Medousa, away from the gorgones. I had control in the water. Us cormorants were gifted with the ability to navigate water as well as air.

I stuck only my beak out of the water. My lungs gasped. My beak surfaced, but my eyes stayed submerged under the veil of Poseidon.

I was safe. I kept my eyes under the water, even as the swell rose and fell. Waves rocked my dark, feathered body. Some said I looked like a vulture, who took to the water. In my heart that was never true, for I showed mercy, and I avoided war.

The gorgones watched Medousa. Her back was to them, so she was safe, but I imagined her turning into dark stone, and sinking into the depths. The gorgones didn't notice me next to Medousa. Their white eyes, void of all life, stayed on the girl. Still I was safe, seeing them through the ocean rather than forthright.

I knew the gorgones lived in the center of the kharybdis. That's why I lived in the tunnels near the trenches, it was easy to avoid deadly eyes. I swam far away whenever they came here. Usually I heard the gorgones before I saw them— their tangled scales, slithering bronze breath, or clicking seashell adornments. However, I was so busy underwater, so taken by Medousa, the gorgones caught me by surprise.

Medousa breathed and floated, over the ocean like a bird in the sky. Her shadow cast into the water, where it obscured the shallows, and then dispersed seamlessly into the deep.

She relaxed, like she was sunbathing in a soft meadow. I imagined her golden hair feathering out into grass, like it splayed in the sea. Her body rolled with the waves of Poseidon and the tides of her breath.

Waves rocked Medousa. She surrendered to them, but her trident crested the water. Her pronged, golden staff was light in defiance of the water's heaviness. It floated so much that I wondered, had Medousa thrown her trident into the sky, if it would've floated away.

As breath filled Medousa's lungs, she leaned forwards. Her legs rose over her torso and pushed her under the surface of the sea. She held the trident and kicked her legs.

As she disappeared, I noticed Sthenno and Euryale covering their eyes with blindfolds.

I sighed.

If they weren't going to follow her down, then it was up to me. I closed my eyes and took a breath. I moved with a coming wave, rising and falling into the ocean.

Medousa was sinking when I noticed a shimmering blue rune on her ankle. It was a snake, wrapping around her ankle. The snake didn't seem like a scar, like the one draped over her neck. It glowed, like she had been branded by stars.

I followed Medousa, swimming above her, like an angel in her wake. I paddled my webbed feet together, and as I made each stroke, my entire body undulated. I moved through the water like a sea nymph, or a wave itself.

Grooves in the trench snaked around us. Stones came to life before my eyes, but I knew, no matter how real they appeared, they were frozen forever in time and fear.

Medousa kicked her bare feet, like I paddled my webbed toes. Soon we were so deep the light became scarce. We swam in the shadow of Sarpedon. Medousa swam past silver schools of breams. Though she didn't see it, an octopus eyed her from the craggy rocks. Shadows of dolphins loomed in the water around us. A gentle current pulled us around the island as we sank deeper along the underwater precipice.

After each stroke of Medousa's legs, she let herself sink. Those who traveled the deepest did so with minimum effort. She was like me, and every cormorant in the Aegean before me, because Medousa melted into the ocean.

Her golden trident illuminated rocks around us. It was like a torch. It illuminated the swishing silver tails of schools swimming away from us.

Suddenly her trident started to sink. Medousa lurched down. There was something witchy about that trident. I wondered if it had been wrought with levity— with a spell that backfired in the deep. It pulled Medousa rapidly deeper. I followed with haste. In the cliff, faces looked back at us as if to mimic our terror, and others were unseeing, eroded by Poseidon.

We reached the bottom of the shelf and I flapped open my wings. There was so little sunlight, the trident had almost nothing to reflect. It was no longer like a torch, but more like smoldering ash.

Dark rocks blended into the wine-dark depths.

Medousa landed against the seafloor. Her stomach trembled for air. I watched her quake. I also felt a longing for air, but I had deeper urges. I wished to see why she had come here, and if she would need my help.

Silver scales flashed in front of the trident. Medousa didn't hesitate. She quickly launched her weapon through the water.

The fish was too fast and the trident was too heavy. The trident scraped its scales, there was a small spurt of blood, and it disappeared into the darkness.

Medousa recovered her trident as it clanked against the seafloor. Silver appeared in the dark water, and I thought the fish had returned.

It wasn't the fish.

A sea nymph looked at me. She had the milky white face of Medousa, but her skin was formless. It had a ghostly iridescence, like the shady gorgones who waited for Medousa up on the surface.

I looked into the mermaid's blanched eyes. I felt my heart shudder. I felt the silence of Poseidon's deep sea in my ears.

The sea nymph's bronze tail surged through the water and wrapped around Medousa. The shrill whine of metal scales scraping against each other pulsed through the ocean. Medousa tugged on her trident, but the sea nymph, who wore bronze gloves like the gorgones floating above, tried to win over the weapon. I heard the click of her metallic fingers against gold. Watching the sea nymph and Medousa fight was strange. The misty sea nymph appeared like a twisted version of Medousa who crawled out of a wicked mirror.

The mermaid didn't only remind me of Medousa. She reminded me of the soul beneath my own feathers, for in the heart of every cormorant was a nymph bound for the sea.

In the same shadow of Sarpedon, where the silver sea nymph

blended into dark water, I had once metamorphosed. The very same shadows which hid her once hid my own transformation.

It was many moons ago, when there were far less stars in the sky. I watched the seas spin. Winds pulled weary sailors to these rocks. I tried not to watch as they sailed towards Sarpedon. I tried not to become emotional as they neared their demise.

Until one day when I saw stars in the sailors' eyes. My heart broke. I imagined their vibrant eyes freezing into dark stones. *Was it an unchangeable fate?*

As they approached, angry tempests filled their sails. I wondered if they had a chance to turn around at all.

I didn't want to see. I didn't want to watch them float through the misty tunnels, towards the gorgones who would turn innocent men to stone.

I escaped underwater. I swam deep into the sea, into the same nook, in the same dark trench where Medousa battled for her golden trident.

I lost my feathers for flesh and I grew a tail. It wasn't bronze, but rather, I had true scales. I changed into an organic sea nymph, not metal and mist. My tail shimmered green like leviathans who circled the seas.

I realized then, that perhaps as a sea nymph, I might distract the men in the ship and throw their course.

My emerald tail propelled me towards the sky. The tail was the exact color of the dark sheen that came off my feathers when the sun hit me.

I surfaced in front of the bow. I was sure that the men saw my torso. They must have taken me as a woman, lost in the sea.

Of course, they would help. Chivalry was in their very nature. I watched them work together to steer against the currents. Their ship veered in my direction. I heard them shout, but most of their words were lost to the sea. One word, *Ulysses*, carried over the waves.

I swam in a leeward direction. I swam in a way so they could channel the energy of the tempests in the air, but move their boat towards me. We moved in a gradual arc, turning away from Sarpedon.

They followed me into the far ocean, where the winds died down. I sent them on their way in a safer direction, then I dived down and disappeared into the deep. As I swam back to Sarpedon, my feathers grew back and my body shrank. As Ulysses' ship sailed towards land, I turned around, to once again inhabit Sarpedon.

In the shadow of the same dark rocks, Medousa struggled for her trident. I could tell she needed to breathe. Even in the golden light reflected from the trident, and the golden light from her hair, Medousa's lips started to turn blue.

Medousa let go. She surrendered. The misty, metal mermaid disappeared, trident in hand. Medousa kicked off the seafloor.

At that moment, I heard crashing waves above us still. The kharybdis had stopped spinning.

Medousa moved frantically. She was not being judicious to conserve air. She panicked. Her spine curved, sporadically, as she swam. She quivered like an arrow through the sky. Her body was begging for air.

Medousa was too deep. She needed to breathe.

As we darted towards the surface, I swear, below us, from the dark water, I heard a hiss. I felt a warning crawl up my spine and push me to the surface.

The sun, steady as always, became brighter as we climbed through deep water.

The sun was always there, but the trident would never glow over Sarpedon again. It was lost to the deep, and the kharybdis was still. Ever since I was a young bird, currents had their way around Sarpedon, curving along the rocks. Mysteriously, when the trident traded hands, the currents were gone.

Suddenly, I noticed that Medousa strayed behind me. I looked back and she was held against a rock. The bronze chain from her neck looped around an outcropping. It caught the nose of a long-passed sailor. Medousa tried to go up, but she was stuck. I saw the bronze chain dig into her scar. The chain rubbed open her wound and a thin veil of blood cloaked the water. It tethered her to the rock, to the realm where she could never breathe.

Midway up the cliff, I had to turn back. I wondered what curse Medousa suffered, and what fate laid ahead of her. She seemed at odds with an unlucky god. I whipped around to free her.

My beak, hooked like a warship, nudged her chain from the stone. I set Medousa free. Her green eyes squinted through salt.

Medousa kicked, but there was something off in her movements. It wasn't the same fluid girl who had swam her way down. She twitched. Her body became limp and breath leaked from her lips.

I feared that at that moment Medousa couldn't feel anything. I swam to her, and hooked my wing under her arm. She felt weightless against me. It was easy to bring her up.

I carried Medousa— empty handed and barely alive— back to air.

Medousa broke the surface, but still she did not breathe. She was somewhere else, somewhere where she hadn't yet realized that she could breathe, that she had survived the dive.

On the surface I felt immediately disoriented. I struggled to hold Medousa up as my mind whirred. I'd grown used to the perpetual wail of the kharybdis and the haunting moans of tempests. Winds ceased and the ocean was like glass.

"Medousa?" a whisper from bronze lips.

"Have you returned?" a gorgones asked.

I darted back below, into the shadows of the sea. Surely they would lower their blindfolds. I didn't want to hear the gorgones' metallic gasps when they saw Medousa, sleeping on the surface.

23. Raven

"It's quiet," a metallic whisper carried over the water. Sthenno's voice whistled into my stony ears.

"Too quiet…" Euryale mused.

"Where have the tempests gone?" Sthenno asked.

"Perhaps they're resting," Euryale suggested.

"Sister, I do not even hear the sea churning," Sthenno said.

If I was still made of flesh, I would have winced. Her bronze lips whistled so sharply over the 's' in her words, that I wanted to flinch. But I couldn't flinch anymore– not since I looked that very gorgones in the eye. I never did much of anything anymore, but watch.

I'd been cast aside from the living world.

The gorgones couldn't see through their blindfolds, but I saw the surface of the ocean. It was unusually calm. The waves simply died and collapsed into each other. For the first time since I became trapped in stone, wind stopped caressing my solid feathers.

I wondered how strange it was that tempests stopped whirring, all while Medousa was underwater.

I wondered what happened between her breaths.

Then, I saw a ripple. A bubble, an exhale from Medousa reached the surface.

"What was that?" Sthenno asked.

"Shh!" Euryale said.

The water broke. Medousa surfaced. Her lips had turned blue, and the scar which draped over her neck trickled with fresh blood. I caught sight of a cormorant's tail. He must have helped Medousa surface, but wished to avoid any deadly eyes.

I didn't blame him. How could I?

If I was alive, I would've cawed to tell the gorgones what made the noise, that Medousa needed their help.

"Medousa?" a whisper from bronze lips.

"Have you returned?"

Medousa couldn't answer. She was frozen in a trance, put to sleep by the water. She was as silent as me, who had been turned to stone. She floated wordless on the surface. Her breath didn't come, and it didn't go.

I loved hearing the breath of dolphins, and the balance between their inhales and exhales. I missed breathing like that. However, I resented the gorgones. They inhaled but never exhaled, for they had lips with no lungs. Every breath they drew dissipated across their misty form. The stars told me their secrets. Bronze lips failed underwater. Sthenno and Euryale floated on the surface, and I knew they couldn't go deeper. They were shades who couldn't fit in with the rest of the dead.

I imagined that both gorgones were jealous of Medousa for the width of her breath.

They could never exhale, never let go.

At that moment they worried about the girl. They dared not pull down their blindfolds and risk turning her to stone.

Medousa opened her eyes at last. I heard her heartbeat quiver and restore itself. She inhaled with a gasp. I heard a rattle in her breath. In one fluid movement, her green eyes opened, and she crawled from the sea, onto the stony surface of Sarpedon.

The gorgones fawned over her, as soon as they heard her breaching breath. They rushed over the surface of the glassy water, and reached for her, seeing only the backs of their blindfolds. The gorgones rubbed their bronze fingers over Medousa's cheeks, as her breath rattled. Their blindfolds had a reddish shimmer in the sunlight.

Broken-up stones cradled the girl and the gorgones kneeling beside her.

Medousa's lips got their blood back and flushed to pink, but the gorgones couldn't see. Their eyes were covered, of course, to protect Medousa.

"Medousa, what happened?" Sthenno's words were frantic.

"Sister, are you hurt?" Euryale asked.

Medousa coughed and a wave purged from her mouth. She coughed again and waves kept coming. She gasped before each flood left her lips.

Eventually Medousa was free. Her breath lost its rattle.

She inhaled, clearly, and said, "I'm not hurt."

Both of the gorgones were worried about Medousa, so it wasn't until she was breathing, speaking, and safe that they noticed something was missing — something of theirs.

"Sister… Where's our trident?" Sthenno asked, reaching for Medousa's empty hand.

Medousa's green eyes looked between her sisters' blindfolds.

"It was stolen," Medousa admitted. I watched blood trickle down her neck, over dark stones, and into the sea.

"Stolen?" Euryale's face contorted with rage. I watched her bronze fingers twitch, like she was about to pull down her blindfold, but immediately thought better of it and continued, "Who? Who stole our trident?"

"I-I-" Medousa could not speak. She bent forwards and wailed. It shook the stones like thunder.

"Medousa, you need to rest," Sthenno said.

"Rest? Are you mad? Medousa will not rest until she goes down and gets our trident!" Euryale said while her voice bounded up to a scream.

"Leave the girl alone," Sthenno insisted.

"She's a traitor," Euryale said, "She handed our trident over to Poseidon. Look around you! Our kharybdis has stopped spinning!"

"Ignore her. You have gone very deep," Sthenno said, stroking Medousa with bronze hands.

"Come to your senses Sthenno! How do we know she hasn't hidden it down there? She's saving the trident for herself," Euryale stood and crossed her arms.

"It's not true!" Medousa said with tears welling in her eyes. They were green, not like the grass of a soft meadow, but like the depths of a stormy sea, "The trident was stolen. Besides, it stopped floating. It sank. That damned trident is the reason I went so deep."

"Do not curse our tri—" Euryale started, but she stopped speaking.

A booming splash resounded over the ocean. Medousa, on her back skyward, couldn't even see the splash. Of course, neither could the gorgones.

Only I saw the splash which silenced them.

It was the thief, a silver and bronze sea nymph, leaping over the sea like a dolphin. The trident glittered in her grasp.

Sunlight struck the shade, right down to her iridescent bones.

Euryale was breathless, wordless, beside Sthenno. Both gorgones harbored suspicions about the splash. They stepped, in unison, over Medousa, towards the horizon.

With Medousa at their backs, both gorgones lowered their blindfolds.

The sea nymph leapt from the water again and I heard the gorgones' sharp inhales.

The shade knew, somehow, to keep her eyes closed as she leapt through the air. I wondered if Poseidon's whispers told her who she had stolen from, how to protect herself, and the best way to mock them.

"Hold on," Euryale paused over her words, "She looks familiar. That sea nymph happened to have Medousa's face…"

"She looks like you. Didn't you see her bronze hands?"

"Not quite. It's her hair," Sthenno said, "Didn't you see her curls? Euryale, don't be tricked by silver and bronze. That's Medousa! It's her shade!"

A dawn of recognition passed over Sthenno. She let out a small hiss, which sounded much like an audible withdrawal of hope.

"She passed the trident onto herself," Sthenno stated in a humbled whisper.

"I told you so," Euryale said.

Medousa crawled back onto the rocks and closed her eyes. Tears brimmed on her lashes.

"We let you use our trident to hunt— to satiate your mortal hunger," Sthenno said.

"You took what we gave you, and ruined it," Euryale finished.

"You were colluding with a shade!"

"Your own shade!"

"What? That wasn't me! I'm right here," Medousa said.

"You're a pharmakis— just like Hekate. We'll never trust you."

"We both saw your shade! That was your own dark soul, running free with our trident into the shadows of Poseidon."

"I have no idea what you're talking about. I never wanted to—" Medousa pleaded.

"Liar!" Euryale cut her off. Both of the gorgones were standing over Medousa. Neither of them wore their blindfolds, but Medousa didn't open her eyes. Sunlight pierced through the gorgones misty wings, their ethereal bodies, down onto Medousa curled on the ground.

"Goodbye Medousa," Sthenno said.

"You're not welcome in Sarpedon anymore," Euryale added.

"Stay in these tidepools. Live here, on the edge of this ocean you colluded with," Sthenno spat into the flat water.

"Come any closer, and we'll turn you to stone."

"We cannot trust you."

"You belong to the kharybdis now"

Both gorgones unfurled their misty wings and launched themselves into the air, and I heard the scrape of bronze-threaded slippers leaving the earth. They charged deeper inward towards the center of their stony labyrinth. I always felt jealous when they flew overhead. Their misty wings were silent as my stony pair.

The gorgones flew away from my sight. I could only see Medousa, perched on a stone outcrop. Her toes tipped into the ocean. A tear rolled down her cheek.

I couldn't believe they betrayed her. They knew as well as I did, that tides were coming in.

Medousa was exiled to sleep in rising water by women who never slept for one night in their deadened lives.

Even though we were separated by water and air, life and death, my frozen heart ached at the sight of her tears falling from her green eyes. They were like dew on grass. The lapping tides came in, and as Medousa's eyes streamed with pearly tears, my eyes fell under the surface of the water.

My frozen body submerged with every rising tide. I was used to ebb and flow, stuck forever between air and sea. My mind and eye had been taken over by Poseidon.

Medousa howled in anguish.

Laughs rained down from the sky on bronze lips. I knew the gorgones were above. I heard fury and jealousy in their laughter, though I could not look up to see them.

Medousa sat upright. She choked back a sob and closed her eyes. Her face was wet with tears, like the Nile's seven-streamed delta, coursing towards her jaw.

Splash.

It wasn't a ripple from Medousa's tears. They hadn't yet crested the edge of her face. Something fell from above, from the sky.

There was a shrill bang in the water. Bubbles foamed before me. I couldn't see through the effervescence to see what fell, and for a moment, I wondered if another bird had turned to stone.

"We're not thieves," Sthenno said.

"Right! We're not like you."

"We ought to give you back your goods, *sister*!" Sthenno called from the sky.

Medousa was frozen, sitting upright, with her eyes closed. Her heart thudded, climbing towards her bleeding throat.

"We'd rather not be haunted by you," Euryale laughed.

"Or any of your faces. How many do you have anyway?" Sthenno mocked.

I heard the gorgones' chatter carry towards the labyrinth in which they lived.

The water stilled. I finally saw what the gorgones delivered to Medousa.

It looked like Medousa's face, like the sea nymph, but bronze. A reddish gleam coated the mask, except for its eyes. They were white like the stony gaze of the gorgones who killed me, like hot flashes of lightning from the sky.

I realized that this mask was like no other— it could kill. I realized that, maybe, the gorgones dropped the mask off here with malicious intent. They expected Medousa to fall beside me. They expected her heart, her lungs, and her soft skin to harden.

I looked at the mask and studied its details. The mask's cheeks blushed ruby in the light of the sun. Snakes sprouted from the bronze face, like the hair of a gorgones. They shimmered in the sea like they were alive. Wings sprang from the mask's temples. Its feathers were so intricate, I wondered if a real dove had been gilded. They reached outwards, opening the mind of the mask.

But those eyes— those eyes never changed from deadly white. That's how I knew, like only a frozen soul recognized, that the mask was deadly.

Medousa sighed, a long hefty breath, and laid flat on her stomach. She reached into the tidepool with eyes clamped shut.

She reached into the dark, blind unknown. Her hand slipped underwater. In those moments, I supposed that suspense and fear distanced her from her pain. Teardrops stalled on her face.

I watched her blindly fumble through the tidepool for the mask. She reached past stones. They each had their own lives, some of them probably watched her, just like me, from a corner of their trapped souls.

The snakes were cast from bronze, and they weren't real. They couldn't bite her any more than me. However, I could tell her mind was playing a trick on her. I could feel her fear. Her heart, beating against dense rock and reverberating into the sea, drummed like it was inside my own frozen ears.

Fear crinkled her face.

I said a silent prayer, thankful I had been frozen with both eyes open, thankful I could see what happened, and that my mind couldn't trick me like hers.

Medousa inched forward and her fingers finally touched the bronze.

I heard her gasp— not from the surprise of finding a metal mask. She knew it was there, but it was finally reaching it which startled her.

Medousa lifted her mask from the sea. She opened her eyes, but it didn't kill her. Her eyes were so full of tears, no gorgones gaze could reach them. She opened her eyes, seeking to be frozen, but she was protected by her own pain.

"A monster indeed," Medousa said. Her green eyes took in every feature of the bronze, though it must have been warped by her tears. It must have been warped by the same forces of Poseidon that distorted my view of her, as I watched her from below the water's surface. I watched her fingers trace scales and feathers.

It may have been possible that the deadly gaze of the mask had warped Medousa's tears too. For when they fell, they weren't ordinary tears.

They weren't like anything Greece had ever seen.

Medousa took a deep, steadying breath, and her tears retreated. She placed her mask on the stone. Then, with free hands, she started to rip apart her robes. I watched her muscles tense and her body shake as she pulled apart fabric. Eventually threads loosened, and Medousa had a sheet. She closed her eyes and wrapped the mask. I watched her crawl over the rocks and set the mask as high as she could reach on a craggy cliff, atop a murder of frozen crows.

Then she sat down and opened her eyes. A sob echoed from her chest.

The teardrops which protected her from the mask, from her own white, deadly gaze, streamed down her face. They fell from her jaw, ran down her neck, and rolled all the way into the sea. They fell in the same way seafoam wafts off of waves.

I didn't know it then, but in that moment, her teardrops served as seeds.

When her teardrops hit the surface of the water, they bursted into smoke. Fumes swirled over the tidepool. The smoke became solid, living, and green. It sprouted stems and leaves. They were such a deep shade of hunter green, I wondered at first if I was imagining something. Sarpedon was not a green island. The only green I'd ever seen here was in the pools of Medousa's eyes.

Roots came to life underwater. I watched them snake through the tidepool. They were pure black, dark as the abyss. I shivered. I remembered forests of black poplar back on the mainland. Not even black polars were as dark as the roots of Medousa's tears. Roots were normally brown, never black as coal.

The roots were black like the rage of Medousa. This botanical property of the plant itself was like a bad omen towards Poseidon. She scorned the powers of the sea, she must have, for she was feeling the wrath of injustice. I knew that her twisted tears wanted to poison Poseidon with those black roots.

Somehow the mysterious plants could lap up saltwater and thrive in the wind. They grew above me and around Medousa. Sarpedon, in a matter of minutes, transformed from a desolate gray island into a lush meadow.

The plant matricized through the tidepool, filling the sea with writhing black roots. I could still see Medousa through the tangles of knots. She was crying, sobbing, so hard I wondered if she even understood what was going on. Her pain brought the island to life.

I knew what birthed this plant, because more than anything else, all ravens understood wrath. This familiarity was not because it was an emotion of our own, but an emotion that had been thrust upon us.

In black roots, I saw my past. I saw a flash of living raven's wings. In those black roots, I saw the swiftness of the night. I saw a dark edge, the burnt ashes of a scorned lover.

Turning to stone was not my first transformation.

Before I was a black bird, I was white as snow.

I was the messenger of the gods. I soared between all the peaks of Greece and relayed gossip between gods. I had white feathers for eons; I had them before any of Hera's pure white peacocks made it to these shores.

It was Apollo who scorched me.

I brought him a message, and I suppose, that it was a message he did not want to hear.

Apollo's face contorted with rage. He flinched at my caws. He turned me, and every raven in Greece black. He burnt one of us, and so he burnt all of us. We all felt the pain of the fire, the depth of his rage.

Our feathers were plated with ashes.

Those roots were dark omens. All roots searched for water, which is what Medousa feared the most. The black feet of the plant sought to curse Poseidon, and make him feel her wrath. I could recognize any dark omen, because I'd been transformed into one.

Medousa's duty, through shedding her tears, was to poison Poseidon. It was like Apollo who tried his best to poison me. The plant would wage revenge through darkness, wherever it met water.

Medousa looked around, tears still rolling down her cheeks. I could hear the roots splashing in the water and saw stems snaking towards the sky.

As the day went on, white flowers erupted from the tip of each stem. Pale buttercups blossomed and drooped. The buttercups looked down with sweet nodding heads. It was like they were looking at the sea and the stones. The flower, so lucid, yet grounded, called the sturdy stem to arc towards the earth.

I watched them with awe. I'd been petrified in Sarpedon for so long, I forgot about the beauty of a flower.

Those white flowers dotted the land like stars dotted the sky. They aged quickly and fell into the sea, where their pollen dissolved alongside salt. Others sprouted in their place. It was a perpetual bloom.

I flew, and nobody, not even Hera in the clouds could see me. I was invisible, like the wind which never touched the waves, but sculpted them from above.

I never thought I'd fly again, but when the black-footed buttercups came into my senses, my wings suppled. I flew as far away from the ghastly island of Sarpedon as I could.

Or at least I thought that was happening, until my stony body grew used to the effects of the black-footed buttercup, and I found myself petrified once more.

24. Quail

While winter melted into spring, I heard the night sky sing down to me in a celestial chorus. The dark abyss behind the stars taunted, teased, and played. It saw everything. The dark sky promised there was something going on, something it knew I would want to witness for myself.

It whispered stories of a girl, *Medousa,* who was about to slip into another realm.

The night sky had my attention, for I'd been waiting to cross paths with Medousa.

I stretched my wings, set my eyes on the blue horizon, and flew away from Delos. There were no winds, and the sea was peculiarly still. I flew quickly in the quiet night.

I flew towards the star of Algol.

This wasn't the first time the night sky sang to me. The sky told me to uproot, to venture out into the sea before. I wasn't a bird, but a girl back then.

It was a long time ago. The sky was younger, and no stars shone in the night. I remember nights with no stars, only a lonely moon. While I didn't cast the stars myself, I bore the witch who burned them.

I had fallen into good graces with Hera, who at the time, resided at the peak of Mount Pelion. She carried me there, upon a cloud, to live in the peak's golden light. Days on the mountainside were rich, but the nights were dark.

In those dark nights, I took a lover.

At first, he was like a beacon of light to me. But I was mortal, and he was not. Life stretched to infinity before him. I was a flash, too short-lived for him to commit to, and there was much beyond me for him to care about. He quickly moved on and found someone new.

He left me with scorn in my heart.

My heart broke, and I had no idea how to move on. I wished, more than anything, to flee the mountain. I simmered with jealous rage. For there was a man, whom I had loved, but he loved another. He betrayed me down to my bones. I wished to leave him, leave Pelion, so he could be a flash in my mortal past.

I wept in secret, without his shoulder for my tears. I cried over marble statues. I cried to stone and I cried in deep, personal ruin. I itched to crawl out of my skin.

There was something calling to me, over the sea. I needed to chase it. I didn't know how. All I heard was Poseidon, where he met the dark sky in the night, calling to me. I had to go.

I hardly knew how to make my way down the mountain. The cliffs were tall, steep, and at the time there was no trail. The ocean was so far away, I could not see it, but I could feel it. Crashing waves rioted against the chambers in my heart. I longed to fly free. I wanted to leap into the sky.

Every fiber in my being said, go to the ocean.

I didn't know how. The mountain was craggy and rigid. I was scared to walk down, for the boulders were loose. I was scared to plummet down a cliff like stones underfoot.

Instead, I looked to the sky. I prayed to transform. I asked Hera to hear my cries. Since she had brought me here, I asked if she might be able to find me a way out.

I fell to my knees. I prayed to leave behind the man who brought me shame, I prayed to be reborn, and start a new life.

For souls who are pushed down long to rise. They long to fly free. I watched finches flitter through the air around me. I curled my human knees towards my chest.

It was dark.

On that fateful night, there was no moon. I prayed in darkness from the crown of Mount Pelion.

Though my lover was gone from my heart, he left his seed in my ripe body. I bore his fruit. I was pregnant. The child would be taken care of, on my own. I had to get away. How could I find my way off the mountain?

Help me.

Oh, I was desperate.

I had to leave. I had to get down the mountain. My heart strained for the sea, deeper than it had ached for any lover. But there was no way for me to get to shore.

It felt like the baby growing in me heard the calls of the dark night, too. She demanded I get down the mountain. She wished to be born at sea.

I had to have saltwater in my lungs. The mountain air was too thin, and I was too forlorn for hillsides. I needed waves. I needed to move.

The night sky wasn't speaking in whispers, it was screaming.

Go to the sea.

Hera appeared before me. Her fingers were knotted together in a solemn stance. Her amber eyes scanned me, not with kindness, but with justice. She sensed a wrong had to be made right.

"You wish to flee Pelion?" Hera asked.

Her brow arched.

A stork stirred on the mountain below me.

"You're with child," Hera's expression lit up.

I nodded. Hera knew things I had never told her. She was always like that, peering into the inner crevices of my mind with a moment's glance.

"You must head into the sea. Only there will you find the right home for your child."

"How?" I asked Hera.

"You will have to give up your humanity," Hera said. She looked me up and down, but I didn't flinch.

"Very well..."

Hera's eyes looked straight into mine. I fell into them like a vat of precious honey. Mount Pelion disappeared.

I felt a transformation bubble over my skin. It rained down from my skull, like hot blood, and tickled my every pore. My hair morphed into a feathered crest. My tunic became streaked wings.

Hera transformed me into a quail.

"Do as the sky tells you to do," those were Hera's parting words for me.

Before she finished speaking, I had sprung into the air. My newfound wings took flight, and I hurled myself towards the sea. Wind ruffled my feathers and tousled the waves.

With a new moon, and no stars, the ocean reflected a barren sky. I knew not *where* to fly. I only flew.

I reached an island, and finally took some rest. As soon as my claws scraped the sand, I heard Hera whisper, all the way from the mountain from which I fled, *Delos*.

I found my home.

The sun started to rise, and I saw, the island had been abandoned. It was perfect. For, I had wanted so badly to run, and I finally reached a safe haven.

I made my nest, in anticipation of a baby girl.

Finally, I laid my egg, a Hekatean egg.

She was my child, but she was not mine to nurture. As soon as the egg was laid, a snake appeared.

I thought, at first, that I should curse the serpent and peck out its eyes. I assumed the snake was a threat to my new child, who waited to hatch.

The snake lifted its head, looked at me, and let out a soft hiss. It was as warm and nurturing as a hiss could've been. The snake was there for good.

I held back my beak and my claws. I watched it take over the nest, and wrap around the egg.

Though the snake coddled her, the egg itself was mine. I birthed her, out in the sea. I formed her. I brought the dark witch into the world. It took a bird, with dark streaks in her feathers, and a round crest, to summon the Pharmakis of the Dark Side of the Moon.

Still, it took a snake to hatch my egg.

The serpent stayed coiled around the egg, until one dark night. After the moon had come and gone, and was missing once more, the egg hatched to reveal a girl.

She was born when destruction melted down from the stars, not as a comet, but as the wax that falls from a candle as it melts, slowly, towards the earth.

Yes, she was born with horns on her head. Dark as she was, Hekate was born with a sliver of moonlight, glinting off her crown.

She used her horns to crack open her egg, and they stayed with her forevermore.

I welcomed my child. I revered her.

So the sky had called me to Poseidon before, once to free myself and my daughter from Pelion, and the second time to look upon Medousa.

Of course, the first time the night sky called to me, I flew in darkness. When I flew to Delos for the first time, there was no moon or stars in the sky. But when I flew to Medousa, constellations and comets were springing up from nothing at all. There were enough stars to light up the sea, and the moon was close to being full.

I grew weary during my approach of Medousa at Sarpedon. I wasn't concerned about Medousa, but the two gorgones sisters always made me nervous.

They struck me as unstable. I heard that they sent ships full of men to their deaths. I never saw a gorgones head-on, so I could not see if their eyes carried regret or if they were true savages. Hekate shook Poseidon's hand, and brought the gorgones sisters back from death.

The gorgones became shades who couldn't go into the sea, shades willed out by Poseidon. He took their lives, and since Hekate animated them, did not allow them to return in their living deaths.

They became shades, but not quite. They could never descend into the Underworld. Their bronze lips would kill them beneath the surface. If they swam into the Underworld, they would drown, but never die. Medousa was different. She was born from real flesh, a mortal who could meet her end.

I did not fear her.

I found her on the outskirts of Sarpedon. I caught sight of her, because her hair glinted like true gold. She was sitting up, resting on a submerged sea cave. It was crafted from a murder of crows, frozen by gorgones.

I poised myself atop one of these crows. My sharp claws grazed over the stone, slowly, in silence. I had to stay quiet; Medousa need not know that the grandmother of the stars was watching over her.

I sat, on Sarpedon, for the first time in shade.

Flowers shielded me from starlight.

Sarpedon was almost unrecognizable. The whipping winds had died down. The ocean was flat as glass. Where there was once a barren landscape of dark stones, emerald leaves unfurled themselves and white flowers drooped. I even saw dark roots cracking the rocks.

The tide was high, and water crept towards Medousa's jaw. The surface of the flat water sliced over her neck. She looked at first like a head emerging from a glass mirror.

I knew she was a mortal shadow, she wouldn't live forever like her sisters. I knew this, because it was the rule of thirds. Whatever the first two were, she would not be. Medousa was destined to die.

She initiated a cosmic shift. I'd been paying careful attention to the stars ever since the moon grew full and Hera whispered to me her name. *Me. Dou. Sa.*

Stars that were once constant, started to flicker. It was like they were winking, as if the stars themselves were in on a trick.

Algol smoldered like burning embers clinging onto heat. That particular star had been flickering since the full moon. Alpheratz disappeared all together.

Things were about to change.

Stars shone in Medousa's eyes. I watched her reach towards a pure, white blossom. She plucked the flower from its stem. As it broke off the stem straightened, produced another, and drooped over again.

Medousa held the flower in her palms. Without touching it, I could tell the petals were buttery. They were tinged with silver, lit by the moon and stars.

Medousa sniffed the flower. I watched a flurry of pollen twirl into the air, and like comets darting across the sky, flush into Medousa's nose.

In moments the pollen took hold of her soul.

Her eyes, once green as the flower's emerald leaves, turned into inky black. Her pupils overtook her eyes and she started to sway in the water.

She made ripples over the surface, cast from her own movement, and then stared at them, as if mesmerized.

It was like looking into the past. This moment with Medousa mirrored the night when Hekate was initiated as a pharmakis. The black poplar tree sprouted from Hekate's skin. It leapt from her body and burrowed into the ground.

Within moments, the seed sprouted. Its branches wrapped around my daughter's fingers. Its leaves mimicked the grooves on her skin.

I remember Hekate's gray eyes fogging with mists of the dead. Then, her eyes darkened like Medousa's after she sniffed the buttercup. I remembered Hekate, alone with me on our island, whispering secrets from the Underworld.

Hekate was never the same after she merged with poplar.

The poplar opened Hekate's senses. She became inquisitive, and she learned how to change the world around her. Hekate harnessed moonlight with glass and metal.

She heard mercury creep through stone, so she extracted the ore. She calculated the phases of the moon.

My daughter discovered her burning glass. She used it to burn fires in the sky, so far away, they appeared as mere specs to our eyes. She led sailors across the sea, inspired human souls to look up at night, and led men to pursue astronomy, all with her torches burning in the sky.

Hekate, of course, offered to share the burning glass with Hera. She grew up on my island; she understood the nature of nature. She understood that nothing was whole without another. Hekate recognized herself in darkness, thus she sought a reflection in light.

Hekate talked to the plants, and they told her their secrets. The poplar taught her how to become the Pharmakis of the Dark Side of the Moon.

Of course, the black-footed buttercups were widening the perception of our dear Medousa.

Medousa started to laugh. She threw her head back and chuckled at nothing but the stars. She laid back into the tidepool and watched the constellations. I knew, with her eyes as black as mine, the stars were telling her more than usual.

I sighed and nestled into the stone. A buttercup hovered over me, drooping, longing to see its own reflection in the sea.

I stared into its center, following the pattern of white petals leading towards yellow stamens. They bursted from the center like shooting stars.

The petals started to bewilder me. They made me feel as if my feathers were gone, as if they had floated away without me. I wondered how on earth I was flying, with my gaze still fixed to a flower.

I blinked my eyes and begged, please let me stay. I did not wish for flight, not at that moment.

Buttercups carried me away. I was lost in petals, until the flower broke from its stem. The seduction failed, and I came to my senses.

It was only a trick of my mind. My feet were still standing on stone; I had not flown away. I exhaled sharply and broke my gaze with the flower. I looked to the stars, collected myself. Medousa was looking to the stars too, I saw her, and for a brief moment, I understood her gnosis.

I couldn't dive to the bottom of that pool. I saw what I came to see, the initiation of Medousa. I wished to allow her to stargaze, without any interference.

I took one last glance at the girl with golden hair, the silver gibbous moon watching her, and the flowers that blossomed like stars over the island. As the girl looked up to the sky, a scar revealed itself over her neck.

As I look back, and wonder, about signs from the body and its scars, the bloody ribbon over Medousa's neck foretold things to come.

I flew out into the night, knowing that if I didn't leave precisely then, I may have been overtaken by flowers too. In the sea, I was guided by stars which Hekate held in the sky, like burning torches. Oh how easy for lost birds to navigate in the night after the stars had been burned.

25. Nightingale

Medousa was chased by a shadow, a boy trying to kill her.

I'd been waiting to act on Hera's behalf, to sing a sweet song in her sleep, to warn her. I'd been waiting for the moon to grow fuller, to catch light from the sun, and fill into a complete circle like those pinprick stars.

Perseus was on his way to Medousa. The moon wasn't quite full, but I sensed it was time to act. I had to be faster than a sailboat. I had to cross the ocean in only a few strokes.

Miraculously, I did.

The winds were on my side. It felt like Hera's clouds ushered me with a heavenly breath.

The sea glistened beneath me. I watched each wave disappear and a new one reappear.

Hera's winds pulled me towards Sarpedon. I moved so quickly, I felt like a comet flying through the sky.

On my way over the sea, I came across another bird. A quail passed me on my right.

Certainly, she was a quail. She had brown stripes over her wings, lined with white streaks that looked like shooting stars. Surely, the quail meant that stars were about to be born. She was an omen any other bird could read.

I had a feeling stars would also disappear. I shuddered. In the past moon phase, stars had been appearing and disappearing. It was an eventful time in the skies of ancient Greece.

But I didn't come to meddle with the stars.

Once I reached the island, and saw dark tentacles and stones snaking through the open sea, Hera's hand stopped pushing my wind.

The air was still and misty with salt.

I'd expected winds at Sarpedon. It was supposed to be the home of the kharybdis. I'd heard legends of tempests, but all was still when I reached the island of stone. All was still, save the gust which carried me across the sea.

I peered through plants, seemingly bursting from the sea and the stones. It was a strange sight, for I assumed the island would've been barren. Humble white blossoms, sweet buttercups, drooped towards the sea. They careened downwards, pulling on their emerald stalks, as if admiring their own reflections in the water.

Black roots caught my eye. I was coming to warn Medousa about Perseus, and tell her to keep him safe, but I didn't have anything else to say.

I didn't know how she was going to thwart him.

However, as soon as I saw those dark roots, I realized Sarpedon was blooming with a witch's plant.

Medousa would have to become an enchantress to trick Perseus. A pharmakis' plants can trick anyone. They brought people into the Underworld, animated the world in fantastic ways, and created myths in the minds of men.

She needed to use the buttercups to her advantage.

I realized that these plants were not here by accident. I could sense that they had sprouted from Medousa herself. Maybe they even came from her dark heart, from a crack where seeds sprouted from her soul.

Luckily, that pain was going to save her.

A plan came to me all at once. I realized how, exactly, Medousa could go head-to-head with Perseus without losing her head. She could be an enchantress— a pharmakis. She could change the world around her with a magical plant.

At last I saw the girl. I heard her tired heart. What a shame, to hear a beautiful song of sorrow. I had spent my whole life singing it, but to hear it in another felt all the more tragic. She was clearly in trouble. She slept over spiny stones in tattered robes. Tide was high, and lapped towards her neck. As soon as I saw her, I recognized her. The same thing happened to me. Though I'd never fallen asleep inside of a sea canyon, I'd been exiled too.

She rested on rocks, between towering green stalks. Medousa was still. She slept in the tidepools. Her body was submerged, but her head was propped up on a leaf, against a stone.

Medousa only moved to breathe, as her chest rose and fell out of the ocean. Her eyes were closed. Golden locks curled around her. They were rough with matts and salt. Curls snaked down her body, and when they met the sea, they became free. I watched hair flutter around her underwater, as if Poseidon gave Medousa's hair a mind of its own.

I looked around. I couldn't see much, but green stalks and drooping, white buttercups disappearing into the mist. A canopy of stalks reached towards the stars, and mangled stones. Bodies which had been frozen, and slowly eroded by Poseidon, were cracked by black roots.

I wondered how far into the labyrinth was the stony hive where the gorgones lived, and why they forced Medousa out here. She could have slept on solid ground.

I was too quiet to arouse suspicions from the legendary khimaira, the guard of Sarpedon. When nightingales fly, we blend seamlessly into the night.

As I got closer, I saw her neck bore a strange scar. Someone must have held a knife to her throat, but didn't quite cut all the way through. I imagined Perseus arriving in Sarpedon, finishing the job, and claiming his prize.

I couldn't let that happen. No. I vowed to stop it.

Below her neck was a chain made of bronze. Its pendant was hidden under her dark robes. Still, with her soft breath, I heard the chain rustle in the quiet, windless night. Her skin looked silver in the moonlight, and so did the ripples in the sea.

Medousa slept with the sea as her blanket. It lapped against her chin. She breathed in her sleep. I wondered how she could rest, between living and drowning, so casually like she had done this all before. Her breaths lapped out into the sea before her. I wondered what, in her waking hours, could have prepared her to rest between stones and sea.

I'd been hurt in my life, so much so that I could sense pain in others. I sensed she always lived under a shadow of danger. I sensed she lost gold to Poseidon, and she nearly lost her life.

She'd been betrayed. I sensed that all she had left, in all of Greece, was Poseidon, the very one who hurt her.

The sea may have been a thief, but it cradled Medousa in its grasp nonetheless.

That was the way of the ocean— impartial. Poseidon didn't feel guilty for anything. He didn't mind that she was scared of the deep. He would hold her just the same. Water was soft, for enemies and for lovers.

I saw a certain grace in Medousa. It reflected from her face over the tidepool. She struck a chord in my soul. I was graceful like her, a long time ago.

I had once been a princess named Philomela. I was not perfect, but I kept my grace through my life, even after mutilation.

Though princesses were revered, and said to be lucky, misfortune befell me. Crimes were committed against me. My body was ravaged by a lustful, braggadocious man. Then, my tongue was stolen. A not-so-honorable king used a curved blade, and he cut it from my mouth.

A king, a man of true power, was scared of what I had to say. He cut my tongue, but I still carried his secret, I still endured what he had done.

He didn't understand his actions. He didn't understand the fire of revenge he lit within me. The tables turned. When he tore out my tongue, it didn't mean I had to stay silent.

Without a tongue, I didn't worry about *what* to say. I had to figure out *how* to say it.

I wove my horror into a tapestry. I turned pain and suffering into a lament, into art. The truth was out. My tapestry revealed the atrocities of the king. Atrocity became artistry. As Philomela, I never lost my charm.

Hera saw me. She saw my tapestry, my missing tongue, and she understood. I was no longer happy as a princess, not without my tongue. Hera turned me into a nightingale, so I could sing forever. A new song made up for my lost words.

As a nightingale, my song would enchant the mind's of poets and maidens, even ones with dark sides like Medousa.

I fluttered down from the sky and landed in the sea right next to her ear. Through her ear, I could see into the darkness of her soul. Dark, yes, but perhaps Medousa harbored a darkness worth protecting. I felt salt against my feathers. I felt the bubbling buoyancy of the sea. After one long, lofty inhale, I started to sing.

I sang a rhapsody for Medousa.

It was like creating a tapestry, where each note was a thread. Everyone knew I was the best singer of all the birds. So, my song was rich and full of meaning, just like the tapestry from my last life.

My song penetrated her dream, while my body floated in reality.

I wove a story for Medousa. Threads started to come together, and I pulled different narratives in and out of each other.

A boy is coming for your head.

I sang.

The flowers can save you.

I swear those black-footed buttercups understood my song. A drooping flower fell into the water beside me and Medousa. It twirled on the flat water like a dancer.

Medousa, please hear my song.

An insight ruffled my feathers. Medousa had killed someone before. Or— many people. This truth surfaced in the space of dreams, an ugly fact in the face of my lovely song.

I didn't stop singing, but I shifted to a bridge. My song changed to something more sorrowful and Medousa, with parted lips over the sea, exhaled into a deeper sleep.

Why should I help a killer?

I questioned myself. It was my duty, given to me by Hera, and I was loyal to her. She told me to warn Medousa, and so I would. Perhaps Hera had a master plan. In turning princesses into birds, she had watchful eyes over Greece.

I kept singing. I sang my disbelief. I sang everything I was too scared to understand.

How could this girl in front of me be a monster?

For, it seemed sad to me, that she slept out here, alone in the sea.

Then I questioned myself again.

What if she was young, impressionable, and taught to be afraid?

With my throat's echo, the burst of my feathers, the nod of my head, I went deeper into her dreams.

I knew Poseidon hurt her, stole her breath, and nearly took her life. But she froze, in her sleep, underneath a blanket of her fear. The ocean rippled against the sleeping girl, curling to her every breath. I saw another side to their relationship, between Medousa and the sea.

Poseidon was her home and her villain. Medousa was born from the ocean. Into his arms, she would return.

I lamented her suffering, and all its complex layers, with my song.

Underneath a canopy of stars, I ushered Medousa into a deeper sleep. I sang and my melody caught, beyond the veil. She drifted away, into the night, together with my song. My warbled cries, controlled chirps, strums like the strings of a heart sent her a message. I wailed the sounds of beautiful sorrow. We had both lost something, and in that we were not alone.

Though my song was clear, it was also mysterious. I couldn't give Medousa instructions through song alone. I had to talk to her with human flesh and tongue. Medousa needed to be warned by another girl from the sea.

I could take on any form in the realm of dreams. I didn't have to be a bird, or a princess who lost her tongue. I became a beautiful reflection of Medousa.

I asked myself who Medousa would be if there wasn't a single drop of monstrosity in her blood.

Medousa's dream started to form. I stepped inside, into the timeless body of Aphrodite.

Her eyes were the same kelp green as Medousa, but deeper, kinder.

With my song, I wove together the threads that bound Aphrodite to Medousa. It was easy, for they were both girls who bubbled up from the sea.

In her dream, Medousa emerged from the ocean, rising over a wave. She came from the water until seafoam fell down her back and materialized into a stunning white horse beneath her. He was fiery and alive, seemingly made from the stars. He appeared so white that he was blue.

Medousa tightened her grip on a pair of gold-spun reigns and sat up, looking around.

The beach appeared everywhere she looked, but when she looked down at the round pebbles, she saw a woman. It was me, Philomela as Aphrodite, in a heavenly body. I felt the weight of braided, hazelnut-colored hair falling down my back.

Recognition dawned in Medousa's eyes. It was like watching mist fall from the sea as morning melted into a hot afternoon.

I appeared in front of her. I sang my essence into a being, a being just like Medousa, a girl who had crawled out of the sea.

Well, I suppose Medousa wasn't *just like* me.

As Aphrodite, my hair was plaited, and though it touched the salt, it didn't become stiff. Aphrodite smelled of the flowers who preferred to be battered by sea breeze, but Medousa smelled of salt. There was a shadow in Medousa's pulse, so unlike the Lady Aphrodite whose heartbeat was clear as crystal.

She looked quizzically down at me from the back of her dreamy horse.

"Fear not, Medousa. I'm the sea's maiden, just like you."

I spoke to her in my alternate form, which felt like stepping into my old life.

Medousa's dream-body blinked, which was strange. Normally

dreamers stared with their eyes wide open. Normally they forgot to wet their eyes in the dreaming realm, for there was no need. Nothing was real.

Medousa blinked again.

She was different. Something in her was destined to be a shadow, to obscure light.

"Poseidon aged me, just like he did you," I assured her, reaching a hand towards Medousa, "We were both born at sea."

"Who are you?"

"Aphrodite," she smiled, "I'm here to warn you about–"

"I know the ocean is dangerous, it's already tried to kill me! It stole from me! Don't waste your breath!" before Medousa finished speaking, she kicked her horse.

I was gone from her sight, gone from her dream.

I wished to tell her more. I wished to tell her that the ocean was carrying a danger she didn't know about yet, that a sailor was coming for her head.

Back in reality, I changed my voice, begging to soothe her. I tweeted a soft hum, which drifted into the eerie night air of Sarpedon's tidepools. My lullaby waxed and waned, it changed and morphed, but it didn't stop.

Her dream morphed too. I followed Medousa into another scene.

Suddenly we were in a small wardrobe. Poppy-rich smoke hung in the air. I shivered in Aprhodite's bones. Medousa was there too, still on her horse. Without the limits of reality, he sat proudly, astride a horse larger than the wardrobe itself.

We were looking at our reflections in a bronze mirror. We were warped with red and brown. Medousa's emerald eyes had a tinge of fire. Her hair was still golden.

Her horse beat its mighty hoof at the ground. Sparks flew from the strike. Even in the bronze reflection, he stayed white, as pure as the stars.

The wooden floor shook, and the small room fell away. I lost the scent of poppies.

In reality, my singing pitch danced with the changes.

This was Medousa's dream, so Aphrodite held her breath. My song warbled in Medousa's ear and encouraged her to find the next space. I sang louder to tether her to the night. I was not scared of waking Medousa, disturbing the khimaira, or attracting the attention of the other gorgones. My song never woke an ear nor stirred a soul. I called in rhythm with the night. Only dreamers heard my song.

We were at Sarpedon in an illusory mirror of reality. Her horse had vanished, lost somewhere between dream scenes. The tidepools were like glass around us, yet so soft they rippled with calm air. Everything was the same, but where the moon shone in reality, the sun was shining.

In her dream, a crow watched Medousa. He was perched at the base of the tidepools. He was neither in air nor water. His inky chest feathers puffed out. His beady eyes were fixed on her.

I felt, deep in my soul, that the crow was there for a reason. This bird, too, was a reflection of reality. When Perseus came to Sarpedon a crow was destined to watch over Medousa. What better bird to help a girl pull off a trick?

Medousa stood barefoot on the stone, next to me as Aphrodite. She tiptoed between gnarly roots and bursting stalks.

In her dream, the sun wobbled.

Suddenly, the dream started to shift. Plants came to life.

Stalks swayed, as if dancing. They moved in time with the murmuring sea. Leaves flapped like the wings of birds. Roots writhed in stone. The meadow of flowers tangled themselves together, as if to form a webbed matrix.

My vision warped, as I was seeing this dream through Medousa, through the darkness of her ear. There were remnants of green in the corners of my sight, green like the irises of Medousa.

"There's magic in these plants," I said. My voice as the dreamy sea-maiden Aphrodite was as beautiful, as charming, as my birdsong.

Medousa nodded, wonderstruck by dancing foliage. The flowers started to use their petals to fly upwards into the sky. We both watched in awe. They floated so high, they looked like stars in the daytime. As soon as one blossom bursted from its stem, another appeared.

These black-footed buttercups were the secret means to save Medousa from Perseus. Hera hadn't told me to expect them, she may not have even known. This was the key to helping Medousa keep her head.

"The flowers are blooming to help you," I said.

"Help me do what?" Medousa asked.

"A boy is coming to Sarpedon," I answered.

"Why?" She asked.

"For your head," I said.

"My *head*?"

"You must give it to him!"

"Are you mad?" Medousa grabbed Aphrodite's shoulders.

"Or so he must believe that he has your head," I said, "Consider giving him your bronze mask."

"What kind of fool would mistake a mask for a head?" Medousa asked.

"A fool who is too scared to look closely at it."

Medousa was silent. Her green eyes looked into mine. The buttercups drooped in my blurred vision.

"Medousa, you must promise not to hurt the boy," I said, "Let the innocent travel the seas. You do not have to be like gorgones. You can spare a life."

"I promise," Medousa blinked and her eyes watered.

She still held my shoulder, connecting us deeper in the dream world. I felt desperation in her fingertips, digging into my shoulders. When she touched me, I felt something else too. I felt the carvings of Poseidon, blending between her fingers and my dreamy skin. Her eyes were wide and glowing like stars. The dream started to warp inwards, where Medousa's green eyes moved and shifted like the plants around us.

"You'll have to use these flowers," I said to Medousa, "They'll convince Perseus that the gods are on his side. These flowers will give him invisibility, flight, and total trust in you."

"Really?" Medousa asked.

"Not exactly. He won't truly have help from the gods," I explained, my words coming from Aphrodite's pink lips, "The plant will become his god."

"So, that's what happened to me? After I smelled a buttercup?" Medousa looked back to the plants, "I thought I could fly, I thought I had vanished."

"These buttercups reach straight for the sun to cast a deep shadow," I explained, "These flowers droop with the weight of all they've seen, and all they have to share. The black roots are the source of the stalk, there is no branching, there is no wavering. This plant is a straight shooter, but shoots a deceptive shot."

Medousa looked back at me, the sing-song intruder of her dreams.

The two sea-maidens stared at each other, in some ways a reflection, in other ways a poisoned potential.

"Agh! What's that?" Medousa leapt from the stone. She motioned to her leg and I looked. Roots took hold of her ankle.

"We have to be a little tricky to guard against being tricked," Aphrodite cooed, with eyes like rushing water, drowning Medousa. I wove a plan together with her, like a princess may encode a tapestry with secrets. We moved threads back and forth and elements of a plan came together.

"The milk!" Medousa shouted, and her ankle was free. The plant let go, as quickly as it had taken hold. As the stalk slithered back into the dancing matrix of roots, I saw a blue glimmer, a snake swallowing its tail into infinity, glistening on Medousa's ankle.

"What milk?" I prompted. She had to speak her ideas, out loud, in her dream. That way, she would remember them when she woke up.

"The root— it grabbed me to tell me something," she said, "I can trick Perseus with the khimaira's milk. Surely she is eating up the buttercups now. Her milk will be rich with the magical properties of these flowers, richer than the flowers themselves. When he arrives, he will be just as thirsty as I was after making the journey to Sarpedon."

She paused.

"And, fresh from his journey over the sea, Perseus will drink whatever I give him," Medousa said.

Thoughts arranged in Medousa's mind. She realized that she could tell her own story.

I left her dream. Aphrodite fell back into my imagination, and I was once again a bird floating in the sea. The sea-maiden was a successful disguise. Medousa's dream had been intercepted.

Hera's mission had been carried out.

Medousa gasped and swallowed the dream into her mouth.

At the last moment, I wondered if she came with me into reality as I took the form of a bird, and flew into the void of night. I darted away from Sarpedon.

As I flew into the open sea, back towards Greece, I crossed paths with a fool. He had eyes like a shallow sea, the bravery of youth cherrying his cheeks, and looked about as thirsty as a stray dog in the summertime. It was Perseus, on course to meet Medousa in the night.

26. *Crow*

Medousa woke from her sleep as tides fell and the nightingale flew away. It was the middle of the night, but the moon was so bright that it seemed to be a silver day. Tides lapped away from my feathers. I wondered if Medousa was meant for the sea or the sky. I knew for myself, as a crow, that the sky was always my home, even when I was trapped in stone and held beneath Poseidon.

I heard a sharp exhale behind me, and the scrape of claws over stone.

I recognized the beast, though I could not have turned my head to look.

I heard the huffy exhale of a lion, the soft bleat of a goat, and the sneaky, flickering tongue of the serpent.

It was the khimaira.

Medousa leaned over me and drooping buttercups tickled her scarred neck. She whispered to the khimaira, "I'm expecting a guest."

The khimaira started to purr. Her rumble reverberated through stones.

"I wish to offer him your milk," Medousa said.

She cocked all three of her heads towards Medousa, listening intently. There was levity in the khimaira's movements. I could tell black-footed buttercups were having their way with her. All three heads had probably been sniffing pollen all night.

The pollen was affecting me as well. Though my body was trapped in stone, it felt like I could've floated away into the dark night.

Medousa leaned into the tidepool, and withdrew a spondylus shell. Its spikes glistened in the starlight, and for a moment, looked as if they were reaching for the stars with alabaster fingers.

Upon hearing the splash of Medousa withdrawing the shell, the khimaira roared. It was a small roar, but rumbled with lucidity. The khimaira was certainly tainted by flowers, and I realized then, that her milk carried the charms of buttercups too.

Her ears were pricked. The blind lioness leaned forward to rub her face against Medousa's shoulder. Then she leaned back, sniffed the air, and stood in wait.

With her back to me, Medousa knelt before the khimaira. I heard milk stream and Medousa sigh.

Once the shell was full, Medousa stood.

"Thank you," she whispered to the khimaira.

With that, the khimaira leapt from the stones and jumped into the tidepool. Where any other creature would splash, the khimaira slipped inside the glassy water without a ripple.

Medousa took careful steps. She made her way to the very edge of the tidepool. It was as deep as she could stand. I knew if she took one more step, she would either be floating or sinking. Medousa stood on the edge of the pool, staring into Poseidon's expanse. Without the sun, the ocean was impenetrable. One had no idea what lurked beneath.

Medousa held her gaze at the sea. She held her prized potion like other women would've held a baby in her arms. Wind played with her hair. For a moment, she reminded me of the gorgones with snakes as tresses.

I looked at her, silhouetted against the stars. She stood there, until a new star seemingly appeared on the horizon.

It was, of course, Perseus, and the flash of his linen sail.

Medousa turned and ran towards a stony shelf. She carried the shell, and disappeared from my view. I knew she was around. I heard her heartbeat, and her breath, but she was hidden behind another rock. I felt her fingertips, electric, and pressed up against another stone. I swear, I felt her pulse coursing through the entire island.

My stony heart reached across the sea, into the mind of the young boy Perseus.

The black-footed buttercups allowed me to fly, from my own psyche, and into another's. Of course my eyes opened, and my perception widened, ever since the black-footed buttercups took hold of my stony form that night.

Perseus traveled in the middle of the night. Golden, lucky stars watched him in the dark sky. The boy was born lucky, he was bound to have his wishes come true. Perseus was so enmeshed with luck, he got what he wanted, even if it meant regretting his wish. Such was the finicky nature of the luckiest among us.

I saw him approaching, my stone eyes, lucid with black-footed buttercups, could take in the night. The sea was so flat that I wondered if he was in the air or the sky. The horizon and sky melted together, a blending of heaven and hell.

Only a boy with the courage of a thousand men could've traveled the wine-dark ocean by himself. Only young boys were foolish enough to be that brave. A leather strap cut into his shoulder, and I saw a massive bronze mirror strapped to his back. His wheat-colored hair had been tousled by his journey. Sounds carried over the sea. I caught wind of the beat of Perseus' heart, in a shrill echo magnified by his shield.

He did not have the heartbeat of a warrior, or even a sailor. He had the heartbeat of someone fastened to an idea, inflexible in his plot. His pulse suited the shrill bronze. He was on an impossible task, and bronze, the metal between living and dead, neither promised him success nor brought him peril.

We were at the slack of the low tide, when the ocean hardly moved. The kharybdis had stopped its torrential whirring.

Winds were weak, yet fate begged a sailor to come forth. Never had any man ventured to Sarpedon on his own free will before. They were usually lost, wheeled in, and caught.

Perseus sailed with will alone. I watched the boy, and so did the moon and its reflection.

Perseus persisted in zig-zags over the open ocean. He adjusted his sail for his course.

Fate brought him here, but so did his own free will. Fate and free will were like two entwined serpents. You could hardly untangle one from the other. He chose his fate, but it also chose him.

I felt a touch of admiration for the boy, but I also wondered if he was a fool. Even as a stone, I never got rid of my ways as a crow. I still felt keen to judge the world, even if I was trapped in magnetite for eternities.

On a sea so flat, it took a small breath of wind to carry Perseus. He moved quickly, and as he got closer, I realized he knew not how to slow down his ship. His curved bow cut his path across Poseidon's palm. He faced no resistance, no waves pushing him back. The boy tacked his sail, made a haphazard turn, and headed straight towards the sea cave I watched over.

If I was still a real bird, I certainly would've chuckled.

There was a puffiness under his eyes. He was dreary from travel; his gaze was hazy. He was clearly dehydrated and disoriented.

Perseus acted with haste, but he acted too late. He hurried to unclip a hatch. I heard the heavy scrape of an anchor against wood. Perseus must have been about to cast it overboard, but without waves to alert him to the shallows, he rammed into a shelf of frozen souls.

Crash.

His hull scraped against the cliff on the outermost edge of Sarpedon. Although I hadn't moved in centuries, I felt the crash of his boat rattle my statue skin. It felt like thunder. The boy was sent flying back, and had to grip his rail to keep from being flung into the sea.

I felt Medousa, hidden somewhere in the rocks, bursting with excitement.

The boy had no idea he was being watched, by me or Medousa.

Through my frozen eye, I saw Perseus' living fear as he found his balance.

With his small boat smashed up against the rocks, how could he sail back? Would he ever return from whence he came? I watched worries swirl around his blue eyes like a whirlpool.

Salt licked Perseus' ruined craft. I'd seen this island eat so many wooden boats, so many sunk by the stoned weight of their men, but never had one crashed on its own accord before.

Suddenly, a shadow fell over my eye. My vision was momentarily occulted, as if a blindfold had been placed over me. The sensation was strange, for I hadn't blinked since many moons ago, when I was a living crow.

It was the fleeting foot of Medousa. I watched her dive, faithfully into the channel. She leapt as if no stone could scrape her milky skin. She embraced Poseidon, in the clear, calm channel.

Like a cormorant, she swam beneath the surface. Her body moved in flow with the water. When she came up for air, I saw a blindfold, wrapped around her eyes.

Medousa covered her own eyes, but what for? She did not have a deadly gaze.

That's when I realized she was going to trick him. Even though she couldn't see before her, she saw what was about to unfold.

Of course, she had secrets. She was a girl masquerading as a monster.

I looked underwater at Medousa's hand behind her back. She held a makeshift satchel, cut from the same fabric of her robes. I knew what was inside— her deadly mask. I watched her bundle it up right there, in the sea canyon, and hide it among the stones.

Medousa seemed tricky. What better bird than me, to see that in her?

She swam, easily in the water, with her undulating spine and slow kicking feet. She reminded me of a snake, so at one with the water it could coil around every corner of the sea. As Medousa shimmied up onto a rock, I saw her other hand. She held the spondylus shell. She had submerged it, and lost not a drop of milk. I supposed that the khimaira's milk was so heavy with charms, that water couldn't draw it from its container.

At that moment, I felt black-footed roots carving through my stony body.

I saw Perseus, peering into the bronze mirror, with his back to the island.

"Hello?" Medousa called into the darkness behind her blindfold.

"Are you Medousa?" there was a quiver in Perseus' voice. I still heard his heart, magnified in the bronze mirror.

"Perhaps I am," There was a smug whistle in her words that carried to my frozen ears, "Who are you?"

Perseus swallowed and steadied himself on the rocking boat. There was chaos between waves and water, heart and man.

I heard the beat of Medousa's heart, too. It was magnified by the water lapping against her chest. Though I knew human's couldn't sense it, their heartbeats had fallen into sync. It was not with perfect timing, not a resonance of hearts singing together. It was more like an echo. Medousa's heart was just one step ahead of Perseus'. Such was the nature of the trickster, leading another behind her.

"Well?" Medousa coaxed, "Who are you?"

"I am Perseus."

"From where have you traveled, Perseus?" Medousa said his name like a lullaby. I swear her eyelashes fluttered beneath her blindfold. She may as well have been a sea nymph for the way she rested, on her belly, on the rocks.

"I set sail from Larissa," Perseus said.

He licked his chapped lips. They grew saturated, and quickly dried out again before a moment had passed. His nose and cheeks were a floral shade of pink, kissed and burnt by the sun.

"Hmm," Medousa purred, "Larissa… I've never heard of it. Perseus, tell me, what do you seek?"

"At the moment, I only seek water. It was a long sail and I ran out of sweetwater," Perseus said.

He was thirsty.

"Why don't you drink this?" Medousa asked.

She stretched the spondylus shell towards Perseus, with spiny ornaments stuck between her long fingers.

Perseus still had his back to Medousa. He stared at the bronze reflection, even though it darkened and warped the real girl.

To accept the drink, he had to face her.

I saw the want for water in his tired body. He could not resist. He shook, his trembling fingers like a sailboat's lines straining against the wind. I heard the wobble of bronze, his shield picking up every prick of his pulse.

Perseus saw, of course, that Medousa covered her eyes. He lowered his mirror, turned, and reached for the shell.

Of course, it was not water she offered him.

Perseus lifted the shell to his lips. I swear he did not look at the liquid. It could have been water or wine.

One sip turned into a heaving gulp. He threw back his head and downed the contents of the shell. Medousa smirked. He dropped his head and looked at her.

Perseus wobbled, absorbing the much needed liquid. Immediately, his lips filled, the spaces under his eyes glowed. He seemed to recover from dehydration quickly, aided by the charmed khimaira milk.

Perseus pursed his lips. He flicked his tongue on his palate.

"Thank you. But, oh my, what a bitter aftertaste..." his voice disappeared into lulling waves.

Of course, khimaira milk was sweet. If it tasted bitter, then the black-footed buttercups had, indeed, tainted the milk.

Perseus passed the empty shell back to Medousa, which she dropped into the tidepools. Medousa sighed. Her enemy willingly drank her elixir, and her head was still on her shoulders. Medousa, the girl who seeded poisonous flowers from her tears, spun the world between her fingertips. Her plan fell steadily into place.

Medousa and Perseus stood in the chamber of my sea canyon. One had performed a favor for the other.

The tide, ever so gently, pulled out. It happened to topple the stem of a black-footed buttercup over the wet stones. The petals floated through the water, towards Medousa in the shallows, looking up at

Perseus in his ship on the rocks. Ivory petals brushed against her dark cloak, and the splotches of her skin revealed by tears and seams. The dark fabric around Medousa moved in the water like smoke in the air.

Hair curled in Perseus' eyes as he leaned over the edge of his boat to closely examine Medousa.

"Ovid warned me that you would carry a trident," Perseus said, "Are you sure you're really Medou—"

Medousa hissed at him.

It was a hiss so full of malice, that it was obvious that Perseus had struck her nerve. She had no trident. Her hiss was bruised and bitter.

Perseus drew a scythe, tied behind him in a loop on his belt. Before the whoosh of the curved blade in the air, his blade had been a secret.

He truly came for blood, there on the fateful edge of my skeletal island.

Medousa hissed, her voice was like an angry ocean. She hissed at the metal and the man who held it. I could feel the wildness of her voice. Even as a stone, I feared her.

Perseus trembled. I saw the hairs on his arm standing upright.

The reflection of Perseus' blade glowed. Moonlight reflected from the scythe over Medousa's forehead. She looked like she had been christened with horns of the moon.

"Are you really Medousa?" he asked, like it was a prayer, like he wished she would deny it.

"Yes."

"How c-could it have been you?" Perseus asked, still trembling, sending light flickering off the mirror which rested on his back, "You welcomed me with both eyes blindfolded. Do you wish to spare me? How could you kill a hunter with hands so dainty?"

The shake in his voice stirred Medousa. The tears, streaming down his face, tempted her to bite him with her words.

"You've mistaken me, just like Orion. You see my curling blonde hair and you've missed my edge. My dainty hands summoned beasts from the earth."

"Prove that it was you! Prove that you killed Orion!" Perseus' face puckered with fear and grief.

"He gave me this scar!" Medousa threw back her head, putting her complete faith in the cowardice of Perseus, in his inability to plunge his scythe through her exposed throat.

She smiled. Her eyes crinkled on the edges of her blindfold. They were both so different. Medousa started fires, and Perseus put them out.

He lifted his scythe towards Medousa. The tides were in her favor, and everyone but Perseus knew it. I heard her heartstrings harden. I saw her face stiffen with defensiveness. I saw her knuckles as she gripped the mask behind her back.

On her face, Medousa remained stoic. She seemed as impartial and unattached as the sea.

Behind her back, I saw her rage. I saw the urge to end him, evident in the shudder of her fingertips and her bone white knuckles.

"You stole Orion's life!" Perseus said.

"You were not there. Maybe I had every right!" Medousa asked.

Perseus lowered his arms. I could tell he was confused, and although he was on a quest, he wasn't certain if it was the right thing to do. Perseus stepped off his craft and onto the rocks of Sarpedon.

His feet were bare, just like Medousa's.

"What if Orion was guilty? What if I was only defending myself? What if a monster came to my aid and I didn't kill him at all?"

"I bet he saw you as a monster! I bet he knew right away that you were evil! I heard about your trials with Ovid!" Perseus shouted, "You've already become an evil legend across Greece. I was warned, never to look in your eye. That's why the kentauroi gave me this."

He stretched his shield overhead, as if to shade himself from the stars.

He held up the bronze mirror. Even in silver light the pure bronze mirror looked red, like a gleaming flash of fire. How funny it is, to call bronze pure. For bronze, by its very nature, was made of different elements. It was an alloy, a conglomeration.

Nonetheless, that mirror burned red under silver moonlight.

I watched Medousa peek from her blindfold, which was a bluff to begin with.

The mirror surprised her. She dropped the blindfold around her neck. A rogue flurry of wind grabbed the light fabric, and sank it into the ocean.

Medousa didn't notice her blindfold swallowed by the ocean. She was in the grip of her emotions.

"You stole that from Hekate!"

What an accusation, I thought to myself. I peered at carvings on the mirror. Though they were illuminated by moonlight and stars scattered across the sky, the bronze reflected them as red and golden.

Perseus saw that her blindfold was missing, and swiveled around, quickly. He went back to gazing at her through the mirror.

The circular border of the round mirror depicted stars, hounds, quails, and comets. Of course, Hekate, the hermit witch of the woods, burnt her story into her own mirror, to see herself in herself.

"Well, then you're a thief," Medousa scowled, bronze gilding her expression's reflection, "no better than me."

"It's not the same. You stole men's lives. Kentaurois gave this to—"

"And you accepted it, knowing it was stolen from my mother."

"You have no mother," Perseus sneered.

He could not hide his thoughts, not from me. He resented her. It stemmed from his own fear, out of his own desire to become a man. To Perseus, it seemed like she was the only thing standing in the way of manhood and heroism. His psyche was clear to me, especially as buttercups made him more and more vulnerable.

He certainly did not want to kill her, and he hated the part of himself that felt that it was his only honorable choice.

She looked at her own face in the mirror. Her gaze lingered on the white streaks of salt that dried over her cheeks. She looked at the matted golden hair that framed her face. Her eyes moved to Perseus, who looked at her in the reflection.

Of course, I knew it was a bluff. I knew her emerald eyes were a danger to no man. Perseus however, thought his life was hanging by a thread.

He came for blood, but I watched confusion sprout in his eyes. It was more than a secret he could keep with the sea. I could see the veil crossing before his pupils. He adopted a haze of hesitation.

The black-footed buttercup started to change Perseus' mind and his eyes. His pupils started to dilate. The bitter, black-rooted plant took hold of his perception. Medousa could cast stars into his eyes, for she had successfully darkened them. I was sure Medousa saw the emptiness, the impressionability in his pupils. There was darkness there, which she could illuminate.

Perseus lowered Hekate's bronze mirror, and it fell, once more, upon his back. He walked from the stony sea canyon and into the water beside Medousa. Under her charms, Perseus melted away. He held the sickle limp by his side.

Perseus sighed as his body met the sea. His linen clothes floated around him.

I watched his feet, nimble as any worthy sailor, step on white buttercup petals. The soft flowers cushioned his steps. Perseus didn't walk upon souls trapped in stone. The flowers took him to new heights. Buttercups absorbed into his soles. He became ripe for the uncovering of mysteries.

"I feel like I can run over the sky," Perseus said, "like I am wearing winged sandals."

Medousa and Perseus were standing in the tunnel, face-to-face, enraptured by salt and Poseidon. I heard a subtle whistle, an echo between them.

Medousa became Perseus' priestess.

She understood the ways her plant changed him. I knew she had experienced the effects of the buttercup that same night. The wonders of the stars in the sky were open, in the early night to Medousa, but as the night changed, Perseus opened his eyes to spirits too. She guided him on the experience. She stayed with him, in the water.

In a haze of black-footed buttercups, Perseus seemed to forget that Medousa's eyes were meant to be deadly.

Perseus and Medousa locked eyes. She enchanted him, just like she would enchant every seeker in Greece with seeds that sprang from her sorrow.

Perseus dropped his silver scythe. It fell into the ocean without a clatter. Poseidon silently absorbed stones and swords.

For a moment, the boy forgot all things. He had forgotten his mission and the danger. He had forgotten that his ship's hull was cracked and hoisted onto rocks.

I was sure, as the black-rooted plant took hold of Perseus' soul, he lost sight of himself. In the strangeness of the island, and the loss of his way back home, I'd bet he started to wonder if he was in fact dead, if he had already been turned to stone.

Perseus had been captivated. To me, it looked like he was drowning in Medousa's leafy eyes.

"Everything I heard about your eyes," Perseus said, "was a lie."

"Oh Perseus," Medousa suggested, "how mistaken you are."

I watched Medousa's seemingly dainty fingers pull the strings of mischief yet again.

She walked towards him, in the water, with one hand still behind her back, holding her deadly mask.

Her other hand reached towards Perseus, and caught his hand in hers. His heart beat faster; his sunburnt cheeks flushed.

"Who told you not to look into my eyes?" Medousa whispered.

"Ovid. And he told me where to find you," Perseus said.

"Is that so?"

"Yes, and the kentauroi built my ship," Perseus said. It was like he was seeing the light of death and wanted to unmuddy the waters around his actions.

His voice trailed off and he looked down into the sea.

"I'm invisible," Perseus gasped.

If my throat was still hollow, if I could caw over the sea, I would've been sent into maddening laughter. I sensed the silent murder of crows wishing to laugh, too. We'd all been corrupted by black roots. We understood the tricks in Perseus' mind.

Perseus swung his shield over his shoulder, held it between himself and Medousa, stared into its reflective surface. He screamed.

Apparently, his reflection was missing from the mirror too.

Well, not to me. I saw all three of Perseus' heads clearly. I saw his real face, hovering over the water. I saw his reflection, gilded by reddish-orange bronze and warped by the contours of metal. And I saw his face, lit up by the moon and stars, reflected in the sea.

Perseus disappeared from his mind alone.

There was another side of Perseus that I picked up in the dewy air. It was the side which Medousa saw. She saw him as someone worth sparing.

Perseus fell silent and Medousa dropped his hand.

"Where did you go?" Medousa played along.

I heard the tension in Perseus' breath ripple over his bronze mirror, until he lowered it and the strap caught it against his back. Then I heard his heart, and its echo, thudding like drums.

"There's no way to kill you with my eyes," Medousa said, "if I cannot see you."

Perseus came closer to Medousa, so close that mere drops of water separated them. He faced Medousa head-on. They stood, together, immersed in Poseidon, upon petals of white buttercups.

"You have killed me already," Perseus said.

"That's not the case," Medousa said.

"Oh, undoubtedly, you have killed me. My pursuit of you has brought me here. I wrecked my ship. Am I not dead without it?"

"I'm sure you'll be able to fly home," Medousa said, "Have you already forgotten your winged sandals?"

Perseus grinned.

Then some understanding came over him, he lowered his gaze, and he whispered, "I made a vow. I gave my word to collect your head."

It was an admittance. His whisper stagnated on the water and sank into the shallow tidepool.

"You're a man of your word?"

Tears brimmed on Perseus eyes, tears that magnified the blue around his enlarged pupils.

"Yes, of course," he admitted, "I gave Ovid my word, but Ovid lied. He said you were a monster. I can see you are no monster. When I arrived, you were blindfolded for my protection! You offered me water! You don't wish to kill. Ovid probably made the whole drunken story up."

Fish skittered across the tidepools, but Perseus did not notice. He was lost in the eyes of Medousa.

"And as for Orion, I never met the man," Perseus said, "He could have been a monster. All I know, all that I could swear by the stars, is that the monster is not you."

In that brief moment, I had no idea what was in store. Would Medousa abandon her plan? Were the black-footed buttercups still altering her world, too?

"Your life is worth more than my word," Perseus said.

Perseus bared his heart, but a trick was unfolding. There were more steps to come. After one, quick breath, Medousa submerged herself underwater. She was gone.

He looked around at frozen stones and lonely stars.

Perseus stood by himself, on a bed of enchanting petals, protecting him from treading on a submerged mountain of the dead.

"Medousa…" Perseus whispered under his breath.

Her name flew over the tidepools towards the horizon. There was not a ripple in the water, save the steady flow emanating from Perseus' inhales and exhales.

He spoke her name like it was a wish he'd hoped would be granted by Poseidon.

I witnessed, for the first time on Sarpedon, an act of mercy.

She could've killed Perseus in an instant. All it would've taken was a mask and a glance. He could've turned into stone like the rest, like me.

Medousa spared him. In a ruthless ocean, atop an island of sacrificed souls, Medousa let Perseus live.

The boy was alone, waiting to become a man. He'd lost his weapon, his will, and his reality.

Medousa shot out of the water, like a flying fish against the wake of a hippokampos. She soared through the air, and landed onto a stone. She had a spring in her step.

In one hand Medousa held the scythe, and in the other, her bundled mask. Of course, she retrieved the single, silver staff from the water. Where Poseidon stole her gold, he granted her silver.

Medousa scraped the scythe against Sarpedon's rocks. The stony, round skull of a man hissed. Friction sharpened the blade. There was a curve in the scythe, like the bow of Perseus' ship, like the horns of the moon, like everything wicked in the world had a smiling edge to it.

Moonlight struck the blade.

The moon was so close to being full in the sky. The scythe curved, ever so slightly, so that I imagined the thin silver blade was the missing chip off the moon. As if, when Medousa emerged from the tidepool with the scythe in hand, the moon's reflection over the water had produced the weapon for her.

"Medousa," Perseus whispered once more.

He stood waist-deep in the tidepool, looking up at her. Medousa stood out of the water, just out of his reach.

Medousa angled the scythe to rest upon her neck. I could see her fresh scar throbbing against the blade. I watched the curved edge fit over the arch of her throat, and the scar that ran across her neck.

Of course, Perseus, imagining himself as invisible, thought he was the culprit.

With the scythe, Medousa reaped the dead in Perseus' imagination, by his own unseen hand.

She pressed the scythe, ever so slightly, against her throat. The blade flexed against her hardened blood and asked for a few drops to rain in front of the boy.

"No!" the boy screamed.

Perseus wasn't even touching her, or the weapon, but he suffered from the illusion. The plants made him think he was cutting off her head. He hallucinated. I could see horror etched on his face. I knew, though he wasn't seeing clearly, he would remember this illusion forever. I was sure, from the waver in his pulse, the submission of his aura, he was being tricked.

Perseus looked at Medousa. Blood trickled down her neck and morphed in his distorted vision.

"You were once beautiful," Perseus cried, "now I've slayed you like a beast."

He wept. Perseus stood motionless as his tears fell into the sea.

Of course, Medousa was not dead. She merely opened a wound which was already there.

Once the buttercups realized Medousa's trick, they started to blush, all across the island. The edges of their ivory white petals turned pastel pink. With blushing petals in Perseus' periphery, he mistook the flush for more blood.

The water, and the reflection of the moon over the tidepool changed. It marbled and faded. Rosy pink streaks bloomed through the water with every drop of Medousa's blood.

She turned the moon's reflection pink.

Who sprang from the rosy reflection of the moon, but the khimaira. She walked, with the claws of a lion, over stones towards Medousa. I could feel the scrape of her claws through the dense rock, resonating through me and my murder.

The khimaira greeted Medousa, nuzzled past her, towards the buttercups. The khimaira took to the emerald stalks like a barn cat to catnip. Its bushy lion's head rubbed against the bursting forest. I smelled pollen falling through the air and heard the khimaira purr. The goat's head reached from the lioness' back and grew busy incessantly gnawing away at foliage. The serpent tail coiled around the stems, as if she could channel warmth from the foliage to her cold heart.

I could see as Perseus saw, because the black-footed buttercup sprouted from both of our minds. His emotions were so intensified they bled into mine. The same enchantments ensnared us. I'd been drowning in it all night, I'd grown used to the enchanting trick. I understood exactly what was going on and I could spring into his mind.

Perseus saw the khimaira. It flashed before his psyche's eye.

But he didn't see three-headed creature, not really.

He couldn't trust his own eyes, that a three-headed beast stood before him. His mind's eye had to project something familiar upon the khimaira, something more believable.

Perseus watched the khimaira morph into a winged horse.

The lion's head, with long flowing hair and forceful exhales, became a horse's face and mane.

The goat sprouting from the khimaira's back became a pair of majestic swan wings.

And the khimaira's swishing tail became that of a horse.

"A winged horse," Perseus shouted, "sprang from Medousa's

blood."

I heard Medousa laugh, but she quieted herself quickly. She still wished to trick him. She had to be as silent as stone.

I saw the horse, glowing and real, in Perseus' psyche. It wasn't real like the khimaira, but the winged horse was real to Perseus.

The khimaira broke away from the plants. She raised all three of her heads in unison, and looked off towards the deep sea. With a bound, and without a splash, the khimaira was underwater and gone.

Medousa flung Perseus' scythe towards deep water. I heard a splash carry the whisper of silver. I wondered if it sank into the Underworld, to reap fields of barley at the bottom of the sea.

Medousa scuttled down the rocks, as sprightly as a fish in water. She swam behind Perseus. When she wrapped her arms around him, buttercups convinced Perseus that the ocean held him. They stood there together, gazing up into the stars, lost in the moment.

Medousa reached around Perseus, and dropped her mask into his hands. He grabbed for it, and I could see his muscles strain against the unexpected weight of bronze.

"You did it," Medousa whispered in Perseus' ear, "You've secured the head of Medousa. Soon, you'll be a hero to everyone in Greece."

I was sure, as the buttercups took over Perseus' mind, he perceived her voice as the gods themselves.

"I did it?" Perseus wondered aloud, "I came to Sarpedon and collected Medousa's head?"

"Yes Perseus," she assured him.

"I must never look," Perseus said, tying yet another knot in the makeshift bag. I saw the wobble of his fingers, the nervous fritter of his youthful soul.

He wept for the girl he thought he murdered. He did not run from Sarpedon with haste, but grieved in place. Perseus was frozen in not fear, or turned to stone, but frozen in regret.

Medousa snuck away, and perched herself on the rock shelf. She looked at the horizon. She seemed wild, crouching like a lioness, or a sneaky khimaira, before the sea.

She pulled her bronze chain off her neck. I saw a key, crafted with carvings of snakes and wings, dangling from a chain. Bronze, untainted by silver cast from the moon and stars, shone bright red. She cupped the key, held it to her lips, and gave it a lucky kiss.

With a swift motion of her arms, like she were swimming in the sea, she removed the chain from her neck. Medousa was free.

She tossed the chain and key into the ocean.

I watched the ornament swing and spin over the glassy water.

It skipped— two knocks before it sank into the land of dreams.

The key opened gates to the Underworld, every murder of crows knew that. Medousa sacrificed it to Poseidon, on her way to the stars.

She sprang forward into the sea, as if chasing her sinking key.

When she dived, Medousa did not make a sound or a ripple. She was like the khimaira who merged seamlessly with the sea or a drop of water Poseidon was welcoming home.

There was a fizzle, a glow of blue light, as she submerged.

Medousa disappeared.

When she vanished underwater, she appeared in the stars.

The shade over Algol and Alpheratz had been lifted. Together they branched out into a diamond, and formed a great rectangle. Alpheratz and Algol resonated with each other and flickered, stabilizing for a moment.

It was the beginning of a new cycle, a change in the stars.

When she leapt into the sea, the wine-dark unknown, Medousa reflected into the night sky. In her sneaky way, she wrote her own myth. Medousa asked Poseidon to put the winged horse into the stars. She took the trick from Perseus' mind and made it real. She was the trickster, the storyteller, and the star-weaver.

"The winged horse is flying away!" Perseus shouted, pointing at the stars, "Come back for me!"

I heard a splash, but I couldn't turn my head to see it. It was beyond my frozen periphery. I heard the snort of a creature, not like the khimaira or any of its heads, but like the billowing exhale of a forward horse. It snorted again and I imagined fire coming out of its nose. It caught Perseus' attention.

"Oh, winged horse," Perseus said, "please take me back to Greece!"

Perseus swam from the channel, out of my sight. Medousa's new incarnation would not be revealed to my eyes, but I saw her reflection, as a starry horse in flight.

27. Swan

I've kept secrets for a long time. They've been aging on my tongue.

I'm afraid stars have shifted, moons have passed, and it is time to spill the mysteries. The mute swan has found her voice at last.

In the following pages, I've been called to unmask what I've covered up. I've hidden it under my ivory feathers, so it's not a bad secret; it's not dark at all.

I witnessed Medousa's second emergence from the ocean.

As the moon filled in the sky, stars begged me to wake up. I heard them whisper. I woke before the call of dawn, before the rooster's chariot raced across the sky, before the stars, remarkably, had finished unfolding.

The stars wished for me to cast my shade onto salt. They asked me to swim in the sea.

So, I flew to Magnesia, where a craggy coastline seemed to reach for the sea. I normally avoided salt and waves, but the water was eerily flat, like a lake. In the wilds, I swam. My webbed feet propelled me through the water, but on the surface of the ocean, I floated as easily as a cloud in the sky.

I swam in circles in ocean water. Stars twinkled above me, and randomly, on one of my circles, I noticed new stars peeking from the ether.

Like a foal born in the dark night, a horse had appeared in the sky. He sprang from the sea, connecting Algol to Alpheratz, and flew into the night.

I noticed a new tree, which certainly hadn't been here when I flew overhead last spring. It was fully grown and towered on the edge of a cliff. Roots snaked between stones. Alongside the eerie new roots, sage, which had always been there, laced over the cliffs.

I heard from the stork that Medousa came from this beach, where cliffs shielded the cove from waves, like birds in a nest huddling from raging tempests.

In the magical hour before morning, when the sun and moon danced, Hekate walked towards the beach. I caught a sniff of ambrosia and bitter wolfsbane before I spotted her. She peered over the beach, with eyes like the pebbles.

Her hair was tousled around her horns of the moon, her eyes were hazy, and she had rosy cheeks. Her skin had the plump glow that followed a long rest. She seemed like, perhaps, she might have slept for several days and nights.

Hekate kept her gaze on the sea, until her eyes caught the new constellation.

"Alpheratz has returned," Hekate gasped.

The witch stood on the beach, and I felt her surprise ripple over the bay. She was giddy, confused, and spellbound by the stars.

"Hera has been weaving?" Hekate asked herself.

I saw her reach for her pocket. I heard a slosh of water.

"Impossible," Hekate said.

I paddled through the water, watching her cloak ripple over the coming dawn like a shadow over the stars. Her crescent horns of the moon, forever crowning her forehead commanded my attention, like they wished to point my gaze towards heaven.

Hekate looked from me, to the new constellation leaping from the sea, to the star's reflection in the water. We both recognized the sea as a mirror, positioned to reflect the sky. The pharmakis and I breathed in misty seawater, on the edge of two worlds, guided by the same stars above.

The water was so still, I could count the stars over the sea. I careened my long neck to admire their reflections. I left no wake. We spent time like that, with the witch watching me swim in circles around the cove.

Beneath the star of Algol, upon the flat line where sky met sea, something approached. At first, I thought it was the white sail of a ship. As it got closer, I realized that couldn't have been true. There was no brown blemish, no wooden hull. The spec was pure white, but so white it seemed blue. I mused, and circled before the witch, wondering if we were being chased by a fallen star.

Hekate saw it too. I watched her sway as she stood, bewitched by the spec that grew ever closer.

It vanished, beneath the seafoam of a wave.

I blinked. Hekate stood perfectly still. For a few moments, we both held our breath. The cove was so still and silent that it had seemed that all the pebbles on the beach held their breath too.

A ripple appeared, between me and the witch.

The pale white ears of a horse sprang from the sea.

As its ears emerged, we both saw a head. Then, the arching neck of a stallion rose from the water. He glittered, like the reflection of a star.

The pharmakis gasped.

"Alpheratz…" I heard Hekate whisper.

Feathers breached the surface. They were like a magnified mirror of my own feathers. The horse walked onto the beach. For a moment, I was too surprised, I missed a stroke of my underwater paddles. My circle veered as I looked at the stallion.

Wings sprouting from his withers. I saw Hekate's jaw drop.

He rose further out of the water to reveal a pearly, white tail and shining, silver hooves.

I suppose observers warp stories, but I swear that horse's feathers were kin to my own. They had the long alabaster arch, like the feathers tucked along my body, shielding me from salt.

Perhaps it was my reflection in the starry water, but I recognized myself in the grace of the winged horse. He had been painted across the sky with a swan's wings. The stars spoke, but not everybody understood. They were like us birds, in that way.

Stars could not speak, but they always told the truth. In the starlight he seemed smug, never telling, never revealing the true side of Medousa in ancient Greece.

Before the winged horse touched stone pebbles, I blessed his baptisma with trumpeting notes. They skipped over the sea like smooth stones. I closed my red mouth, red hot and burning with the things I wished I could've said to the world.

Though men named me mute, I trumpeted. Such a round, perfect squawk never betrayed any secrets. Some said I sounded more like a singing whale than my fellow birds.

Somehow this fateful morning twisted over time and retellings. As stories passed from different lips, my trumpet became a flute.

Upon hearing my song, a black root sprouted from the horse's ear. The horse shook his massive head, and freed himself from the dark root.

I watched the root fall from his ear, and burrow between pebbles. Then a green sprout sprang from stone. One sprout turned into another. Each emerald stalks blossomed with a white flower. The plant merged with sage and spread towards the horizon.

This happened, all in a matter of breaths.

Hekate ran towards the horse. She jumped over and between the black roots like a cat.

An ordinary horse would've balked at Hekate's billowing cloak rushing toward him. However, this winged horse merely took a deep breath. He did not startle. When the pharmakis reached him, she stroked his face.

"Alpheratz?" Hekate whispered.

He lowered his magnificent wings to reveal a sleeping boy, draped over his back. The horse snorted and the boy woke. His eyes were wide, mostly black, with a tinge of blue. His giant pupils were black as the root that sprouted from the horse's ear. The boy rolled off the back of the horse and stood.

Hekate's platinum hair flicked over her shoulder as her eyes darted back and forth.

"I did it!" Perseus shouted.

"Did what?"

He ran his hands over his body, then stopped.

Perseus revealed a dark sac.

"I retrieved the head of Medousa," Perseus said.

He wasn't boasting. His words were ripe with regret. A somber look overtook his face.

Under the light of stars, I saw emotions creep over Hekate's face, but she swallowed them. Her brow arched and she cocked her head to look at him. I watched Hekate take a long inhale through her nose.

"Is that so?"

"Yes," Perseus said, "I shouldn't have done it."

"Why did you?" Hekate asked.

"As soon as I met her, I didn't want to kill her. She's just a girl!" Perseus wailed, "But I met gods at Sarpedon! I was forced to do it. I became invisible and I lost my own will. It was not me who brought my hands upon the blade!"

Perseus' voice cracked. For a moment, all was silent, save the whir of my circles around the cove. I watched everything unfold. My webbed feet paddled me through the water, eavesdropping with a swan's innocence.

"I should have never gone to get her head! I should have never shook Ovid's damned hand!" Perseus cried.

"How did you do it?" Hekate asked.

"Medousa couldn't hurt me, because I turned invisible. I did it! I got her head! Can you believe it?"

Hekate waited for the boy to continue.

"The gods have their way on that island. As soon as I cut her head, her blood sprang into a winged horse. There! You can see him!"

Perseus gestured towards the heavenly beast.

Hekate nodded slowly.

"Pegasos," she named the creature. The name of Medousa's new legend sprang from Hekate's lips over the magnetic lands of Magnesia. It shook the black poplar trees and floated over the glassy sea. *Pe. Ga. Sos.*

The boy was awestruck by what happened, or what he thought had happened. He was in a mood, humans, songbirds, and dolphins found themselves in, where one must speak and take something incredulous off their chests. He had to tell what happened at sea. He was brimming with excitement. Perseus hardly believed any of it was real. I was awestruck too. I watched the horse stand calm beside Hekate and Perseus, marveling at his magnificent wings.

"You have Medousa's head, you say?" Hekate asked.

"Yes," Perseus said.

"If you carry this with you, Perseus, you will put many people in danger. You're better off leaving it with me."

"Oh, I cannot give her head away," Perseus said, "I promised to give it to Ovid."

"Sweet boy," Hekate said, "Sometimes you must be the trickster to avoid being tricked."

"What do you mean?" Perseus asked.

"If you truly walk with Medousa's head," Hekate said, "People will hunt you, and try to take it from you. They'll find you, before you ever reach Ovid. You'll never be safe again, and when her head is stolen, all of Greece will be in danger."

"Oh…" Perseus' face fell.

"That is why you found me, Perseus, to guide you. I am the goddess Athene," Hekate said.

Hekate's lie was yet another secret that rested on my scorched beak as moons went by. I circled in the cove, understanding the power of a well-placed lie.

Realization swept over Perseus' face. He fell to his knees and bowed his head.

"I-I had no idea I stumbled upon the Temple of Athene," Perseus said, "I meant no dishonor. Of course, you are Athene! Of course, I will give you Medousa's head."

He placed the heavy bronze sac in the pebbles at Hekate's feet. I heard the dulled clank of cloth between metal and stone.

"Nobody will doubt your deed," Hekate said, although I knew the witch and the double-meanings of her words. She, herself, doubted his deed. Still, she enchanted him.

"I must make a confession," Perseus said, "I used this mirror to trick Medousa. I beg for help from Athene. Can you return this to Hekate? I'm afraid it was stolen from her, and that was upsetting for Medousa."

He pulled the strap from his shoulder, raised the mirror over his body, and laid it at Hekate's feet. The rim brushed her leather hunting boots and I heard a twang.

So, Hekate stood in mockery of Athene, with a shield, and the supposed head of Medousa.

"Thank you, Athene," Perseus said, "I must go now, I must tell Ovid his monster is gone, and her head is safe in the hands of a goddess."

He ran for the mainlands, desperate for a city. I could sense his emotions, for they were so strong, and brimming from his chest. The supernatural nature of wilderness had been driving him mad. His perceptions were overwhelming him. The boy, rather close to becoming a man, needed a relaxing drink in his hand, and willing, mortal ears to hear his mighty stories.

Perseus left Hekate with the winged horse, the mirror, and the mask. He hastened his way over the cliffs, and into the woods. He left Magnesia exactly as he had set out on his journey— carrying only a small sac.

Hekate examined the mask. She held it up to her face, as if willing to see through the dark fabric, to truly understand what was bundled inside.

She had her suspicions, naturally.

She sniffed it once more. I saw her eyes light up. I thought, with a funny recollection, that this master of metallurgy could've surely smelled a mask made of pure bronze.

Then she looked back to Perseus, darting through her magnetized woods.

Her gray eyes hardened into marble.

Hekate reached into her pocket and withdrew her burning glass. If I am to bear all my secrets, I will say that at first I mistook it for a dark magnetite stone in her palms. Her orb was the perfect opposite to the white moon above.

Hekate lifted the burning glass to her eye with a steady hand and long, nimble fingers. The early light prismed around the perfect circle, like a drop of water casting a rainbow. It glimmered, though it was dark, and the day was just breaking.

Stars came to light, where Hekate looked from the boy to the sky. She burned them with her glass.

Hekate must have been warmed by the boy, struck by his honesty, so she made him into a legend. She asked him to stand in the sky, beside the next incarnation of Medousa.

She cast his living soul into the stars. In that way, she made him half-god and half-boy. For, while his mortal soul continued to roam Greece, and one day his body would die, Perseus ruled over the sky. He carried Algol, the head of Medousa from whence the winged horse sprang, and a curved blade forevermore.

Hekate watched Perseus run for Athens. He had legends on his lips. She watched him, with fire in his step, on his way to tell a story of the gods. He ran in fear, in admiration, he ran because he served Athene and returned his own honor.

You've probably heard about the rumors, about what Perseus did with the head of Medousa. However, I feel it's time to spill those secrets too.

As the black-footed hellebores started to bloom in Greece, so did the stories from Perseus' lips. The flowers became entangled with his story, and rightfully so.

The flowers became a doorway to mysteries. When witches brewed their roots into wine mortals became acquainted with gods. Of course, these things couldn't be written down outright. People called the black-footed buttercups *the head of Medousa*. This is yet another secret I've been brewing in my beak.

The plant was so powerful that it revealed mysteries, but also took lives. Of course, given the dose, any potion became a path to poison. The plant with black feet allowed mortals to step one foot into myth. Sometimes it was so enchanting, they stepped with two feet. Then their souls were reaped and they never went back. The black-footed buttercup became infamous.

Those with malicious hearts brewed especially strong doses, and men turned to stone. A metaphor passed through tongues and pages in books, became truer, in the eyes of many, than the truth.

Therefore, the head of Medousa became responsible for deaths. People fell dead, celebrating at weddings, when they 'saw into her eyes'. All of Greece blamed her mythical head, but those in secret circles who drank special wines knew the meaning, knew the truth.

The flowers took over the beach, too. They wormed their way through all the pebbles with night-dark roots.

She watched the horizon, the woods where Perseus disappeared. Her forest had already been overtaken with emerald stalks and white flowers. The plants were like a dark, green cloak over the lands, dappled with blossoming buttercups.

So, Perseus ran away from the beach, and into an altered Greece. The black-footed buttercup had made its way across the mainland, escorted by the winged horse.

The witch looked away from her forest. She looked at the blue eyes of the horse and watched him stretch his wings.

The Pharmakis of the Dark Side of the Moon slid her burning glass back into her robes. I knew her secrets and her arrangements with Hera. Swans saw into the hearts of witches, where their secrets festered into lies.

"It seems we give proof from which origin we are sprung," Hekate said to the winged horse, whose cerulean iris flickered, "Alpheratz became Medousa, who became you."

The horse watched her, and I watched them both.

"Medousa has flown from her own life," Hekate spoke to the horse, "into yours."

The pharmakis looked up at the sky and her eyes traced lines between stars. She navigated between Algol and Alpheratz and I heard her heart soften with every beat.

Pegasos stomped his mighty hoof into the ground. He jerked his head towards the stars, as if to say, *I am there too.*

I heard the distant screech of a rooster call in the day. The sun started to lighten up the morning. The stars overhead, even the newly burned, started to crackle and fade away.

As the sun rose, so Pegasos became more clear on the beach, and his stars faded from the night sky. Under the glinting sunlight, I noticed he was not completely free.

He wore a golden bridle. It was as yellow as the stripe on a finch's wings. I wondered if his bridle was spun from the hair of Medousa. Pegasos was so unlike the ghost horses of Magnesia who ran across the forest on bronze shoes. This was a holy beast, who would never be chained by the Underworld. The shrill twang of bronze did not suit him.

Pegasos was tethered to the sky by gold, not by bronze in the Underworld.

"You've been crafted by Poseidon's hand," Hekate whispered as her fingers traced the bridle, and a string of pearls across the horse's forelock.

Against the golden bridle, Pegasos seemed like a defiant, blue shade of white. He was white, so white he could trick the eye into taking him as blue. There was an iridescence to the horse, like he had truly come from the essence of stars. I caught streaks of purple and blue in his shadow. His fur was like the feathers of ravens, before they were scorched by Apollo.

The raven's dark feathers had violet and emerald undertones, but they were once lighter birds. Pegasos looked like the early ravens, before their feathers caught on fire, who glistened with pastel purple and teal.

Then, Hekate looked up at the sky.

Hekate jumped. It seemed that the plump moon caught her off-guard.

"Hera..." She whispered.

I knew the ways of witches. Hekate was meant to be a day's ride away, at the peak of Mount Pelion. She had an appointment to keep, at a castle, in the clouds.

I heard the pharmakis curse under her breath. I wondered if she knew how many days she slept.

Surely, Hekate could ride the winged horse to Hera's golden gates.

Hekate closed her gray eyes. With one inhale, she jumped, threw her leg over the white horse, and sat astride Pegasos. The moon was waxing. Sunlight was about to strike it full. Hekate took a chance, a moment, and seized it.

Pegasos unfurled his wings and snorted. His exhale formed misty, silvery vapor in the morning light.

The horse stood up on his haunches, and launched into the sky. Pegasos returned to the stars with a pharmakis on his back.

Hekate tamed the winged creature. She used his bridle to guide him. With the slightest touch of Hekate's hand, upon gold, she led Pegasos over the cove.

I saw black cloth fall from the horse's back. Hekate dropped the mask of Medousa into the cove of Magnesia. She gave it to Poseidon who, of course, reversed the curse.

I heard, from the cormorant, when the golden trident was wielded underwater, its spell reversed. It sank instead of floated. Likewise, when the mask of Medousa was wielded by Poseidon, it did not turn life into stone.

Poseidon changed the nature of Medousa's mask.

He turned stones into life.

I careened in the water, arching my dance to see.

Underwater rocks turned purple, pink, and yellow. They transformed into coral, the animal which mimics stone. I swam through the water and watched in awe. Coral came over each pebble and hardened like splashes of dried blood.

After that day, Hekate forever saw Medousa in the ocean. But at that particular moment, Hekate didn't notice the coral. She was riding astride the winged horse. She flew upwards, into the clouds, high enough to disappear from my sight.

I heard the giddy laughter of Nephele. Clouds rained down with joy.

I left the cove and flew into the wildly enchanted lands of Magnesia. A new Greece was being born. There was more to the story. There was truth in the stars, but it was a truth with black roots.

I knew better than to take constellations at first blush. Mute swans understood the mysteries, and took note of which flowers were in bloom.

Acknowledgments

If not for my brilliant husband, Terry, this book would simply not exist. I must thank him for sharing his fascination with Medousa, Algol, Joseph Campbell, and mythology in general. Before I met Terry, I thought that mythology was just a collection of silly stories.

This book has been made possible by the tireless work of Brian C. Muraresku, Carl Ruck, R. Gorgon Wasson, and Albert Hoffman. For anyone interested in the botanical themes of this novel, I suggest reading *The Immortality Key* by Brian C. Muraresku.

I would also like to thank my high school astronomy teacher, Mr. Chap Percival. His passion for astronomy is contagious. I'm certain that every student who took Mr. Chap Percival's astronomy class was supplied with lasting interest in the stars.

About the Author

This is Alice Abyss' debut novel. Her worldwide pursuit of birdwatching, diving, and riding horses gave her the experience necessary to write this immersive novel.
Keep an eye out for her future releases.

Email: info@ascelpius.press

Visit Aslcepius.Press for blogs, short stories, and links to Alice Abyss' social media.

Made in United States
North Haven, CT
18 July 2024

54952655R00168